STAR WARS®

THE CESTUS DECEPTION

STAR WARS

THE CESTUS DECEPTION
—(A CLONE WARS NOVEL)—

STEVEN BARNES

BALLANTINE BOOKS · NEW YORK

A Del Rey® Book
Published by The Random House Publishing Group

Del Rey is a registered trademark and the Del Rey colophon is a trademark of Random House, Inc.

www.starwars.com
www.delreybooks.com

ISBN 0-345-45898-2

Manufactured in the United States of America

First Edition: June 2004
First Mass Market Edition: March 2005

OPM 9 8 7 6 5 4 3 2 1

For my new son, Jason Kai Due-Barnes.
Welcome to life, sweetheart.

CLONE WARS
TIMELINE

With the Battle of Geonosis (EP II), the Republic is plunged into an emerging, galaxywide conflict. On one side is the Confederacy of Independent Systems (the Separatists), led by the charismatic Count Dooku, who is backed by a number of powerful trade organizations and their droid armies.

On the other side is the Republic loyalists and their newly created clone army, led by the Jedi. It is a war fought on a thousand fronts, with heroism and sacrifices on both sides. Below is a partial list of some of the important events of the Clone Wars and a guide to where these events are chronicled.

MONTHS
(after *Attack of the Clones*)

0	**THE BATTLE OF GEONOSIS** *Star Wars:* Episode II *Attack of the Clones* (LFL, May '02)
0	**REPUBLIC COMMANDO** *Star Wars:* Republic Commando (LEC, Fall '04)
0	**THE SEARCH FOR COUNT DOOKU** Boba Fett #1: *The Fight to Survive* (SB, April '02)
+1	**THE DARK REAPER PROJECT** The Clone Wars (LEC, October '02)
+1	**THE BATTLE OF RAXUS PRIME** Boba Fett #2: *Crossfire* (SB, November '02)
+1.5	**CONSPIRACY ON AARGAU** Boba Fett #3: *Maze of Deception* (SB, April '03)
+2	**THE BATTLE OF KAMINO** Clone Wars I: *The Defense of Kamino* (DH, June '03)
+2	**DURGE VS. BOBA FETT** Boba Fett #4: *Hunted* (SB, October '03)
+2.5	**THE DEFENSE OF NABOO** Clone Wars II: *Victories and Sacrifices* (DH, September '03)
+3	**MISSION ON QIILURA** *Republic Commando: Hard Contact* (DR, November '04)
+6	**THE DEVARON RUSE** Clone Wars IV: *Target Jedi* (DH, May '04)

CLONE WARS
TIMELINE

MONTHS
(after *Attack of the Clones*)

+6	**THE HARUUN KAL CRISIS**	
	Shatterpoint (DR, June '03)	
+6	**ASSASSINATION ON NULL**	
	Legacy of the Jedi #1 (SB, August '03)	
+12	**THE BIO-DROID THREAT**	
	The Cestus Deception (DR, June '04)	
+15	**THE BATTLE OF JABIIM**	
	Clone Wars III: *Last Stand on Jabiim* (DH, February '04)	
+16	**ESCAPE FROM RATTATAK**	
	Clone Wars V: *The Best Blades* (DH, November '04)	
+24	**THE CASUALTIES OF DRONGAR**	
	MedStar Duology: *Battle Surgeons* (DR, July '04)	
	Jedi Healer (DR, October '04)	
+29	**ATTACK ON AZURE**	
	Jedi Quest Special Edition (SB, March '05)	
+30	**THE PRAESITLYN CONQUEST**	
	Jedi Trial (DR, November '04)	
+30	**LURE AT VJUN**	
	Yoda: Dark Rendezvous (DR, December '04)	
+31	**THE XAGOBAH CITADEL**	
	Boba Fett #5: *A New Threat* (SB, April '04)	
	Boba Fett #6: *Pursuit* (SB, December '04)	
+33	**THE HUNT FOR DARTH SIDIOUS**	
	Labyrinth of Evil (DR, February '05)	
+36	**ANAKIN TURNS TO THE DARK SIDE**	
	Star Wars: Episode III *Revenge of the Sith* (LFL, May '05)	

KEY:

DH = *Dark Horse Comics, graphic novels*
www.darkhorse.com
DR = *Del Rey, hardcover & paperback books*
www.delreydigital.com
LEC = *LucasArts Games, games for XBox, GameCube,
PS2, & PC platforms* www.lucasarts.com
LFL = *Lucasfilm Ltd., motion pictures* www.starwars.com
SB = *Scholastic Books, juvenile fiction* www.scholastic.com/starwars

DRAMATIS PERSONAE

CORUSCANT GROUP
Obi-Wan Kenobi; Jedi Knight (male human)
Kit Fisto; Jedi Master (male Nautolan)
Doolb Snoil; barrister (male Vippit of Nal Hutta)
Admiral Arikakon Baraka; supercruiser commander (male Mon Calamari)
Lido Shan; technician (humanoid)

CLONE COMMANDOS
A-98, "Nate"; ARC Trooper, recruitment and command
CT-X270, "Xutoo"; pilot
CT-36/732, "Sirty"; logistics
CT-44/444, "Forry"; physical training
CT-12/74, "Seefor"; communications

CESTIANS
Trillot; gang leader (male/female X'Ting)
Fizzik; broodmate of Trillot (male X'Ting)
Sheeka Tull; pilot (female human)
Resta Shug Hai; Desert Wind member (female X'Ting)
Thak Val Zsing; leader of Desert Wind (male human)
Brother Nicos Fate (male X'Ting)
Skot OnSon; Desert Wind member (male human)

FIVE FAMILIES OF CESTUS CYBERNETICS
Debbikin; research (male human)
Lady Por'Ten; energy (female human)
Kefka; manufacturing (male humanoid)

Llitishi; sales and marketing (male Wroonian)
Caiza Quill; mining (male X'Ting)

CESTUS COURT
G'Mai Duris; Regent (female X'Ting)
Shar Shar; Regent Duris's assistant (female Zeetsa)

CONFEDERATION
Count Dooku; leader of the Confederacy of Independent
    Systems (male human)
Commander Asajj Ventress; Commander of the Separatist
    Army (female humanoid)

VOLUME 531 NUMBER 46

HoloNet News

13:3.7

Baktoid Closes Down Five More Plants

TERMIN, METALORN—In a statement issued to shareholders, Baktoid Armor Workshop confirmed that it will close down five more plants in the Inner Rim and Colonies as a direct result of Republic regulations that have hindered its battle droid program.

Baktoid plants on Foundry, Ord Cestus, Telti, Balmorra, and Ord Lithone will close by month's end. An estimated 12.5 million employees will be laid off as a result.

Legislation passed by the Senate eight years ago forced the disbanding of the Trade Federation's security forces, the largest single consumer of Baktoid's combat automata and vehicles. Further licensing restrictions on the sale of battle droids made the purchase of such hardware prohibitively expensive for most of Baktoid's clientele . . .

1

For half a millennium Coruscant had glittered, a golden-towered centerpiece to the Republic's galactic crown. Its bridges and arched solaria harked back to ages past, when no leader's words seemed too grand, no skyscraper too spectacular, and titanic civic sprawls boldly proclaimed the rational mind's conquest of the cosmos.

With the coming of the Clone Wars, some believed such glorious days were past. Whether the news holos spoke of victory or defeat, it was all too easy to imagine flaming ships spiraling to their doom beneath distant skies, the clash of vast armies, the death of uncounted and uncountable dreams. It was almost impossible not to wonder if one day war's ravening maw might not envelop this, the Republic's jeweled locus. This was a time when the word *city* symbolized not achievement, but vulnerability. Not haven, but havoc.

But despite those fears, Coruscant's billions of citizens kept faith and continued about their myriad lives. A flock of hook-beaked thrantcills flew in perfect diamond formation through Coruscant's placid, pale blue sky. For a hundred thousand standard years they had winged south for the winter, and might for yet another. Their flat black eyes had watched civilization force Coruscant's animal life into inexorable retreat. The planet's former masters now scavenged in her duracrete canyons, their natural habitats replaced with artificial marshes and permacrete forests. This, others argued, was a time of marvels and marvelous beings from a hundred thousand different worlds. This was a time for optimism, for dreams, and for unbridled ambition.

A time of opportunity, for those with vision to see.

The red-and-white disk of a two-passenger *Limulus*-class transport sliced through Coruscant's cloud-mantle. In the morning sun it glittered like a sliver of silvered ice. Spiral-dancing to inaudible music, it had detached its hyperdrive ring in orbit, slipping through wispy clouds to land with a *shush* as gentle as a kiss. Its smooth, glassy side rippled. A rectangular outline appeared and then slid up. A tall, bearded man wrapped in a brown robe stepped into the doorway and hopped down, followed by a second, clean-shaven passenger.

The bearded man's name was Obi-Wan Kenobi. For more years than he cared to count, Obi-Wan had been one of the most renowned Jedi Knights in the entire Republic. The second, a startlingly intense younger man with fine brown hair, was named Anakin Skywalker. Although not yet a full Jedi Knight, he was already famed as one of the galaxy's most powerful warriors.

For thirty-six hours the two had juggled flying and navigational duties, using their Jedi skills to hold their needs for sleep and sustenance to a minimum. Obi-Wan was tired, irritable, famished, and felt as if someone had poured sand into his joints. Anakin, he noticed, seemed fresh and ready for action.

The recuperative powers of youth, Obi-Wan thought ruefully.

Only an emergency directive from Supreme Chancellor Palpatine himself could have summoned the two from their assignment on Forscan VI.

"Well, Master," Anakin said. "I suppose this is where we part company."

"I'm not certain what this is about," the older man replied, "but your time will be well spent studying at the Temple."

Obi-Wan and Anakin continued down the skywalk. Far beneath them the city streets buzzed with traffic, the walkways and ground-level construction occasionally interrupted by wisps of cloud or stray thrantcills. The web of streets and bridges behind and below them was dazzling, but Obi-Wan noticed the beauty little more than he had the height, the fatigue, or the hunger. At the moment, his mind was occupied by other, more urgent concerns.

As if his Padawan could read his thoughts, Anakin spoke. "I hope you're not still annoyed with me, Master."

There it was, another reference to Anakin's rash actions on Forscan VI. Forscan VI was a colony planet at the edge of the Cron drift, currently unaffiliated with either Republic or Confederacy. Elite Separatist infiltration agents had set up a training camp on Forscan, their "exercises" playing havoc with the settlers. The most delicate aspect of the counter-operation was repelling those agents without ever letting the colonists know that outsiders had assisted them. Tricky. Dangerous.

"No," Obi-Wan said. "We contained the situation. My approach is more . . . measured. But you displayed your usual initiative. You weren't disobeying a direct order, so . . . we'll mark it down to creative problem solving, and leave it at that."

Anakin breathed a sigh of relief. Powerful bonds of love and mutual respect connected the two men, but in times past Anakin's impulsiveness had tested those bonds sorely. Still, there was little doubt that the Padawan would receive Obi-Wan's highest recommendations. Years of observation had forced Obi-Wan to grant that Anakin's seeming impetuosity was in fact a deep and profound understanding of superior skills.

"You were right," Anakin said, as if Obi-Wan's mild answer gave him permission to admit his own errors. "Those mountains *were* impassable. Confederacy reinforcements would have bogged down in the ice storm, but I couldn't take the chance. There were too many lives at stake."

"It takes maturity to admit an error," Obi-Wan said. "I think we can keep these thoughts between us. My report will reflect admiration for your initiative."

The two comrades faced, and gripped each other's forearms. Obi-Wan had no children, and likely never would. But the unity of Padawan and Master was as deep as any parent–child bond, and in some ways deeper still. "Good luck," Anakin said. "Give my regards to Chancellor Palpatine."

A hovercar slid in next to the walkway, and Anakin hopped aboard, disappearing into the sky traffic without a backward glance.

Obi-Wan shook his head. The boy would be fine. *Had* to be fine. If a Jedi as gifted as Anakin could not rise above youthful hubris, what hope was there for the rest of them?

But meanwhile there was a more immediate matter to consider. Why exactly had he been called back to Coruscant? Certainly it must be an emergency, but what *kind* of emergency . . . ?

The appointed meeting place was the T'Chuk sporting arena, a tiered shell with seating for half a million thronging spectators. Here chin-bret, Coruscant's most popular spectator sport, was played before hundreds of thousands of cheering fans. Today, however, no expert chin-bretier leapt in graceful arcs across the sand; no pikers vaulted about returning serves. No cerulean-vested goalkeepers veered like mad demicots, hoisting their team's torch aloft. Today the vast stadium was empty, cleared and sequestered, hosting a very different sort of gathering.

As he emerged from the echoing length of pedestrian tunnel, Obi-Wan scanned the tiered stands. Most of the rows were as empty as a Tatooine desertscape, but a few dozen witnesses were gathered in the box-seat section. He recognized a scattering of high-level elected officials, some important but ordinarily reclusive bureaucrats, a few people from the technical branches, and even some clone troopers. Instinct and experience suggested that this was a war council.

Over time the Clone Wars' initial chaos had settled into a tidal rhythm; loyalties declared, alliances formed. The galaxy was too vast for war to touch all its myriad shores, but at any given time battles raged on a hundred different worlds. While that number represented an insignificant fraction of the billions of star systems swirling about the galaxy, due to long-standing alliances and partnerships, what happened to millions of living beings had the potential to affect trillions.

Already kingdoms, nations, and families had been ravaged by the wars. As the numbers grew and weapons inevitably became more and more powerful, devastation might well spiral out of control, offsetting the countless eons of struggle that had finally birthed a galaxywide union. The labor of a thousand generations, vanished?

Never!

Lines had been drawn: Separatists on the one side, and the Republic on the other. For Obi-Wan as well as many others, that line was drawn with his own life's blood. The Republic would stand, or Obi-Wan and every Jedi who had ever strode the Temple's halls would fall. It was a simple equation.

And in simplicity there was both clarity and strength.

2

I'Chuk arena's sand-covered floor was empty save for a pale, slender humanoid female. She wore a white technician's cloak, and her black hair was cropped short. She stood tinkering with a gleaming chrome hourglass-shaped construct that Obi-Wan found a bit puzzling: it looked more like an edgy work of art, a Mavinian cluster-wedding organ, or perhaps a Juzzian colony marker, than anything dangerous enough to concern a Jedi. Rows of narrow pointed legs at the base were the only apparent means of locomotion.

What in the thousand worlds was this about?

The technician fiddled with the device, running various wires from it to a pod at her waist. Perhaps it was some sort of advanced med droid?

The audience grew increasingly restless as she detached the wires, then turned and addressed them.

"My name is Lido Shan, and I thank you for your patience," she said, ignoring their obvious lack of same. "I believe that our first demonstration is ready for your graces." Shan gave a little bow and swept her hand toward the gleaming construct. "I present the JK-thirteen. To demonstrate its prowess, we have selected a Confederacy destroyer droid, captured on Geonosis and reconstructed to original manufacturer specifications."

The JK stood chest-high with a glassy finish, aesthetically pleasing in ways few droids ever managed. A child's toy, a museum display, a conversation piece, some fragile and delicate bit of electronics, perhaps. On the other hand, the black, wheel-like destroyer droid looked comparatively primitive, battered and patched, but still as menacing as a wounded acklay.

With a hiss of compressing and decompressing hydraulics, the destroyer droid rolled forward, crunching the sand into tread ridges as it did. The JK model hunched down, gleaming, but in a strange way seemed oddly helpless. It seemed almost to *quiver* as it crouched. The impression of helplessness was reinforced by the size differential: the JK was perhaps half the battle droid's mass.

At first Obi-Wan wondered if he was simply to witness another demonstration of destroyer droid power and efficiency. Hardly necessary: he still carried scars from the blasted things. No, that was an absurd assumption: Palpatine couldn't possibly have summoned him from Forscan for so mundane a purpose. In the next instant the destroyer droid rolled within five meters of the JK, and all questions were answered.

In a single moment the JK divided into segments, assuming a spiderlike configuration. In that instant its pose seemed less of a cowering leaf eater than one of those cunning creatures that mime helplessness to lure their prey into range.

The destroyer droid spat red fire at its adversary. The sand rippled as the JK projected not a single force field, but a series of rotating energy disks that absorbed the blasts with ease. That was a surprise: typically a machine required less sophistication to *deflect* energy than to *absorb* it. This display implied some kind of advanced capacitance or grounding technology. The attacking droid continued its rain of fire, unable to comprehend that its pure-power approach had proved inefficient.

Like most machines, it was powerful but stupid.

Obi-Wan's eyes narrowed. Something . . . *something* unusual was happening. The JK sprouted tentacles from the sides and top, tendrils snaking out so swiftly that the destroyer droid had not the slightest chance of evasion. Now Obi-Wan, and indeed most of the witnesses, leaned toward the action as the war droid struggled helplessly in the JK's tentacled grip. Initially the tendrils were thick and ropy. Even as he watched they grew thinner, and then thinner still, webbing the attacker with fibers that finally reduced to an almost invisible fineness.

The tendrils chewed into the destroyer droid's casing like hundreds of silk-thin fibersaws. The droid finally seemed to comprehend its peril and commenced a desperate struggle, emitting disturbingly lifelike keening sounds.

The droid's struggles ceased. It quivered, vibrating in place until it threatened to shake itself apart. Smoke oozed from its slivered casing. Then, like some piece of overripe metallic fruit, it simply divided into sections. Each crashed to the sand in individual chunks, spitting sparks and leaking greenish fluid. The pieces rattled into the dust, trembled. A second later, stillness and silence reigned.

For a moment the crowd was stunned into silence. Obi-Wan could well empathize. The tactic had been unconventional, the weapon deadly, the result indisputable.

"Droid against droid," the globe-headed Bith beside him scoffed. "Games for children. Surely *this* is not worthy of a Chancellor summons."

Beneath them, Lido Shan was unruffled. "Your indulgence, please," she said. "We wished merely to establish a baseline, a reference point against an opponent both familiar and formidable. This class four combat droid was stopped in less than . . . forty-two seconds."

Behind Obi-Wan an amphibious Aqualish's translation pod gargled a question. "But what of *living* opponents?"

The technician nodded, as if she had anticipated such a query. "Our very next demonstration involves an Advanced Recon Commando."

On cue, a single clone trooper, a commando in full battle armor, armed with an infantry-grade blaster rifle, stepped forward from his hiding place beneath the lip of the arena wall. Clone Commandos were specialized troopers. They had been modified from the basic trooper template to allow for specific training protocols. A blast helmet concealed his features, but his posture bespoke aggressive readiness. An uneasy mutter wound its way through the crowd.

The amphibian seemed taken aback. "I . . . would not wish to be responsible for a death . . ."

The technician fixed the Aqualish with a pitying gaze, as if every response had been anticipated. "Don't worry." Her motions were measured and relaxed as she manipulated a few controls. "The machine is calibrated for nonlethal apprehension."

Although that pronouncement quieted most of the witnesses, Obi-Wan felt even more uneasy. This droid, with its ethereal beauty and unconventional lethality, had something to do with his mission. But what? "What exactly is the trooper's objective?" Obi-Wan called down.

The corners of Lido Shan's lips pulled upward. "To fight his way past the JK and capture me."

The muttering witnesses regarded her with disbelief and something more disturbing: *anticipation.* They knew they were about to witness something memorable. But which did they desire most? The JK defeated, or this snooty technician given her comeuppance?

The trooper edged forward warily until he was about two dozen meters from the creature . . .

Obi-Wan shook his head. *Creature?* Had he really done that? Thought *creature* instead of *droid*? What had triggered that?

The trooper raised his blaster to his shoulder and fired a crimson bolt of light. The spinning absorption disks reappeared, sucking the energy bolts with a liquid crackling sound.

But the mere fact that the droid needed a force screen seemed to encourage the trooper. He feinted to the right and then rolled to the left, sprang nimbly off his shoulder to fire again, repeatedly changing position as the droid continued its defensive action.

Obi-Wan opened his senses, stretching out with the Force. He could almost feel the man's racing heart, taste his nervousness, sense the choices weighed as he wove his evasive web. Left, right, left . . . the next move would be to the—

Left again.

As the great Jedi watched, the JK spat out a webbing of strands as thick as his small finger, ensnaring the clone helplessly in midleap. He might have been no more than a wounded thrantcill, bagged by any musk merchant with a net. The timing was superb. No. More than superb: it had been *perfect*. What kind of programming made such precision possible? Obi-Wan could swear that the aim had been almost precognitive, almost . . .

But that was impossible.

Struggling in the net as the JK dragged him closer, the trooper pulled his blaster around to draw a bead on the technician. Obi-Wan's eyes flickered to the technician: she seemed unconcerned. In the moment before the barrel would have fixed on her, an orange spark flowed out along the tentacles. The trooper rocked with a single hard, violent shiver, thrashed his heels against the sand, and then lay still. The JK pulled him close, one tentacle lifting his trunk high enough for a second, more slender probe to flash a beam of light against the trooper's closed eyes. The JK lowered the trooper back to the sand, then stood still and watchful.

For a moment the crowd's every intake of breath seemed frozen in their collective throats. Then the JK's web unraveled, flowing back into the droid. The trooper groaned and rolled over onto his side. Another moment and he levered himself to his knees, wobbly but unharmed. Another trooper helped him retreat beneath the arena wall's curved lip.

The audience applauded, with the exception of Obi-Wan and another Jedi who edged his way through the crowd to stand beside him. Obi-Wan felt relief as the familiar form approached, and also as he saw that the newcomer was no more inclined toward applause than he.

The newcomer was two centimeters taller than Obi-Wan, yellowish green in skin tone, with the ropy cranial sensor tentacles and unblinking eyes typical of a Nautolan. This was Kit Fisto, veteran of Geonosis and a hundred other lethal hot spots. He neither smiled nor applauded the JK's actions: no Jedi would ever look at another being's injury, no matter how superficial or temporary, as entertainment of any kind. Was it mere coincidence that the Nautolan was here, or had he, too, been summoned?

Kit looked down at Obi-Wan's hands, noted their tension. "Such displays are not to your liking?" he asked. His voice had a moist sibilance even when speaking of mundane issues. The surfaces of Fisto's unblinking black eyes swirled. This was repressed anger, but few non-Nautolans would have known that.

"I see little regard for the trooper's welfare," Obi-Wan said.

Kit gave a humorless chuckle. "The reefs of policy and privilege make war seem merely some distant entertainment."

The globe-headed being in front of them turned his head 180 degrees without moving his shoulders. "Come now, sir. It's just a clone, after all."

Just a clone. Flesh and blood, yes, but bred in a bottle, merely another of 1.2 million clone troopers born with no father to protect them, and no mother to mourn.

Yes. Merely a clone.

Obi-Wan had no interest in arguing. To these, who had little fear of dying in combat, whose offspring would also be spared a soldier's terrible choices, clone troopers were a supreme convenience. This troglodyte had merely spoken his honest opinion.

"Excellent, excellent," said another witness, a leathery creature sporting a cyclopean cluster of eyes in the center of his head. "Excellent. I now understand how the JKs earned their reputation among the criminal class."

The two exchanged a swift, odd glance, piquing Obi-Wan's curiosity. "Which is . . . ?"

The two turned back to the arena, pretending not to hear his question. Obi-Wan was not so easily fooled. Alarm trilled along his spine. These waters ran deep indeed.

The leathery one spoke again. "You wish us to be concerned," he said to Lido Shan. "We are prepared to acknowledge the potency of such a device. But . . . ahem . . . we are fortunate enough to have Jedi among us today. Would it be impolite to request a demonstration?"

Obi-Wan watched as dozens of eyes turned toward them, evaluating, triggering whispers. He watched fingers, tentacles, and claws touch furtively, and was certain that credits were changing hands. Gambling on the outcome?

Kit Fisto leaned closer without ever looking directly at him. "What do you make of this?"

Obi-Wan shrugged. "I've little urge to satisfy their curiosity."

"Nor I," Kit said, and his tendrils swirled with a life of their own. He then turned and addressed the technician. "Tell me," he said. "Does *JK-thirteen* have meaning beyond a standard alphanumeric designation?"

There it was, the question Obi-Wan himself had hesitated to ask.

A thin current of whispers rippled in the arena. The technician shuffled her feet hesitantly. "Not officially . . . ," she began.

"But unofficially?" Obi-Wan prodded.

The tech cleared her throat uncomfortably. "Among smugglers and the lower classes," she said, "some call them 'Jedi Killers.' "

"Charming," he said, more to himself than anyone else, momentarily too stunned to answer. *Jedi Killer?* What was this obscenity?

Beside him, Kit doffed his cloak, face set in its implacable pale green mask. His cranial tendrils, Obi-Wan noticed, were restless even as his unblinking eyes focused on the droid.

"What are you doing?" Obi-Wan asked, knowing the inevitable answer. In fact, almost certainly, this was why Kit had been invited: his volatility and courage were renowned.

"I would feel this thing for myself," Kit said, voice deadly calm. He then raised his voice in challenge. "Technician! At your pleasure."

The Nautolan's head sensors wavered in the still air. The droid regarded him without reaction. With a single glance back at Obi-Wan, Kit somersaulted to the floor of the arena with a poise and fluidity no chin-bret point guard could have dreamed of, landing without a sound.

He stood a dozen meters away from the JK. As before, the droid seemed harmless. Master Fisto's lightsaber flashed in his hand, and its emerald length rose from the hilt, scorching the air as it blossomed.

The droid emitted a hum that climbed in pitch and intensity until Obi-Wan's skin crawled. It remained motionless except for its surface, which once again segmented into an arachnid configuration. It seemed to sniff the air. Its insectile whine changed, as if it were wary of its new opponent.

It extended tentacles again, but this time they wiggled in an oddly sluggish fashion. Strange indeed. Although previously appearing flexible and alert, was it now about to use the same tactics it had used against the commando? Perhaps the droid was not so advanced as he had initially feared . . .

Kit's lightsaber swatted the first tendril from the air with contemptuous ease. Obi-Wan found his attention straying from the JK, focusing instead on Kit, admiring the strength of his stance, the clarity of his angles as he chose lines of engagement. Kit favored the Form I style of combat, a fierce—

Wait.

Warning sirens howled in Obi-Wan's mind. Something was terribly wrong. Intellect raced to keep pace with intuition. The JK's repetition of previous patterns had lulled him into complacency. *The tendrils were only a feint.* Where, then, was the real attack?

He leaned forward, examining the droid more carefully. Its *feet.* The spiky protrusions were sunken in the sand. And projecting outward from the treads themselves, burrowing under the surface . . .

Were more tendrils, color-camouflaged to resemble sand. This thing attacked on two levels simultaneously, a strategy beyond most *living* warriors. Even more disturbing, it was deliberately misleading Kit by performing at multiple levels of tempo and efficiency, literally juggling its tactics, luring him to overconfidence.

The sand tendrils were within centimeters of their target before Kit sensed them. His lidless black eyes grew wider still as the sand erupted. A stalk snaked around his foot, trying to yank him onto his back. Other vines raced to assist the first group.

The onlookers gasped in amazement as they realized that they were about to see the unthinkable: a mere droid defeating a mighty Jedi!

But Kit was far from vanquished. As if he, too, had merely been playing a game, he crouched and leapt forward, spinning on his body's vertical axis like some kind of carnival acrobat, surging directly at the JK. He rode the JK's yanking motion instead of fighting it, slipping between the tendrils, the Nautolan's sense of timing faster and more precise than conscious thought.

Whatever its powers, the droid had not anticipated such an assault, nor could it adjust in time. It released him and retreated up a step, all tendrils lashing at the Jedi. Kit's lightsaber rained sparks. Tentacles flopped onto the sand, some of the larger pieces twitching, more like separate creatures than severed limbs.

The Nautolan hit the sand, rolled, and bore in again instantly, his face tightened into a fighting snarl.

Now the JK battled at maniacal intensity, and Obi-Wan wondered: *What is it trying to do?* Again and again the tendrils lashed at Kit's head. Had Lido Shan failed to give the droid proper inhibiting commands? If so, and the gleaming monstrosity had a single opportunity, it would slay the Nautolan. Obi-Wan's hand crept toward his lightsaber, the weight of thirty-six grueling flight hours banished from his limbs. If the need arose—

But Kit had entered lightsaber range. At this more intimate distance, the droid was at a disadvantage. Now Kit was the predator, the JK reduced to the role of prey. Hissing, it retreated on its slender golden legs, tentacles wavering, as if it couldn't crunch data fast enough to counter the unorthodox attack. Kit's emerald lightsaber blade was *here, there,* everywhere: unpredictable, irresistible. The spinning energy disks no longer absorbed the strikes: now they merely deflected them, sparks raining in all directions.

Kit accelerated into a blur of motion complex and rapid enough to baffle even Obi-Wan's experienced gaze. The Nautolan Jedi's lightsaber wove between the energy shields, descending on the JK's housing for the first time. The droid emitted a painfully thin shriek. Its gleaming legs shivered.

It collapsed to the sand. It twitched, struggling to rise. And then spilled onto its side, spewing smoke and sparks.

The arena was silent as the crowd absorbed what they had just witnessed. Doubtless, some had never seen a Jedi in full action. It was one thing to hear whispered stories about mysterious Temple dwellers; another thing entirely to see the almost supernatural skills for oneself. A century hence, some might be regaling their great-grandchildren with tales of this demonstration.

But there was another aspect of the affair that most eyes had missed, a strange phenomenon that had manifested first with the trooper, but seemed even more pronounced with Kit Fisto: the JK had *anticipated* the Nautolan's responses.

A bitter metallic taste soured Obi-Wan's mouth, a sensation he recognized as the first whisper of fear. "What is this device?" he asked. "I note that the shields absorb, rather than deflect."

The technician nodded. "And what does that suggest to you, Master Jedi?"

"It is no battlefield implement. It is designed to protect its environment, even from ricochets."

"Excellent," she said.

"And judging by its cosmetic appearance, the JK is some manner of personal security droid."

Lido Shan held up her hands, requesting silence. "That concludes the demonstration," she said. "There will be briefings for some of you. As for the others, the Supreme Chancellor appreciates your presence."

The crowd drifted away, a few of them pausing to congratulate Kit. Perhaps they had considered descending to shake his hand or slap his back, but neither gesture seemed appropriate given the tightness around Kit's dark, unblinking eyes.

Obi-Wan jumped down from the stands and handed the Nautolan his cloak. Without a word Kit accepted it, and together they walked up the stairs toward the exit. Obi-Wan looked back at the sand, where service droids were still vacuuming up oil and fluids. What would he, Obi-Wan, have done given the same challenge? He allowed himself no doubt that he would have emerged victorious, but simultaneously realized that Kit's chaotic, unpredictable approach had given the Nautolan an advantage against the machine. Obi-Wan's own more measured response might well have proven less effective.

On their way out they passed a knot of troopers, all carved from the same rock, all with the same broad shoulders and shielded faces, the same military bearing and polish. With surprising tenderness they cared for their defeated brother, and Obi-Wan wondered . . .

The Nautolan's tendrils lifted and Kit turned, seeming to read his mind. "Obi-Wan?"

"For a moment I wondered if I had met him before."

"And?"

"And I realized how foolish that thought was."

"Foolish?" Kit asked.

"Yes. I've met every one of them."

True enough. Yet watching them caring for one of their own as if none of the witnesses existed, he wondered if he, or any outsider, really knew them at all.

3

The Chancellor's briefing room was as tall as four Wookiees, its marble ceiling supported by massive duracrete pillars. Its vast bay window peered out on Coruscant's magnificent skyline: the Bonadan embassy and revolving Skysitter Restaurant were directly across the avenue. The dense duracrete forest conveyed a sense of grandeur that impressed dignitaries from the Outer Rim but always left Obi-Wan wondering if something more productive might have been done with the space.

At the moment a cluster of scaled and emerald-eyed Kuati dignitaries busily exchanged formal pleasantries and good-byes with the Chancellor and his robed assistants. The two Jedi stood in a corner of the room as the ambassadors executed elaborate ceremonial bows.

As they waited, Obi-Wan noted that Kit seemed a bit ill at ease. "Are you all right?" he asked quietly. "Did the droid come too close for comfort?" In truth, he could not remember Kit ever seeming other than utterly self-possessed.

"My life does not revolve around comfort," the Nautolan said. "Still . . . it was, as I've heard humans say, a 'close shave.' "

And strangely, even those words told Obi-Wan how challenging the JK had been. That last statement was as revelatory as the Nautolan Jedi had ever been.

As the diplomats exited the room, Supreme Chancellor Palpatine finally addressed them, his broad, strong forehead creased with worry, lips drawn into a thin, tight line.

"My pardon for the inconvenience and mystery, my

friends," he said. "I hope that you will shortly understand the need for both."

"Chancellor," Obi-Wan said, in no mood for formal pleasantries. "Are you prepared to share this 'Jedi Killer's' secret with us?"

The Chancellor winced. "I admit to being mystified. Even our lowest citizens would not find such a vulgar appellation amusing." After a pause for thought, he continued. "In the interest of providing context, please indulge a digression." Palpatine waved them toward a pair of chairs. The Chancellor sat at his great desk, rectangles of light and shadow dividing his face into quadrants. He turned to the short-haired female technician, who had silently entered the room while the Chancellor spoke. "Lido Shan?"

"With pleasure, sir," she said. "When this device first came to our attention, our first priority was to determine exactly how it performs in such an unusual manner. Ordinary scans showed little of note in the inner workings, save for a completely shielded central processor unit."

"Naturally, that processor was the focus of your investigations," Obi-Wan said.

"Naturally," Lido Shan replied, allowing her pale lips to curl into a smile. "Opening the processor invalidates the warranty, but we thought it worth the risk."

Kit canted his head. "And what did you find?"

"Please," Lido Shan said, imitating the Chancellor's tendency for oblique discourse. "In time. Let us begin with an assessment based on its displayed skills." She paused, gathering herself. "The JK is a Force-sensitive bio-droid of a type previously considered impossible. For much of the last year, they've been sold throughout the galaxy. Even at inflated prices, they sell faster than they can be manufactured."

"Force-sensitive?" Kit scoffed. "Absurd! Why haven't we seen these droids before?"

"Because," she replied, "they are the most exclusive, expensive personal security droids available."

"And exactly what is this cost?" Kit asked.

"Eighty thousand credits." Shan gestured, and a hologram

maze of droid circuitry blossomed in the air around her. She ran her hands along the internal structure, tracing various features, then took a deep breath.

"And now," she said finally, "we come to the heart of the matter. The secret of their success is a unique living circuit design incorporating organics into the core processor, allowing greater empathy with the owners and superior tactical aggression toward intruders."

"Living circuits?" Kit asked.

Lido Shan seemed to match the Nautolan's ability at unblinking attention, but Obi-Wan watched as a yellowish mucosa filmed her eyes and then swiftly dissolved. "The processor is actually a life-support unit for a creature of unknown origin."

The hologram flickered, darkened. A coiled, snakelike, eyeless image appeared. A comparison scale suggested that the creature was the size of Obi-Wan's clenched fist. "And this gives the droid its special qualities?" he asked.

"Yes," Lido Shan said. "We believe so. We made a direct request for information from the manufacturers, but they refuse to discuss their secrets."

"And this manufacturer is . . . ?"

"Cestus Cybernetics. Are you familiar with Ord Cestus?"

Obi-Wan scanned his memory. "The homeworld of Baktoid Armor?"

"Excellent," the Supreme Chancellor said.

Lido Shan nodded. "Our Cestian contacts tell us that the animal is called a dashta eel. This dashta appears to be nonsentient, which in some ways is even more amazing, representing the first nonsentient creature ever found with a profound level of . . . well, of Force sensitivity."

"Dashta eels?" Obi-Wan glanced at Kit, who shook his head.

"Possibly natives of Cestus's Dashta Mountain range," the Chancellor said. "Combined with the JK's unique armament, they give the droid an anticipatory advantage in combat. We have tested it with a variety of opponents, and you, Master Fisto, are the first to prevail."

Kit bowed fractionally, the only sign of his acknowledgment or pleasure.

"For that reason," the Chancellor said, "Master Fisto's thoughts would be invaluable."

Kit Fisto pursed his lips for a moment, as if reluctant to give an unconsidered answer. "Life will always have greater Force-harmony than any machine," he said. "However . . ."

However indeed. The Nautolan's swift, worried glance revealed the rest of his thoughts as clearly as a shout.

"When did these Jedi Killers first appear on the market?" Kit asked.

"About a year ago," Palpatine replied. "Soon after the Clone Wars began. Extensive Trade Federation contracts created a boom on Cestus, which subcontracted for the Baktoid Armor Workshop. After the Battle of Naboo, the Trade Federation distanced itself from the workshop, creating economic chaos. Financially desperate, Cestus turned to the Republic and requested our help. We made a substantial order—" He winced. "—but unfortunately we were spread too thin economically, and payment was not prompt. More chaos resulted. We may have misjudged the importance of this small planet. Lido Shan," he said. "Speak of the Gabonnas."

Lido Shan sighed. "As soon as the war began, we placed certain highly important technical parts on restriction. Among these were Gabonna memory crystals, used by Ord Cestus in the manufacture of high-end Cesta security droids, its most famous nonmilitary product prior to the introduction of the JK line."

"And how did that lead to the current situation?" Obi-Wan asked.

"With the restrictions," Shan said, "Cestus's rather delicate economic balance shifted to the negative. Gabonnas are the only memory crystals fast enough to power a class five personal security droid." She said this flatly, perhaps supposing it to be common knowledge. "Most battle droids are class four, and can run on less extreme hardware."

The Chancellor shook his graying head. "Cestus was . . .

unlucky, and perhaps foolish to place so many of its cocoons in one hutch."

"I see," Obi-Wan said.

Kit Fisto spoke for both of them. "So . . . the situation is quite unstable. Cestus no longer trusts us."

The Chancellor nodded. "You are doubly tasked, my Jedi friends. I have consulted with the Senate and the Jedi Council and we agree that you are to contact the Cestian Regent, one G'Mai Duris. Regain her trust by taking any necessary steps to preserve their existing social order. We must bring them back into the fold and stem the flow of these obscene Jedi Killers." His mouth twisted, as if merely speaking those last words left a bad taste.

"So," Obi-Wan said, attempting to mentally reconstruct the time line. "To the Cestians, the Republic has twice caused economic chaos. I assume they appealed to the Trade Council?"

"Indeed, and we tried to reach a compromise, even offering another, more lucrative military contract."

"And?" Kit asked.

"Negotiations collapsed."

"Because?"

"We were told that payment would have to be in advance." The Chancellor's face grew long. "This we cannot do on a contract of such magnitude."

"Perhaps it is merely my ignorance of commerce," Kit growled, "but surely the Cestians know they flirt with disaster. How can the sale of a few thousand droids be worth such risk?" He leaned forward, his dark eyes swirling with intensity. "Explain."

Lido Shan closed her own eyes for a moment, and then spoke. "The JKs themselves represent only a fraction of Cestus's total economic picture. But they've become fashionable, high-status objects, increasing the value of their entire product line."

"Of course, there are additional problems," Palpatine admitted. "The lower-class population, which of course constitutes ninety-five percent of Cestus, is descended from . . . how do I say this delicately?" He pondered, and then abandoned the effort to be politically correct. "They are descended from uncivilized aboriginals and criminals, and inherited their forebears' unfortunate antisocial tendencies. The wealthiest families, and duly elected government, might well be thrown into turmoil and collapse if a proper solution is not found."

Obi-Wan nodded to himself, thinking that there was much left unsaid here. "Why is the situation so severe?"

"Because Cestus is a relatively barren world, which cannot support its current population without importing soil nutrients, food, medicines, and supplies. Every drop of water consumed by an offworlder must be carefully processed."

"I see."

"So. The first JKs appeared on the market, priced at a premium. This was noted, but was hardly something to be alarmed by. And then a second piece of intelligence reached us."

"That being?" Kit asked.

"That the Confederacy had made an offer to buy thousands of these security droids. Perhaps tens of thousands."

Obi-Wan was stunned. "Has Count Dooku access to such wealth?"

"Apparently," Palpatine said with obvious regret.

Kit Fisto's black eyes narrowed. "I'd assumed that such bioconstructs could not be mass-produced."

"We'd made that assumption as well, Master Fisto. Apparently, we were wrong. We don't know how, but we know why."

"They will be used as battle droids," Kit said.

Battle droids. Obi-Wan winced. "How can this be allowed? Certainly selling military ordnance to the Separatists is forbidden."

"Yes," Lido Shan said. "But there are no laws against selling *security* droids to individual planets in the Confederacy, which is, technically speaking, all Cestus is actually doing. It's irrelevant that the JKs can be converted into lethal implements merely by substituting memory crystals."

Obi-Wan hoped that his face concealed his thoughts, because his most primary emotion was dismay. The idea of bio-droids being converted to death machines was alarming. Such devices might even nullify the slight precognitive advantage enjoyed by Jedi in combat.

It could not be allowed.

"We've learned that Count Dooku offered to supply Cestus with its own Gabonnas, allowing the assembly lines to resume production. He also offered to supply technology allowing Cestus to streamline and increase production of droids and dashta eels."

"Cloning?"

"Yes. The rumors suggest superiority to Kaminoan technology. Techniques that create endless colonies of living neural tissue, allowing their factories to production-line a process that was once quite exclusive and expensive."

"Those who place profit above freedom," Kit said, "generally end with neither." He paused, sensor tendrils waving gently. Perhaps, like Obi-Wan, he envisioned a battle against thousands of machines, each as dangerous as the metal opponent battled on the sands of T'Chuk coliseum. A terrifying wave of precognitive juggernauts.

The Chancellor seemed encouraged that they so swiftly grasped the situation. Indeed, to Obi-Wan's way of thinking, it was the Chancellor himself who barely understood the difficulties ahead. Wise in politics he might be, but Palpatine was still a novice in the ways of the Force.

Obi-Wan found himself thinking aloud. "It might take a special decree to deny Cestus the right to manufacture and sell these droids."

"And meanwhile," Kit said, "the galaxy waits, and watches."

"Indeed," the Chancellor said. The light from the overhead window divided his face. "If the Trade Council dominates precious little Cestus, we will seem like bullying thugs. Before things deteriorate to that level, I, the Senate, and the Jedi Council insist we try diplomacy."

"With a lightsaber?" Kit asked.

The palest of smiles crossed the Chancellor's face. "Hopefully, it won't come to that. My friends, you will travel to Ord Cestus and begin formal discussions. But the negotiations cover your other purpose: to convince Cestus, and through them the other interested star systems, that Count Dooku is too dangerous to deal with."

"And our resources, sir?" Kit asked.

And now, finally, the Chancellor's smile grew certain and strong. "The best of the best."

4

Three hundred kilometers below, the ocean was quiet. From this peaceful vantage point, one would never guess that within those watery depths courageous soldiers were fighting, striving, slaying. Dying.

A steady stream of single-person capsules erupted from the sides of the troop transport ships, blazing their fiery trails down through the atmosphere. Within the transports, corridors surged with unending streams of uniformed troopers. The hallways buzzed with activity, like blood vessels bursting with living cells. The troopers wore not blast armor but flexible black depthsuits. They ran in perfect order and rhythm, knees high and heads erect, heading toward their rendezvous with danger, perhaps death. Each stood exactly 1.78 meters in height, with short black hair and piercing brown eyes. Their skin was pale bronze, with darker variations among those who had spent more time in the sun. Every face was identical, heavy eyebrows and blunt noses prominent above strong narrow mouths.

Clone troopers, every one.

A few were not common troopers, although at the moment few outsiders could have told them apart. These were the Advance Recon Commandos. Representing a tiny fraction of the total clones grown in the Kamino cloning labs, the ARC troopers were the deadliest soldiers ever created.

Contrary to popular belief, even a standard trooper was not merely a mindless shock troop or laser cannon fodder. Trained in a wide spectrum of general military disciplines ranging from hand-to-hand combat to emergency medical techniques, they were also graded from basic soldier to commander based upon field performance. Theoretically, all troopers were equal, but experience and tiny variations in initial cloning conditions inevitably made some more equal than others.

Within one of those ships, the *Nexu,* ran a man whose armor sported the blue captain's color. His helmet and neck chip designated him A-98, known as Nate to his cohort. Although in other times and places he had led his brothers into combat, now he was merely one of identical thousands trotting to their destiny.

The next clone in line locked himself into a cylindrical drop capsule, trusting Nate to do a spec check on the external monitors. Nate went through a mental list as familiar to him as the pattern of creases on his hard right hand. With a brisk, flat slap of that callused palm on its outer wall, he pronounced the capsule sound and secure. Through the heat and shock-resistant plate he could see his brother's eyes. His own eyes, reflected back to him.

With a bump and a *chunk,* the eyes retreated as the capsule sank into the wall, joining the conveyer belt.

He turned, nodded at the next trooper in line, and locked himself into a tube. The man checked Nate's settings, as Nate had a moment before for the man ahead of him. He heard the *bang-slap* against the capsule wall. A comforting sound. To blazes with all the flashing lights: there was nothing more reassuring than another trooper's approval.

The capsule, used on numerous previous drops, stank of sweat—and not his own, although the previous occupant had been a genetic twin. Nate detected traces of antiviral medications designed for functioning in an alien environment. He inhaled deeply, one part of his mind completely on autopilot as the rest of him went through his metal coffin's checklist.

That smell. Sweet, sharp, and organic. *Triptophagea,* he figured. Triptophagea was a drug used to prevent fever on half a dozen planets he could name offhand. Only one of them was the site of recently hot action, and he figured that

that meant the previous occupant had been on Cortao within the last month.

On a deeper level, he was aware that those thoughts were merely distractions from the drop's danger. Risk was always a factor. Fear was a soldier's constant companion. No dishonor in that: what a man *felt* mattered not at all. What he *did* meant everything. He was one of the few ARC troopers in all the galaxy, and as far as Nate was concerned, there was no better existence.

The capsule juddered as it began to move down the transport line. The speaker in his helmet burped to life. *"This is control to Trooper A-Nine-Eight. Estimated time of ejection one minute twenty-four seconds."*

"One minute and twenty-four seconds," Nate repeated, and clenched his fist in invisible salute. "One hundred percent," he said, ARC-speak for *perfect*.

One minute twenty. About eighty heartbeats, long enough for a thousand ugly thoughts to worm their way into an unguarded mind. He'd learned a hundred ways to deal with them, none more powerful than the personal ritual of his cohort meditation. He submerged in its comforting depths, shifting mental swatches of color and shape as he had since childhood, taking solace in the simplicity and beauty of each geometric pattern. He listened to his pulse as his heart slowed to forty beats per minute in response. Chanted the fourteen words engraved on his soul: *It's not what a man fights* with, *it's what he fights* for *that counts*.

Nate fought for the honor of the Grand Army of the Republic, and to him, that obligation was a thing of beauty.

Some thought clones could not appreciate beauty, but they were wrong. Beauty was efficiency and functionality. Beauty was purpose and a lack of waste.

Most equated beauty with effeminacy or lack of utility.

Troopers knew better.

Bump. Another capsule gone. He lurched left as the capsule shifted right, rattling closer to the end of the line.

Bump.

"Fifty seconds," control warned.

BUMP. The shuddering became a hollow swooshing sound, felt in the bones more than heard in the ears. The capsule was moving along more smoothly now, and A-98 took the time to check his settings. There followed a moment of piercing silence. He held his breath, quieting his nerves, finding the place within himself that needed this, that lived for the moment to come.

Then thought ceased as his capsule was spewed from the side of the ship toward the ocean below. Acceleration slammed him back against the capsule walls.

Nate had time to check his visuals. This model was better than his previous capsule, which had kept him in darkness for most of the ride. This one had viewscreens: one giving a view from the capsule's outer skin, the other on some kind of main feed from the *Nexu,* giving an entirely different perspective.

From the perspective of the drop capsule the *Nexu* was a gigantic, angular flat metal shape, bristling with weapons and antennae, capable of carrying twenty thousand troops or megatons of weapons and supplies. Function at its finest.

Then that view was lost, and A-98 was plunging down into Vandor-3's outer atmosphere.

The capsule shuddered as friction warmed its skin to two thousand degrees, heat that would have fried him in an instant if not for the thermoenergetic force screen that sucked heat into the capsule batteries.

Nate checked his equipment as he plummeted toward the dark, churning ocean below. Sensors related the temperature, position, and acceleration. Tiny steering repulsors used the capsule's stored energy to keep him on target.

Everything was fine. Nothing to be done now. Nothing but to fall, and fight, and win. Or die.

His stomach rocked with the sudden vibration as his capsule began to decelerate, the repulsors blasting as sensors warned that they had reached critical distance above the swelling waves.

Within thirty seconds the capsule jolted again as he struck water. The capsule lights switched from yellow-orange to red emergency as some of the lesser systems began to fritz. Zero perspiration: glitches like that were to be expected. The miracle would have been if all systems had remained *intact* through the entire descent.

Sensors revealed that the capsule's skin temperature was dropping rapidly: he was plunging deep now. Nate clenched his mouthpiece between his teeth, testing it to make sure that the cool wind of life-giving oxygen flowed freely. In just a few moments it would be too late to make adjustments. In a few moments, the game would commence.

The comm crackled with intercepted chatter: *"We lost one in quadrant four, another in quadrant two. Stay alive, people!"*

"Sounds like a plan," he muttered, as much to himself as anyone who might have been listening. And there was no reason to mourn when the next moment might well extinguish his own flame: his own warning light flashed. His capsule had malfunctioned. Cold water gushed in through the cracks, flooding him from ankles to knees.

"Warning!" his emergency system brayed at him. *"Hull breach. Warning! Hull breach . . ."*

Thanks for the heads-up, he thought, his entire right side already sopping wet. Well, Nate reflected bitterly, that was what happened when contracts went to the lowest bidder.

"We have breaches in three units on the left flank. Emergency procedures in effect. Request permission to terminate operation."

"Negative!" the commander said, not the slightest centigram of pity in his voice. Nate both admired and resented that quality. *"Proceed to objective."*

The first voice tried again. *"Request permission to implement rescue operation."*

"Negative, Trooper! Designated units will provide backup support. Stay on target."

"One hundred percent," the trooper replied.

Claustrophobia and the caterwauling of doomed men would dismay most, but Nate completed his emergency checklist with machinelike precision, punching buttons and pushing levers even as rising water increased the air pressure until his head threatened to explode.

As the pod juddered and shook, a red diode at eye level counted down to zero. Air hissed into his mouth as the pod's outer hull broke away and water engulfed his world. The pod split along its longitudinal axis: the top half flipped away into the deep as the pod's lower half transformed into a sled.

All around him, hundreds of his brothers floated into formation. He was merely one of an apparently endless multitude maneuvering through the murk. As far as the eye could see, troopers swam and sledded in endless geometric array.

He adjusted the grip and the steering, happy to regain control of his fate. A strange kind of contentment enfolded him. *This* was the life for a man. His destiny in his own hands, flanked by his brothers, spitting in death's bloody eye. He pitied those timid beings who had never experienced the sensation.

Each sled was fitted with its own nose cam, transmitting images into a low-frequency network, generating a fist-size hologram Nate could rotate to examine from any angle.

Trooper formations had the geometric precision of snowflakes or polished gemstones. One might easily have assumed such complex and beautiful patterns to have been rehearsed in advance, but that assumption would be incorrect. The formation was merely the inevitable outcome of countless troopers responding to simple instructions ingrained during their intense, truncated childhoods.

Nate turned his attention from the overall patterns to his own specific tasks. All he needed to do was protect six troopers: those above and below, left and right, front and back. And, of course, trust that they would do the same for him. If he did that, keeping the proper distance, allowing for environmental factors, the clone formations naturally assumed the proper shape for attack and defense. Once battle was actually joined, other core instructions produced other effects.

They moved through the murk, lights flashing out from the individual sleds, illuminating the irregular shapes of plant and animal life arrayed along the ocean floor. Except for the occasional comm crackle in his ears and the thrum of the sled engine, all was silence. All was 100 percent and straight-ahead.

Nate focused on the task at hand, no thoughts of past or future clouding his mind. His arms gripped the handles, his legs kicked a bit, even though the sled had its own propulsion. He enjoyed the sense of his body's impressive resources. A soldier needed infinite endurance, a powerful back, a deep and textured knitting of muscle in the abdomen. Some made the mistake of thinking that it was a trooper's *upper*-body strength that was special. That was all most civilians remembered if they ever saw a trooper without his armor: the densely knotted shoulders and forearms, the thick, blunt, surprisingly dexterous fingers.

But no, the difference was in his legs, capable of carrying twice his own weight up a thirty-degree incline at a steady march. It was in his back, capable of hoisting one of his brothers up and carrying him to safety with no sense of strain. No, a soldier in the field didn't care about how he looked. What mattered was performance under fire.

A voice in his ear chattered. *"We have contact, right flank. Some kind of undersea snake or tendril . . ."*

This was it!

"Evasive maneuvers! Triangulate on sector four-two-seven." A hologram immediately shimmered in the water before his eyes, showing where that sector lay. *Good.* He had yet to see anything that he could call a landmark. The moment he saw something, his training, his "inner map" system, would kick in, but for now he had to rely upon technology.

Something expected but still disturbing cut into his calm: the sound of a trooper's plaintive, truncated scream. Then: *"We've lost one."*

Nate felt the wave of water pressure before his eyes or sensors revealed a threat. All around him his brothers scattered, evading. He watched as a fleshy, cup-lipped tentacle ripped the trooper two rows from his left into the deep, leaving clusters of bubbles behind. The dark clouds billowed in the thousand-eyed glare of their headlamps.

And now he could see what they faced, and cursed himself: how in space had he missed it? The entire ocean floor was covered with immense clusters of what had initially seemed like rock, but were now revealed to be a gigantic, undifferentiated colony of hostile life-forms. Billions of them, a reef stretching in all directions for kilometers, a city of mindless, voracious mouths. Even the tentacles themselves were not mere appendages. Rather, each was composed of millions of smaller organisms, cooperating in some strange way to improve their odds of obtaining sustenance.

His mind combed thousands of information files in a few seconds. *Selenome,* he decided. *Deadly. Native to only one planet, and it sure as space wasn't this one—*

Another voice in his ear: *"How many of these things are there?"*

"Just one freaking big one, enough to kill you if you don't shut up and do your job. Keep the channel clear. Right flank—tighten up. Watch each other's blind spots."

Then there was no more talk, only action. Energy bolts sizzled through the water, freeing vast billowing gas clouds that threatened to obscure their view.

Once again, their understanding and instinct-level programming proved invaluable. If he could so much as see a single trooper, he could estimate the position of others. If he could glimpse the ocean floor, he could guess the size and shape and position of the rest of the formation, and hence determine where and when and *whom* it was safe to shoot.

When a man was sucked screaming into the depths, it tore no fatal hole in their formations: those around him merely closed in and continued to fight. The creature at the ocean floor might have been a self-regenerating horror, a colony creature with no natural enemy save starvation, but the Grand Army of the Republic was its equal. The GAR would live forever, the whole infinitely more durable than any individual part.

"I'm clear! I'm clear!" another voice called.

"We lost another one! Watch your blinds, and cover your brothers!"

"Tendril on your nine!"

"Got it covered."

Nothing about a selenome could be considered routine in the slightest, but Nate, although he had never faced such a challenge, already knew how to fight it. Again, complex behaviors arising from simple instructions.

His blasters were calibrated for underwater combat and demolition. Nate squeezed the trigger in short, controlled bursts, swooping left and right, up and down, evading the searching tentacles. He and his legion of brothers danced to a martial melody, shearing chunks of tentacle until the water was a boiling froth of selenome bits.

We're the GAR, he thought savagely, grinning as one of his brothers evaded a questing tendril by a hairbreadth. *You had no flaming idea who you were messing with, did you, you flak-catching, sewage-sucking—*

A fleshy tendril's grip jolted adrenaline through his veins. Toothed suckers smacked at his sled. Its lights flickered and died. The tentacle chewed at his depthsuit, mouthing at him as it fought to pull him down into the selenome's gaping maw.

Fear chilled his combat fever, and he clamped down on it instantly. What had Jango said? *Put your fear behind you where it belongs. Then blast everything in front of you into splinters. You'll do fine.*

A thousand thousand times he'd repeated those words, and he'd never needed them more.

The tentacle squeezed powerfully enough to break an ordinary man's ribs and grind his spine to paste. Troopers were not ordinary men. Nate inhaled sharply. The captured air transformed his midsection into durasteel, capable of resisting as long as he could postpone exhalation. Like any trooper, Nate could hold his breath for almost four minutes.

Of course, once he was forced to exhale his rib cage would collapse and the selenome would crush him, then devour his shattered body in the darkness. He couldn't concern himself with that. He refused to entertain the possibility of failure. Instead, he freed his rifle and doubled over, firing in short controlled bursts until the tentacle ripped free.

The water boiled black.

"Break off!" the voice in his ear bawled. He didn't know if that was a general order or one intended only for those in his wave, but it hardly mattered. He swam up through the cloudy water. Around him twitched floating chunks of selenome, and pieces of other things he had no intention of inspecting closely. Later, perhaps, in the inevitable dreams to follow.

The ocean floor sloped up to meet him. In a few more meters his feet had traction, and Nate swam and then crawled his way to the surface. Now he towed his broken sled, instead of the other way around.

Nate ripped the mouthpiece out of his lips and sobbed for breath as the waves crashed around him. He wasn't through yet. A quick glance to either side revealed his exhausted brothers, still crawling out of the waves in their hundreds, dragging their equipment behind them. He flopped over onto his back, spitting water and staring in paralytic fatigue at the silvered sky.

The clouds parted. A disklike hovercraft floated down, bristling with armament. Nate closed his eyes and gritted his teeth. This next part he could predict perfectly.

"All right, keep moving," Admiral Baraka called down to them. *"The exercise is over when I say it is."*

Baraka's hovercraft continued down the beach, repeating the same announcement over and over again. Two troopers at Nate's side spat water. They glanced up and shook their heads. "Keep moving?" one said in amazement. "I wonder how fast he'd drag his carcass off the sand if he'd just fought a selenome."

"I'd give a week's rations to find out," Nate muttered.

"How many of us made it?" the other asked.

"Enough," Nate said, and pushed his way up to his feet, collecting his gear and pulling it up the beach. "More than enough."

*   *   *

From his position on the hovercraft, Baraka called down: "Keep moving! This exercise has not concluded! I repeat, has *not* concluded . . ." Admiral Arikakon Baraka was an amphibious Mon Calamarian. Mon Calamari were goggle-eyed and web-handed, with salmon-colored skin and a measured and peaceful manner easy for their opponents to underestimate. But the Mon Calamari warrior clan was second to none, and Baraka held high honors in its ranks. He didn't particularly like clones, but there were prices to be paid for remaining within the Republic's vast and sheltering arms. In one way clones were an advantage: there was no need to conscript civilians or recruit the homeless. That led to an army composed only of professionals.

Baraka heartily supported the notion of experienced, professional tacticians and strategists supplementing Kamino's more theoretical training. After all, when it came down to it the Kaminoans were cloners, not warriors. Baraka had won scars in a hundred battles. Should all that hard-won knowledge die because the Chancellor wanted more of the power collected in his hands? Never! In a soldier, focus and experience reigned supreme: *The tide will slacken, the whirlpool will shrink, the krakana will cower. Such is the power of a focused individual.* Mon Calamari philosopher Toklar had penned those words a thousand years ago, and they still rang true.

So beings like Admiral Baraka came to Vandor-3, the second inhabitable planet in Coruscant's star system, one of many underpopulated worlds where clone training operations were commonly conducted. Clone troopers shipped out to work side by side with native troops on a hundred different systems. They weren't bad soldiers—in fact, he admired their tolerance for pain and ravenous appetite for training.

Destined to be a professional soldier from birth as had his father and grandfather before him, Baraka feared that the birth of the clone army was the death of a tradition that had lasted for a dozen generations.

His sergeant and pilot were both clone troopers, just two more broad-shouldered, tan-skinned human males. Beneath their blast helmets, they had the same flat, broad faces as those crawling from the surf below. "We estimate one point seven percent mortality during these drills," the sergeant said.

"Excellent," Admiral Baraka replied. *Clones are cheaper to grow than to train.* Even he was appalled by the coldness of that thought, but was unable to generate a smidgen of guilt. All along the beach, he saw nothing save hundreds and ultimately thousands of troopers crawling from the waves, their wet, ragged tracks like those of crippled crustaceans. They were an officer's dream: an absolutely consistent product that made it possible to plan campaigns with mathematical precision. No commander in history had ever known *exactly* how his troops would react. Until now.

Yet still . . . still . . . there was a part of Baraka that felt uncomfortable. Was it just the idea of being rendered obsolete? Or was it something else, something even more disturbing that resisted labels?

He couldn't decide. Admiral Baraka had a distant sense that his lack of respect for the clones' dignity and worth had decreased his own, but couldn't help himself.

"Keep moving! Keep moving!" he squalled into his microphone. "This exercise has not concluded. I repeat, has *not* concluded until the objective has been taken . . ."

He flew on, quietly noticing his pilot's and sergeant's helmets turning toward each other. If they hadn't been trained so exactingly, his disdain would probably make them hate him. Considering the killing pressure he placed them under, lesser troopers would have gladly roasted him alive.

But not clone troopers, of course.

As laser cannon fodder went, they were the very best.

5

His day of drills thankfully completed, Nate lay back against the transport's waffled floor as it flew him and fifty of his brothers back to the barracks. Vandor-3 was the severest training exercise he'd yet endured. According to rumor, the mortality rate had edged close to the maximum 2 percent. He did not resent that statistic, however. Nate understood full well that ancient axiom: *The more you sweat in training, the less you bleed in combat.*

He and the other troopers were wounded and weary. Some still trembled with the aftereffects of adrenaline dump. A few chewed nervesticks; one or two sat cross-legged and eyes closed. Some slept, and a few chatted in low tones, mulling over the day's events.

To outsiders, they were all the same, but clones saw all of the differences: the scars, the tanning, the difference in body language due to various trainings, vocal intonation variations due to different service stations, changes in scent due to diet. It didn't matter that they'd all begun life in identical artificial wombs. In millions of tiny ways, their conditioning and experiences were different, and that created differences in both performance and personality.

He peered out of one of the side viewports, down on one of the towns at the outskirts of Vandor-3's capital city. This was a small industrial burg, a petroleum-cracking plant of some kind, surrounded by square kilometers of barren, unused land. This was where the barracks had been built, a temporary city built purely for housing and training fifty thousand troopers.

The barracks was modular, built for quick breakdown or construction, and he had been camped there for the last week, waiting his turn to go through the training drop.

Clone troopers who had already suffered through the drop gave no clue as to the rigors ahead. He'd seen their suction-cup wounds, of course, but the troopers who had already survived the selenome quieted when a trooper lacking a Vandor-3 drop ribbon approached. Early warning of any kind would inevitably degrade the experience. To an outsider such a warning might seem a courtesy, but troopers knew that prior knowledge reduced the severity and emotional stress of the exercise, and therefore decreased a brother's future chances of survival.

The transport dropped them off in front of a huge gray prefab building, housing perhaps three of the troop city's fifty thousand.

Floating on a haze of fatigue, Nate dragged his gear from the transport and through the hallways, nodding sardonically to the troopers already sporting the drop ribbons as they applauded, thumbs-upped, or saluted him, acknowledging what he had just endured.

They had known, he had not. Now he did.

That was all.

He caught a turbolift up to the third level, counting down the ranks of bunks until reaching his own. Nate dropped his gear onto the floor beside his bed, stripped off his clothes, and trudged to the shower.

Nate glimpsed himself in mirrored surfaces as he passed. He had no vanity as ordinary men considered such things, but was intimately aware of his body as a machine, always on the alert for signs that something was wrong, out of place, compromised, damaged. Always aware that the slightest imperfection might negatively affect performance, endangering a mission or a brother's life.

Nate's body was a perfect meld of muscle and sinew, balanced ideally along every plane, optimally muscled, with perfect joint stability and an aerobic capacity that would have humbled a champion chin-bretier. His skin sported recently acquired bruises and abrasions, new wounds to be patched or healed, but such trauma was inevitable.

A-98 entered the refresher station, moving along to the steaming tile-floored confines of the shower room. He leaned against the gushing water, gasping as it struck his new abrasions. After emerging from the ocean onto the bloody beach they had spent another six hours struggling up a hill to capture a stun-gun-protected flag, working against captured or simulated battle droids. A full day of glorious, grueling torture.

The soap squirted out of one of his brothers' hands, and Nate caught it. Then, to the amusement of those around him, he tossed the slippery bar from one hand to another like a carnival performer.

That action triggered a brief wave of spontaneous silliness and dazzling jugglery as the troopers flipped the bars of soap back and forth to each other almost without watching, as if they were linked by a single enormous nervous system.

It went on for several hilarious minutes, then died down due to shared exhaustion. They soaped themselves, wincing as astringent foam flowed into cuts and bruises.

This was his life, and Nate could imagine no other.

Kamino's master cloners had ensured that the troopers were no mere ordinary rank-and-file infantry. Ordinary sentient soldiers the galaxy over could be trained from ignorance to basic skill in six to twelve weeks. Standard clone troopers went from infant to fully trained trooper in about nine years, but in waves numbering in tens of thousands. Clone Commandos were a specialized breed, trained for special operations, recruitment of indigenous troops, and training. The Advanced Recon Commandos were a level higher still.

Ablutions completed, Nate left the shower room and returned to his bunk. Troopers were quite economical in terms of space: they slept in pods when there was no room for individual quarters. They were simultaneously a multitude and a singularity, thousands of identical human units cloned from a single physical and mental combat paragon, a bounty hunter whose name had been Jango Fett.

Their lives were simple. They trained, ate, traveled, fought, and rested. Occasionally they were allowed special stress relief, leading to interaction with ordinary sentient beings, but their training had prepared them for the simplest, most direct experience of life imaginable. They were soldiers. They had known nothing else. They dreamed of nothing else.

Nate found his bunk capsule, kicked his gear into the slot beneath it, and tumbled in, covering his nakedness with the thermal sheet. It automatically assumed seventeen degrees Celsius, the perfect body temperature to provide comfort and optimal healing: one of a trooper's few luxuries in life.

Almost immediately, crushing fatigue bore him down into darkness. As it did, where other men might have released into sleep or tossed and turned, mulling trivial matters, Nate closed his eyes and entered rest mode, rapidly dropping toward dream time. Sleep would come quickly when he decided to let it: another valuable part of his training. No tossing and turning for a trooper. One never knew when an opportunity for sleep would come again. When necessary, Nate could sleep on the march.

But before slumber he was trained to use the thin edge of consciousness, the place between sleeping and waking, to organize information. His subconscious resurrected the day's events, everything from his ascent to the *Nexu* to the initial mission briefing, the drop, and the battle with the selenome, struggling onto the beach, and storming the hill afterward.

Recalled information flowed into preselected mental patterns for storage, contributing to the overall chances of survival and, even more important, of successfully completing assignments.

He remained in this state for fifty minutes, as the tug of the day's fatigue grew more insistent. He could stave off that fatigue for unnaturally long periods of time, but saw no reason to do so. He had performed well, and deserved his rest. And anyway: his dreams would continue to evaluate and organize, even if mostly in symbolic form. That was good enough.

A-98 surrendered consciousness and allowed his body to heal itself. After all, tomorrow was another day.

Best be prepared.

6

In the Jedi Temple's Archives, Obi-Wan Kenobi and Kit Fisto studied their assignment, the industrial powerhouse known as Ord Cestus.

Obi-Wan found Cestus an interesting study, a relatively barren rock rich in certain ores, but miserable for most agricultural farming. Much of its surface was desert. The native life-forms included a hive-based insectile people known as the X'Ting, and a variety of large, deadly, and reputedly nonsentient cave spiders.

The current population stood in the millions, with several advanced cities unsustainable without imported resources: fertilizers and soil nutrients, medications, and spices used to modify the water supply for non-natives.

"Dangerous," Kit said, studying at his side. "A simple rationing drove them into Count Dooku's arms. That could never have happened to a self-sufficient people."

This was simple truth. In war, secure supply lines were as crucial as trained soldiers.

Three hundred standard years before, the relatively primitive X'Ting—a single colony with multiple hives spread around the planet—had contracted with Coruscant, offering land for a galactic prison facility.

At some point Cestus Penitentiary began a program designed to train and utilize prisoner skills. This became *really* interesting when a series of financial scandals and an industrial tragedy on Etti IV sent a dozen minor officers of Cybot Galactica, the Republic's second largest manufacturer, to prison for twenty standard years. The twelve hadn't been on

Cestus for two years before cutting a deal with prison officials to begin research and fabrication of a line of droid products. Access to vast amounts of raw material and virtually free labor released a flood of wealth.

The twelve were quickly and quietly work-furloughed into opulent homes. Select guards and officials became wealthier still, and a corrupt dynastic conglomerate was born: Cestus Cybernetics, producing an excellent line of personal security droids. The next events were difficult to sort out. Large tracts of land were purchased from the hive at fire-sale prices. Then, following terrible plagues among the X'Ting, Cestus Cybernetics gained almost complete control of the planet.

Still, life, even for the average offworlder, had been rough before Cestus Cybernetics subcontracted to the fabulously wealthy and successful Baktoid Armor Workshops. It retooled completely, tapping into an interstellar market in high-end military hardware. The economy expanded, and then crashed when the Trade Federation cut ties after the Naboo fiasco . . .

Boom. Then, crash. Cycles of growth and decay followed one another with numbing regularity.

Obi-Wan scanned the roster of current leaders. Following last century's plagues, after the near destruction of the entire hive, the office of planetary Regent was still held by one of royal X'Ting lineage, one G'Mai Duris. Was this office elective? Hereditary? Was Duris a figurehead, or a genuine power?

Another reference an hour later caught Obi-Wan's eye: mention of a group of guerrilla fighters called Desert Wind. Most of the surface farmers were poor, descended from the rank-and-file prisoners after their parole. Protesting a century of oppression, Desert Wind had sprung up twenty years back and tried to force Cestus's industrial rulers, a cabal of wealthy industrialists called the Five Families, to the bargaining table.

Desert Wind had been crushed in the past year, but there were said to be a few left, still mounting raids on company caravans.

The more deeply Obi-Wan and Kit peered, the more the truth of power on Cestus, and its delicate relationship with Coruscant, evaded them.

"It's like digging through a sponge reef," the Nautolan snarled after eight hours of study. "We'd need a wizard to sort through this nonsense."

"I don't know many wizards," Obi-Wan replied, "but I think a good barrister would be invaluable, and I know just the one."

"Excellent," Kit said. "And another concern. If negotiations go poorly, we may wish to . . . *pressure* this Duris person."

Obi-Wan flinched. The Nautolan was correct, but Obi-Wan preferred caution. "Have you a suggestion?"

"Yes. You and the barrister deal with the politicians. We have—" He searched his screen for the information. "—two contacts on Cestus, a human female named Sheeka Tull and an X'Ting named Trillot. Between them, we should find the necessary leverage."

"If they are trustworthy," Obi-Wan offered.

Kit laughed. "Are you suggesting we can't trust our own people?"

That question hung in the air, tension increasing every moment. Then Obi-Wan laughed. "Of course not."

"Good," the Nautolan said. "As I was saying, I'll take an ARC and a few commandos and recruit native troops for emergency use."

Obi-Wan grasped the logic instantly. If they brought Desert Wind back to life, the regent and these Five Families would be more nervous, less secure, possibly more receptive to Republic overtures. It wouldn't do to have a trooper's body captured: its genetic signature would be evidence of Coruscant's manipulations.

For hours the two friends pored over the files, discussing possibilities and strategies, until they were satisfied that every action and counteraction had been considered.

The rest would have to wait for actual arrival on Cestus.

7

Ten hours later A-98 reawakened, his recovery cycle complete. Nate glanced at his sleep capsule's heads-up screen, which reminded him to report to the op center for orders.

Thirty seconds was spent in a quick mental survey of his body. Another half minute was invested in his morning mental ritual, completing the shift from deep sleep to full waking. True enough, in an emergency he or any trooper could make that shift in seconds, but he enjoyed more leisurely transitions as well.

Self-inspection complete, he threw off his blanket and swung his feet down to the floor. After visiting the 'fresher, washing his face and brushing his teeth at the communal sink, he packed his few belongings into a duffel. According to Code an ARC trooper must be ready to go anywhere, do anything, at the beck of the commanding Jedi or Supreme Chancellor. One hundred percent of Nate's self-image was invested in being that perfect trooper.

There was no other choice, no other existence. A-98 was ready. He had a few small mementos of previous military actions in his rucksack, his equipment, and three days' rations of food and water.

Nate had been raised on Kamino, of course, one of a simultaneously decanted cohort of a thousand clone troopers. A dozen had been designated as Advance Recon Commandos. They had been trained together, taught together, and suffered their first missions together. Half had been chosen for personal training by Jango Fett himself, and had returned to their brothers bruised but steeped in lethal wisdom. ARC clusters were encouraged to develop their own traditions and identity, which was useful during competitions with other cohorts. Although they had initially shipped out together, over time that original cohort had broken, as most ARC troopers worked alone.

He found himself seeking identification on the troopers he encountered, helmet or neck chips that told the time and place of decanting. A cohort brother could be relied upon to remember certain ceremonies and shared perils, always good for a bit of extra companionship. Family within family, a touch of home on a distant, hostile world.

He fondly remembered twenty-kilometer training runs with his cohort, tried not to remember how many brothers he had watched die during his two extended campaigns and dozen smaller actions. In most instances ARC tactics were a blend of lightning attacks and applications of overwhelming force, with punishing combinations of aerial bombardment and devastating ground engagement.

But as satisfying as those victories had been, he longed to take more personal and subtle action as well. He felt that there were aspects of himself yet untapped. He did not fear death, but one thing he *did* fear was the possibility of ending his life without discovering the depths of his abilities. That, as he understood such things, would be a waste.

Nate shrugged his rucksack over his brawny shoulder and headed to the op center, wondering what the day's conversation would bring.

Ten minutes later he was ushered into a small office tucked away beneath an ammo dump and a people-mover ferrying workers back and forth to the city.

His commanding officer, a Mon Calamari major named Apted Squelsh, sat hunched over papers when Nate entered, and for a moment seemed not to realize that she had company. Then she looked up. "A-Nine-Eight?"

"Yes, ma'am?"

"Take a seat, please."

Nate did so, easing into a hard-backed chair of densely

veined Corellian hardwood. He ran a thick thumbnail along the arm's grooved channels as the major finished reading the screen, and then folded her hands to speak to him.

"You performed admirably during yesterday's exercise," she began. "Your unit had a fifty percent reduction in both genuine and sim casualties, with no loss of speed or efficiency. That's what we like to hear."

"Thank you, ma'am."

"I have a new assignment for you," Major Squelsh said, blinking her huge dark eyes. "I assume you are prepared?" Not a real question, but a bit of ritual byplay.

"One hundred percent, ma'am." The ritual response.

"Very good. You will accompany and assist two Jedi to a planet called Ord Cestus. Do you know it?"

"No, ma'am, but I'll get up to speed immediately. My support?"

"Four men," she said.

At last! Actions like these were the doorway to advancement, sought after by any ARC trooper worth manka spit. "Ma'am?"

"Yes?"

"It concerns Admiral Baraka." He paused. "Is the admiral aware of the fatality statistics?"

"Of course." Squelsh's eyes were level, her plump broad lips pressed together tightly.

"And did he say anything you might want to share with us?"

The major paused for an intense moment, then replied, "He said, 'Well done.'"

Nate held his face steady, unwilling to display his emotions to a commanding officer. "Thank you, ma'am."

"That is all."

Well done. They'd left flesh and blood and brothers all over that beach and in the pitiless depths, and "well done" was the best they could get.

Typical.

Nate left and took the beltwalk to the hololibrary to put in a few hours researching the target planet. True, he'd get a briefing packet before he left, but he found it valuable to do his own research as well. Briefing packets were generally quite specific to the mission, and prepared by researchers who had never humped heavy ordnance up a cliff.

Nate was so immersed in his research that he barely noticed when another trooper began reading over his shoulder.

"Hmmm," said the other trooper. "I'm Forry. I was near that sector last month."

That perked up his interest. "Nate. Do you know a planet called Ord Cestus?"

"Heard of it, Nate." Forry peeled a nervestick and bit off a shallow chaw. "Makes droids? Didn't they manufacture those MTTs?"

Multitroop transports. Nearly unstoppable, their armor and twin blaster cannons had cut quite a swath on Naboo. "Maybe so," he said. "Anything else?"

"Only know that much because of that demo yesterday. They made the JK model that Seven-Three-Two went against."

A trooper had gone up against a droid of some kind? Not surprising, but the conversation suggested that it had been an exercise, not actual combat. "I hadn't heard. What happened?"

Forry shrugged. "He was captured. JKs are some kind of special security model. It only took about twenty seconds, and he's still in the infirmary."

Now his whole attention was riveted. "Do we have vid footage?"

"Sure," Forry said. "I'll call it for you." He began to brush crystals on the desk in front of them, and holoimages blossomed to misty life.

"Thanks. Planet's interesting. Generations ago Cestus was a prison rock."

"Truth?"

"One hundred percent. The descendants of those prisoners eventually settled there and became miners or farmers. They were exploited by the descendants of the prison guards, who owned the company."

Forry shrugged again. "It's the same all over. Ah! Here we go . . ."

The footage had been recorded in the T'Chuk arena, no more than forty hours earlier. He watched as the trooper made standard evasive moves, and even a few admirably tricky broken-rhythm maneuvers. Ultimately, none of them worked. Their brother went down, hard, in just a few miserable seconds.

Disturbing.

"You go up against, better zap it from a distance."

They watched a replay. "Fast," Nate said. "As a Jedi?"

"Faster," Forry said. "But speed isn't everything. Look at this . . ." He hit other controls. The footage of a Jedi with protruding head tentacles appeared.

"From Glee Anselm," Nate said. "Don't see many Nautolans around. Jedi, eh?"

"Who else would use one of those archaic light sticks?"

They shared a good laugh at that. The Jedi were awesome fighters, but their adherence to illogical quasi-spiritual beliefs was beyond Nate's comprehension. Why would a fighting man trust anything beyond a steady eye, a strong back, and a fully charged blaster? He examined the Nautolan Jedi's image again. "So a Jedi actually came down from the Temple and rolled the dice. And?"

"Watch for yourself."

Nate triggered PLAY, and together they watched as the Jedi not only stood his ground against the JK, but actually forced it into retreat. Nate inhaled sharply as the Jedi beat the thing at its own game. In some ways his tactics weren't that different from those attempted by the trooper, but the results were impressively superior.

"Beat it."

"Umm-hmmm." Forry clucked admiringly. "Did you see that timing?"

"Uh-huh. Never seen reflexes like that, either. You're right: the machine was faster, but it didn't make any difference."

"Jedi." Forry laughed. It was hard to say whether the laughter was bitter or admiring. Perhaps a touch of both. "So they watched a trooper go down, and just had to get down there and show off."

Nate caught the implication: the Jedi might have even programmed the droid. How could the droid move faster and still lose? Unless it was *instructed* to lose . . .

Nonsense. They both knew a Jedi would never do such a thing. This was nothing but lingering unease, a defensive technique to hide the slight feeling of inferiority troopers sometimes felt around Temple dwellers.

"They beat Jango," both of them said simultaneously. These three words were almost a litany. Whatever they could say about Jedi being strange, or egotistical, or bizarrely esoteric, in an arena on Geonosis they had slain the clone troopers' template, and that meant they were worthy of respect.

"Good hunting," Forry said to him.

"Good hunting," Nate replied. Then he paused. "You been given your next op yet?"

"Nope," Forry said. "Dealing me in?"

"If you want it."

"One hundred percent. Let me check in and out, get my sack and tac."

"You'll have orders within the hour." A crushing handshake, and Forry went his way.

Brother gone, Nate opened a window. "Request status." A moment's pause, and then medical stats blurred past. He nodded in approval. CT-36/732, nicknamed Sirty, had not been wounded by the JK. His nervous system had been momentarily overloaded, and he had consequently suffered a few hours of irregular heart rhythm. Nothing alarming, but of course he had been taken to a med droid for observation.

Sirty would be in fighting shape soon, and would make a perfect team member: the only trooper who had fought the JK.

"Special request CT-36/732 be seconded to the Cestus operation."

A *"Request approved"* message bleeped, and then the screen closed.

For hours he studied, trying to get the kind of random

background intel never covered in standard tac briefings. One just never knew which bit of data might save one's butt once the capacitors started sparking. Nate himself would be dead now, blown to jelly in the battle on Geonosis, if he hadn't studied power-cell recharge cycles and subsequently recognized when one of the wheel droids was entering a reflux pattern. Its capacitor's whine was barely audible, but he'd taken a chance, leapt from cover, and blasted it, saving five of his cohort.

That little maneuver resulted in a week's free food at the base cantina and a fast track to his captaincy.

He dictated notes into his personal file for transfer to the Cestus-bound transport ship. For hours he continued, fiercely maintaining focus.

The lives of his brothers and, more important, the honor of the GAR were his to protect. And even more than that— this was his game, the game he was born and bred to play. In a way that no outsider could ever understand, this was *fun*.

8

Only two hours remained.

Nate and six of his brothers stood in a bricked, walled-off area outside the ribbed arch of the barracks, beneath Vandor-3's densely starred night sky, performing a cohort ship-out ceremony. Whenever a trooper headed off on assignment, his cohort wished him not only good luck, but good-bye. In the context of a trooper's life, this was more practicality than pessimism.

If he did return, congratulations on a job well done.

If he did not, well . . . what needed to be said had been said.

"It is the proudest duty of a trooper to serve and seek a good death," said Glorii Profus, their Kaminoan mentor.

The graceful, silver-skinned Profus was a combination psychiatric and spiritual adviser. Although clones never yielded to their fear, it would be wrong to think that they never experienced it. Emotion was as valuable as blasters and bombs, death an inevitable part of war itself. No trooper could, through any amount of skill or strength, avoid that unpleasant reality. And always, on all planets and through all times, soldiers had asked the same question: *What if I die?* And for a trooper, the most comforting answer was: *You will die. But the GAR goes on forever.*

The Kaminoan gracefully arched his long silver neck and raised his cup, brimming with Tallian wine, the finest in the quadrant. His voice was cultured and comforting. "From water you are born. In fire you die. Your bodies seed the stars," he said, the ritual words that had comforted a million clones before they marched to their deaths, and might comfort a billion more.

They raised their cups as one. "We seed the stars!" they said, together.

And then they drank.

9

The Jedi Temple dominated Coruscant's cityscape for kilometers around, its five towering spires piercing the clouds like a titan's outstretched fingers. Within the countless hallways and corridors, the lecture halls and exercise yards, libraries and meditation chambers were all designed with an intrinsic grace and flow. Within them, even the least gifted were sensitized to contemplate that Force binding the universe into a single organism.

The Council itself met in chambers less prepossessing but no less dignified than those of the Chancellor. Its arched walls and hangings had been created by the galaxy's finest craftspeople. Such richness would cost a fortune to reproduce, but most of the furnishings were gifts from rulers and merchants whose lives, wealth, and honor had been protected by Jedi skills over the millennia.

Obi-Wan had long since grown accustomed to the opulence, and gave it little notice as he stood at ease before the Council, awaiting their pronouncement.

Master Yoda's wizened head tilted slightly sideways as Obi-Wan Kenobi and Kit Fisto consulted with them.

"These are confusing times," Obi-Wan said. "In many ways, our former mandate has been suspended, and much of our authority curtailed."

"Strife changes many things," Yoda said. "Unpredictable these Clone Wars prove to be."

"But now I am sent on a sensitive diplomatic mission, involving treaties on multiple levels—such complexity that we require a barrister just to sort them out." Obi-Wan considered his next words carefully. "I have never refused a mission, but must tell you honestly that I feel ill prepared for this . . . this maze of commerce and politics."

Master Yoda frowned. "Worry I do. No longer may Jedi look to the words and actions of Masters past for their guidance. Strange new times are these." The other Jedi in the room nodded in agreement. This subject had been debated long and hard, but in the end, the Jedi were obliged to fulfill the Senate's and the Chancellor's wishes.

At the moment, Mace Windu's face resembled a somber mask sculpted of onyx duracrete. Of all the Jedi, it was Master Windu who held status closest to that of Yoda. "I agree, but the Republic has never been tested so severely. If asked to accept new roles, we must respond. If we cannot protect the Republic, to whom should the responsibility fall?"

"It augurs well that Palpatine still seeks diplomatic solutions," Kit said.

"Then why not send diplomats?" Obi-Wan asked, realizing as he did that he already knew the answer: diplomacy was only the first layer of the Chancellor's response. Palpatine knew that a Jedi's mere presence was a durasteel fist in a furred glove.

"The war goes well," Master Windu said, "but we are forced into too many unfamiliar roles. If we are not careful, we may lose our clarity of purpose and intent. Too often, lightsabers are required where once words alone sufficed."

Yoda nodded. "Once, Jedi had only to appear to quiet a crowd. Now common brawlers we become."

"It is the matter of Antar Four, and even the Battle of Jabiim," Windu said. Those grim memories triggered a murmur of regret.

"There have been more victories than failures," Obi-Wan reminded them.

"I agree," Master Windu said, "but the maintenance of social order requires both myth and reality." Once upon a time it had been difficult for Obi-Wan to comprehend Windu's meanings. The Master Jedi's profound meditations lifted him to a realm few could dream of, let alone experience. But in more recent years Obi-Wan had begun not merely to appreciate these pronouncements but almost to anticipate them. "And the myth has been fractured: only the reality remains. This situation on Cestus is delicate, and involves these Force-sensitive droids. Ultimately, a swift and clear resolution would save many lives." He leaned forward and fixed Obi-Wan with a gaze that might have cut diamonds. "Whatever misgivings you may have," Master Windu said, "you are asked to accept this mission with your usual integrity and commitment. Master Kenobi, Master Fisto, for every conceivable reason, you must not fail."

Kit Fisto bowed, and his sensory tendrils wavered eagerly, like sea fronds in an invisible current. "I gladly accept."

"I also accept," Obi Wan said, then added, "I will bring Ord Cestus back into the fold. We will end these Jedi Killers."

Yoda's eyes glowed warmly. "With the Force as our guide, into peace war may yet transform."

10

For three hours Obi-Wan lay in his cubicle's hard bed, slowing and synchronizing his body's rhythms to maximize the restorative benefits. Where an ordinary mind and body wavered in and out of the mental and physical zones of recuperation, every minute spent in this extreme state was worth three minutes of ordinary slumber. He emerged rested and ready, packing his gear and rendezvousing with Kit for the flight to Cestus.

In the Temple's communal dining hall, the two Jedi shared a meal of thrantcill pâté and hawk-bat eggs. While eating they spoke in quiet voices of trivial things, understanding that the days ahead would be intense. Memories of such quiet times were sustaining.

They took an air taxi out to Centralia Memorial Spaceport. The port was one of Coruscant's oldest, some of its older pads actually preserved as monuments even as the rest of the spaceport expanded out into one of the galaxy's most modern facilities. There awaited the Jedi a refurbished Republic cruiser, its scarlet skin panels open at the aft wing as technicians made last-minute adjustments to the fuel atomizer cone and radiation dampers.

They'd half finished supervising their ship's loading when a military shuttle arrived, its triwing configuration folded for docking. Five troopers in gleaming white armor exited.

If Obi-Wan was entirely honest with himself, he had to admit that large groups of clone troopers made him slightly uncomfortable. Easy to understand and explain away. One factor was the fact that they were the absolute image of the notorious bounty hunter Jango Fett, who had come within a hair of killing him on three separate occasions. More disturbing still was the fact that, although genetically human, they had not led human lives: clone troopers were born and bred purely for war, without the nurturance of a mother's embrace, or the safety of a father's loving discipline.

They looked human . . . they laughed and ate and fought and died like men. But if not human, what exactly were they?

"General Kenobi." The trooper saluted. "CT-Three-Six/Seven-Three-Two reporting. May we take your gear, sir?" His bearing and attitude were clear and crisp, his eyes guileless. A memory floated to mind. Hadn't CT-36/732 been the trooper who'd fought the JK? The young man seemed healthy. No slightest gesture betrayed physical or emotional pain of any kind. Remarkable.

"Yes, please stow it in our cabin." With admirable ease the trooper slung his gear over his left shoulder, a nod his only response.

Obi-Wan was surprised by his slight aversion. It mirrored the prejudice he knew some others to feel, people who treated the troopers as if they were little more than droids. This was unworthy of him, of any Jedi. These terribly young men, no matter what their origin, were prepared to die in service to the Republic. What more could anyone ask? If their progenitor had been evil (and Obi-Wan was not entirely certain that that word fit the complex and mysterious Jango Fett), his clones had died already in their thousands. How many deaths would it take to wash away an assassin's stain?

"Oh my, oh my," a falsetto voice cried behind them. Obi-Wan turned, recognition filtering its way through his other thoughts. Approaching slowly was a creature with a great flat turquoise shell covering a wet, fleshy body. The creature crept along on a single many-toed foot. A yellowish mucus trail glistened on the ground behind him.

Obi-Wan smiled, all discomfiture vanishing. This one, he knew. "Barrister Snoil!" he said with genuine pleasure. Politicians Obi-Wan distrusted, and in most cases their minions were even worse. Regardless, Doolb Snoil was one of the three or four finest legal minds of his acquaintance, and had proven worthy of trust during sensitive negotiations on Rijel-12. Of Vippit extraction from the planet Nal Hutta, Snoil had attended one of Mrlsst's renowned legal universities before beginning his initial apprenticeship in the Gevarno Cluster. A celebrated career and a reputation for exhaustive research and absolute reliability had led Snoil to his current berth. If anyone could make sense out of this Cestus mess, it would be Snoil.

"Master Kenobi!" he said, twin eyestalks wobbling in delight. "It's been almost twelve years."

Obi-Wan noted the new rings and deposits on the turquoise shell, clear evidence that Doolb had been able to afford regular treatments and shipments of his native viptiel plants, high in the nutrients his people used to prepare themselves for the rigors of householding. In another few years, he reckoned, Snoil would return home to mate. If Nal Hutta's economics were anything like Kenobi remembered, Snoil would have his pick of the most desirable females. "I see by your shell that you have been prosperous."

"One tries." His eyestalks swiveled around. "And—Master Fisto! Oh, my goodness. I did not know that you were accompanying us."

Kit clasped Snoil's hand. "Good to have you along, Barrister. I know your home. Once upon a time I spent a week trench diving on Nal Hutta."

"Goodness gracious! So dangerous! The fire-kraken—"

"Are no longer an issue." Kit smiled broadly and continued up the ramp.

Snoil raised one of his stubby hands, then the other, and rubbed them together eagerly. "Fear not!" he cried in his tremulous falsetto. "When the right moment arrives, Barrister Snoil will not be found wanting."

Snoil crawled the rest of the way up the landing ramp. The Vippit was followed by five troopers moving equipment and armament aboard. They acknowledged the two Jedi and continued their work.

A trooper displaying captain's colors saluted sharply. "General Kenobi?"

"Yes?"

"Captain A-Nine-Eight at your service. My orders." He handed Obi-Wan a thumbnail-sized data chip.

Obi-Wan inserted the chip into his datapad, and it swiftly generated a hologram. He studied the mission résumé and skill sets, and was satisfied. "Everything is in order," he nodded. "This is my colleague, Master Kit Fisto."

The trooper regarded Kit with an emotion Obi-Wan recognized instantly: respect. "General Fisto, an honor to serve with you." Fascinating. To Obi-Wan, the trooper had merely been polite. His body language toward Kit suggested a greater level of esteem. Obi-Wan swiftly guessed why: the clone had seen vid of Kit's droid encounter. If there was one thing a soldier respected, it was another fighter's prowess.

"Captain," Kit said. Obi-Wan said nothing, but he noted that, in some way that had escaped him, Kit and the clone trooper had made an emotional connection. This was a good thing. Kit was raring to go, always. Obi-Wan was cursed by a constant urge to understand the reason for his missions—Kit merely needed a target. He envied the Nautolan's clarity.

The trooper turned to his four men. "Get the equipment aboard," he said, and they hastened to obey.

Kit turned to Obi-Wan. "They are utterly obedient," he noted, perhaps again anticipating Obi-Wan's own thoughts.

"Because they have been trained to be," he said. "Not out of any sense of independent judgment or choice."

Kit looked at him curiously, his sensor tendrils twitching. Then he and the Nautolan entered the ship and prepared for their journey.

Within minutes all the gear was stowed, the checklists completed, the protocols passed. The ship hummed, and then hovered, then with an explosive acceleration broke free of Coruscant's gravity and lanced up into the clouds.

Obi-Wan winced. His voyage from Forscan VI was gruelingly recent, but that was preferable to flying with a stranger at the controls. Better still was simply staying on the ground.

Obi-Wan found his way up to the nose of the ship and settled into an acceleration couch as the ship rose. The clouds gave way to clear blue. The blue itself faded and darkened as they entered the blackness of space.

Around the horizon's graceful curve hovered twelve giant transport ships, shuttling clone troopers from Coruscant bunkers to Vandor-3, the second most populous planet in Coruscant's system. He'd heard that Vandor-3's ocean was a brutal clone-testing ground. Officials had spoken of it as if discussing profit-and-loss balance sheets. Obi-Wan found that obscene, but still, what was the alternative? What was right and wrong in their current situation? The Separatists could turn out endless automata on assembly lines. Should the Republic recruit or conscript comparable living armies? Jango Fett, the GAR's original genetic model, had gladly placed himself in the most hazardous situations imaginable. A man of war if ever one had lived. Was it wrong to channel his "children" down the same path?

Kit had appeared behind him. "They do nothing but prepare for war," he said, again mirroring Obi-Wan's thoughts.

Obi-Wan smiled. That Jedi anticipation, manifesting in a different arena. He found himself relaxing, hoping now to be able to take advantage of Kit's sensitivity in the trying days ahead. "What manner of life is this?"

"A soldier's," Kit replied, as if this was the only possible, or desirable, answer.

And perhaps it was.

Of course, he himself had left enough tissue about the galaxy for Kamino's master cloners to have created quite a different army. And if they had, to what purpose might it have been put?

He laughed at that thought. And although the Nautolan arched an eyebrow in unasked query, Obi-Wan kept his darkly amused speculations to himself.

11

For two hours Obi-Wan Kenobi and Kit Fisto had practiced with their lightsabers, increasing their pace slowly and steadily as the minutes passed. The cargo bay sizzled with an energized metallic tang as their sabers singed moisture from the air.

A Jedi's life was his or her lightsaber. Some criticized the weapon, saying that a blaster or bomb was more efficient, making it easier for a soldier to kill from a distance. To those who reckoned such things statistically, this was an important advantage.

But a Jedi was not a soldier, not an assassin, not a killer, although upon occasion they had been forced into such roles. For Jedi Knights, the *interaction* between Jedi and the life-form in question was a vital aspect of the energy field from which they drew their powers. Ship-to-ship combat, sentient versus nonsentient, warrior against warrior: it mattered not. The interaction itself created a web of energy. A Jedi climbed it, surfed it, drew power from it. In standing within arm's reach of an opponent, a Jedi walked the edge between life and death.

Obi-Wan and Kit had been engaged for an hour now, each seeking holes in the other's defense. Obi-Wan swiftly discovered that Kit was the better swordfighter, astonishingly aggressive and intuitive in comparison with Obi-Wan's more measured style. But the Nautolan gave himself deliberate disadvantages, hampered himself in terms of balance, limited his speed, emphasized his nondominant side to force himself to full attention, the kind of full attention that can be best accessed only when life itself is at risk. To relax and feel the flow of the Force under such stress was the true road to mastery.

A Master from the Sabilon region of Glee Anselm, Kit was a practitioner of Form I lightsaber combat: it was the most ancient style of fighting, based on ancient sword techniques. Obi-Wan's own Padawan learner, Anakin, used Form V, which concentrated on strength. The lethal Count Dooku had used Form II, an elegant, precise style that stressed advanced precision in blade manipulation.

Obi-Wan himself specialized in Form III. This form grew out of laser-blast deflection training, and maximized defensive protection.

For hours the two danced without music, at first falling into a preplanned series of moves and countermoves learned in the Temple under Master Yoda's tutelage. As they grew more accustomed to each other's rhythms, they progressed into a flowing web of spontaneous engagement. Slowly, minute by minute, they increased pace, stuttered the rhythm, increasing the acuteness of attack angles and beginning to utilize feints and distractions, binds, rapid changes in level, and to introduce random environmental elements into the interaction: furniture, walls, slippery floors. To an observer it would have seemed that the two were trying to slaughter each other, but the two knew that they were engaged in the most profound and enjoyable aspect of Jedi play, lightsaber flow.

At a crucial instant Kit hissed, more to himself than Obi-Wan, then stepped back, disengaged, and switched his lightsaber off.

Obi-Wan switched his off as well. "What is it, my friend?" he asked.

"The bio-droid," Kit said, anger heating his voice. "I should have performed better."

"You were brilliant. What more could you have done?"

Kit sat heavily, his smooth green forearms resting on his knees, sensor tendrils curling and questing like a nest of angry sand vipers. "I should have gone closer to the edge," he said, the irises within the unblinking eyes expanding until they appeared to glow. "Released myself into the Force, become more unpredictable. More . . . random."

Obi-Wan heard the concern in the Nautolan's voice. Form I was wild, raw . . . and deadly. It also required too much emotional heat for Obi-Wan's taste. "That would have been dangerous," he said, choosing his words carefully. "Not to your body, perhaps, but to your spirit."

Kit looked up at him, irises contracting again. "It is the way of Form One."

And here Obi-Wan knew he needed to tread softly. Combat style was an exceedingly personal choice. "Agreed," Obi-Wan replied, "but Form One represents greater risk to you as well, my friend."

Kit said nothing for a time, and then slowly, almost imperceptibly, nodded. "We all take risks."

That simple truth momentarily silenced Obi-Wan. There it was: Kit knew that Form I placed him in greater jeopardy, but his sense of duty made it worthwhile. In that moment Obi-Wan's respect for the Nautolan rose to the highest levels.

For now, the best thing that he could do was help get Kit's mind off the subject. He stood, briskly slapping his palms together. "But come!" he said. "If our ruse is to succeed we must practice a while longer. Then I need to get back to work on the lightwhip."

That seemed to lift Kit's spirits. "When will it be ready to test?"

Obi-Wan sighed. "I've never actually built one, but saw a bounty hunter wield one once, in the Koornacht Cluster. The theory is clear enough, and I found a diagram in the archives. Just remember: if covert action becomes necessary, all suspicion must fall on Count Dooku. If you are seen wielding a lightsaber, you'll be identified as a Jedi."

"Less conversation." Kit grinned. "More practice."

They returned to their dance, each sensitive to his differences but comfortable in them as well. On and on they went, until exertion drove all thought from their conscious minds, until all discussions were forgotten, and all that remained was a pure joy of moving, separately and together, in the way of the Force.

12

Concluding his practice session, Obi-Wan freshened himself and donned a new robe. He then went out to the lower deck lounge. There, in a more comfortable environment than the formal dining room just fore of them, he found Barrister Snoil studying at two computer workstations, each of his eyestalks engaged with a different holographic display.

"A useful skill," Obi-Wan said, just behind the barrister's right ear. "You comprehend both simultaneously?"

Snoil turned, startled. "Master Kenobi! I didn't realize you were there. As to your question . . . yes, my people can split attention between sides of their brain," he said. "The full reintegration will not take place until sleep tonight." Genuine concern creased Snoil's glistening face. "Actually, I am glad you are here. I was hoping we might confer."

"On what matter?"

"These treaties!" His falsetto rose to a squeak. "A nightmare! Ord Cestus was never supposed to be a major industrial power. When it was initially set up, Coruscant granted it quite favorable trade terms. The point was for the prison to be self-sufficient, and not a burden to the Republic."

"And now?"

"And now the prison exists as a legal fiction only, a definition expanded to include the entire planet. Cestus markets goods under a corrections license."

Snoil paused, eye stalks wavering almost hypnotically. He canted his head slightly to the side, as if considering a new thought. When he spoke next, his voice sparked with renewed enthusiasm. "Delicate. Delicate. If we threaten a suspension of activity while their status is reevaluated, that should panic them."

"Right into Dooku's arms," Obi-Wan said, and shook his head. "Hardly a desirable outcome."

"True," the Vippit replied, then lowered his voice. "I was actually more concerned about another subject."

"That being?"

"Well . . . it is my Time," he said, emphasizing the last word.

"For children?"

Snoil nodded emphatically. "Oh yes. Master Obi-Wan, I am so happy you called me. For years I've owed you a great debt."

Obi-Wan laughed. "We're friends. You owe me nothing."

"You saved my life," he said fervently, and his twin eyestalks bobbled. "I was under contract on Rijel-Twelve when the clans revolted. If you hadn't evacuated Republic staff, my empty shell would lie there still."

Well, yes, Obi-Wan had handled a bad bit of business there, but . . .

Snoil would not be denied. "Until I repay the favor, I cannot marry."

Obi-Wan couldn't *wait* to hear the explanation. The galaxy's wonders never ceased to amuse and amaze him. "No? Why not?"

Genuine anguish filled Snoil's voice. "Because you can call upon me for a service whenever you wish. No well-born female would bond with me until I have cleared this debt, because I cannot negotiate wholly with her."

"This is your people's way?"

Snoil nodded.

Obi-Wan laughed heartily. "Well, my friend, my confidence in our mission just soared. It seems you have more reason to see this job through than I."

13

Over the three hundred years since initial entry into the Republic, Cestus's native population had decreased by 90 percent, while the immigrant population had increased to several million. Their needs were so different from those of the original inhabitants that, without interstellar commerce, that population would starve or be forced into migration and poverty.

Hundreds of years earlier, Cestus had been a world of amber sands and coppery-brown hills, mostly rock with a few blue pools of surface water and the scaled ridges of continental mountain ranges. Its poor soil was home to a thousand varieties of hardy plants whose root acids constantly struggled to break down rock into absorbable nutrients. Most notable among its vegetation were some eight hundred varieties of edible and medicinal mushrooms, none of which had ever been exported.

However poor it might once have been, with the rigorous filtering of Cestus's water and addition of various nutrients, the planet's soil offered up two dozen vegetables suitable for consumption. After fifteen generations of cultivation, significant patches of green now stretched across the brown expanse, some few of them visible even from space.

From high orbit, it would have been difficult to see the industrial areas that produced the Baktoid armor or dreaded bio-droids, or see any reason at all to think that this secluded planet might become a crucial balance point in a drama playing out across the galaxy. However difficult to believe, it was a sobering truth.

*   *   *

Their transport cruiser made its initial descent to a section of the Dashta plain selected for the tiny amount of electromagnetic activity in the area: evidence that there was little or no entrenched population. The offworlders wished to avoid prying eyes. Ahead lay work best done in privacy.

For an hour the troopers humped crates and rucksacks full of gear out of the ship. Kit insisted on carrying his own equipment, and the troopers were happy to let him do it: the Jedi was as strong as any two of them. For half the trip Obi-Wan had labored on the weapon now coiled at Kit's side. Kit had a reputation for improvisation, and within hours he handled the lightwhip as if he had been spawned with it.

Obi-Wan turned to Kit and extended his hand. "Well," he said, "this is where we part."

"For now," Kit said. "We'll set up base camp in the caves south of here, and should be ready for operations in a day. After that, we'll be ready for whatever comes."

"I'm sure you will," Obi-Wan said. "Communication on astromech remote maintenance channels shouldn't alert their security. We'll disguise our conversation as modulations of the basic carrier frequency."

Kit nodded, but the smile on his lips didn't reach his eyes. "A good idea. May the Force be with you."

There was little left to do save play out their hand as dealt. Obi-Wan stood, looking out at the horizon, at the dust devils spinning and churning. Beyond those, a rust-colored cloud crept across the ground, peaceful and lovely at this distance, one of the sandstorms that made surface living on Cestus such a hazard. Obi-Wan understood perfectly why Cestus had been chosen as a prison.

The four remaining clone troopers stayed behind with Kit. Obi-Wan walked back up into the ship, and the door sealed behind him.

He strapped himself into the empty chair next to CT-X270, checked to make sure Doolb Snoil was safe, and then nodded. "Let's go, Xutoo," he said.

*   *   *

Kit checked the instrumentation on his Aratech 74-Z speeder bike, modified military hardware as maneuverable as a hawk-bat and capable of speeds up to 550 kilometers per hour. Riding one reminded the Nautolan of storm-swimming, one of his favorite sports.

The four directional steering vanes were well adjusted and responsive to a touch. The repulsorlift engines purred like demicots and had no problem handling the heavy cargo bags strapped to the sides. All fuel cells were full, all diagnostics live. Good. He raised his hand, and the clone troopers mounted their own speeders as if they had practiced that single maneuver for a month. He breathed deeply. Fire burned his veins as his twin hearts went slightly out of rhythm with each other, preparing him for action. This was the moment that he lived for, the calm before the storm. Like swimming the surface during one of Glee Anselm's mammoth hurricanes, or the practice of Form I, it was the storm itself that was the test, the challenge to see if he could maintain his balance in the whirlwind. Never had he fallen. One day he would, as all mortals did. *But not today,* he grinned fiercely. *Not today.*

He triggered the speeder. The purr became a growl as it lifted.

In perfect formation the five sailed through the gullies and along rivers through a tumble of low brown scrub brush.

Although most nearby objects whipped past in a blur, those more distant remained clear. Kit drank in the scenery, noting the far-off line of a caravan out along the scrub rock. The speeder bikes traveled too low to be seen, low enough for the speeders behind him to be swallowed in the storm of dust particles, baffling scanners.

At one moment they passed a small knot of nomadic X'Ting, the insectile people who had once dominated the planet. While still holding some political power, they now numbered but a few tens of thousands. The nomads raised their crimson arms and pointed at the line of speeder bikes as they raced past.

Again, nothing to really worry about. He convinced himself that this wasn't an omen. Encountering the Cestians in the midst of such a desolate area was just happenstance. Nomadic native Cestians tended to be nontechnological, used no devices that emitted radiation anywhere in the electromagnetic spectrum. Nothing to worry about . . .

Cestus called to Kit. In this landscape he sensed the struggle of life against an unsparing nature. It reminded him of his homeworld's surface territory, a land of great harshness, but one that bred a people of tremendous courage. Except for a lack of vast and roiling oceans, he might have been born here.

On the next speeder bike behind him, Nate traversed the same landscape, occupied by his own thoughts. The ARC captain scanned everything, searching for ambush spots, possible strongholds, lines of sight . . . everything he saw, everything he thought was connected to his duty. There was room in his mind for nothing else. Nor was anything else needed.

Kilometer by kilometer, they progressed toward their goal, the Dashta Mountains far to the west.

14

After assuming a trajectory plausible for a ship approaching from Coruscant, CT-X270, "Xutoo," reentered Cestus's atmosphere. The cruiser's communications array fired, automated docking signal receivers decoding instructions for landing.

They headed straight for Cestus's capital city, ChikatLik, an X'Ting word meaning "the center." Xutoo handled the controls with supreme confidence, as if he had been born piloting ships.

Then again, for all practical purposes, he had.

They descended through the umber heart of a swirling kilometers-wide dust cloud that obscured most of the surface beneath them. The guidance computer projected wireframe animations of their target, and revealed more of the surface detail than Obi-Wan's naked eyes. One of Cestus's primary features was the vast network of tunnels, created by volcanic activity, water erosion, and millennia of digging by the once vast X'Ting hives. It was these caves that had made it such a perfect choice for a prison planet, and it was into one of the larger lava tubes that their ship descended.

As they entered its mouth, the air cleared, and for the first time during their descent visual cues revealed valuable information. After a few seconds the sides became pleasantly painted and sculpted. Obi-Wan caught a few briefly snatched glimpses of graffiti, and then networks of pipe and steel, mazes of rigging clearly the product of endless generations of workers.

He noticed also that the laborers seemed to have done

everything in their power to keep a sense of the original beauty, and he admired that. As much as the works of mortals could be, and often were, quite beautiful, there was always something about the natural world that touched Obi-Wan even more deeply, as if a testament to the truth and depth of the Force that conscious efforts could never approach.

They zoomed down another tunnel and turned left. Artificial light reflected around the corner. For a moment he was blinded.

ChikatLik's offices and apartments blended with the volcanic structures so perfectly that it was difficult to see where they ended and mortal workings began. He saw a thousand elevated roads and pedestrian paths, but little aerial travel. Many of the curved, apparently stone paths streamed with slidewalks, a local transport system that seemed to have grown organically over the years until the entire city bustled like a close-up, impossibly intimate view of a living body's interior.

Their ship spiraled down through the towers and roadways, heading to a central landing pad at the outskirts of their destination, some kind of major living complex. Where volcanic rock was obscured the walls had the texture of rough gray or black duracrete, perhaps some compound produced by the digestive systems of hive builders.

As the ship came softly to rest, one of the side screens showed a line of uniformed human males standing at attention. Obi-Wan knew that Xutoo had already killed the main engines so that no stray heat or radiation would spoil the approach.

Doolb Snoil's emerald eyestalks quivered with excitement. "Look at the honor guard!"

"Yes," Obi-Wan replied. "It must be rare to see representatives from Coruscant out here on the Rim. I fear that this has more than mere business significance."

"Ah," Snoil said. "I would expect some aspects of hive politics to survive. Expect complex, confusing social interactions, Master Jedi."

Obi-Wan laughed. It was true: no longer was he a mere

peacekeeper. Today he was an ambassador, an envoy from the central government. Like it or not, he would have to accept that role.

The guards were near-human Kiffar, who immediately snapped to attention as the door opened and the ramp touched down. "Master Kenobi, it is my pleasure to welcome you to ChikatLik," the nearest guard said. "I've only just received word that the Regent is on parlay. Hive business. She returns tonight, and will meet with you tomorrow."

Obi-Wan nodded sagely, and Snoil's eyestalks bobbed with pleasure.

A band composed of assorted droid musicians blared a medley of melodic bleeps and hoots, doubtless the Cestian planetary anthem, as Obi-Wan, Snoil, and their astromech unit descended. The band next performed a passable rendition of the Republic's official anthem, "All Stars Burn as One." Once upon a time that song had quickened his blood, but for the last months Obi-Wan had begun to bristle whenever he heard it.

After their rendition was complete, the Kiffar guard saluted again. "Thank you," Obi-Wan said, and Snoil's eyestalks ceased waving in accompaniment to the music. In truth, it *had* been stirring.

"Welcome to Cestus. General Kenobi, Barrister Snoil."

Obi-Wan nodded. "Thank you, Sergeant. I hope that all business can be completed quickly, that I might have an opportunity to appreciate the beauty of your world before I return home."

The words flowed so smoothly that Obi-Wan laughed to himself. In truth, he might have made a passable politician. Peacemakers and power brokers had to meet to find common ground, and if he had chosen that path . . .

With that thought in his mind, and a resultant half smile curling his lips, Obi-Wan allowed himself and Snoil to be escorted to a railway running above the free-flying transport lanes.

"Few buildings on the planet's surface," Snoil asked. "Why?"

"The natural caverns were easy to exploit for prison space, and safer from dust storms and raiding aboriginals. That was long ago."

"And now?" Obi-Wan asked.

"And now?" Their guide shrugged. "The plagues left a lot of hives empty. We just moved right in."

As they followed the cart, a pair of droids carried their luggage from the ship and placed it in a separate cart, to follow them. Many of the buildings and structures were themselves imitations of stalactites and stalagmites, but there were flashes of different artistic or architectural movements as well, angular areas, evidence of a hundred different cultural influences.

They approached a particularly large and beautiful expanse of carved rock wall. Only on a second look did it resolve into a building. "Our destination," the guard said.

"What is it?" Obi-Wan said. It was almost a kilometer across, one of the largest city constructs Obi-Wan had seen on a Rim world, so enormous that at first he had mistaken it for an organic part of the overall structure.

"The Grand ChikatLik was the first actual prison building built here," their guide said. "It was converted fifty years ago, and now serves as our finest hotel."

He could see it all more clearly now: a few hundred years of constant rebuilding, one apartment and cubicle grafted onto another had been smoothed into an overall design that was somewhere between a kind of insect hive and a gigantic office complex, something that transcended either artificial or organic design. Impressive.

Their cart zagged right, entered what appeared to be a lava tube, and emerged in the hotel lobby. The interior was quite literally cavernous, a lobby built around a luminous natural hot spring, lift tubes thrusting up through cascading shelves of frozen limestone.

The silvery protocol droid concierge approached them, fairly shivering with excitement. "Welcome! You are now guests of the most luxurious hotel on Ord Cestus."

Snoil's fleshy lips curled in appreciation. "After days on the shuttle, it's good to have a room, not a cabin," he squeaked.

Two X'Ting attendants materialized just as their luggage cart appeared behind them. The X'Ting were dull gold, with oval bodies and thin, apparently spindly legs. "Show these two very special guests to their accommodations," the droid said. Perhaps fantasizing about generous tips from the distinguished guests, the attendants eagerly carried their luggage to droid carts, then guided the carts to the turbolifts. Obi-Wan noted that one of the X'Ting wore a name tag reading FIZZIK.

The lifts rose along the cave's internal wall, rising rapidly but smoothly, then rotating so that the wall slid open to disclose a hallway.

The X'Ting attendants unloaded their luggage and carried it into the suite. The droid bowed. "I hope that these lodgings will prove satisfactory, sirs."

Obi-Wan found himself answering more to the attendants than the protocol droid. "I'm certain that they'll be fine."

"You may wish to explore the city in the time before the lady arrives."

"Very considerate. I'm certain we can entertain ourselves."

The protocol droid left, motioning for Fizzik and the other X'Ting to leave with him, and they did.

Doolb Snoil began to speak, but the Jedi raised a single finger, bidding him to silence. Their astromech began a sweep of the room as Obi-Wan unpacked, every motion slow and controlled.

"Which room should I take?" Snoil asked.

"Whichever has the better view," Obi-Wan said. "I remember you said you wanted to see the sights here . . ." He was prepared to continue in that vein, but fortunately their astromech unit beeped its *"all clear"* signal.

"I believe it's safe. This room is free of any devices or eavesdropping scans. Our mech will tell us if this changes."

"Thank the Broodmaster," Snoil said, wiping one of his

brows. "I tell you honestly, Master Obi-Wan. I find this spying-about most uncomfortable."

"You needn't worry about any of that," Obi-Wan said. "Just do your job, and I'll do mine."

"And how do you see things proceeding?"

"As we said before—" He sat near Snoil, putting his own thoughts in order as he tried to incorporate what he had seen and heard since landing. "—we go to court, and see what there is to be seen."

"And if our entreaties are ignored?"

"Then," Obi-Wan said thoughtfully, "then things get tricky."

15

Kit Fisto, Nate, and his three brothers had arrived stealthily, making their initial surveillance of the Dashta Mountain region specified by their mysterious contact, Sheeka Tull. Tull had designated a cave hidden beneath an overhanging rock shelf, opening onto a broad, flat stone theater that could be used as an emergency landing zone, although for security, the main staging area was located hundreds of meters downhill from the cave entrance.

On first glance the cave looked ideal, but Kit entered gingerly, sensor tendrils tingling. The shaggy desiccated body of some four-legged mammal half the size of a speeder bike lay just inside the cave. There were no immediately apparent wounds . . . had it simply crawled into the cave to die? He nudged the body aside and took another step forward. Nothing living to be seen. Side tunnels stretched off in multiple directions. Cave birds and some membranous reptilians flitted about overhead. Moss and old dusty webbing clotted some of the corners, but he found nothing alarming.

"There might be something here," Nate said, coming up behind him.

"Perhaps we should find another cave," CT-12/74 said. His nickname was Seefor.

"Not until we make contact with Tull," Kit said.

Here in the shelter of a craggy valley almost completely devoid of all but the simplest vegetation, they spent the first hours building their base camp and sleeping quarters, assembling sections of modular housing. They were so engrossed in their work that they barely noticed when the first of the cave spiders appeared.

Kit cursed himself for not recognizing the webs or the ragged, furry, desiccated corpse for what they were, but when the first eight-legged monstrosity bounced out of the shadows to leap onto Sirty, the Nautolan moved instantly. The spider screamed as his lightsaber seared through a leg, then the trooper bucked it off, putting three shots into the beast before the body hit the ground.

They hardly had time to congratulate themselves: six cave spiders of equal size crawled from the darkness.

Kit ordered the troopers into perfect square formation, shoulder blasters at the ready as their eight-legged attackers emerged. Somewhere back in the caves was a nest, pure and simple, and they had responded to the challenge for their territory. No time to regret. This was action.

A cascade of cave spider silk jetted toward the trooper diagonal from Kit. Nate. The trooper shoulder-rolled and came up to firing position, blasted the rocks above the spider's hiding place. As stones rained down on the unfortunate creature Nate rolled again and ran to one of the speeder bikes.

Fleeing? Absurd. In the GAR's short, spectacular history, no trooper had ever shirked duty, fled a battle, or even disobeyed a superior's order. But—

Immediately behind him a great shaggy eight-legged beast hissed and leapt. Kit pivoted, lightsaber singing. The spider bounded out of the way, landing in a crouch. It bounded again, spitting venom. Kit dodged to the side, lightsaber swatting one of the caustic greenish gobs, and the fluid erupted into searing steam. The rocks before them rustled, and a swarm of young spiders, no higher than Kit's knee, crawled out, their shining eyes hungry, envenomed fangs dripping.

He glimpsed movement and turned to see a gigantic red female, half the size of a bantha, crouching in the shadows, watching, her glowing eyes fixed on him. A general, directing her troops.

This Kit could understand. Well, as of the commencement of the Clone Wars Kit Fisto was a general as well, and he had his own troops. *Come on!* he snarled silently, irises expanding. He set his feet in a wider stance for balance, and waited.

Nate's speeder bike started instantly. Under his expert hands it leapt off the cave floor and ran in a tight circle, buzzing the shadows, turning tight corners, drawing out the spiders. They spit silk and venom at him, and every time they did, his brothers below got a better fix. Incandescent laser bolts and the howling of Kit Fisto's lightsaber filled the cave as the spiders fought back, casting bizarre, distorted shadows against the walls. The arachnids jumped, leapt, and crept. They spit venom that burned through armor, and sticky silk that threatened to bind arms and legs together. But nothing they did broke the Geonosis Square, a tactic that maximized the impact of both aggressive and defensive fire.

The trooper wove, using the speeder bike's maneuverability to confuse the spiders. Their eight-legged adversaries were quicker on the ground, but seemed baffled by this high-flying tactic. General Fisto gave a whistle so loud and high that it rattled Nate's ears at twenty meters. The other troopers broke for their speeders, and within moments the cave was filled with screaming, dipping, blasting speeder bikes.

Nate laughed aloud, loving this moment. It was like being back with the selenome: *You didn't know what you were messing with, did you?*

His laughter died as another row of arachnids crawled out of the top cavern. *What in space—?* They must have stumbled into the largest breeding ground in the entire mountains. This was the worst, what troopers called 10 percent, but it was too late to curse fate. Little to do now but fight.

At least six of the large spiders, and dozens of the smaller ones, had perished in blasts, lightsaber strokes, and showers of falling rock before they retreated shrieking into the caves. The largest, the enormous red-furred female, protected the others as they fled.

The troopers started to pursue, but the general raised his hands. "No!" he called. "They're broken. Let the brood go."

The female locked eyes with the general. Surprisingly, she

lowered her head as if making obeisance, then backed into the shadows and disappeared.

The troopers landed their craft, peering into the darkness to be certain no mistake had been made before holstering their weapons.

"Perimeter sensors up *immediately,*" General Fisto said.

"So we're staying here, sir?" Nate asked.

General Fisto's answering smile was not pretty. "Might as well assume all these caves are spider-infested. At least we know this one is clear."

"Besides that," Sirty whispered to Nate when General Fisto turned away, "we fought for it. It's ours."

As the others set up in the cave, Kit Fisto carried his broadcasting unit a kilometer out to a completely desolate area with no line of sight to their new camp. There he triggered his beacon and sat in wait.

After five seconds he turned it off. He waited five minutes, then broadcast for another five seconds, and set the automatic monitor to continue in like sequence: five minutes off, five seconds on.

After an hour he heard an answering squeal in proper coded series. He turned off the monitor and waited.

The sun was nearing the western horizon when a battered cargo ship appeared from the south. It flew in a slow, groaning circle and then settled toward the ground, frying the underbrush as it did. That thermal inefficiency implied an older model, and in merely adequate repair.

The panel door opened and a ramp descended. Kit heard a bleeping sound, and then a human female appeared at the top.

Kit had few standards by which to assess human beauty. Based on her movements and posture, however, this female was in excellent physical condition, her unblemished black skin and lustrous short hair suggested a healthy immune system, and she seemed quite aware and alert. Good. They would need these qualities to successfully implement their plans.

The woman studied Kit, her expression one of exasperation. "A Nautolan. Pretty far from an ocean, aren't you?"

The Jedi was unamused. "I'm waiting," he said.

She rolled her eyes. "No sense of humor. All right: 'Alderaan has three moons.' "

" 'Demos Four but two,' " Kit replied without hesitation.

She nodded as if he had confirmed more than identity. "Name's Sheeka Tull. I was told to expect you."

"What precisely were you told?"

She scuffed her toe across a line in the ground, raising a tiny plug of fine, dry dust. "They said if I helped you, certain things in my past would be forgotten. That right?" She looked back up at him, defiance sparkling in her eyes. He nodded, and she seemed relieved. "So. What do you need?"

"What I *need* is a reliable contact. There were cave spiders."

She shook her head. "There are spiders all through these mountains, but I didn't see any when I checked out that cave. Sorry."

Kit locked eyes with her, a test of wills. Was she telling the truth? She was his contact, given by the Chancellor's most trusted tacticians. Trust was his only option. "Very well. I must speak to the anarchists known as Desert Wind," he said.

"They took quite a beating last year," Sheeka Tull said. "What do you want with them?"

"You have no need to know that," he replied.

"No." Her eyes narrowed. "That is *exactly* what I need to know. If you won't tell me, I can't help you. I wouldn't dare."

Kit watched her. If he had known her longer, he might have determined if she was telling the truth, or bluffing. A useful ability, but again, calibration was everything. He had to make a field decision, one that was tough no matter how he looked at it. "We need to create an effective force capable of sabotage and deception, in case the government needs to be overthrown."

He knew that his words rocked her, but she hid her flinch very well. "Well. Thanks for the honesty."

"You can take us to Desert Wind?"

"No. But I can take you to the people who know them."

"Fair enough."

"After you're finished here, you never heard of me." She stood with her small fists balled against her waist.

"Fair enough."

She nodded, and drew a little circle in the dust with the point of her toe. "All right, then," she said. "Time for you to meet *Spindragon*."

16

The insectile Cestian's name was Fizzik, and at the moment he was at his most aggressively ambitious, in the peak of his species' three-year cycle between male and female genders. In his current state, the coursing of masculine hormones was a nerve-dulling intoxicant, and made him willing to take almost any risk to obtain the medicine that would balance the hormones more smoothly. The plant capable of easing, or even accelerating, the transition was called viptiel, native to a world called Nal Hutta. Far too expensive for a mere hotel attendant.

And that was why Fizzik decided to sell his soul to his distant brother Trillot. He waddled his bright gold oval through the crowd until he found a certain alley, disguised as a minor lava tube. Everywhere, the walls were slathered with promotions for various exhibits and attractions, and both flat and holographic commercials attempted to lure stray credits from unwary pockets.

Fizzik had not been here for a year and a half. If there were a few who might have recognized him, they probably failed due to the fact that he had been female the last time he had passed this way.

Once, hundreds of standard years ago, the planet had belonged to the X'Ting, who had driven their only rivals, the spider clans, into the distant mountains. But the coming of the Republic had changed everything. At first hailed as a triumph for the hive, in time the offworlders controlled everything. Regardless of what anyone said, the last century's plagues had been no more or less than attempted genocide:

the hives had all but collapsed, and Cestus Cybernetics became the planet's de facto ruler. Most surviving X'Ting were relegated to cesspools such as this wretched slum. Some, of course (for instance, that worthless drone Duris, or Quill, the current head of the hive council), had sold their people out in exchange for power. Those traitors were the pampered pets of the Five Families.

In his female persona, Fizzik often secured domestic work amid the offworlder upper classes. When he cycled back to male, most offworlder employers found his powerful pheromones sufficiently unpleasant to terminate his employment. So . . . down to the gutter again, scraping for a living until his emerging feminine persona earned him a better berth. Moving between social tissues over the years had earned him a wide network of contacts—a net wide enough, in fact, to have snared a valuable bit of information: that the Grand ChikatLik's newest arrivals were critically important visitors from Coruscant. There was every chance he might be able to sell such information to one of the most powerful X'Ting in the capital, the being who held the threads connecting the criminal underworld to the labor organizers to the true masters of Old Cestus: Fizzik's brother Trillot.

In a few minutes he arrived at a heavy, oval iron door set in a shadowed corridor off bustling Ore Boulevard. In one sense, it was important to know the code words. In another, those who came to this door and sought entrance without having funds to spend or something to sell would find themselves on the wrong end of a flame-knife.

The guards, one blue-skinned humanoid Wroonian and a gigantic furred Wookiee, glared down on Fizzik with no discernible shift in their facial expressions.

"Need to see my brother," Fizzik said, and added a code word known only to hive siblings.

The guards nodded blandly and opened the door. One walked ahead of him, although he looked around as they moved down the shadowed corridor.

The hallway was lined with small alcoves, in which various galactic life-forms reclined in shadow, alone or in pairs, staring out at him with vast, glassy eyes before sinking back into whatever thoughts or dreams had occupied them.

"What you need Trillot for?" the Wroonian asked.

"Got information. His ears only."

The guard grunted. "What you say? You want to eat diamonds?"

Fizzik despaired. One would think that a being of Trillot's wealth and power would employ the very best help, but that rarely seemed to be the case. "Just take me there."

"His brood-mother *what*?" the guard said, turning. His face now betrayed a trace of emotion, and it was not at all pleasant.

Fizzik realized the trap he had entered. The alcoves around him rustled with curious eyes. This was nothing less than a shakedown. He thrust his hand into his pocket and pulled out a handful of credits. His last. Oh, well, life was a gamble. If this one paid off, in a few minutes he would be flush. If not . . . well, the dead had no use for money.

As soon as the credits touched the thug's hands, the Wroonian smiled broadly. "Oh!" he said. "Oh! You want to see *Trillot*." He made the credits disappear, and then swept a curtain aside.

At first Fizzik could see only a broad couch, but as his eyes adjusted to the darkness, he was able to make out his brother.

Trillot was three broods senior to Fizzik. Like Fizzik, he was a minor child of a noble but impoverished brood-mother, his only inheritance a yearning for the wealth and power of ages past. Unlike Fizzik, however, Trillot had talent and a willingness to take risks. After a false start working in communications for Cestus Cybernetics, he found his niche in labor relations. Trillot's three-year cycle between male and female personae tended to keep his immigrant opponents and rivals slightly off-guard. Fizzik knew that, unlike most X'Ting, Trillot used an imported cocktail of viptiel and other exotic herbs to collapse the monthlong breeding period at either end of the gender cycle into mere hours of numbed transformation. No incapacity, no fertility. No mewling grubs for one as ambitious as Trillot.

Five years later Trillot had proven his worth to a local Tenloss syndicate, and two years after that he resigned from Cestus Cybernetics to work directly for the overboss himself.

A mysterious series of tragic accidents had cleared the way for Trillot's ascension. Well, unexplained as long as Trillot himself chose not to comment.

Everything that followed was almost preordained. Seeing Trillot's utter ruthlessness and perhaps sensing the inevitability of his ascension, the overboss fled Cestus, leaving the power in Trillot's capable hands.

It was too little, too late. The overboss met with an accident, almost as if someone wished to ensure he would never return to attempt to claim what had once been his.

Trillot's power in ChikatLik had never really been challenged. Were he not cautious, such a challenge have might come in the lethargic monthlong transition between genders suffered by most of his kind. Another motivation to use the illegal viptiel cocktail that allowed him to make this transition in a single painful night. Trillot was aggressive at all times.

In the twilight zone between labor and management, between white and black market, between upper and lower class, between offworlder and X'Ting hive council, there was no fixer like Trillot, and everyone knew it.

Like most male X'Ting he was a deceptively delicate, insectile creature. His every motion seemed as carefully cultivated and pondered as a master's game of dejarik. A high, crystalline brow over faceted eyes and an elongated oval for a body gave the impression of vast intelligence and great gentility. Fizzik knew that only the former impression was correct.

But Trillot's thorax was red and swelling, a clear sign of feminization. Such a rapid shift had to be agonizing, and Fizzik wondered what herbs and drugs Trillot used to control the pain. And then more to clarify his mind from all the oth-

STEVEN BARNES   91

ers. And then more to protect himself from the toxic effects of the previous dosages. And then more . . .

Fizzik was dizzy just thinking about it.

Trillot spoke to the guard in a clicking, popping language that seemed odd emerging from his strangely prim mouth. The guard answered in the same indecipherable tongue. Then his head pivoted to face his guest. "Ah. Fizzik," he said. Fizzik had heard more warmth and welcome in the voice of an execution droid. "It seems you have information for me. Ah, come along. No, no. Of course, if your information is sound, there will be compensation."

"I wish only to serve my elder brother." Fizzik lowered his eyes respectfully.

"Ah." Trillot's body seemed to move one section at a time, so that one part of it always remained still while the rest was in motion. It was unnerving to watch. Although of the same species, Fizzik had never possessed such plasticity. Trillot walked a bit awkwardly, his swelling egg sac unbalancing his stride. They traversed a dark corridor lined with alcoves, from which the glittering eyes of a dozen species watched them pass. Trillot seemed to have attracted Cestus's entire underclass. Fizzik knew that the offworlder majority on the planet had dominated many of the other species to the point that less than 3 percent were native Cestians.

The passage through the corridor was punctuated with low, respectful bows from Trillot's coterie of hideous bodyguards. Suddenly Trillot stopped and sniffed the air. Now for the first time, Fizzik saw something like emotion cross the golden face. If he had to make a guess, he would have said that his elder sibling was unhappy. This would not be pretty.

"I smell Xyathone," Trillot said. He looked at the guard. "Do you smell it?"

"No, sir," the guard replied in a Bothan dialect that Fizzik actually understood. Trillot was rumored to speak more than a hundred languages, and Fizzik was inclined to believe it.

"I do." He moved closer to one of the alcoves. A thin tendril of steam wound its way from beyond, and Fizzik pulled the curtain aside.

Two Chadra-Fan were curled into the darkness, inhaling vapor from a boiling flask. Trillot sniffed again, deeply. He spoke to them in their own language, and then turned. "Guntar!" he called.

The guards hustled, and for that moment Fizzik thought Trillot had forgotten him completely. They returned shortly, dragging a fat little gray ball of a Zeetsa behind them. Trillot looked down on the sphere as it prostrated itself. "Did you sell my guests the mushroom?"

Lips appeared on the sphere's surface. "Yes," Guntar babbled. "Of course. Nothing but the best—"

"And why then has it been cut with Xyathone?"

The little Zeetsa was the very picture of outraged innocence. "What? I did not know, I swear—"

"Do you indeed? Then perhaps your senses are insufficiently acute. You should have smelled it. Tasted it in the mixing. Do you say that that insignificant nose and tongue of yours aren't up to the task?"

There was a pause, and Fizzik tensed. There would be no happy resolution to this matter.

"I . . . I suppose . . ."

"You know how I loathe inefficiency." To his guards: "See that the offending organs are removed."

The ball screamed as the guards dragged him away. Trillot turned back to the Chadra-Fan. He spoke to them in their chittering tongue. They replied, and he drew the curtains shut. To the guards: "See that they get the best. From my personal stock."

"Yes, sir."

Trillot pulled the corners of his mouth into something approximating a smile. "Come with me now, Fizzik. It will take a few minutes to reach my sanctum. I suggest that you use them composing your report. After all—" From somewhere in the darkness behind them echoed a stomach-curdling scream. "—you know how I loathe inefficiency."

17

For hours the clone troopers had busied themselves in the cool, deep shadows of the Dashta Mountains. They glued, fitted, and welded, joining together hundreds of preformed durasteel sections, melding them with native materials to create the nucleus of a fine command center.

"So where's our first strike?" Forry asked Nate as they worked.

He shrugged in response. "Give me a spot-weld, right here." Their astromech unit extended a soldering probe. "First of all," he said, shielding his eyes against a bright, sharp shower of sparks, "there's reason to think we might not get used at all. General Kenobi's supposed to *protect* the entrenched political and economic forces."

"Yeah, right," Sirty said.

"But if it does go down?"

Nate grunted. "Then I'd guess we'll hit Cestus Cybernetics."

"Sounds like a plan."

Their comlink bleeped; a tone said that they'd be expecting friendly visitors in a little under a minute, and they were not to respond with force. That beacon triggered long before they heard the distant but distinct *swoosh* of air. A few seconds later General Fisto's speeder bike appeared.

Nate wandered out to the pad, feeling loose, dangerous, and satisfied. In a matter of hours they had turned this mountain hole into a reasonable headquarters.

He watched the Nautolan's speeder glide over the smooth and jagged rock surfaces, heading north. Nate followed on foot, arriving in time to watch a cargo ship arrive on the open spot they'd chosen as their secondary landing zone.

The door opened, and the walkway extended. A dark-skinned human female exited, following Kit back up toward the cave. Nate saluted as Kit passed. The woman glanced at him with little curiosity as she and Kit entered the cave. The Jedi received salutations from the other clones. He briefly evaluated the work that they had already performed, then took the woman to a scanner and showed her some material. They conferred briefly, and Kit said: "Captain, Forry, I wish you to accompany us."

"Yes, sir," they said simultaneously.

Spindragon was a suborbital YT-1200 medium freighter. She was old, melded with parts from other similar models, with a rounded hull and an elongated, tubular cockpit. Nate spent a few minutes examining the welds. Although it was obvious that a dozen different soldering mixtures had been used, as well as a bit of Corellian epoxy, they seemed strong enough to stand up to high-g turns, and he gave his approval.

The interior was barely more than functional: little bits of decoration suggested an attempt at aesthetics, but nothing frilly enough to decrease utility.

The woman cocked her head sideways at the ARC trooper, trying to peer through his helmet. "I didn't catch your name," she said.

"Trooper A-Nine-Eight."

She snorted. "Is there a short version of that?"

"Call me Nate," he said. Curiosity flickered in her dark eyes, and her lips pursed as if Sheeka Tull was tempted to ask a question. She didn't surrender to temptation, but he guessed that she hadn't shuffled him into the *nonbeing* category to which most citizens automatically relegated clones.

Within minutes they were all strapped in and ready to go. She rose from their landing pad and spiraled up into the sky, flying southeast for about fifteen minutes, then north for another ten.

A small manufacturing complex lay before them. Nate

made a quick tactical assessment: several mine dropshaft shacks, living quarters, a small refinery, some shipping docks, landing docks, water filtration equipment, and communications towers. Next to a series of condensation coils nestled a blue bubble that he figured was a polarizing hothouse, using shielded plastics to change their sun's spectral range so that a wider variety of plants could be grown. Typical settlement. Fragile. Easy to destroy.

But he remained silent. A major part of his job was just being visually impressive. Most citizens had never seen clone troopers, although they had doubtless heard tales.

He and Forry were first down the ramp when it extended, followed by Sheeka Tull and the Jedi.

The community seemed to have turned out for them, but he noticed that there were precious few X'Ting in the crowd. Most were humans, a few were Wookiees, and there was a smattering of other species. No doubt many of them were descendants of the original prisoners.

The farmers and miners relaxed noticeably when Sheeka appeared, and she waved to them. She was known here. Good. That would make things far simpler than if they had to establish either trust or dominance.

"Greetings to all of you," she said to them. "I'm glad you showed up, though I can't say I'm sure what this is about. But these are the people I told you to expect. I won't vouch for them. Keep your ears and eyes open, and make up your own minds."

They nodded, and Nate had to respect her speech: Tull might be willing to bring them here, but even whatever leverage the Republic had upon her could not force her to sell her honor by pretending friendship. Good. He liked her more all the time.

General Fisto stood at the bottom of the ramp and raised his hands. His tentacles curled and coiled hypnotically.

"Miners!" he called. "You harvest ore from the soil. You transport, refine, and manufacture. You are this world's heart."

The faces were doubtful, but intrigued. Nate noted that

several of the younger ones looked at him as well, studying him as if wishing his helmet were transparent.

"You stir the tides of commerce," the general went on. "It is your hands that hold the materials, skills, equipment, and raw material to build their luxuries."

When several of them nodded, he knew General Fisto was speaking their language. The only question was whether or not they truly cared to hear his words.

"But despite this fact, how often have you been included in their decisions?"

"Never," someone muttered.

"How often have you shared in their harvest? Do you grasp that their droids are among the galaxy's most prized possessions? There is nothing wrong with growing wealthy, but the wealth should be shared with those who do the dirtiest, most dangerous work." As he proceeded, the emotion in his voice grew more and more pronounced. "Your ancestors came here in chains. For all the power you wield, you may as well wear them still."

He had their interest now, but he would need far more to make this gambit successful.

"Even now, your masters court war with the Republic."

This triggered a series of gasps and ugly murmurs. A few of them might have had no love for the Republic—the kind who might automatically side with Cestus against the strength of a thousand-ship fleet. Others felt no such bravado, and shifted nervously from foot to foot, as if fearing they stood in a bantha trap with closing jaws.

"Why are they doin' that?" an older woman asked. The wind stirred the tips of her gray-streaked hair.

"They sell these deadly droids to the Confederacy. They will be modified and used against the Republic." At this, Nate stood just a hair taller, and noticed that his brother Forry did as well. Eyes focused upon them. What thoughts flitted through their minds? Did they regard the troopers as potential enemies? Imagine them dying? Or killing? Studying them as potential allies? Wondering what it might be like to fight at the side of an ARC trooper? Certainly, some here had blood hot enough to crave such an adventure, such a test.

"In fact, we have information suggesting that they plan to mass-market these droids offplanet, once the secret is secured."

"What? It couldn't happen. The Guides—" a female miner began, but then the farmer to Nate's right gave her ribs a painful elbow thump, and she fell silent.

Interesting.

"Yes," Kit continued, as if he could read both Nate's mind and that of the woman who had just spoken. "You have been told that it is impossible for more than a few hundred of them to be produced, because of the dashta eels."

The group was even more uncomfortable now, but Nate intuited that the problem was multifaceted. Some were afraid, a few outraged, and in one . . . two pairs of eyes he saw a skepticism so deep that he knew automatically: *These know something.*

"But they are willing to gamble with your survival in order to make their fortunes."

"How do you know that?" one young blond-haired man asked. "The Five Families live here. You can't sink half a sand-wagon, Nautolan."

"Yes. They live here, but are not *trapped* here. Wealth makes many things possible. Those owning the designs will grow fat. You must ask yourself—would those who already restrict you to a subsistence living hesitate to beggar you completely?" An ugly murmur rumbled through the crowd. "You tell me: over the last years and decades, have they treated you as if your lives, your families, your needs and wants are of concern to them?"

And now there was a wider range of nodding and agreement.

One X'Ting female, a tuft of red fur vibrant between thorax and chin, her body broad with internal egg sac, stepped forward. This was rare. Where once millions had swarmed the hives, no more than fifty thousand X'Ting remained on the entire planet. She was larger than most of the human males, who gave her a wide berth. "What you want from us?" Her clumsy speech marked her as a low-caste. Her dusky face reddened with emotion, and her secondary arms fidgeted. "No more pretty-pretty talk. Heard them before. What you offer us, and what you want from us?"

"I offer you nothing save what every planet in the Republic has been promised: a fair voice in the Senate, access to the shared resources of a thousand star systems, and our support in forcing your government to share the wealth with those who produce it. What I ask in return is this: if I prove my point to you, if we can prove that your leaders are prepared to sell your birthright, to betray the Republic, to leave you drowning in the ash of a war-torn planet while they escape to the stars with your children's heritage—if I can prove these things to you—"

General Fisto's unblinking black eyes fixed on several of the young males in the group, and a few young females as well. To Nate's pleasure, he noted that they drew their shoulders back. They rocked back and forth, glancing at each other, as if tempted to step forward even now.

At this cue Nate and Forry doffed their helmets and stood more rigidly. Their identical faces always caused a stir: some thought them twins; others had heard of the clone army, and just needed to put a face to the mental image.

Sheeka Tull's eyes snapped wide. She stepped backward as if she'd been slapped. She looked from Nate to Forry and back again three times, and then retreated until he couldn't see her.

"—that you allow your best and brightest to join us if they so choose," the general concluded.

"That all?" the X'Ting woman asked.

"That is enough. Do not reject my words out of hand. Let us find whatever support there is to be found. We wish nothing that you do not want to give."

The people chattered among themselves, then ventured new questions. Nate guessed that the most important issue was whether or not they had an actual choice in this matter. And he silently congratulated the general for deliberately—

or instinctively—choosing the right tactic to appeal to these disenfranchised people. He noted that their young men and women were listening most closely, measuring General Fisto's words as if they were handfuls of gravel with gems possibly hidden in the mix.

The general promised to keep the farmers posted as to progress, and they continued on to the next group. As they returned to the ship, Sheeka Tull took the Jedi aside and spoke to him urgently, gesticulating at the two clone troopers. Nate couldn't hear the conversation, but when it was done she looked a bit shell-shocked. She walked past Nate and Forry without looking at them, and took the pilot's seat without another word.

For the rest of the day they followed the same routine. The dark-skinned woman would introduce them, and General Fisto went into his spiel while Nate and Forry stood tall. The general made no direct reference to the clone troopers, but he knew they had to be wondering if these were the troopers they had heard so much of—and was there, possibly, a role for them in the planetary militias currently being organized in every corner of the galaxy?

Nate knew the answer to that question, the same answer that generals and conquerors had known since the beginning of civilization: there is always room for another willing warrior.

After the third talk, the Nautolan was engaged by a group of miners who seemed entranced by this exotic visitor from the galactic center. The general interacted with the group privately, with the result that four of them were invited to sup with the hosts and their families. A rumbling belly told Nate he'd placed his physical needs on hold for too long. Both from habit and because it added to their mystique, he and Forry ate apart from the others. A group of the miners' children pointed at them and giggled.

To his surprise Sheeka Tull chose to sit beside him. Nate ate quietly for several minutes before he found himself studying the play of the dark skin of her neck against the red-and-white stripes of her pilot's jacket, and found himself intrigued.

He decided to try a conversational gambit. "Good meat," he said. "What is it?"

"Not meat," she said. "It's a mushroom bred by the X'Ting, adapted for human stomachs. They can make it taste like anything they like."

He stared at his sandwich. The fungus had striations like meat. Tasted like meat. He bet it had a perfect amino acid profile, too. He chewed experimentally, and then just relaxed and enjoyed. "Why are you here?" he asked.

"What do you mean?"

"You weren't born here," he said.

"And how do you know that?" She seemed genuinely curious.

"Your pronunciation is different. You learned Basic *after* your native tongue."

She laughed, but it was a long, low laugh, without derision. A good laugh, he decided. "Where'd you learn to think like that?"

"Intelligence training. There's more to soldiering than just pulling triggers."

"Now now, don't be so touchy." She grinned.

He took a deep and satisfying bite of his sandwich. The mushroom was spicy and hot, juicy as a Kaminoan fanteel steak. Too often, ARC field rations were a flavorless gruel or lump, as if lack of genetic diversity justified a lack of savory variation in the mess tent. "So . . . how about my answer? How'd you end up here?"

She leaned her head back against the tree. Her hair was full-bodied, but did not fall to her shoulders. It was worn in a short puff, almost like a hedge growing from her scalp. "Sometimes I feel like I've been everywhere, and done everything," she said.

There was silence for a minute, and Forry went to fill his mug a second time. Nate caught Sheeka looking at him with what he supposed was approval, but still as if she had some sort of secret. She studied his face almost as if . . .

As if . . .

He managed to focus his thoughts. "Where's your family?" Why in space had he asked *that*? It was none of his business, and worse, it opened the door to potentially embarrassing personal questions.

"My birth parents?"

"You're not a clone, are you?" He meant it as a joke.

Her face hardened. "Yes. I had parents."

"You lost them." It wasn't a question. Looking down the hill, he could see the elders gathered around General Fisto, whose gestures were simultaneously measured and sweeping.

For more than a minute she said nothing, and he hoped his words hadn't offended. Then finally, speaking so softly that at first he mistook her words for a trick of the wind, she began to speak. "A range war on Atrivis-Seven," she said. "It was a bad time." She stared down at the dirt. He couldn't imagine what it would be like to know war was coming, to feel it raging all around, and not have the skills to lift arms and join the fray. He hoped he never found out.

She went on. "Maybe I was attracted to Ord Cestus because it was so . . . isolated. So far from the hub. I guess it wasn't isolated enough. I met someone."

Something in her voice caught his interest, made him look at her more carefully. "A man?"

She shrugged. "It happens," she said. "A miner named Yander."

"You fell in love?" he asked.

Her mood lightened. "That's what they call it. You understand love?"

He frowned. What kind of question was *that*? "Of course," he said, and then reconsidered. It was possible, of course, that she meant something that he did not include among his own definitions.

"It wasn't just him," she continued, now locked in her own private world of memories. "It was his three children, too. Tarl, Tonoté, and Mithail. His whole community." She glanced away from him for a second, then back again. "I fell in love with all of them. We married. Yander and I had four good years together. More than a lot of people get."

Something caught in her voice, and he cursed himself for invading her privacy. Then in the next thought he wondered why she had allowed herself to be questioned if the questions so obviously triggered pain. Finally, he managed the simple words "I'm sorry."

"So am I." Sheeka Tull sighed. "So, anyway, I'm raising his kids. Never had a lot of family . . . I want to raise the one I have now. That's why I'm willing to take the chance to help you guys. Clean up my record."

"What leverage do they have on you?"

She shook her head. "Maybe when we know each other better."

When? Not *if* ? Interesting.

"Does your new family live near here?"

Again she shifted evasively, and he sensed that he had touched on a sensitive topic. "No. Not here. With their aunt and uncle. A fungus-farming community. It's just scratch, but we like it."

"Scratch?"

"They make enough to feed themselves, and a little to barter, but not enough to sell."

So. She worked to care for her adopted family, who lived with the miner's brother and sister. She was reticent to discuss . . . the children? Or their location? Hard to say. Interesting.

As he came out of his thoughts, again he had the sense that she was staring at him, and this time he felt uncomfortable. "Why do you look at me that way?"

She shook her head. Then, as if she thought herself the biggest fool in the galaxy, she shook with peals of deep, rich laughter. "I suppose I keep expecting you to remember me. That's crazy, of course." She laughed again, and Nate just felt more confused. "You have to pardon me."

"I don't understand."

"I suppose I should have told you before. I knew Jango Fett."

He didn't quite believe what he'd heard. Worse, he wasn't sure how to react. "You did?"

She nodded. "Yes, twenty years ago, in quite another life. Seeing you was kind of a shock. When you took those helmets off—wow!" Her laugh was throaty and vibrant. "It's him, all right, and just about the age he was when we first met."

Nate's head spun. "I should have expected that, I suppose. Certainly some of my brothers have also encountered people who had known him . . . I've just never spoken to one."

"Wow." She scratched in the dirt with her toe, drawing another of the little symbols, and then scratching it out again. "Well, wonders never cease. How'd this happen? And the other troopers . . . they're all little Jangos?" He bristled, and she laid her hand on his arm. "Just a joke. You know, joke?"

Finally he nodded, sensing that she meant no real harm. "The Republic called for a clone army," he said, and recited the words that he had heard and said a thousand times before. "They needed a perfect role model for a fighting man. In all the galaxy they found only one, Jango Fett."

"Oh, he wasn't perfect, but he was a serious chunk." Her smile grew more mischievous. "And he's now the father of a whole army of bouncing baby clones. What does he think of that?"

"He's dead."

The pause that followed might have swallowed a decent-size star cruiser.

"How did it happen?" she whispered. "I supposed I always knew that Jango was too intense to last forever. And yet . . ." Her voice trailed away.

"And yet what?" Nate asked.

"He always seemed invulnerable, like nothing could get to him." She shook her head. "Stupid. My heart didn't want to believe what my head already knew."

The happy music of children singing and playing wafted to them.

One, one, chitliks basking in the sun.
Two, two, chitlik kista in the stew.
Three, three, leave a little bit for me . . .

An odd song. Of course, young clones sang on Kamino. They sang mnemonic tunes, imprinting the subconscious with recipes for explosives, ordnance manuals, equations for lines of sight and windage, and anatomical vulnerabilities for a hundred major species. Of course there were songs, and games. But these rhymes seemed merely concerned with the day, and the sun, and the world about them without specific instructions on the art of survival or death. He had never heard a ditty like that, and it intrigued him.

"How much do you know about him?" Sheeka asked.

He straightened his posture a bit, and again spoke words that had crossed his lips a hundred times. "He was the greatest bounty hunter in the galaxy, a great warrior, an honorable man. He accepted a contract and stuck with it to the end."

"But how *exactly* did he die?"

Nate cleared his throat, surprised to find it more constricted than he thought. "One of his clients was a traitor. Jango Fett didn't know this when he accepted the contract, and once he had given his word, there was no other choice. It took a dozen Jedi to kill him." At least, that was what Nate had always heard. Pride surged through his veins. There was no shame in what Jango had done. In fact, in the current decadent world, where most promises weren't worth bantha spit, he was proud to be the offshoot of so deadly and honorable a fighter.

He looked at her sharply, expecting her to challenge his words.

"So Jango was killed by the Jedi." She jerked a thumb at Kit Fisto. "And there they strut. Bother you?"

He shook his head slowly. "No," he said. "No. We are under contract as well, a contract made with our blood. We were born to serve, and in that service find life's greatest gift: a meaningful existence."

She shook her head, but there was no mockery in her expression. "He'd howl," she said. "Jango wasn't the philosophical type."

Curiosity overwhelmed him. True, he had met Jango, been educationally bruised and battered at his hands. But no trooper had much idea what he was like as . . . well, as a *man*. Mightn't such knowledge make Nate a better trooper? "Tell me more," he said.

Sheeka Tull cocked her head sideways, evaluating him, mischief alight in her eyes. "Maybe later," she said. "If you're good."

"I'm the best of the best," he answered.

"That," she said, dark face speculative, "remains to be seen."

18

At their next stop on the plains west of the Dashta Mountains, members of two different farm communities had assembled to listen to the Jedi. There was no one hall large enough to hold them all, and General Fisto pulled Nate to the side. "You've had recruitment training?"

"Yes," Nate confirmed. "Recruitment and training of indigenous troops."

"Good. I want you to handle the smaller group. Report back to me how things go." The Jedi held his hand out.

Nate took the offered hand and shook hard. "Yes, sir."

Nate's group met in a prefabricated hut used to house cargo ships making overnight hops to the outlying fungus farms. About fifteen hundred males and females of a dozen different species crowded beneath its arched metal ceiling. All had come to see the representatives from the galaxy's core.

The ARC captain strode to the makeshift podium, noting the number of fine young human males whose broad shoulders and thick arms might easily have swelled a trooper's uniform. It was not so easy for him to evaluate female and nonhumanoid training material. What were the fitness standards for a Juzzian? Whether sedentary or the hyperactive mountain-hopping variety, they appeared to be little more than cones with teeth.

There was great value to the all-clone army, but he could also feel that these people had a strong connection to their farms. Given the right motivations, they might fight like demons to protect their land and families. "Citizens of the Republic!" He spoke as clearly as he could, projecting his voice as if trying to be heard above the din of battle. He looked to his left. Sheeka stood there, watching him. Reporting back to General Fisto? Or . . . ?

"I come to you today not with empty words or promises. I have no soft phrases to place you at ease." They stirred restlessly. Good, it was important that he catch their attention.

"It's time to choose sides," he said. "Your leaders' ambitions will drag you into ruin, but courageous action now will save you. There will be rewards for those who side with the Republic, and possible military careers for those with ability." That last comment was true enough, but lacked shading or depth. The Grand Army of the Republic was 100 percent clone, but local militias were often recruited to supplement it.

His comments created a stir in the audience. Nate hoped to build upon it, continuing after a brief pause for effect.

"People of Cestus! There is honor in honest labor, but there is also glory to be gained through risking life and limb to preserve those principles you hold dear. Let your actions now speak to what you dream of being, and not just what you have been."

He noted that the young men looked at each other, and knew that Cestus's vast desolate spaces did not breed cowards. A hard life bred hard men. And women, too, he noted. More than a few of the young females had squared their shoulders. Clearly, they did not relish a life in obscurity, here in the Republic's hinterlands. He had to walk carefully, though, not to offend the elders, and shaped his next words to that effect.

"I do not come to take your children, who should remain with you to learn the ways of their ancestors. But those who are of the age of consent, those who seek a different life and may have been trapped by a greedy corporation that would drain your life and youth and give nothing but empty promises in return—for those I offer another way."

One strapping farm lad glanced to either side, shoulder-length yellow hair riffling with each motion. The man beside him had the same flat, broad face and yellow hair, but was at least twenty years older. Care and toil had rounded his shoulders, caused him to cast his eyes downward. *Father.* He may have been beaten, but his son was neither broken nor bowed. "Sounds awfully good to me," the boy said, and spat into the dust. "Name's OnSon. Skot OnSon. Lost our farm when those Five Family executives cut our water supply out by Kibo Sands."

That last comment generated grumbles, but most were sympathetic. Clearly, OnSon's was no isolated case. "I don't need even that much motivation," another said. "Parents died last year of the shadow fever. I've been working the farm by myself—I'd kiss a cave spider to get off this rock."

Nate held up his hand as the agreement swelled. "Citizens!" he called. "You will be given a rendezvous. There, we will determine which of you have the strength to assist your Republic in its hour of need."

He stepped back from the podium and listened to them as they argued. Passionate and opinionated, the discussion might rage for hours. There: he'd lit a torch. It would be up to others to fan the flames.

19

From rug to translucent ceiling, every centimeter of Obi-Wan's suite was designed for optimal luxury. Considering the weeks in the jungles of Forscan VI, Obi-Wan had initially found it charming. As the hours passed and Snoil hooked into Cestus's core computers, spending hour after hour absorbing mountains of legal data, Obi-Wan began to feel positively stifled. Snoil was researching when Obi-Wan finally surrendered to sleep, and was still at it when the Jedi awakened in the morning.

Obi-Wan was aware that their every move was being watched—by forces loyal to the government, and perhaps spies for the Five Families, that ruling group he was certain lay behind what he now considered a puppet Regency. Governments came and went, but old money kept its influence through one administration after another, weathering them as mountains weather the changing seasons.

Other eyes were probably on him as well, some of them unfriendly and unofficial. Cestus had a highly developed criminal class, many of its leaders descended from the hive that had once controlled the entire planet. They would have tendrils everywhere.

Snoil's eye stalks wavered. He seemed to be fighting panic. "Never have I seen such a tangled web," he said. "Master Obi-Wan, it might take months just to dig out the actual power structure. Everything is owned by legal fictions, every treaty not with individuals but councils or corporations with no corporeal identity. My head hurts!"

"How about this Regent? Would you say she has real power?"

"Yes, and no," Snoil said. "G'Mai Duris represents a sop thrown to the remnants of the hive. After all, the original contracts were all with the X'Ting, so any survivors have to be honored. My guess is that she has public power, but takes orders in private."

"From who?"

The Vippit's head bobbed side to side. "Probably these Five Families."

Then the air blossomed before them. A blue Zeetsa with elongated lashes bobbled politely. "The Regent has requested the honor of your company," she said. "Will you be able to attend?"

"With pleasure," Obi-Wan replied, and stopped pacing.

"An air taxi will arrive for you shortly," the Zeetsa said, and disappeared.

"Good!" Obi-Wan brightened. "Time for the real work."

Obi-Wan helped Snoil polish his shell—a communal activity among Vippits—and soon the barrister was ready to leave. They descended to the lobby as their air taxi arrived, and were soon zipping along the city's periphery, arriving at the throne room within minutes.

Set in a cave large enough to comfortably hold the interstellar cruiser that had brought them to Cestus, the throne room was rather modestly furnished, less ostentatious than the Supreme Chancellor's own quarters. After all, Cestus was honeycombed with caverns both natural and hive-rendered. And if these had been formed by natural processes rather than hive activity or mining, then in a way this was merely an expression of Cestus's natural beauty.

Here in this marble-tiled chamber the hive council met, and group meetings with the representatives of the guilds and various clans took place. Because of the small size of the day's audience, the room looked even more immense than it actually was.

A tall, broad X'Ting female with a pale gold shell sat on the dais, and Obi-Wan recognized her immediately as Regent Duris. She was said to have worked her way up through years of service and talented politicking. Her reputation was strong and honest, and her face, though unwrinkled, was grooved with the kind of deep, mild smile lines that suggested a serious and steady disposition.

Even seated on her throne, she radiated power, her expression polite but stern. So: this was to be a formal encounter.

G'Mai Duris traced her ancestry back to the original hive queen, but only tangentially: the direct lineage had died out during the plagues. Still, considering Cestus's current situation, that qualified her.

She rose, primary and secondary hands pulling her voluminous robes across her broad hips and thorax like shadows across a sheltering valley. This being carried herself with the regal pride and confidence that came only from generations of scrupulous breeding. "Greetings, Master Kenobi. Pardon the delay. Allow me to welcome you to our world. I am G'Mai Duris, Regent of Cestus."

Obi-Wan bowed. "Supreme Chancellor Palpatine sends his greetings," he said.

"This is gratifying to hear," she replied. She was watching him very carefully, her faceted green eyes intense. "I was not certain there would be sympathetic ears in the Senate. We have gone so long with no sign that our problems or people were understood."

Was there some hidden meaning behind her words? Obi-Wan sensed that the stresses upon Duris ranged beyond the normal.

"When you meet him," he said carefully, "and I am certain that one day you will, you will find the Chancellor to be a man of supreme understanding. He empathizes with your plight, and hopes as much as you to find some kind of peaceful solution." *There.* He, too, could speak on multiple levels. The question was whether he had read Duris properly, and whether she could respond.

"That would be my fondest wish," she said. "But make no

mistake, Master Jedi: my people's welfare is my highest priority. More than my office. More than peace. More than my own life."

Obi-Wan nodded, pleased with her. Although this meeting had been days in preparation, he was satisfied with the connection. This being was astute. "I can understand how you came to power. Your clarity on the responsibilities of office is admirable."

G'Mai Duris nodded in turn. "Let this be the beginning of a deeper and more satisfying relationship between Ord Cestus and the rulers of the Republic."

Obi-Wan held up a gently chiding finger. "The Republic has no rulers. Only custodians."

"Of course," Duris said, bowing her head.

Snoil spoke for the first time. "I am Barrister Doolb Snoil, representing the Coruscant College of Law. I make my case as clearly as possible," he said in his soft, high voice. "By both treaty and tradition, Cestus is a signatory to the Coruscant Accords. Although technically Cestus Cybernetics sells nothing illegal, we believe that the JK droids will be modified and used to kill Republic troops."

"So you say," Duris replied.

Snoil continued on unfazed. "Therefore, it is with greatest respect that I request you to cease production and/or import of any such droids as mentioned in part two paragraph six of the primary docufile."

A knee-high blue sphere rolled forward. The Zeetsa who had sent the holo? Duris bent so that the creature could whisper in her ear. She listened intently, then studied several readouts of various documents floating in the air before them.

Snoil continued to speak for almost another hour, citing Republic treaties and what he had come to understand of the current legal status of Cestus Cybernetics, the Five Families, the production of security droids, and possible repercussions. Duris responded with admirable clarity: she was an encyclopedia of legalities, always firm, never impolite, intelligent and strong.

But, Obi-Wan knew, much of this was artifice. She had to be utterly terrified. An X'Ting of her station, more than anyone, understood the concept of extermination. History told her more than she wanted to know about what might happen should politics end and devastation begin.

He hoped that it would not come to that, that this time that rarest of miracles would happen: people of goodwill would resolve conflict without violence.

20

In any recruitment operation, the ultimate question was: how many would respond? It was one thing for youthful would-be warriors to cheer in the fading warmth of a fine speech; quite another to rise the next day, after a night of dreams or nightmares, dress, and travel a distance to the place where they would be trained to lay down their lives for the Republic.

The first prospects arrived before daylight the next day, when Nate and the commandos were getting the morning brew going over an open fire and finishing their breakfasts. The first to arrive was the tall, broad-faced young man with yellow hair named OnSon. Only a few steps behind him walked another boy, shorter but even thicker across the shoulders. They had been told to bring food to eat and share, and their backpacks were packed with dried meats and preserved vegetables. Nate immediately thought of a dozen field recipes that would transform the new supplies into mouth-watering collations.

The newcomers were invited to rest at the fireside and share the brew. They had barely begun to speak when they heard a rolling roar, and a speeder bike whizzed by. A rough-looking X'Ting female doffed her helmet. She smoothed her upper thorax's tufts of red wiry fur with her primary hands, dismounted from her speeder, and strode over to them, throwing a coarse-clothed sack onto the ground. When she spoke, the roughness of her words reinforced her lower-caste image. "I Resta," she said. "Own farm 'bout hundred klicks south of ChikatLik. Resta on same power grid, and they

raise juice price so high husband have to take job in mines."
There was not a shred of self-pity in her blazing, faceted
green eyes. "Husband die in mines. Now Resta losing farm,
and all so that power can go to some Five Fam' fun-fun place.
Resta sick to death of backin' up. Resta not backin' up no
more." She added, "Gotty problem?" to the miners and farmers around her. Challenge rolled off her like heat waves
dancing above a desert mirage.

Nate struggled to interpret the words. Apparently, due to
the opening of some Five Family vacation spa, the price of
power had soared, driving Resta into poverty.

"She don't belong here," one of the miners grumbled,
triggering a wave of muttering.

Nate approached her and took her red-skinned hands in
his, examining each of her four palms in turn. Thick calluses
over the chitinous flesh. Broken nails. This female had struggled with Cestus's poor soil for decades. Most of her surviving people had been driven into the wastelands, but not this
one. She was tough enough, and good enough, assuming that
she could pass the tests.

This female would despise soft words. "You'll do" was all
he said.

He turned to the complainer. "One more word and you can
pack and leave. This fight is for all Cestians with heart. Close
yours to this one, and you're gone. This is her planet more
than yours."

The man tried to stare Nate down, not realizing that it was
impossible. Within moments he dropped his eyes, muttering
an apology.

All that morning a steady stream of arrivals heartened
them, until there were almost two hundred prospects. Fine.
Nate knew that General Fisto was off slinging more recruitment speeches. It was up to the troopers to turn these farmers and miners into fighters, unless they wished to leave
clone protoplasm scattered incriminatingly about.

Throughout the last days the troopers had labored to build
an obstacle course. As the morning's shadows shortened they
ran the recruits through their paces, forming them into lines

by height, dividing them into four groups so that they could compete against each other. Running narrow rails, suspending themselves from overhead bars, lugging rocks back and forth across a field until they puked from exhaustion, the recruits suffered through standard trooper field training.

During the sun's waning Forry added calisthenics, and more running, jumping, and carrying. Nate was pleased to see that every one of the new prospects was game.

For some reason he was especially pleased to see that Resta was keeping up with the offworlders. She might have been a bit slower, but she was as strong as a Noghri, and seemed to have an unquenchable tolerance for pain.

By the time they broke for rest and food, only ten of them had dropped out, trudging home with heads down. One, Nate noted with pleasure, was the miner who had complained about Resta.

Good. The first day's grueling schedule was designed to make about half the group quit. From then on, those who remained could consider themselves tough, fire-breathing survivors. It was the kind of thing that bred camaraderie, the most important factor in a combat unit.

After the meal break, his brothers began to divide the recruits into smaller units, testing them again and again. Not one had picked up a weapon of any kind. It was not yet time.

Spindragon arrived when the day was halfway done, ferrying General Fisto back to camp. The Nautolan asked tersely how many recruits had come and how many had survived the early training, then retreated to the cave for whatever mysterious preparations or planning Jedi indulged in.

Sheeka herself watched the recruits' exertions and frowned. "Why all of this?" she asked. "Jango used to say it took months to get someone into real shape."

He smiled and lowered his voice conspiratorially. "Gives us a chance to observe them. See who fits in and who doesn't. Who can handle physical pain? Fear? Fatigue? We've got no time for dilettantes."

She nodded, as if she might have already anticipated such a response. She seemed an interesting woman: pilot, step-mother, galaxy-spanning wanderer, and former girlfriend of the immortal Jango himself.

Sheeka interrupted his thoughts. "You told me what the army says about Jango. But there is always more than one way to look at a story, right?"

"Yes."

"So there are other people, who say other things."

Of course there were. Always. He had heard their snide comments, had watched their eyes narrow and the corners of their lips turn down when a clone trooper passed. "Yes," he said.

"And what do *they* say?"

"What do they say? That he was a criminal, a bounty hunter, an assassin, a traitor to the Republic." The snidely whispered words echoed in his ears, and he found himself slightly annoyed just to remember them. Had he no original thoughts of his own to offer? "It is our duty and honor to erase his stain."

"Is that how you feel?" she asked. "Is that all there is?" A short, hard laugh. "He was a man who walked between the worlds, but when I knew him he was honorable, and brave, and a great . . . fighter. Bounty hunter." She shrugged. "Whatever. Not too smart to learn everything possible about someone from his enemies."

He thought about this for a few moments before answering. "What would I have to do to be more like him?"

She looked him up and down, from his spit-polished boots to his chiseled face. And her smile softened a bit, grew more contemplative. "Not be afraid of being human," she said. "Not be so scared of feelings. He rarely showed them, but he had them. Not be so scared."

Nate bristled. What in the world was this woman prattling about? "I'm not scared of anything."

She barked laughter. Despite his anger, he admired its clarity and timbre. "Bantha spit," she said. "I've been watching you and your brothers. You're afraid of everything. Of saying the wrong things. Feeling the wrong things. Probably of dying in the wrong position."

There it was. Thank the cloners that troopers had no such prejudices! "You don't know anything about my life, or my death. Of course, that never stops civilians from judging, does it?" The last emerged as something very close to a snarl.

Nonetheless, she was completely unshaken. "Who's generalizing now?" she asked.

He glowered at her, but no more words came to mind.

"No?" she asked. "Then accept a challenge."

"A challenge?" Despite himself, he was intrigued. Distantly, he heard the shouts and grunts of effort. It was almost time for him to go and relieve the others.

"Yes," she said. "You know how to be a soldier. I've seen that. My challenge is for you to react to the world as just a human being. When you see a sunset, do you think of anything but night-vision lenses? When you see a sunblossom, do you only imagine the poisons that might be extracted from it? When you see a baby, do you think of anything except what kind of hostage it might make?"

Nate stiffened. "Advance Recon Commandos don't take hostages," he said.

Sheeka's lovely face managed to darken even further. "Don't be so blasted literal!" she said in frustration. "I'm trying to communicate with you, and all I can touch is your shell. Who *are* you?"

The sounds of children playing seemed to have receded, grown farther away. "I know who I am." He paused. "As much as any of us ever do," he said, rising. "These mushrooms taste like dirt," he lied. "I'm getting some meat." He tossed his food into a trash container, and then rejoined the exhausted recruits.

For the rest of the day Nate attempted to focus his attention on the trainees. He kept a wary eye on how they did on the obstacle course, discerning which of them were in the best physical and mental condition, which ones had the best emotional control, which might have leadership potential.

But every few minutes he broke concentration and scanned

the entire craggy area, as protocol directed. And he noticed that no matter when he did so, his eyes sought the face and form of the infuriating Sheeka Tull. Sometimes he found her beneath a rock overhang, sometimes helping with the food. Once he glimpsed her interacting with General Fisto, and pointing in the direction of her ship. And once, when he didn't see her at all, he felt a strange disappointment.

That lasted but a moment: Nate wrested his attention back to the task at hand.

As the day rolled on, trainees were presented with an endless series of sweaty, torturous obstacles. Invariably the clones negotiated the tests first, with a level of agility and effortless ease that made the Cestus volunteers shake their heads in disbelief.

Child's play, for one who spent his childhood in the training rooms of the Kamino cloners.

By the day's end, 40 percent of the volunteers had quit. Those remaining were a hard, tough lot who glared at each other and cursed under their breaths at the troopers, but they cursed as a group. They had survived the best that these armored sadists from Coruscant could offer. They were ready for the next level.

Nate organized his thoughts and made his report to General Fisto. As he approached the back of the cave a meter-long thread of light blazed briefly, snaked and coiled through the air, then died again. The strange phenomenon repeated. His nose itched with the stink of burning metal, and the glare of the flexible line hurt his eyes until he had to turn his head away.

When General Fisto heard his approach, the light disappeared, and he pivoted with a loose-limbed adroitness so smooth that he might almost have turned inside out, seemed to flow *through* himself.

"Yes?"

"We've concluded the day's testing."

"And?"

"I believe that we have forty-eight good recruits."

Something like light glowed in the depths of the general's unblinking eyes. "This is good. And tomorrow?"

"We'll pick up a few more. I can either accompany you in recruitment, or stay here and continue training."

"Continue the training," General Fisto said after a moment's consideration. "Divide them into groups according to day and time of initial recruitment. Allow those who enlisted first to have the greatest status."

"Yes, sir," Nate said. The general was underestimating ARCs if he thought that such a hierarchy was not already part of their command structure. On the other hand, it was not his place to educate or correct Jedi.

For some reason, that thought made him think of Sheeka Tull again, and her insolent evaluation of him. There was something about her he found almost unendurably irritating.

He wandered back outside the cave, and without telling his feet what to do, they headed in the direction of Sheeka Tull's ship. After all, the day's work was completed. His three brothers would take care of any cleaning of weapons or policing of the obstacle course area. He could take a few minutes. *Just a stroll,* he lied.

He found Sheeka at a folding table outside her ship, scrubbing at the rust on one of *Spindragon*'s Corellian flux converters and enjoying the stars. She didn't seem surprised to see him, but didn't hail him until he came closer. "Nate," she said.

"And how do you know that it's me, and not one of the others?" he challenged.

She laughed. "You walk a little differently. By any chance have you got a leg wound?"

He stopped for a minute. A broca, a huge reptilian creature that haunted the swamps of a misbegotten black hole called Altair-9, had nearly torn his hip away. He had thought the damage healed. Interesting. This woman was as observant as a trooper!

"Yes," he said, but kept the rest of his thoughts to himself.

She smiled at him, went back to her cleaning. "How did the day go?"

"Some good prospects. We pushed them hard and lost only forty percent. Strong stock on Cestus."

Sheeka smiled again, evidently pleased with his answer. She went back to her cleaning, and he just sat, watching the stars. He knew that many of those blazing orbs had planets of their own, and wondered how many would be embroiled in battle before the Clone Wars ended.

After a time her attention returned to Nate. He felt content merely waiting for her to speak. When she did, her question surprised him. "What do you see when you look at me?" She chose that moment to yawn and stretch a bit, and for the first time he felt the impact of her as a woman, and was surprised at the fierceness of his reaction. Nothing male and humanoid could fail to notice her mesmerizing meld of strength and softness, the long elegant lines of her legs, the delicate arch of her neck . . .

Nate stopped himself, remembering that she had asked him a question. He searched, found one answer that bordered on the obscene, and subsequently edited himself. Finally he said, "A human female whose skin tone matches that of General Windu."

"Who?" She laughed. It was rich and deep, and he realized that his first sense of being mocked was completely wrong. He found that he admired her laugh; it was warming to him in a way that let him reduce emotional control for a few precious minutes. Interesting.

He found himself asking a question before he had stopped and evaluated it. "And what do you see when you look at me?"

Almost instantly he regretted saying it, because that smile softened, became wistful and a bit sad. "The shadow of the best—" She paused, as if changing a word in midsentence. "—best *fighter* I ever knew." She reached out and brushed her hand along his jaw, then rose as gracefully as a sunblossom spinning in the solar wind and returned to her ship.

21

After the first few days, the stream of newbies had slowed to a trickle. Therefore, Nate was surprised to see a group of lean, dirty men and women approach. They arrived in a motley variety of battered hovercarts dusty enough to suggest they had hauled far more ore than passengers. Their apparent leader was a tall old red-bearded human male who looked wide across the shoulders and loose in the gut, well weathered and deeply tired. "We want parley with your leader," he said.

Sirty looked him up and down. "And who makes this request?"

"Name's Thak Val Zsing," the newcomer said.

"You're looking for me," Nate said, stepping forward.

Thak Val Zsing looked from Sirty to Nate, and a humorless grin split his face. His teeth were broad, cracked, and brownish.

"Recruits, sir?" Sirty asked.

Val Zsing 's expression soured. "Didn't say that."

"Well then—?"

"We're Desert Wind, and if we like what we see, we're here to fight."

So. *These* were the anarchists who had been so brutally crushed by Cestian security forces just months ago. If they were even a quarter of their former strength, he was a Jawa. And they were ready to fight again? Brave if not smart. "Even Coruscant has heard of your courage."

Thak Val Zsing nodded, satisfied by that answer. "You know who we are. We're not so sure about you yet." The men and women behind him nodded. Nate scanned their clothing and armaments. Old. Badly patched. Their skin was ragged from fatigue and malnutrition. It looked as if their weapons were in better shape than they were. Still, tired and half broken they may have been, but these were people holding a serious grudge.

"Every one of us is prepared to die to overthrow this decadent system."

Ah, then. They had every reason to blame the government for their problems, but he couldn't use Desert Wind in its present form: they were too brittle and angry. This was a delicate situation, and he had to play it carefully. "Maybe you've misunderstood our intentions," he said. "We're not here to overthrow the legal government. We are here to ensure that that government obeys the Republic's rules and regulations. As citizens of the Republic, you have full right to redress of grievances."

Thak Val Zsing pulled at his crimson beard with his fingers and spat into the dust. "The Families couldn't care less about your rules. You talk pretty, and offer us nothing."

That was a perfectly accurate answer, and Nate felt a bit flustered.

The Jedi suddenly appeared behind him. "I offer the opportunity to serve your Republic," General Fisto said. Nate had been so fixed on the members of Desert Wind that he hadn't heard a sound.

The vast dark pools of the Nautolan's eyes captivated the anarchists. Thak Val Zsing was the first to break out of the trance; the others followed swiftly and began to grumble. "Serve how?"

"Come," the general said urgently. "Fight with us."

"In other words, take your orders."

"Be our comrades."

The sincerity in his words was mesmerizing, his Nautolan charisma doubly effective on this desert world. Most of Desert Wind's ragged members seemed to feel it like a blow to the chest.

Most, but not all. Thak Val Zsing shook his head. "Nope.

Don't like this. We've heard enough promises, and taken enough orders. We'll win our own freedom."

"If you act on your own, you become common criminals," Fisto said. "With us, you are patriots." Hard words, but these folk were at the end of their resources. They had nothing to lose.

The ragged members of Desert Wind looked from Thak Val Zsing to Kit Fisto and back again. One devil they knew, one they didn't. Like most creatures, they went with what they knew. They would continue to harry the government, and they would be eventually caught, or jailed, or killed.

And that was the end of it, with nothing that anyone could really do to stop it.

General Fisto extended his hand to Thak Val Zsing. "Wait," he said.

"What?" Val Zsing was tired, but also proud.

"I could offer your people clemency if they work with us. When our job is complete your crimes will be expunged, and you'll return to your mines and farms and shops. I would not have you throw your lives away."

Nate knew Val Zsing had to be warring with himself. This was a good man, but too weary to have much optimism left in him; he had been told too many lies to believe a Jedi, or a Jedi's clone soldiers. He could hear the old man's thoughts as clearly as if he spoke them aloud.

"What do the others say?" General Fisto asked.

"They say they trust *me,*" Thak Val Zsing said, puffing his chest out. "And I don't trust you. I only came here because they asked me to. But now that I've seen ya . . ."

The general gazed across the faces of Desert Wind, then turned back to Thak Val Zsing. "These are your people. How did you win their hearts?"

"By blood," he said. Nate could see it in Thak Val Zsing's eyes. Despite his bravado the man wanted to believe, but couldn't.

"I see," the Nautolan replied.

"There might be another way," Thak Val Zsing said slowly. The battered warriors straightened and stared at him.

They looked at each other as if the confrontation was about to turn into something physically unpleasant, and then Thak Val Zsing's shoulders slumped.

Once, perhaps, the old man had been a great fighter, but those days were long past. Still, the members of his group looked up to him, and respected him as they would a father. Doubtless he'd shepherded them through more than one tight squeeze.

How could the dynamic be altered? What resolution could there be?

More than anyone else, Thak Val Zsing seemed to understand the stakes. One last action. One last judgment. It might mean destruction or salvation for his ragtag band. But what to do?

"Thirty years ago I took command of this group," Val Zsing said, his eyes locked with the general's. "You could guide them, if you were willing to pass the same test."

"Test?"

He nodded. "Brother Fate?" he said quietly.

A gray-tufted old X'Ting male in brown robes walked over. He was accompanied by a somewhat bulkier X'Ting female, also in brown robes. They carried a woven reed basket suspended between them.

The basket was large enough to hold a human infant, and that was what Nate initially supposed it held. He had heard of extremist groups who worshiped some child or infant, supposing it the avatar of a god, or the reincarnation of some sacred soul.

But a moment later he realized he had made an error. Whatever lay in that basket was nothing human. It weighed more than an infant as well: perhaps ten kilos. And it hissed. The basket wobbled slightly, and from their efforts to keep it balanced, he knew that there was something moving in there, something serpentine.

"Will you trust us as you ask us to trust you?" the old X'Ting female said.

"What would you have me do?"

"Place your hand inside," she said.

"And?"

"And then we will see."

General Fisto looked at her, and then at Thak Val Zsing.

Nate held his breath. This was a test of both courage and intuition. Trust and common sense. What was in the basket? The woven sand-reed container was large enough to hold any of a thousand venomous creatures. And if it bit the general, what then? Was Kit Fisto supposed to magically transform the poison within his body? To charm the beast so that it would not bite? Or was this entire thing some kind of an elaborate assassination plan? Whatever it was, he could not repress a hint of apprehension. What would the Jedi do?

General Fisto's expression didn't change, but he nodded his head. "Yes."

The old X'Ting couple laid the basket down. The cover still obscured whatever was inside. The general rolled up the sleeve of his robe and extended his hand into the container. Nate noticed that the pace of entrance was neither slow nor fast, but continued at a single unvaried medium rate.

General Fisto's eyes never left the old woman's. His arm had disappeared up to the elbow, and the witnesses watched carefully.

And yet . . . what was he missing? There was something happening here that defied definition.

Finally one of the other old females nodded, and the general, using the same slow, steady pace, withdrew his arm from the basket. Its underside glistened with something wet. He rolled his sleeve down without wiping the wetness away. The Nautolan's face was impassive.

The two brown-robed X'Tings retreated to a neutral position and sat cross-legged, primary and secondary arms folded in a prayer position, foreheads leaning against each other. The others formed a wall between the clones and General Fisto and the basket. They were hunched over and seemed to be studying something.

Then they returned. "He tells the truth," the woman said. And the others nodded.

Thak Val Zsing exhaled mightily. Nate could tell that he was relieved, but his pride wouldn't let him speak it.

"Very well, then," Thak Val Zsing said. "The Guides . . . have never been wrong before. All right. I yield the leadership of Desert Wind." He paused. "And I hope I'm not making the biggest mistake of my life."

As Kit Fisto walked back up to the cave, Nate ran up next to him and spoke in a low voice. "What did you feel in the basket?" he asked. "Some kind of rock viper?"

"I do not know," Kit said, barely moving his lips. "It did not try to harm me. But I felt . . . something. A presence I have sensed before." When Kit said no more, Nate accepted that and rejoined his brothers.

Thak Val Zsing shook his head as they walked toward the cave. "I wouldn't have believed it," he said. His eyes burned with challenge. "I'm not the one who's trusting you, Jedi. Remember that."

"I will," Kit promised.

"Well," he said, scratching his head. "A promise is a promise."

"It is good that you are a being of your word."

"Sometimes," said Thak Val Zsing, his shoulders slumping, "his word is all a man has."

"You bring more than words," Kit replied. "Eat with us?"

Thak Val Zsing and his people jostled to find seats at their rude table. As steaming platters heaped with fresh meat, mushrooms, and hot bread were placed before them, he turned to Kit again. "We haven't had a good meal in a week. Can you . . . ?"

"All you can eat," Kit said.

Thak Val Zsing and his people attacked their plates ferociously, bolting down their food like starving Hutts. Finally they slowed, belching and laughing, and it became possible to speak with them.

"I have read the files," Kit said, "but I'd like to know your views. What happened on Cestus?"

"The story's an old one," Thak Val Zsing said. "I probably

look like a miner, by now. Truth is, I was a history professor. Lost my job when the government cut social programs and utilities to the outlying areas."

"The elected government? The regent G'Mai Duris?"

He snorted. "She's not the real power here, star-boy. Better play catch-up. Anyway, I went to work in the mines. The rest, as they say, is history." He grinned. "Look. Old story. You have oppressors and the oppressed. That was true before the Republic ever found these people: the X'Ting drove the spiders into the mountains, and probably exterminated some others who were gone before we ever arrived. We came, bought land from them for a few trunks of worthless synth-stones, and a couple of hundred years later some mysterious 'plagues' killed about ninety percent of 'em. Convenient, eh?"

"Extremely. You think these plagues no accident?"

Val Zsing snorted. "There's no evidence you could trouble your precious Chancellor with. Any prison cramming together species from around the galaxy is a forcing ground for exotic disease. Let's just say that the Five Families weren't heartbroken."

Thak Val Zsing tore a great chunk out of a roasted bird and chewed as juice ran down through his beard and onto his shirt. "Maybe my great-grandfather laughed about it, but it's not funny now. The Five Families own everything. Those of us at the bottom barely have enough bread. Our babies cry in the night."

"I thought Cestus Cybernetics was wealthy," Kit said.

"Yes. But precious few of those credits make their way to the bottom."

"We're gonna change that," Skot OnSon said. "Overthrow the government, take back our world."

Our world, Kit thought. And just whose world was it? The Five Families? The immigrants? The X'Ting hive? What about those wretched spiders the troopers had driven into the dark? He was sorry to have taken their cave now, but happy to have restrained the troopers from pursuit.

22

Obi-Wan and Barrister Snoil hadn't left their apartment since returning from the throne room. The attendants seemed to hover around them, hoping for tips, bringing them food and rather clumsily trying to overhear their conversations. Finally Obi-Wan had to ask the hotel's management to solve the problem.

Snoil had an unquenchable appetite for work. The Vippit rarely ate and never slept. He pored over documents, consulted with Cestian legal minds, relayed communications through their cruiser to Coruscant for second and third opinions.

Through it all, Obi-Wan sensed not desperation but a kind of joy at having an opportunity to discharge his old debt through excellent performance. If he could just find a way through this legal warren, understand the path that might lead to peaceful resolution, they might all leave Cestus happy.

Obi-Wan helped where he could, offered advice, tried to take some of the burden from Snoil's shell, but in the end he felt almost useless. Their next meeting with G'Mai Duris was in no more than eighteen hours, and as of yet they had no ammunition to turn the tide.

But something would come up. Something always did . . .

23

Three hundred kilometers northeast of the command base stood the saw-toothed expanse of the Tolmea mountain range. Its tallest peak, Tolmeatek, rose thirty-two thousand meters from the valley floor, its snowcapped summit a gleaming beacon for the adventurous. Only within the last hundred years had any non-native managed the climb without rebreathing apparatus. The very word *tolmeatek* meant "untravelable" in X'Ting. The lesser mountains were of the same inhospitable disposition, stark inclines and flash storms making the entire region too dangerous for casual travel.

And ideal for clandestine activities. Within the shadow of mighty Tolmeatek nestled another landing pad, also hidden from chance observation.

A three-X'Ting delegation gazed up into the stars until one of the orbs began to change position. Oddly, it appeared tiny until the last possible moment, when it seemed as if the minuscule object suddenly expanded with impossible speed.

The greeters waited at their places, unmoving. Two wore shadowy robes, one a recently acquired offworlder style cut for an insectile X'Ting. A narrow landing ramp descended from the shining ship. A female humanoid appeared in the doorway. She wore a floor-length cloak and was clearly visible only in silhouette, but what they could see made them hold their breath.

The cabin behind her was dark. Her profile was clean-shaven, with a skull both symmetrical and large enough to suggest formidable intellect. The pale skin covering it was so clear and flawless as to be almost translucent. Six knife-shaped tattoos were arrayed on each side of her head, daggers pointing at her ears. She seemed to sparkle a bit, as if with some inner radiance. Doubtless, a trick of the light.

As she descended, they saw that her eyes were a flat and expressionless blue, briefly examining Fizzik without any comment or judgment. He was so far beneath her notice that he barely registered at all, neither threat nor ally. For all the change in her expression he might have been an astromech droid.

Fizzik was afraid of this woman, and found the sensation oddly delicious.

He stepped forward, prepared to offer his planned greeting. "Ma'am . . . ?"

The woman tilted her head slowly sideways, staring at him as if he were an unaccustomed form of lower animal life. That odd sensation within him, the fear-thing, swelled. Fizzik went silent.

She took two more steps and then touched her belt. All around the ship, in a giant circle with a radius of perhaps twenty meters, the sand sizzled. Fizzik had noticed a line of tiny sandwasps crawling across the sand, mindlessly carrying their burdens back to their nest. Where that line crossed the sand, half a dozen of the tiny creatures had curled into smoking balls. The others on either side of the line were unharmed.

For the first time, she spoke. "If your people approach my ship," she said, "you'll need new people."

"Yes, Mistress."

"*Very* good," she mocked. "Take me to Trillot."

Fizzik opened the back of a little snub-nosed tunnel speeder to her, and she entered without another word. Her movements flowed, as if she were more felinoid than humanoid. A savagely beautiful predator.

The tunnel runner hovered and then pivoted, heading into one of the nearby entrances. The little geebug was built for swift maneuvering in the warren of tunnels beneath Cestus's surface.

These tunnels had been built by hive technicians eons ago,

but had only been electronically mapped fairly recently—a few standard decades, perhaps. The geebug was also equipped with the very latest and most powerful scanning equipment and skittered through the tunnels like a thrinx on a griddle.

Fizzik sat beside the pilot in the front seat, but took a chance to cast a glance back at the rear seat, to see, perhaps, if their guest was at all discomfited by the series of near misses as they negotiated the warren.

She seemed unflappable, her piercing blue eyes amused, full pale lips curled up at the edges as they scraped through an especially close call. She scanned the cave walls as they flew past, noting everything. Their passenger turned and looked at him, curiosity lighting her face at last. "So the Five Families fear to meet with me openly."

"It is considered risky. But you will be with them soon."

She snorted derisively. "What is all this?" she asked, gesturing at the walls.

He found her voice a kind of coppery music. "The planet is honeycombed with mines and tunnels. They are the easiest way of traveling without detection."

She chuckled, although what might have piqued her amusement was beyond him. She turned at last to face him. "And you are—?"

"Fizzik, brother to Trillot, who awaits your arrival."

When she offered no introduction in return, he shrank back. He stared at her, and as he did her eyes grew vast and dark. "Perhaps," he said, "I should just let you rest from your no doubt long and arduous journey."

Their passenger closed her eyes. And no matter how abrupt their spins and turns, what jolts the tunnel runner got from near misses, she did not open them again until the vehicle came to a halt.

The instant the vehicle *shush*ed to stillness her eyes snapped open, and Asajj Ventress was as alert as a Gotal on the hunt. Her short nap had apparently refreshed and renewed her. That is, if such a creature required refreshment and renewal.

They had arrived in a cave below the heart of the city. Five of Trillot's most trusted aides awaited them. Whereas she had exited the ship like a queen or some kind of dark princess, here she opened the front of her cloak and assumed another aspect, which Fizzik recognized as that of a military leader. Beneath the black skintight suit her body was as sinewy as a snake, only her breasts and hips feminizing an otherwise androgynously muscular physique.

Trillot had briefed Fizzik about Commander Ventress, of course. Rumors had floated about, and even his brother wasn't certain which to believe. Some said she was a Jedi herself; that she had left the ancient Order, taking her weapons with her. Others said that she was an acolyte of some shadowy group superior to even the feared Jedi Knights.

The ring of greeters parted, and they stepped to a turbolift platform large enough for four. He noted that the aides did not deign to step aboard, as if they wished to keep a safe distance. The two rode up together.

She smelled of acid fruit.

Darkness enfolded and then released them as they reached the upper level.

As they emerged into Trillot's headquarters, the hard, cold creatures who awaited them seemed to part like shallow water. No one dared touch her; none approached her. A kind of silence descended over the entire floor as he escorted her to her meeting.

Trillot was seated at his desk as she entered his office. He was bloated now, his transformative hormones in full effect, accelerated by the alien herbs. He squirmed and fidgeted almost continuously, as if he could find no comfortable position.

Oddly, Ventress seemed somewhat deferential. From a pack so cunningly hidden upon her taut body that he had missed it entirely, she withdrew several items and politely placed them on the table before Trillot.

The golden gang lord's faceted red eyes moved back and

forth across the items, and he waited. The air shifted, and he smelled the slightest musky tang. Trillot, he knew, exuded musk from neck glands when going through the Change, but that smell intensified when he was nervous. In all the years he had known his brother, Fizzik had smelled it only twice before.

The woman nodded deeply. The bag shuddered. Something black and red thrust its head out of the flap, forked tongue flickering as if tasting alien air.

"Gifts," Ventress said. Was that the very tiniest trace of mockery in her voice? "Of salt, water, and meat."

Trillot stared, uncertain what to do. Ritual meals were common, a highly developed art in X'Ting hive politics. But Trillot was no royal, not even a noble. What could he make of this? Mockery or not, he dared not respond impolitely. His gaze shifted to Ventress and then back to the table. The red-and-black head proved to be the head of a banded snake, emerging from the bag slowly. No . . . it wasn't a snake. Its small stubby legs paddled as it attempted to escape its confines. It moved sluggishly, as if it had been drugged.

Trillot looked at his protocol droid, and then back at the crawling creature . . . no, *creatures,* because a second had emerged.

The protocol droid bent and said quietly: "I believe that you are expected to ingest the windsnakes. With relish, sir."

Yes, that was definitely a tiny smile on Ventress's face, but whether genuine or artificial he couldn't say.

Trillot studied her for a moment, and Fizzik wondered what his employer was going to do. Again, an unexpected flash of emotion. This woman became more intriguing with every passing moment.

With a movement swift enough to baffle sight, Trillot's hand snapped out, grasped one of the windsnakes just behind the head, and dashed its body against the table. Even more swiftly the second time, he repeated the maneuver with the other one.

"Send for Janu," he said. A droid scurried out of the room, and a moment later an enormous brown creature with a distended chin and a raised, horny crest dividing its head wad-dled into the room, great dusky folds of skin cascading down to the floor. "Yes, sir?"

"Water, salt, and two succulent windsnakes. What recipe can you concoct?"

Janu tilted his waffled head sideways as if measuring. He picked up the limp bodies and sniffed them, bringing them close to his flat, wet nostrils. Then, suddenly, his thick lips split in a grin. "Ah! Glymph pie. Windsnakes come from Ploo Two, and the Glymphids are famous for a variety of casseroles. I can procure fantazi mushrooms—"

"No," Trillot said, voice cracking a bit. Fizzik sharpened his eyes. Ah! The vocal change was another dead giveaway: his brother was thick in the shift toward his female state. Soon his eyes would change from rust-red to emerald. "I will need my wits about me this evening."

As he said this, he glanced at Ventress, who remained mo-tionless, squatting on the balls of her feet, back perfectly straight, immobile as a stone. Again, Fizzik had never heard his brother discussing his private practices or habits with an outsider. Or at all, when it came right down to it. An almost perverse fascination bubbled within him.

"Fine," Janu said. "Then I will use . . . banthaweed."

"That should suffice." He waved at the tray, and the enor-mous Janu lifted it and carried it away.

"I thank you for your gifts," Trillot said. "I assure you that I will enjoy them to the full."

Ventress inclined her head with palpably false modesty. "A small gift from Count Dooku," she said. "A delicacy. Take heart: the Yanthans who remove the venom sacs rarely make a mistake." She smiled. "And even if they do—it is said to be a good death."

Fizzik wasn't sure he wanted to know how a creature like Ventress might define *good*. It was difficult to tell whether she was serious, or merely enjoyed tormenting her host.

In either case, the results were fascinating.

"I trust that your journey was pleasant?" Trillot asked.

Her expression did not change. "Irrelevant. I wish to know

why I was not met by the Families. At the least, why I was not brought immediately to their presence."

"We have a new guest in the capital," Trillot said, attempting to placate. "Until we know his precise business, a measure of additional discretion was thought wise."

She gazed at him, and although Ventress did not speak, Fizzik felt he could hear her thoughts. *Miserable cowards.*

Fizzik had observed Trillot's immense bodyguards as they watched their boss defer to this woman. There were also a dozen lean young male X'Ting around Trillot's nest: thugs trying to get rich easy, looking for someone strong to follow. Not necessarily bad, but lost, and lost in dreams of glory past. There was no way of telling how they might react. They might exhibit typical hive behavior and simply follow. The more disloyal might sense an opportunity to jump track, to find a way to ingratiate themselves to a superior power. But there was another reaction as well, and Fizzik could see it brewing in the filmed eyes of one of the smaller bodyguards, a member of the X'Ting assassin clan. His name was Remlout.

"Excuse me," Remlout said in the high, reedy voice he assumed when speaking Basic. "I've heard a story about you."

She rose and turned to him. Again the corners of her mouth raised, as if she already knew what he was going to say, and welcomed it.

"In all politeness," Remlout sneered, "I've heard that you never, ever turn down a challenge. Is that true?"

She glanced at his shoulders, his hands, his eyes. "You've been to Xagobah," she said. "To learn Tal-Gun?"

"Yes," Remlout said, confused. Not many X'Ting ventured offplanet.

Asajj Ventress smiled. "Your neck is pale: their blue sun's burning has faded. You've been away from your teachers a long time."

He nodded, mouth slightly open in surprise.

"Count Dooku told me that if I wished to progress in the arts, it was vital to take every challenge." She cocked her head lazily at Trillot.

Her smile widened. She turned to Trillot. "Would this displease you?"

Trillot looked back and forth between Ventress and Remlout. Fizzik knew what his brother was thinking. Trillot did not like this woman, but for a variety of reasons was bound to honor her wishes. Fizzik had witnessed Remlout's skills, but was uncertain they would be enough to defeat Ventress, and didn't want to lose a bodyguard. On the other hand . . .

Challenge simmered in the air.

Trillot leaned back, grimacing as he strove to make his swelling egg sac less uncomfortable. The gang lord—not quite *lady,* not yet—templed his fingers together. "If both participants are willing, then it is not my place to say no."

Ventress nodded and turned to face Remlout, pivoting as if on ball bearings. Her fingers crooked like claws.

Now Trillot added, "But please, Commander Ventress. It is hard to find good bodyguards."

"I won't kill him," she promised. "At your pleasure," she said to her opponent.

Remlout bowed. His vestigial wings fluttered with warning, and he spread his primary and secondary arms. The creatures who served at Trillot's pleasure backed against the walls.

Now the two of them were in a cleared space. Remlout stepped in an arc, circling Ventress.

Remlout cartwheeled, and then balanced on his primary hands, his feet tracking Ventress as if they were scan detectors. Those primary hands were as broad and strong as most feet, and Fizzik knew that Remlout could stand like this for hours.

Fizzik had seen this once before: Remlout making his formal challenge of any visitor who had a similar code of warrior ethics—or seemed to offend his master Trillot. The fact that he had made the challenge so soon was not remarkable in itself, but Fizzik suspected that there was something more going on here. He had seen foes attempt to penetrate

Remlout's defense only to be struck with such nimble violence that Remlout's punishing feet might have been arms.

Most cowered at the sight.

Ventress was another matter altogether, however. She swayed back and forth, ripples surging through her body as if she were some kind of sea frond. Strange: she was clearly female, but she moved more like an X'Ting male.

Remlout made his attack: left–right–left, feet jabbing out in a breathtaking three-strike combination. Ventress never shifted her legs, but somehow avoided the triple threat. Fizzik ran the sequence back through his mind: Ventress had moved bonelessly, with a spinal relaxation so extreme that she could have shifted only a centimeter or less, angling sideways, sliding from the path of each kick as if she had had all the time in the world.

Something else had happened, something obscured by the flash and flex of limbs. Fizzik couldn't see it, but Remlout was on the ground, writhing, face purpling, twisting on his side, hands reaching around for his shell.

The assassin spasmed, the muscles in his back tightening again. Remlout's face grew tauter and tauter, more deformed with strain, and he howled as if in the midst of the most monstrous and debilitating muscle spasm in history. His entire body arched, and with a series of rending *pops* Remlout's supercontracted muscles splintered his own shell. He collapsed, drooling and almost motionless, his head wobbling in aimless circles.

A medical droid rolled forward, performed a swift analysis, and then reported back to Trillot.

Trillot looked at Ventress, eyes gone dark. Fizzik knew that his employer wanted to censure her, to remind her of her promise, but dared not.

Ventress might have read Trillot's mind. "He is not dead," she said matter-of-factly.

"Indeed not," Trillot replied. "And for that I am grateful."

She bowed graciously as several of Trillot's employees picked up the hapless Remlout and carried him away. With every jostle, he screamed. They were not as gentle as they might have been, and Fizzik supposed that Remlout's history as a bully now worked against him.

He noted that, without another word being said, the body language of every creature in that room was suddenly more respectful and alert. It couldn't have worked better for Ventress had she scripted it. She brushed imaginary dust from her spotless cloak and stood before Trillot once again. Fizzik counted the pulses at her jawline, clearly visible but unhurried. A knot of muscle at the base of one tattoo quivered in unhurried rhythm.

Trillot seemed to have moved on, apparently wishing to change the subject as quickly as possible. "And there is one more development," he said.

"Yes?" Ventress stood immobile. The previous moment's violent action might have meant nothing at all. But in the name of the galaxy, what had she done to poor Remlout? And would he, Fizzik, ever have the temerity to ask?

"Yes," Trillot said. "Now. As to the Jedi negotiating with our good lady Regent—"

That, finally, caught the offworlder's attention. "His name?"

"Obi-Wan Kenobi."

Now, for the first time, Ventress's attention was riveted. *"Obi-Wan."* Her blue eyes flamed. Again, Fizzik sensed that it might be worth his life to inquire. "I know this one. He needs to die."

"Please," Trillot implored. "There is business to be conducted. There may not be time . . ."

Ventress cast a scathingly cold glare upon her host. "Did someone request your advice? I think not." She closed her eyes, and in stillness she seemed like the center of a storm. She opened her eyes again. "I don't believe in coincidence. Obi-Wan and I are here on the same business." The tip of her pink tongue wet her lips. "I think I will kill him."

Trillot's faceted gaze met hers, and Trillot lost; looking away. "I brought you here, thinking that with the Jedi in the capital, we need special arrangements before the meeting—"

Ventress's head tilted slightly sideways, and her voice was snake-quiet. "No. Obi-Wan will attempt to subvert the Families. He may already have a spy among them. No. Who knows I am here?"

"The families know Count Dooku is sending a representative," Trillot said. "But not who or when."

"Splendid. Leave it thus. First I will destroy Kenobi. Then I speak business with your precious Five Families."

From her initial flare Ventress had grown abnormally quiet, almost like a negative space, drawing light and heat from the room around her. This woman was as dangerous as a sand viper. Never had he seen her like.

"Yes, of course." What else could Trillot say?

Fizzik mused that he would certainly serve out the rest of his contract, but when it was complete . . . he wondered if the woman Ventress might conceivably need an assistant.

24

Protocol, Chancellor Palpatine had often said, *is the oil greasing the wheels of diplomacy.* After an exchange of pleasantries, they retired to Duris's office for a more private conversation. Three of her advisers accompanied her, and although they refrained from most interjections, he knew they were fully engaged with the negotiation process.

Barrister Snoil was debating a minor point as Shar Shar, the little Zeetsa, rolled forward. Duris bent so that the aide could whisper in her ear. She listened intently, then studied several holo documents projected on a screen before them.

She looked up and smiled. "Barrister Snoil," she said. "You are aware of the case of Gadon Three?"

Snoil's eyestalks retreated into themselves, and then extended again. "Yes," he squeaked. "But there are at least four cases that might have some application here. Please be more specific."

Duris seemed pleased with Snoil's erudition, and held up a finger at what, from their angle, seemed a shadowy silhouette. "A matter of breakaway Kif miners."

"Ah, yes." He composed himself. "Approximately fifty standard years ago, the miners began selling high-energy ores on the open market. Some of these ores found their way to a colony allied with enemies of the Gadon regime. The Gadons came to the Republic for a ruling, and it was adjudged that the intent of the original sale had been above reproach. Therefore the final disposition of the ores was not the responsibility of the miners."

Obi-Wan closed his eyes briefly. That had been a poor decision. The Republic hadn't penalized the miners, because a similar situation was brewing in a nonallied cluster of planets the Chancellor hoped would provide the Republic vital raw material. A lenient ruling here could well make for good friendships elsewhere.

Brilliant politics, but it had now backfired! Obi-Wan felt that long-vanished headache beginning to return.

While he retreated into his mind, Duris and Snoil continued to banter back and forth. He knew this was just the opening salvo, but he was already out of his depth. They spoke of obscure treaties, taxes, rules and regulations.

Legalities be spaced. This had to end!

Obi-Wan waited for a lull in the conversation, and then raised his hand. "Pardon me, Regent Duris." He calmed himself. Could she be so obtuse? "Do you imagine that the Republic will stand by and allow Cestus to manufacture these killing machines?" Obi-Wan was a bit surprised at the strident tone in his own voice. "There is only one way this can end."

For the moment, formality and mannered, measured approach had broken down. Blast! He was no politician. He saw only the death and destruction that would be visited on this planet if he was unable to help them see past their contracts.

"And what is that?" Duris said frostily. She arched her segmented shell and squared her shoulders. Anger boiled beneath her composed surface as well. And something more. Fear?

He steadied his voice. "With no JK droids reaching planets outside the Republic. Perhaps none of any kind leaving your workshops at all."

"Do you threaten us? The Republic had its chance to purchase our products, and chose to neglect payment. Then, they restricted Gabonna crystals. Tens of thousands lost employment, Master Jedi. Our economy was almost crippled. There were food and water riots across the planet." She leaned forward. "Thousands *died*. Now you tell us not to conduct business with planets offering solid credits. Would the Supreme Chancellor authorize equal payments? In advance?"

No. Palpatine would never do that—it would be perceived, rightly, as submitting to blackmail. "I am not here to threaten," he said. "Merely to act as a conduit of communication between the Republic and the good people of Cestus. We know that you are fighting for the welfare of your people—"

"All the people of Cestus," she said. "Not just the X'Ting. Not just the hive council. My responsibilities are to every soul on this planet."

If true, a fine sentiment, Obi-Wan thought. "We, on the other hand, fight for the fate of an entire galaxy. You may rely upon one truth: we will not allow your machines to slaughter our troopers. Whether or not this entails the destruction of your civilization depends upon you."

For a moment there was silence in the room. Duris and Obi-Wan regarded each other intensely, a test of wills.

Then she nodded her head slowly. "Before you destroy us," she said, "perhaps you should better know what it is you will end." Her voice tightened, and this was where her breeding and strength rose to the surface. She would not be rendered ineffective by her emotions, however fearful they might be. "This evening there is a hive ball in your honor. It would please me if you would attend. Perhaps some communication is best facilitated in a more informal setting."

Obi-Wan took a deep breath. He had little taste for such formal celebrations, but then again, protocol was important. "I am grateful for the invitation. I hope that Your Grace will not interpret anything I have said as a lack of respect for you or your people."

"We've both a job to do," she said, and once again he had the odd sense that she was speaking on more than one level at a time. "But that does not mean we cannot be civil."

"Indeed," he said, and bowed.

25

Obi-Wan's formal robe was much like his everyday dress: flowing from floor to shoulder in a cascade of burnt sienna, but woven of demicot silk. Their astromech had buffed his boots to a high shine, and his spare tunic was cleaned.

Snoil's flat shell gleamed, and the folds of his skin were scraped clean of mucus and buffed as highly as Obi-Wan's boots. A pair of flat boxes had arrived for them. When opened, each yielded a flexible mask. The slanted eyes, peaked eye ridges, and flat, wide mouths were clearly a caricature of X'Ting physiognomy. When Obi-Wan pulled it on and viewed himself in a mirror, the effect was striking. "And what is this?"

Snoil was actually blocking the doorway as Obi-Wan completed his own preparations. A bemused smile wreathed the cephalopod's face.

"Master Jedi," the Vippit said. "You are resplendent."

"And you sparkle," Obi-Wan said. "Now, Barrister Snoil, it is important that we understand what is happening here."

Snoil raised one of his stubby hands. "Master Jedi, I know that I may seem ungainly and somewhat gauche, but I have been involved in such missions before. This ball is clearly a tactic, not a social occasion. I will be alert."

Obi-Wan sighed with relief. His companion was acutely aware of these games. More aware, perhaps, than he. In this, it was possible that Snoil would take the lead, and for that he was grateful.

"This is a hive ball," Snoil said, examining his mask. "The

hive may have little real power, but apparently the offworlders enjoy pretending that it does."

"Well," Obi-Wan said, helping Snoil on with his disguise. He extended his arm, and Snoil slipped his own small, firm hand through it. Snoil's arm was pleasantly smooth and cool, moist but not sticky. "Shall we join the fun?"

The music enveloped them silkily even before Obi-Wan and Doolb Snoil had exited their shuttle car. Several hundred guests had already arrived. Most were human or humanoid, with a sprinkling of other sentient species among the bejeweled attendees. Many were in pairs or trios, although at least one clan-cluster hovered around the appetizers. Hospitality droids served food and drink at a prodigious rate. Only a handful were genuine X'Ting, Obi-Wan noted, although all the others wore the X'Ting masks. Respectful custom or ugly joke? He wasn't at all certain.

The masked and costumed attendees parted as Obi-Wan and Snoil moved forward. With polite nods and interested expressions, they let the two pass and suppressed their speculative whispers until the odd pair had gone by.

The cream of Cestus's society had turned out for this gathering, a glittering ensemble indeed. A multispecies band strummed varied wind and string instruments and at least one synthesizing keyboard, producing music that sounded much like the mating anthem of Alderaan's Weaving clans, a perky melody that fairly demanded fancy footwork.

As they entered his eyes found G'Mai Duris swiftly, performing some X'Tingian rhythmics reminiscent of the Alderaan Reel. The couples and trios performing the precision choreography stopped. The music stopped. All of the masked participants applauded the newcomers.

If he was to assume that there was more than one meaning to everything that occurred here, then why had they chosen to welcome him in such an elaborate fashion? One answer came to mind: they hoped that elaborate displays would impress upon a galaxy-spanning traveler the idea that even

here, on the Outer Rim, there was a civilization worth preserving.

These smiles, these bows—they were sincere and hopeful.
These Cestians wanted him to understand the fragile and
lovely society that they had built up over the years, and it be-
hooved him to open his heart to them. If he grasped their nature better, it might be easier to make crucial decisions, or
devise appropriate tactics.

He hoped.

So with that in mind, when Duris approached him with
her mask held to her face, he took her arm with genuine
pleasure. "Master Jedi," she said. "It is such a delight that
you could spare the time to join our little gathering."

"One could not travel halfway across the galaxy," he said,
"and not partake of Cestus's famed hospitality."

Duris seemed to sparkle. Her immense intelligence and
energy filled her considerable frame to bursting. She was the
most vibrant and fully *alive* X'Ting he had yet encountered.

A small crowd of dignitaries formed behind her, all
masked, but some wearing costumes that actually concealed
their profiles. "G'Mai," one woman asked. "Please introduce
us to our visitors."

"Of course," Duris said. "Jedi Knight Obi-Wan Kenobi
and Doolb Snoil of Coruscant, please meet the heads of the
Five Families." A short, slender man bowed. "Debbikin of
research." A half-faced X'Ting mask on the next woman's
imperious face did not disguise the elaborate makeup and
tattooing of her lips. "Lady Por'Ten of energy." The next
man was tall and broad and pale, as if he had never seen the
sun. "Kefka in manufacturing," Duris said. Kefka was possibly human, with perhaps a bit of Kiffar mixed in by genetic
splice. The next man's blue skin proclaimed him of Wroonian extraction. "Llitishi of sales and marketing," Duris proclaimed. The next in line was a slender X'Ting, one of
perhaps five or six in the entire ballroom. "And my cousin
Caiza Quill of mining." He stood taller than Duris, almost
level with Obi-Wan. Quill extended his right primary hand in

a gesture of respect. He had a golden, stick-thin insectile body and vast faceted red eyes.

Each bowed in turn. They made small talk. Then, expressing their eagerness to begin negotiations on the morrow, they retreated to allow the Jedi and Barrister Snoil to enjoy their evening.

Duris led him onto the dance floor. "Are you familiar with the reel?" she asked.

"More in theory than practice," he said politely, momentarily wishing that a band of assassins might attack the party at this moment, giving him an excuse to decline.

He was on the verge of begging off completely when he *felt* something. A sensation like a flux-wire brushing across his spine, and he knew that there was danger in this room. He glanced left and right, seeing nothing but dancers. Then—a glimpse, a silhouette on the far side of the room. A lithe, costumed figure. Male? Female? He wasn't certain, and wasn't even certain why his alarms had triggered. There appeared no obvious threat, but he wanted to be certain. Duris stood before him, waiting patiently for him to answer her implied request. Obi-Wan forced himself to smile. "Shall we experiment?"

She laughed throatily and, he thought, with genuine mirth. He looked back over his shoulder. Barrister Snoil was surrounded by three masked females, one human, a Corthenian, and a Wookiee, who were engaging him in animated conversation. Good. Snoil's torpid locomotion was a perfect excuse for declining dance, but at least he was pleasantly occupied.

With that in mind, Obi-Wan extended his left hand, and she rested both primary and secondary right hands upon his forearm. He joined the line, took his place across from G'Mai Duris, and extended the tendrils of the Force.

The band prompted them to enjoy Cestus's own special dance variant. Even if the original form had been one as universal as the Alderaan Weaver's Reel, they would have their own interpretations. And he knew that the guests were watching to see if he could adapt. This would tell them not only if he was of their social tribe, but how they might expect him to react in the future.

Obi-Wan had dual obligations: to learn this dance as swiftly as possible, and to search out the elusive figure and determine why his senses were screaming at him. *Something is wrong. Danger!*

There. White-smocked, deliberately genderless? Slipping between two humans and a native Cestian servant. Human? No. Extremely fluid in motion—

Then Duris squeezed his arm. "Master Jedi! I had no idea that you were a courtier as well as warrior and diplomat. You dance superbly."

He chuckled to himself. For centuries, dance had been used at the Jedi Temple to facilitate rhythm and timing. On any world of the galaxy, when one found males or dominant females dancing, it was often a warrior art in disguise. Obi-Wan knew the movements of a dozen fierce and beautiful traditions.

"I merely follow your lead, madam," he said, smiling as he focused over her shoulder, seeking the elusive figure.

Gone!

The room swirled and Obi-Wan glided along with it, his Jedi reflexes and coordination drawing admiring glances almost at once.

He remembered his childhood in the Temple. Master Yoda had devised so many ingenious ways to teach vital lessons. He remembered watching the great Jedi perform complex dance steps, admonishing his astonished young students to become "complete" movement artists. *A warrior who cannot dance? Clumsy in both war and peace he is.*

At the very least, an ambassador who could not fumble his way through the Alderaan Reel was a poor ambassador, indeed.

There was nothing suspicious to be seen, and in fact his sense of danger had faded, almost as if it had never been justified at all.

"We're all watching you, you know," Duris whispered, coming closer. "Most have never seen an actual Jedi before."

Obi-Wan chuckled to himself and backed away from her as the music changed. He swirled and passed to the next lady in line, where the dance began anew.

At the first opportunity he retired from the line, and on the pretext of seeking refreshment again scanned the entire room, from stalactites to stalagmites.

Nothing.

As if there had never been anything at all.

Asajj Ventress hurried down the tunnel toward her waiting hovercar, discarding her X'Ting mask as she went. Fizzik awaited her there, in a chauffeur's coat, and none of the guests trickling out of the ball paid them any attention.

"Did you see him?" Fizzik asked.

She laughed mirthlessly. "Of course," she said. "He almost sensed me." For months Count Dooku had taught her the Quy'Tek meditations. It was good to see the result. Her grin was as feral as a kraken's fixed and meaningless smile. "Obi-Wan Kenobi." She settled back into her seat and closed her eyes. "The game is mine."

"Wasn't that very risky?" Fizzik said.

She opened her eyes and gazed at him, perhaps wondering whether her pleasures would be best served by killing him here and now.

"Life is risk," she said, and then turned to watch the buildings flow past. For a moment her face assumed an unaccustomed softness as her thoughts deepened. "Perhaps death, as well."

At that, Fizzik fell silent.

Ventress closed her eyes, laying plans.

Jedi. She'd killed many Jedi, and yet did not hate them. Rather, she hated the fact that they had lost their way, that they had forgotten their true purpose in the world, becoming pawns of a corrupt and decadent Republic.

While most Jedi were discovered in early infancy and raised in the Jedi Temple, Asajj Ventress had been discovered by Master Ky Narec on the desolate planet of Rattatak. An orphaned child starving in the wreckage of a war-torn city, Ventress had clung to anyone offering her hope, and over the next years came to worship the formidable Narec as a father figure. He had groomed the Force-strong child, uncovered and developed her potential. At that time she imagined that one day she might travel to Coruscant and stand before the Council, become part of the ancient Order.

Then her Master was murdered. The Jedi Council, who had abandoned Ky Narec to his fate, now became the object of her blind rage. Consumed with vengeance, she became a destructive force beyond anything her Jedi Master could have dreamed.

It was Count Dooku who discovered her on the Outer Rim. She had attacked him, been defeated and disarmed, but rather than slaying her he took her as an accomplice, completed her training, and set her feet on the proper path. It was Dooku to whom she owed total allegiance, as she owed nothing save death to the ruthless, corrupt Jedi.

Yes. She had clashed with Jedi. Killed many. Faced Master Windu and come within a hairbreadth of defeating him. Faced Skywalker in battles they would both remember. Obi-Wan had escaped her hand twice, but would not again. This she swore by her allegiance to Dooku. This she swore by her dead Master Ky Narec.

This she promised herself, purely for her own pleasure.

Asajj Ventress's closed eyelids fluttered, and her pink mouth curved upward in a smile.

26

The Jedi and his Vippit companion had retired to their shared quarters, but G'Mai Duris was still attending to her ball guests as the music slowed and the lights came up, signaling the evening's end.

She stood at the door, bidding farewell to her guests, when Caiza Quill and his partner Sabit appeared. A few months before, it had been Quill who had been the green-eyed female, Sabit the male, but even then Quill had been intimidating. At his weakest, he was more intimidating than Duris was at her strongest. Now, at his most aggressive, the weight of his pheromones was almost overwhelming.

He leaned over her, exuding his scent. "Don't think that I don't know you're trying to cultivate the Jedi as an ally," he said. "Don't think for a moment that I will tolerate that. Remember what happened to Filian."

She stiffened. How could she forget? Not five years before, Quill and her mate Filian had engaged in a formal combat, what the X'Ting called "going to the sand." And there, before the council, the lethal Quill had slain her love. If she lived to a thousand, she would never forget the sight.

"Do not weaken," he said. "Do not waver. Or you will suffer."

And then he was gone.

G'Mai Duris bid the rest of her guests farewell and took her shuttle back to her apartment. She had loved Filian completely. As they had spiraled through the eternal dance of male and female, each moment and way of being had been, in its turn, exquisite.

But he had died before the fertilization dance could begin. So childless, alone with her empty egg sac, she rocked in the darkness, tears of terror and loneliness slicking her faceted emerald eyes.

27

As the new recruits practiced their maneuvers, Nate watched, noted, and made adjustments in *this* obstacle course or *that* targeting range. Forry approached him at an easy trot, the sort of pace that a common man would find exhausting in ten minutes, and a trooper could continue all day long.

"Sir!" the commando said, saluting smartly. "More recruits arrive."

"How many?"

Forry smiled with satisfaction. "Two dozen, sir!"

Nate felt a warm flush. This was exactly the kind of news he had hoped for. "We'll make a fight of this yet," he said.

Nate was well satisfied with what he saw, and was moving the intensity up a notch when Sheeka approached behind him.

"So?" she asked. "What do you think?"

He was pleased to realize that he felt confident to intuit her meaning.

"Not too bad," he said. "Farm boys and deep miners, but they can take orders."

"They're tough folk," Sheeka said. "A lot of them think it's time to fight."

"And you?"

"I just fly," she said.

"You might do just fine," he said. "Strong legs and back, good reflexes. You might think about signing up."

She laughed. "No experience. And experience counts." Then she glanced at him. "On the other hand, you weren't always the old battle-scarred veteran, were you?"

Nate shook his head. Then with a slight smile, he added, "True. But our simulations are . . . quite stimulating." He moved his shoulders a bit, rolling out the stiffness and re-membering Vondar-3.

"I'm sure they are," she said.

He watched as the training droid's arms flexed in multiple directions, giving each recruit the motivation he or she needed to excel. "They are eager enough—but they'd have their heads handed to them by experienced troops, or battle droids."

"I've watched you with them," she said. "I think the four of you are just the man for the job."

For a moment he thought that she had misspoken herself, then realized that her straight face was only being main-tained with effort. She laughed out loud.

Nate felt his own lips twitching, understanding her joke, and that even though it was at his expense, he appreciated it.

"Yes, we are," he said.

With that, he left her and went down to take a more per-sonal hand in the training. It was not entirely lost on him that he squared his shoulders just a little more rigidly, that he moved a bit faster in demonstrating unarmed combat moves, that he was a hair more alert, because he knew Sheeka was watching. And although he felt a bit absurd for it, at the same time he enjoyed her attention, and hoped that she would be there when the day was done.

28

In ChikatLik, diplomatic operations proceeded at a glacial pace. Snoil spent the mornings and much of the afternoons poring over contracts, and finally twined his eye stalks in frustration. "Ah! I've lost ten years' growth on my shell," he whined. "Have you seen these?"

"What?" asked Obi-Wan, who was working to establish secure communications with Coruscant. This necessitated linking through Xutoo at their docked ship. So far, a solar storm seemed to have distorted the link.

"The little cracks and fissures here where the new chitin is forming." Snoil craned his long neck to look back at his flat shell's attractive curls and swoops. In truth, he was accurate: there were new cracks where the thinnest, newest shell segments should have been forming.

"Ah, yes, I see," Obi-Wan said, distracted. "What does it mean?"

Snoil's eye stalks coiled in distress. "Stress! Stress, I tell you."

"Well, I don't want to add to your burden . . ."

"Oh, please . . ."

The hololink suddenly cleared, and Supreme Chancellor Palpatine floated in the air before him. Snoil immediately quieted.

"Chancellor," Obi-Wan said.

"My Jedi friend. What news have you?"

"I believe that the Regent is of good heart, but fears for her life if she acts her conscience."

"And what do you think her conscience would dictate?"

"That which is best for all Cestus: suspension of manufacture."

"Then what is the problem?"

"I believe the real power is in a group called the Five Families, owners of Cestus Cybernetics. And they think of little save profit."

"Then you may need to take matters to the next level. I believe you were given reliable contacts. Have you used them?"

"I believe Master Fisto has met with one. I meet with the other tonight."

"I wish you fortune, Master Kenobi. Remember: little time remains, if we would avert disaster."

"Yes, sir," Obi-Wan said, but before he could speak further the Chancellor was gone.

He sighed, turning to Snoil. "Barrister," he said. "If you had a wish list of . . . secure documents, what would be at the top?"

Doolb moaned. "Oh, what shall I do? What shall I say?"

"The truth."

His eye stalks twined around each other. "I think I would ask for the original papers of incorporation and land purchase. And, oh—the purchase orders themselves between Cestus Cybernetics and Count Dooku or his intermediaries."

"Will do." He slapped Snoil's shell with the flat of his hand. "If anyone asks, just tell them I'm sampling the native cuisine," he said. "Take care."

And with that, Obi-Wan left their suite.

Obi-Wan was able to slip into an empty room down the hall, and from there to exit through a window unmonitored by the security forces which doubtless kept a long-distance view of all his activities.

He climbed up to the roof and rode a service chute down to the street, landing in an alleyway with his knees slightly bent, cushioning the shock. Three steps and he blended with the crowd, none of whom took the slightest notice of him.

Obi-Wan had heard of other planets that had begun as

prison colonies, but never actually visited one. He was heartened by the overwhelming sense of energy and *aliveness*. Everywhere he looked the streets were filled with milling, thronging offworlders. Although there were only a smattering of X'Ting citizens to be seen, the city did remind him of a hive colony. Commerce was conducted every minute of the day, and every being he passed was trading in one way or another. One out of ten shops was boarded up, but the others buzzed with a frantic sense of activity, as if dancing on the edge of a precipice. How many Cestians understood the game her masters were playing? Even if without conscious awareness, these people seemed a little too bright and aware. This was nervousness, not exuberance.

He hailed one of the cheaper, older air taxis, figuring that they were less likely to be tied into the surveillance grid. Even if they were, technically speaking he was doing nothing illegal or that would overtly damage his mission. The driver's taxi holocard read GRITT CHIPPLE. Gritt was X'Ting, with the red thoracic fur indicating descent from a lower hive clan. "Your destination?" Gritt inquired.

"The Night Shade." Gritt Chipple flinched. Clearly, he knew the Night Shade, and was not entirely happy to travel there.

"Hard credits," Obi-Wan added, and offered the little X'Ting some Cestian chits. The driver's red eyes lit up. The chits were onplanet and therefore easier to change, and not tied into the galactic credit grid like the Republic chits. Untraceable. Avarice overwhelmed fear. "Aye," he said, and they zipped away.

"You Jedi?"

Obi-Wan nodded. He was not disguised, but had hoped that he might avoid notice.

"Then I heard of you. You wan' ride back from Night Shade?"

"That might be good, yes."

The little one made a spitting sound that Obi-Wan interpreted as pleasure. "Then I wait for you. You be careful.

Sometimes offworlders not safe." Another spitting sound. "Sir."

The car had been riding along the side of the vast cave, but then leapt into the maelstrom of ChikatLik. The complex was dizzying even to one who lived in the fabled Jedi Temple. The driver floated through the maze as only one born to a planet could do, and Obi-Wan thought that Anakin might well have appreciated the little X'Ting's facility.

Five minutes' travel brought them to a darker, grimmer section, one set off from the main business districts. This was a place where reputable citizens strayed on only the most disreputable of business. Where in other parts of the city he saw only a few X'Ting per hundred citizens, here, finally, the insectile beings were plentiful.

The driver handed him a triangular holochip. "Trigger this when you want ride," he said, and the door opened. Obi-Wan tipped Gritt handsomely and exited. The tattered little taxi cruised off, leaving Obi-Wan alone.

Following memorized instructions, Obi-Wan approached the door guarded by the two massive X'Ting guards. Females, no doubt. The males were smaller and more lethal, but the females were more intimidating to offworlders, who often failed to realize that much of the bulky body was mere egg sac.

"You wish—?" the larger of them asked in a surprisingly cultured voice.

He spoke a code word, then said, "I have an appointment with Trillot." Not exactly the truth, but he knew that their contacts had warned the X'Ting gang lord to expect him.

"A minute," the smaller said, and slipped back through the entrance, emerging a moment later to hold the door open. "Enter."

Eyes measured him, not all of them respectful. A few were curious, wondering if he was typical of his kind, wondering if the Jedi were as strong as their supporters said, or as weak as the Separatists claimed.

The den was dark, and alien eyes glimmered at him from

the darkness. No one guided him, as if they expected him to find his own way.

He could tell by the body language of the beings he encountered, their posture and expressions, which way through the maze Trillot lay. If this was some kind of a test, he intended to pass it with flying colors.

On every side of him wafted the smells and sounds and sights of an utterly corrupt habitat. Clearly, these were social dregs, yet . . . to be so close to the inner circle of the powerful Trillot, they had to have resources, if nothing other than Trillot's trust. So Obi-Wan might as well consider this the gangster's hive, a place the X'Ting kept for his own comfort, something that reminded him of his own grubhood, even if it demanded the destruction of other beings.

He recoiled at the thought, but kept his thoughts and feelings to himself.

At the end of the corridor was another door, and before this one stood a second pair of X'Ting bodyguards braced at attention. Males this time, and genuinely lethal. They opened the door as he approached.

It took a moment for his eyes to adjust to the interior. Trillot sat perched on a tall cushion, puffing contentedly on a pipe of some kind, long thin vapor curls spiraling from slits in the side of her neck. The swollen thorax, ready to be filled with fertilized eggs, told Obi-Wan that Trillot had completed the swing from male to female.

"Jedi," Trillot said, her faceted eyes fixed on Obi-Wan. "Welcome to my abode."

"Mistress Trillot," Obi-Wan said, and then bowed slightly, reciting a complex series of sounds in X'Ting.

Trillot's eyes glittered. "You are very cultured for a human. Please. Come sit by my side."

Obi-Wan did so as Trillot took several more puffs. "I would not insult a Jedi," she said, "by publicly offering the fruit of fantazi." The implication was obvious.

Kenobi smiled. "We have business," he said. "Fantazi clouds the mind."

Trillot nodded. "But also sharpens the senses."

"We both know why I am here," Obi-Wan said. "War sweeps across the galaxy. Cestus is not immune to its touch."

"War . . . or peace," Trillot said with a deep and evidently satisfying puff. "Either way, I make my profit."

Bluff.

"Not if that war destroys Cestus's industrial capacity. Then there are no workers to exploit. Then you suffer as well."

Trillot nodded slowly, as if Obi-Wan had indeed made an important point. "I wish to avoid travail if that is at all possible."

"I believe it is."

"Then I will listen. What is it that I can do for you?"

Good. Avarice was a useful lever. "My friends on Coruscant say you have a finger on everything that happens here," he said.

Trillot tittered. "How perceptive."

Obi-Wan lowered his voice slightly. "I wish to know the secret codicils between the Families and the Confederacy."

At that, Trillot seemed to be taken a bit aback. "Indeed? Such information would be hard-won."

"I have resources."

"Do you? I have resources as well. I would be loath to endanger them on such a mission."

"I was told that if anyone could reveal the industrial system's weakness, it would be you."

Trillot inhaled deeply. A long, thin stream of smoke escaped her shallow throat-slits. "And if—that is to say *if* I was to share that knowledge, how might it benefit me and mine?"

"In order to keep the peace and keep these devices off the market, the Republic is prepared to offer a generous contract for droids. Your information is valuable in . . . favorably resolving my negotiations. I will give you advance notice of the order's size and specifications."

"And why would that interest me?"

Obi-Wan knew that they were equally aware of the stakes involved. "Because it would give you time to buy and hoard certain components, equipment, raw materials. I'm certain an enterprising lady such as yourself can see the potential."

Trillot exhaled, and her face took on an arrangement that Obi-Wan believed was a smile. "You think like a criminal," she said.

"One of my many failings."

"I like that in a man," Trillot said, leaning close enough for Obi-Wan to catch a whiff of phéromones. Possibly a seductive move among the X'Ting, but to Obi-Wan, Trillot smelled like a tannery.

"So?"

Trillot sighed. "So. Well, then. Yes, it is true. There is a weakness in the system, but only because it would kill those who tried to exploit it."

Interesting. "Explain."

"Radiation," Trillot said. "It is said that beneath the industrial city of Clandes lies a juncture box where the landlines cross. Not all communications are wireless—not since the uprisings a century ago. These landlines can directly access the main terminal, with only minor safeguards. After reconfiguration, that entire area was designated unfit for habitation, and the workers moved out. With the safety regulations no longer so . . . stringent, they saved money on shielding. It would kill you in a few minutes . . . unless you had a class six Baktoid radiation suit."

"Which I assume you have?"

"Let's just say that a lady of my peculiar resources knows how to acquire such things."

"And what might the price of such a wonder be?"

"Such suits are rare, now that the Baktoid factories are shut down," Trillot said mildly. "What you wish done is singular. If and when you commit such an act, any who know of the suit's sale would know to come looking for Trillot."

"What price?"

"It will never happen . . . but let's say half a million credits."

Half a million. More than he planned to pay, but possible. Still, if he gave in too quickly, this gangster would lose respect for him. Future negotiations would be strained. "Absurd."

Trillot might have been reading his mind. "Yes. Isn't it?"

The two bantered and sparred for a few more minutes, and then Obi-Wan softened his stance. "So . . . through this terminal, assuming that the agent did not die of radiation poisoning, the production line could be shut down . . . or crashed?"

"It could happen, yes." Trillot seemed delighted with herself.

"Even if I had half a million credits, I am not yet prepared to engage in sabotage against the Clandes factory," he said. "Let us discuss other alternatives."

"A question," Trillot asked. "If that central computer were shut down, the entire economy goes . . . *pfft*. Not good for business, eh?"

"No," Obi-Wan said, certain of his ground. "The luxury droids would stop. Low-end droids could continue manufacture under license."

"Ah. Then Cestus would fall neatly into the Republic's arms, and business can continue as before."

"So," Obi-Wan said, extending both hands palm forward in the manner of agreeable X'Tings. "We have a deal?"

"Details on the trade agreement?"

"That's all for now. And inquiries concerning that suit."

"It will be done."

He touched palms with Trillot, and then, bowing, he turned and left.

Trillot waited a few moments, puffing again from the pipe. Smoke drifted from the flaps in her neck.

As if on cue, Ventress appeared. Her tattooed scalp seemed almost to glow in the dim light. She seemed thoughtful but not disturbed. "So," she said. "Kenobi wants the notes of Count Dooku's negotiations with the Five Families, as well as secret codicils between Cestus Cybernetics and the hive."

Trillot blinked. "Does this disturb you?"

"No. It excites me." She closed her eyes and smiled, lost in her own speculations. "Obi-Wan and I have an appointment."

Trillot ceased to take pleasure from her draws, and coughed a bit, furious to have revealed her inner mood in such a gauche fashion. Her broodmates would have been ashamed. "What shall I do? If it is that important, then surely I should refuse to supply him."

Ventress's eyes rolled up and lost focus, as if seeking a distant vista. "No."

"I can give him false information—" she tried again.

"No." Ventress had focused again, and was even more certain this time. "He may have other sources. This may be nothing more than a test. If you fail it, he will never trust you again." She paused a moment, and her eyes shivered side to side in their internal search for truth or clarity. "And," she continued, "I think that before this is through, it will prove to be good that he trusts you." She considered, and then the first smile creased those thin, pale lips. "Yes, I believe that that is true."

29

Obi-Wan Kenobi slipped out of Trillot's den. With every step it seemed as if layers of a toxic curtain were lifting from his mind.

Gritt Chipple was waiting for him even before he triggered the little chip he had been given. The taxi driver seemed a bit off-put.

"Sir Jedi," he said. "I got a flash. Asked me to link you to another taxi."

Obi-Wan's eyebrows raised. "Yes?"

"Don't know who. Link you?"

This was interesting. Who would attempt such an unusual contact? "By all means."

The X'Ting driver dithered over a fingerboard, and an indistinct face appeared. Not male or female—it was deliberately obscured for gender and species. The voice was masked as well. "I respectfully request the honored guest meet me at the Cleft Head for a cup of wake-tea and a bit of discussion. I believe he will find it to his benefit." A map appeared.

"Where would this take us?" Obi-Wan asked.

"Im'grant section. Not bad, not good. Strange." Chipple shrugged. "I know not say, sir."

Obi-Wan checked over his recent actions. He didn't recall anything unusually suspicious. So if it was a trap, why not stay their hand until something actually occurred? "Let's go," he said. But as they rose and flew away, Obi-Wan felt comforted by the weight and heft of the lightsaber at his side.

*   *   *

Obi-Wan entered the Cleft Head through a door that re-sembled a quartet of X'Ting hive cubicles. As he crossed the threshold, Obi-Wan heard a raucous scream. The mob of X'Ting and offworlders backed away, giving two combatants room.

Two young X'Ting males circled each other, and then one lunged. The other danced away, and both curled their abdomens: quarter-meter-long stingers emerged. Both male and female X'Ting had stingers, but those of the males were slightly longer, the poison more deadly. Their increased strength-to-weight ratios as they dumped their egg sacs made them far faster.

Their stingers stabbed at each other. Finally, one made a mistake, and the stinger plunged deep. The stricken X'Ting seemed paralyzed with fear even before the toxin took effect. Then he foamed, shuddered and collapsed, shaking. And then was still . . .

The bar's patrons turned back to their drinks, as if this was a nightly occurance.

The Cleft Head wake-up house served a thousand stimu-lants from a hundred worlds, designed to help office workers burn the midnight wick without collapse. It was all legal, al-though Obi-Wan was certain that within its confines access to slightly less legal substances was easily arranged.

He chose a table that allowed him to watch the door and ordered a cup of Tatooine H'Kak bean tea. The fragrant orange-colored extract had hardly been delivered to his table before a bulky figure in an enveloping cloak slipped into the chair opposite him.

"G'Mai Duris," he said, sipping. H'Kak beans were posi-tively wizard at brushing away the heavy, noxious strands re-maining from Trillot's den. "I'd hoped it might be one of your emissaries, but dared not hope you'd come yourself." He kept his voice low. Her face was hidden within the folds of her cowl, but he recognized her faceted eyes at once. If Duris wished to travel incognito among her constituents, he had to assume that she had good reason. Besides, another question needed answering. "How did you find me?"

"I have my own sources, my own spies," she said. "And some report directly to me rather than to the council. Some in low places have found me trustworthy in the past. It was sheer chance that they picked you up entering Trillot's lair."

She cocked her head sideways, and although he could barely see her eyes, he knew they would be hooded with challenge. "I assume you did not go to Trillot in search of intoxication. May I ask your business?"

"Perhaps when we know each other a bit better," he said, buying himself time.

"Perhaps."

She laughed, and he thought its sound more genuine and unaffected than any she had made in her public mode. "This is ChikatLik's immigrant section. They came during our boom days, and now many of them are trapped onplanet, without enough credits to get home. They're more concerned with finding jobs or transport than listening to conversations. They don't pay attention, Master Kenobi. At times, the best hiding place is in plain sight."

"So, then. The Cleft Head bar, indeed."

"I was hoping that you might sneak out. And that if you did, I might be able to meet with you."

Obi-Wan nodded. "Now that I understand your method, perhaps you can enlighten me as to your intent."

"For the first time I can speak freely—" She paused. "Or almost freely, at any rate."

He chuckled. "You have my attention."

"Regardless of what you may think, Cestus's Regency is a sham—governments come and go, but the Five Families who controlled the early droid and armor works—mining, fabrication, sales and distribution, research, and energy—actually control everything. I believe they favor the Confederacy."

"You believe?"

She sighed. "I have no real proof. I am related to the hive's royal house. My cousin Quill is royalty as well, but since he killed my mate, and stole hive council leadership"—she cast her faceted eyes downward—"I am no longer privy to the inner workings of the Five Families *or* the hive council. I no longer know if their decisions are made by vote, or if some one or two of them have taken power. No one knows who holds the ultimate power. No one can pierce the melded corporate veil."

"Corporate veil?" Obi-Wan mused. "More of a family veil."

"True. No outsiders know the business of those meetings."

"What of the planet's other original inhabitants?"

"Its aboriginals?" She shrugged. "Most are dead and gone, or pushed to the Badlands. The spider folk were once strong, but I doubt there is a single intact clan left on the surface."

The buzz of the Cleft Head rose, and then ebbed again, a current that washed over them in waves. "I am afraid, Master Jedi. I see no good way out of this."

"Might they replace you as Regent?"

"No," she said flatly. "I am Regent for life." She lowered her head. "He would take the Regency himself, if that would not so baldly proclaim a conflict of interests. He controls the hive council, and is in turn controlled by the Five Families."

"And what does this mean?"

"It means that the checks and balances that should protect the indigenous peoples are nonexistent. It means that the original contracts with the hive can be manipulated in any way profitable to the Families."

This was ghastly. "And you cannot stand against him?"

"If I go against Quill, he will just challenge me, kill me, and replace me." She paused. "As he did my mate Filian."

"And you are afraid of him?"

"He is one of the hive's most lethal fighters." She shivered at the very thought.

"Why are you meeting with me?"

Her eyes flashed. "When I took office, I found a datapad

left by one of my predecessors, a hundred fifty years ago. It spoke of another Jedi, named Yoda, I believe."

Obi-Wan couldn't resist a smile. Yoda? He didn't recall hearing about the great Jedi Master on a planet named Cestus.

". . . he was marooned here while escorting a prisoner, and did great service to the hive. My predecessor trusted the Jedi, so I trust you. I believe I can speak to you honestly, and receive honesty in return."

"I will do what I can, so long as it does not compromise my mission."

"It does not," she assured him.

"Then we are just two new friends sharing a quiet hour, and a bit of H'Kak."

She took a deep breath. "Thank you. You and I walk through a hall of mirrors, Obi-Wan. Count Dooku's order will force my people to choose between economic collapse and military defeat. I believe those who placed the orders knew it . . . and perhaps even hoped for such a situation."

Reasonable. "For what purpose?"

"I do not know. I fear Cestus is a pawn in a larger, more dangerous game."

Obi-Wan hunched closer. "What manner of game?"

"I do not know. I say only that I sense the hand of a master games player, but do not know the end."

He considered what she had said so far, and realized that there was nothing there that he could not have learned on his own. Was she attempting to manipulate him, or could he trust his Jedi intuition? The Clone Wars had raged for some time now. Wouldn't G'Mai know more than this? She would have an idea what the larger game was.

A game that Obi-Wan, for all of his experience and power, was ill prepared to play.

"It is almost as if a stalemate is actually desired," she said. "I cannot make more sense of it all than that."

"Why are you telling me these things?"

Her shoulders slumped. "I don't know. Perhaps because it

is a lonely knowledge. In sharing it, I become a bit less iso-lated."

If she spoke the truth, then part of her reason for speaking to him was that, being from offplanet, she knew she could trust him as she could no one enmeshed in Cestus's power structure. If she could not see any means out of the current dilemma, then this was a plea for him to unravel a knot cen-turies in the making. He was not here for this! He was here for one reason and one reason only, to keep Cestus from pro-ducing and exporting more JK droids.

The Cleft Head cantina was filled wall-to-wall with stimulant-seeking customers, and it was not difficult for Ven-tress to blend in, again using a portion of her Force energy to shield herself from Obi-Wan's keen senses. He was one of the most powerful Jedi she had ever met. She believed her-self stronger, but was not so certain as she had once been.

Nevertheless, his strength made the taste of her inevitable victory all the sweeter.

Ventress blended seamlessly into Cleft Head's multispecies milieu, observing without being observed. She enjoyed this risky game, shielding herself from Obi-Wan, gliding close until she could feel his awareness flutter, then backing away again, playing with the edge of his perceptions.

The moment was so dangerous that it filled her senses, was more potent than any fleshly pleasure or drug could ever be. This was danger, in its rawest sense. To play with the senses of a master opponent tested the limits of her emo-tions, emotions that she kept under tight control. It was . . . *intoxicating,* yes, that was the word.

There. She came closer for a moment, allowed a bit more of her attention to flirt with the exterior shell of his aura, which flickered in her sight like a field of soft small lights.

In one sense, there was little risk: she could watch him, would know if he was beginning to focus his attention on the exterior and away from his conversation, and had every con-fidence in her ability to withdraw before he became aware.

Delicious.

"Shhh," she whispered, so softly that she could not actually hear her own words. "So close. So easy. He doesn't even know you exist." A sharp uptake of breath. "No. No, there— he almost sensed something, but you were gone before he noticed. He will scan. He will see nothing. You *are* nothing."

She could see that there was some thread of communication growing between Obi-Wan and Duris. Well, it didn't matter.

Whatever he tried, Ventress stood ready. Whatever his plan, she was prepared to counter it. In fact, whatever it was the two of them had in mind, she would use it to lure him into her trap. This time, there would be no escape.

She had yet to meet with the Five Families, but could still use them. Bait, that was the approach. She would have tracking and listening devices attached to their vehicles and persons. They would be followed, their actions and words recorded.

And somewhere in the process, she would trap Kenobi. She could feel it. This was the planet, this was the time.

Obi-Wan Kenobi would be hers.

Delicious.

Twice since landing on this planet, Obi-Wan had felt . . . something. Not quite enough to fully bring him to attention. Certainly not enough to clearly identify. Comprehension eluded him, as if he were groping for an object just out of reach. But although none of his senses could touch such a phantom object directly, the mere withdrawal left ripples in water . . . or in the air. And now there was a ripple in the Force. A *not-presence.* Something withdrawn. Something *missing.*

He did not feel it consciously. In fact, the more consciously he searched, the more it slipped away, as if he had imagined the entire thing. So he concentrated on the conversation with G'Mai, leaving only the slightest sliver of attention, a merest mote, to scan the surroundings, searching not for a presence, but another . . . lack of presence. Yes. Another sense of withdrawal.

It was too small to integrate itself into his consciousness at the moment. Not until later, in the depth of his Jedi meditations, might this small trap bear fruit. But he could wait.

30

For a dozen generations the leaders of the Five Families had ruled as if by divine privilege. So long as ore flowed to the foundries, and those foundries fed the factories creating droids and armor, channeling credits to Cestus coffers, that power might last for generations more.

The trappings of royalty provided what the actuality did not: a lavish wealth of art, fine subtle scents, and furnishings that might have done credit to any office in the Republic. If Cestus could not come to civilization, civilization had indeed come to Cestus.

At the moment, however, some of the conversation in the throne room was far from polite. For hours now the arguments had raged, and although on the surface the words used were polite, there was no mistaking the fierceness beneath them.

"Every event can have multiple meanings as well as consequences," said Llitishi, whose family had sprung from the daughter of an ore miner and the son of a murderer.

"I am aware of this," Duris said.

Quill, the room's only other X'Ting, stood. "The hive is upset that the Republic Senate has declared planets have no right of secession."

The Five Family leaders were arrayed in a semicircle about Duris's throne. In theory, the forces they represented were no more powerful than hers. In practice, of course, Duris was almost completely under their control.

"They are not fools," Duris said. "If Palpatine interferes with our right to commerce, it will drive more planets away."

Quill bore in. "If the Republic offers violence as a means of persuasion, the situation worsens."

Duris sighed, and remained silent as her esteemed guest spoke. It had been a week now, and as Obi-Wan presented his case to yet another group of the Five Families' representatives and barristers, she began to despair that a true consensus would ever be reached.

"I stand before you with a fair and just offer," Obi-Wan said. "We can stop the Gabonna crystal blockade and advance funds to purchase two thousand units of your class JL and JK droids."

G'Mai paused. This offer was new. She knew, of course, that Obi-Wan had been communicating with his Coruscant masters. In fact, some of those communications had already been intercepted and decrypted.

The X'Ting was similarly taken aback. "That might . . . ," he said, then emphasized, "*might* be enough to secure our market position."

Debbikin nodded. "I am willing to believe that this Jedi speaks honorably."

Obi-Wan inclined his head. "A fact noted and appreciated."

Lady Por'Ten's nephew raised his skeletal hand, as if warding off expectations of easy settlement. "But even this offer is risky. The cost of the war mounts. Taxes soar. The central government offers payment in credit bonds, to be redeemed at a later time. Such bonds can be traded for goods, but usually at a lower rate than face value . . ."

Obi-Wan had kept his voice and manner even, but he found the entire discussion dreadful, dull, and exasperating. Time was short, and there was a limit to the tricks he could pull, a limit to the negotiating room extended him by the Supreme Chancellor.

And if he ran out of maneuvering room . . . he shuddered to think of the cost. Perhaps sensing his mood, Snoil bent down and whispered to him. "Time is running out. This is more and more troubling: if the Republic wins, the rebellious planets will face a heavy punishment for their attempt to leave. But if the Republic loses, then planets belonging to the Republic will carry the tax burden."

Obi-Wan felt the patch of cold behind his left ear expand. The stress level was climbing intolerably. "My cephalopodan friend, you are giving me a headache. You, and the sense that Duris may be correct."

"In what way?" Snoil asked.

The Five Family executives were so busy arguing with each other that for the moment, no one seemed focused on them. "This may all be misdirection," he said. "I fear that lack of clarity will haunt me yet."

Duris raised both primary and secondary hands, requesting quiet. "We have an obligation to conduct these negotiations with good faith. I believe my honored associates hold the financial welfare of Cestus Cybernetics closely to heart, as they should. I represent the planet of Cestus, with all its citizens, and the hive, and its interests. Cestus Cybernetics could conceivably move to another planet, whereas this is our only home. Save the squabbling for another time. Our survival is at stake."

There was stunned silence for a moment, and then the discussion began anew, this time with a less argumentative tone.

After the hours of negotiation were past, the Jedi and the barrister returned to their lodgings. The other members of the Five Families packed their docufiles and left, but Quill approached Duris.

"You have blocked me for the last time," he said, seething. "I have spent a lifetime arranging a deal just such as this, and I will not tolerate your interference. Appear before the council tonight. You may end your own life, or you can go to the sand. Those are your only choices."

He leaned closer. "Personally, I hope you choose to fight. It would be good to kill you, as I did your mate. He died begging. I would like to hear those same words from you, smell your surrender."

Quill paused. "Then, of course, I will kill you."

31

In the dead of night, Trillot's people delivered the documents Obi-Wan had requested. Between those and the official records, Snoil had access to enough information to keep a research staff busy for years.

They didn't *have* years.

He absorbed, scanned, noted, summoned up abstracts, and worked well into the night. As far as Obi-Wan could determine, the Vippit hadn't slept since they arrived. Because he was uncertain of Vippit physiology, he wasn't sure whether this was exceptional. Still, he had grown more and more concerned until the hour when an exhausted Snoil informed Obi-Wan that he was ready for sleep.

Snoil crawled into his bedroom and was not seen again for ten hours, when he appeared in the doorway with an enormous smile splitting his face.

"Doolb?" Obi-Wan asked.

Snoil was radiant. "Obi-Wan!" he called. "Obi-Wan! While I slept, the two halves of my brain talked to each other. I've found it!"

"Found what?" he asked.

"Look here," he said, feverish with excitement. "In this document, executives of the Cestus Cybernetics *boast* about the fact that the land was purchased with synthstones. They actually laugh at the ignorant aboriginals."

Venality. Offensive in all its forms. "And?"

"Technically, synthstones represent counterfeit money." Snoil's eyes gleamed. "Follow me here, Obi-Wan. Cestus Cybernetics was a licensed subsidiary of the prison. The prison was constructed and operated under a Republic contract."

"Yes? And?" He still couldn't see where this was leading.

"Obi-Wan," Snoil said in exasperation, "Cestus Cybernetics was at that point a representative of the Republic, held to the same standards as any ambassador. A purchase made with counterfeit currency is no purchase at all. This *nullifies* the original sale. The land beneath every factory on Cestus still belongs to the hive!"

Obi-Wan's head spun. If this information got out, the Five Families were finished. Coruscant would take control of the situation, and only the hive would profit. Great for X'Ting, but if the economy crashed, the water and food shortages might kill millions. So it was a dreadful, last-minute leverage, barely better than an all-out bombardment.

But it *was* better . . .

32

There was a knock on the door. Chipple the driver stood in the entrance, his secondary hands extending a datadisk. "Client say play this."

Obi-Wan inserted the disk in his astromech, and waited a moment as the image field was generated.

G'Mai Duris appeared in the air before them. "Things have come to a head," she said, "and my leadership of the hive council is under attack. There is no one else I can trust, and I ask that you come to my quarters, where we can speak in greater privacy. My condition is dire."

Duris kept an apartment in the penthouse section of ChikatLik. A servant admitted Obi-Wan to the luxurious accommodations.

The inside of her apartment was a blend of technology and traditional X'Ting "chewed duracrete" architecture.

Obi-Wan followed Duris into her kitchen. There, a variety of glowing lights were illuminating a beautiful little garden of various mushrooms and fungi. It took his breath away. This was master-level skill, a lifetime's education in creating a miniature fungus forest.

"Beautiful," he said.

"It is our medicine and cuisine, our meditation and entertainment," Duris said. "Each family has its own mushroom forest, a balance of different species that has been passed through the line for thousands of years."

G'Mai Duris took a twist here, a pinch there, and as Obi-Wan watched put the finishing touches on a meal that seemed created of a hundred different dishes using fungi of varying texture in various ways. Her private forest provided the spice and garnish. Larger amounts of a heavier, meatier fungus were added from a special locker. The aromas were growing almost intoxicatingly delicious when she said, "I am being forced to fight Quill tonight. I've heard of the Jedi—you are said to be the greatest fighters in the galaxy. Can you teach me to fight?"

Obi-Wan bowed his head. "I am sorry. There is no time." He considered.

She kept preparing, but her primary and secondary hands were starting to shake.

"Is it possible that you might have a second?" he asked. "A champion?"

"It is not done," she said sadly. "I had hoped this day would never arrive. So. I knew it was a foolish hope," she added. "Still, I had to try. Would you stay, please, and dine with me? Please?"

She was shaking so piteously that he couldn't deny her.

She served him what she called her "death meal." A last ritual act. As with every official motion and word, her actions were perfect. Her motions were precise, elegant, controlled.

He asked her questions about the hive, and the rituals.

She kept glancing at the chrono, and he knew her time was drawing near.

"I cannot face Quill in the arena, just to be slaughtered publicly. I am afraid of what I might do. I might beg and disgrace my lineage. Better for me to die tonight. In my fungus forest are the plants I need to end my life." She smiled wanly. "There is a saying among my people: *Death is darkness. The children are safe.* It means to have courage."

So things had gone that far. He was appalled that her conversation could have taken such a lethally casual tone.

A thought occurred to him. "What happens if both you and Quill die?" he asked.

"Then the council would be free to make its own decisions. Without Quill, I believe they would be more reasonable."

"Then I have the answer for you," Obi-Wan said. "The answer is in your death meal."

"What?"

"Listen to me," he said, and bent close. "I have the answer, if you have the courage."

Together they took a turbolift down into the depths of the city, below the sections where offworlders lived and worked and thought themselves the owners of a captive world. Down into the oldest sections they went. There, some thousands of X'Ting still lived in something approximating a community.

The caves had been formed by water seepage, not volcanic activity. The walls had been textured with the familiar creases of hive-style chewed duracrete. Here, below, they did things in the old ways.

At the hive council table sat twelve ancient X'Ting, one for each of the planet's hives. How powerful and regal they must have seemed once. Now, their hives broken and scattered, they clung to mere fragments of their former glory. Despite their daily humiliations, the twelve faced their Regent and her offworlder companion with dignity.

Quill doffed his robe, baring his powerful thorax. "So you decided not to take your life," he grinned. "Good. I want the entire council to smell the stench as you die."

Duris trembled so badly she could barely remove her cloak, and almost dropped it as she handed it to Obi-Wan. "Courage," he said softly. "Death is darkness. The children will be safe."

"I have no children," she whispered. It was almost a whimper.

"Every soul on this planet is in your hands," he said. "They are all your children."

G'Mai Duris nodded.

Their arena was a circle of groomed sand twenty meters in diameter. Radiating contempt, Quill began as Duris expected, strutting and boasting. He made short, lightning stinger thrusts, and instead of responding with parry or flight, Duris closed her eyes, folding together the fingers of her primary and secondary hands.

"The answer is in your death meal," Obi-Wan had told her. The ritual death meal, designed to drain all emotion. Only a master, prepared to serve the death meal from birth, could have matched her actions in the apartment. Even though facing the end of her life, G'Mai Duris had been utterly calm.

"This is what you do," Obi-Wan had said. *"Close your eyes. Think that you are preparing your death meal, and be calm. When he stings you, the instant you feel his stinger, sting him. Do not try to survive. Go as one already dead."*

Quill approached her, and she merely waited.

He turned this way and that, trying to frighten her. Nothing he tried worked.

"There is a secret to the warrior arts," Obi-Wan had said. *"One that has nothing to do with training. Nothing to do with fancy movements. It is the willingness to trade lives with your enemy. To never fight for anything you would not die for. Those who fight for glory, or gold, or power, stand on shifting sand, not the bedrock of true courage. Fight for your people. Fight for your mate. For you, dying means winning. The arena is not a circle of sand. The arena is your heart."*

Quill leapt and pranced and shook his stinger. He hissed and circled and made fearsome faces. And through it all, G'Mai Duris merely stood.

Waiting to share death with him.

At last Quill stopped, stupefied, for the first time his mask of confidence cracking. Beneath, was fear.

G'Mai Duris stood, eyes closed. Waiting.

Quill's mouth quivered, and he lowered his eyes to the sand. "I . . . I concede," he said, radiating hatred.

The eldest X'Ting on the council stood and spoke. "G'Mai Duris is the winner. Caiza Quill must yield his seat."

G'Mai Duris drew herself up to full height, folding the fingers of primary and secondary hands formally. "My peers and elders," she said. "My dear friend Master Kenobi has told me an astonishing thing. For centuries we have known that our ancestors were cheated out of their land, land purchased with worthless baubles we believed were legal tender.

"For years we had no means of redress, save to accept whatever sops Cestus Cybernetics threw our way. But that has changed." Her faceted eyes gleamed. "Master Kenobi brought a barrister with him from Coruscant, a Vippit who knows their laws well. And according to the central authority, if we should choose to press our suit, we can destroy Cestus Cybernetics. If we own the land beneath their factories, we can charge them whatever we wish for land usage, possibly even take the facilities themselves."

"What?" the council's eldest said, faceted eyes widening in shock. "Is this truth?"

Quill sputtered. "You would do nothing except destroy the planet! Destroy Cestus Cybernetics, and you destroy our economy!"

The elder looked at Quill with contempt. "The hive was here before Cestus Cybernetics. It is not the hive that will suffer if this company changes hands . . . or even if it dies. It will be those who have sold themselves to offworlders for a promise of power."

"But my lords," Duris said. "I have obligations to the offworlders, people who came to Cestus with skills and heart, and wanted only to build a life here. We cannot use this opportunity to destroy. We must use it to build, and heal."

The elders nodded, as if pleased by her empathy.

Quill quivered. "You have won nothing, Duris! I will block you, I swear. Regardless of what you think you have, what you think you know . . . this isn't over yet." He stormed out, humiliated and enraged.

"Can he do that?" Obi-Wan asked.

"Perhaps. Any member of the Five Families can veto any specific business deal. If he believes it is in his best interest, or just for the sake of hatred, he will try." An alarming thought occurred to her. "He might try to keep you from sending Palpatine this information. Perhaps you should send it immediately."

Reluctantly, Obi-Wan shook his head. "The Chancellor

will use it to shut Cestus Cybernetics down legally. No one wins. I think our best bet is to use this bit of information as final, emergency leverage." He looked at that supposition from every angle he could, and saw no flaw in his logic.

So. Nothing about this assignment was to be easy. "But the Families have thought of all this as finances and politics. So long as they do, they can make decisions based upon ledger sheets. It is time we changed that, time we made their dilemma more . . . personal."

Late that night Obi-Wan had a very secretive conversation with Kit Fisto. "Things are balanced precariously," he said. "I wanted your counsel."

"Obi-Wan," Kit said, "I know that you are uncomfortable with deception, but these people have no idea how dangerous Dooku can be. If a few . . . theatrics can save lives, I believe we must go forward."

Obi-Wan sighed. There was truth there, but he wished he didn't have the sense that Kit was actually looking forward to the coming action. "All right," he said finally. "We go. You'll have all the magcar details in a few moments. More important, have you been practicing?"

"Of course," Kit answered. "Be ready for the performance of a lifetime."

33

Wisps of fantazi smoke snaked through Trillot's catacomb maze like fire-kraken tendrils. Little droids hustled about, serving all: since the crippling of Trillot's bodyguard Remlout, a nervous group of underlings had suggested that perhaps their mistress would prefer to have the dispersement of the various salves and intoxicants under her direct control.

At the moment, though, Trillot felt like she had anything but control. She was struggling to keep her voice and body language neutral as she spoke to Ventress, who stood before her as motionless as if she had grown there, eyes turned slightly upward, hardly aware that Trillot existed. What strange realms her mind might have been moving in, Trillot had no idea at all.

"Do I have to tell Kenobi the truth?" Trillot asked again, fingers of primary and secondary hands fidgeting together.

"Only if you are fond of breathing," Ventress replied. "He will know that you are either lying, or incompetent. In either case you are of no further use."

Ventress's cold blue eyes widened like a chasm between worlds.

The glands beneath Trillot's arms began to ooze surrender pheromones, and she hoped Ventress would not scent her distress. She bobbled her head eagerly. "Yes. Yes, of course. Madam?"

"Yes?"

She cleared her throat. "If I might be so bold as to ask: why is this single Jedi so important? Certainly we have greater—"

Another withering glance.

At that instant one of her bodyguards thrust his head into the room. "He's coming!"

Trillot had turned for only a moment, a bare flickering of her head, but when she turned back, Ventress was already gone.

Obi-Wan entered the pit, breathing shallowly to limit the effects of the noxious atmosphere. And yet . . . there was something in the air that made him want to breathe more deeply. He dared not, knowing that there was a limit to what his metabolism was capable of processing.

"That scent," he said.

"Scent?" Trillot asked.

"Yes. Bantha musk, and . . . something else. Used as a body scent by certain Five Family females, or . . ." He could feel the gears turning in his head. Certainly some members of Cestus's female upper class might visit Trillot's den. Hardly surprising. But he doubted that he was merely reacting to such a casual, if corrupt, interaction. What, then?

This was not good. For some reason, he had felt off-balance since first arriving on Cestus. In the city, at the ball, in the chambers, here in Trillot's chambers, at the cantina . . .

Was there a connecting thread, or was he just tired?

Trillot's mouth twisted. "Well, you've caught me." A vile, conspiratorial smile. "I do have a few, eh, friends among the upper class. I hope you can keep a secret."

Obi-Wan kept his thoughts to himself. What perversions passed for entertainment among Cestus's upper crust were hardly his concern. And yet . . .

"Of course. Yes, surely that is it. Perhaps I caught that scent at the ball. Now." He exhaled, centering himself. "This is what I wish of you. Information."

"On?"

"The subterranean transit system. I assume you can provide?"

"Of course."

A beam of light projected from Trillot's chair. She made a

few brief hand passes through it, and a web of nodes and moving lines materialized. Obi-Wan walked into the middle of it and concentrated. Now, for the first time in days, he felt completely immersed in his plan. Perhaps, after all, his disturbance was mere nerves.

"Here—" He pointed. "And here . . ."

Hours later, Obi-Wan's astromech, using a scrambled technical link, beamed the map to the training camp, where it was evaluated by the commandos and a brooding Kit Fisto.

"—to here," Nate concluded.

The campfire crackled behind them. The training had been going well. They had the fighters they needed, trained to obey orders even under considerable stress. To the credit of the Cestians, their men and women had adapted to military discipline with admirable speed and efficiency.

"That is the whole of it then," the general said, his unblinking eyes reflecting the map, the firelight, and the stars above them. Nate watched him, waiting for word, a sign. He did not understand General Fisto, and knew that he probably never would, but hoped that the mysterious Jedi would be pleased at their progress. For some reason, he craved this Nautolan's approval.

Kit Fisto nodded. "You have done well," he said, and went back to the ship. The troopers nodded among themselves, laughing and sharing jokes and camaraderie, a rhythm that Nate fell into instantly. Forgetting the slight unease he had seen in the general's eyes. Just nerves. So much at stake. Resources so limited. So few options.

And no room for failure at all.

34

*P*lanets died, screaming their pain to the trackless void. Stars exploded into halos of fire, nebulae imploded into black holes. Ships filled with screaming men ruptured, admitting pitiless vacuum.

Lying flat on her back, lids closed, body motionless, Ventress dreamed, her spirit stalking a universe of infinite rage.

She dreamed of Ohma-D'un, the moon of Naboo where she had first encountered Obi-Wan Kenobi. The operation had devolved into a slaughterhouse. She had sorely underestimated the Jedi's courage and intelligence. Ventress was walking the true path that the Jedi had abandoned. Master Dooku had told her, taught her. The galaxy needed order, and the decadent Jedi had forgotten their primary obligation: to the Force itself, not to a corrupt and selfish regime. She had not made that error. Would not ever.

Without preamble, Asajj Ventress awakened and came to a sitting position. The dreams had been the usual, nothing special about them at all. They were, indeed, merely her mind attempting to work out a problem of vectors and resources. She had given her fealty, and with a woman like Ventress, once word was given, there was no other course. She defined herself in terms of her obligations and contracts. There was no deeper identity to cause emotional dissonance. She simply did what had to be done.

Somehow Master Kenobi was central to the problem. But as yet she had no idea what to do . . .

* * *

Just outside her door, Trillot glided away, head aching. She had offered the terrifying Ventress a stateroom in her catacombs, and the creature had accepted. She had intended to spy upon the mysterious Count Dooku's messenger, but those efforts had taken an unpleasant turn. Trillot felt . . . *infected* when her visitor dreamed. She closed her eyes and saw images of death and destruction on a horrific scale.

Fear ran so deep it was like a living creature burrowing through her stomachs. Hadn't she done everything possible to make Ventress happy? Supplied all information? Provided accommodation? Planted tracers on Quill and Lady Por'Ten? She had done all this and more . . .

So why was she still so terrified?

The churning black-and-red cloud behind her eyes throbbed unmercifully as Trillot slunk away. And when she crawled into her sleeping chamber that night and desperately sought the solace of sleep, that headache boiled into a cavalcade of nightmares that multiplied in intensity until dawn came, and she emerged to do battle with another day.

35

Cestus's sun had risen on the eastern horizon, lengthening the mountain shadows until they resembled a mouth filled with broken teeth. Where the shadows did not reach, its fierce light seared the ground with a radiance that was bright and clear enough to curl the plants that would not emerge again until next twilight.

As was his habit, Nate rose and dressed before dawn. He performed a series of ARC drills, bending, stretching, and tumbling, discovering no kink or wound sufficient to bind his motion. Energy felt good. He felt strong, tough, mean, and altogether lethal. *Ready enough.*

He found General Fisto in the main cave, sitting in front of the shimmering map. The general sat balanced on knees and the balls of his feet, buttocks resting on his heels. Nate had seen the Nautolan sit in this fashion for hours, and winced a bit, knowing that his own legs would have cramped within minutes.

"You're ready, sir?"

The general rose. In his hand he held a handle with a length of flexible cordlike material attached. "It is time," the Jedi said.

There was nothing more to say.

36

From the very beginning the pattern had been set: representatives of the Five Families traveled to the central palace for the day's round of negotiations, conversations, and arguments. Some arrived by private aircar or railcar. About a third traveled in a secure, private shuttle on the magcar system using the subterranean network beneath ChikatLik. It was the city's most secure transportation and had never been breached, even during the Uprisings that birthed Desert Wind.

Today Lord and Lady Por'Ten, Debbikin the younger, and Quill took the underground magcar, and they used the opportunity to confer with each other as they sped through the depths.

"And do you believe that the Jedi has reached the limit of his concessions?"

Young Debbikin canted his head to the side, an imitation of his father's customary thinking posture. "It is hard to say. Father's spy on Coruscant says the mood there is unfavorable to negotiation. Palpatine is pure will: he would make war on a disloyal planet." He leaned in closer to the others, as if fearful of being overheard, although the moving car was doubtless one of the most secure locations on the entire planet. "But I feel that this situation, with every eye upon Cestus, gives us several interesting advantages. First: in direct negotiation, we can make an excellent case that we have a legal right to produce the droids. We can also make the case that the war has disrupted our supply lines, threatening our survival. Therefore, we are fighting not for our economic survival, but the very right to feed our people."

Por'Ten's triple-jowled chin wobbled as if he had intimate familiarity with missing meals. "The starving children," he said sadly.

"Now listen," young Debbikin continued. "This means that the Chancellor might be motivated to be generous, if we just have the courage to see this through."

The leaders of the Five Families nodded and smiled, agreeing with the logic. "But you said that there was another motivation . . . ?"

"Yes, indeed." Young Debbikin's voice dropped. "The war will not last forever. When it ends, if the Republic wins, we are in an excellent position: the value of our holdings will multiply greatly."

"Yes . . . ," Quill said. He had said little since the beginning of the ride, and seemed a bit like an intensely dense storm cloud, lightning forking in his faceted eyes. "No matter what happens, we win."

"Even if we leave Cestus, we will still possess controlling shares of Cestus Cybernetics, enough to keep a local veto yet set ourselves up on any world we desire. The Five Families will have leapt to galactic prominence."

"Yes," Quill hissed. "And there is another possibility, can you not see? Whether we deal with Palpatine or Count Dooku, we must have greater leverage in the future. Duris must be removed."

They looked at him coldly. "You were supposed to have that problem under control," Debbikin said. "You were admitted to the Families under that promise. In fact, I hear you have been removed from the hive council. What good are you to us now?"

"I *will* handle things," Quill sputtered. "We have agreements you dare not break. I control the mines, Debbikin. The hive council can unseat me, but I am not so easily replaced." His gaze might have smelted durasteel. "I will bring Duris down, and find a more . . . pliable puppet for the throne, trust me."

Thump.

Suddenly the confident expression melted into one of confusion. "What was *that*—?"

They felt the sound before they heard it, a dull impact on the magcar's roof, a juddering as it changed direction.

The tunnel walls outside the car blurred past, but it was the same blur that they had seen for years, the same strata of rocks that led between their private residences and the palace. Now, even though they still blurred, there was a subtle difference, enough to disturb them. And the direction had changed.

"What is this?" Lord Por'Ten raised his voice. "Conductor?"

The droid at the front of the car turned to him, metallic face expressionless. "I am sorry, but my controls have been overridden by an unknown source."

The representatives looked around at each other, shock plainly painted on their faces.

"Contact the security forces?"

"I am sorry," the droid said again with that unnatural patience available only to the unliving. "I must inform you that the entire car is surrounded by some kind of interference field."

"Well I never!" Lady Por'Ten said and pulled out her personal comlink. After a bit of fiddling, she looked up; all the color had drained from her narrow face, her customary haughty manner muted. "He's correct."

"Where are they taking us?" Debbikin asked.

The droid paused for a moment before answering. "We have taken one of the obsolete tunnel systems and are currently being shunted onto a mine track. I project that our probable destination, based upon information dealing with other kidnap/murder scenarios—"

"Murder?" Lady Por'Ten shrieked.

Ignoring her distress, the droid continued. "I regret to inform you that there is approximately a thirteen percent chance that the intent of this action is, ultimately, the death of every person in this car."

The Five Family executives glanced around at each other, mouths quivering in shock.

The car went a bit farther, made a sharp right turn. It stopped, and then slowly, inexorably, they felt it sink beneath them.

"Yes, as I anticipated, one of the mining tracks. This is not good, as it is not a part of the central system, and therefore may not show up on the maps. If the beacon has been disabled, which is probable, I project our chance of being rescued as approximately one in twelve."

"One in . . . twelve?"

"Yes. Unless you would like the chance of us both being rescued and of all of you being recovered alive. In which case the chance is closer to one in six hundred fifty, based upon kidnap and homicide statistics—"

"Shut up!" Lord Por'Ten roared, and stood. The car had finally come to a stop. Now they could hear footsteps on the roof, their eyes following them as one portentous *thud* at a time, they moved back to the rear, and then stopped.

They glanced at each other, and Quill had opened his mouth to speak when a figure with thick ropes of tentacle wriggling from his head swung lightly down and smashed through the roof's plastine partition. Jagged shards scattered as he landed without a sound, in marked contrast to the heavier tread heard up on the roof.

A Nautolan! But what did he want?

His eyes were huge and black, with no apparent irises, but with a filmy coating that seemed to shift in opacity from moment to moment depending on the angle of light. He was empty-handed, but there was a handle tucked into his belt, and Debbikin knew instantly that it represented a threat of some kind.

"Who are you?" Quill spluttered.

"My name is Nemonus. Greetings from Count Dooku," the Nautolan said.

"Wha-what do you want?"

"You seek to change a bargain," the intruder said.

"What? What are you talking about?"

The intruder turned, so slowly that he seemed like a machine in low gear, a disturbing contrast to the terrifying speed with which he had smashed through the roof. "You must learn that there is no place you can hide. A deal was struck. Those who renegotiate price may find other matters transformed as well."

Although ordinarily the most imperious of men, Por'Ten completely melted before the intruder's molten gaze. "Wha-what are you talking about?"

The intruder came closer. His lips thinned. The tentacles about his head curled slowly, insinuatingly, as he spoke, twitching with their own crazed energy. He whispered, yet in some odd way the whisper was louder than a shout. "My master promised to keep you out of the war. That you would not be involved. That can change, my friends. That can all change."

Young Debbikin glanced at the others, nearing panic now. "No! We have kept our pledges to you. All of them."

The intruder sneered. "Then why have you raised your prices, threatened to withhold shipment without further credits?"

There was a moment of relief as they glanced at each other. For a moment, they had feared that he knew of the negotiations with the Jedi Kenobi! No, this was something completely different, Cestus Cybernetics' demand for a 10 percent surcharge. Llitishi of sales and marketing had sworn that Count Dooku would agree if they but held firm.

"It is the war, the war!" Debbikin leaned closer, trying to establish a sense of intimacy. "Supply lines have been cut . . ."

The intruder was unimpressed. "We have made other arrangements for you."

"Yes, but the timing is off, and we have to buy additional products so that all of the equipment matches. We are proceeding, but everything is taking longer, and therefore more expensive—"

The intruder raised his palm. Although he hadn't so much as touched them, the force of his personality drove them backward into their seats. "You cannot be trusted."

Quill was using his secondary hands to reach stealthily for the little hold-out blaster always attached to his wallet. They knew that he was descended from an assassin clan, and that those skills had been passed from one generation to the next for half a millennium. If their kidnapper made but a single mistake, the blaster would be out, the Nautolan would be dead, and they had a chance to regain control of the car. And Quill, incidentally, would have redeemed himself.

"How can you say that! Our dealings with you have placed Cestus in jeopardy with the Republic. We would not betray you. If we did, we would have no one!" The intruder's back was to Quill. The blaster was almost in hand . . .

Tension crackled in the air. Debbikin kept his eyes on the intruder, striving not to reveal by eye movement or the slightest tremor of voice that anything was amiss.

For the first time the intruder seemed to change expressions. The film over his black eyes swirled. "Your Families need a lesson. The best I can imagine is one written in blood—"

Quill's blaster was out and moving to the level, its tiny gleaming barrel rising to sight at the intruder's back. But without turning, the intruder's hand flickered. The gleaming handle at his belt blurred. Something that looked like a coil of glowing wire suddenly flexed, lashing backward toward Quill's blaster. Three meters long it was, and thin as a thread, wrapping around the barrel. With the slightest twist of the intruder's wrist, the blaster was sliced in half, the grip suddenly glowing white-hot. Quill dropped the blaster, howling from singed fingers, and thrust them into his mouth, sucking and nursing them.

"Now then." Kit Fisto smiled grimly. "Shall we negotiate?"

37

By the time Obi-Wan arrived at the palace, the halls were in an uproar. He was hustled into G'Mai Duris's presence to see the regal X'Ting hunched in her seat listening to the words of a round, short-legged Zeetsa with a very worried expression.

"—Regent Duris," the leathery blue creature said in conclusion. Her stubby arms pointed at a glowing map hovering in the air. Her eyes traced the map with concern.

"Excuse me, Shar Shar," Obi-Wan said as softly as he could. "If there are concerns with the transportation grid that necessitate the postponement of the day's negotiations, perhaps I should return at another—"

Duris glanced up, an expression of surprise and then tears of gratitude overflowing her faceted eyes. "Master Jedi!" she said. "Obi-Wan. I am afraid we have an emergency. Thank goodness you are here!"

"Indeed?" he asked. "How can I be of assistance?"

"The Five Families should have been here an hour ago. Their private car seems to have disappeared."

"Disappeared?" Obi-Wan managed to conceal the pleasure in his voice. "How is that possible?"

"The entire planet is honeycombed with tunnels. Many of them are unmapped. We can only assume that someone, for their own purposes, shunted the car off its route into one of these secondary pathways."

"And as yet you have received no communication?"

"None," she said.

Obi-Wan studied the entire map, his face set sternly. "May

I assume that the other cars traveling along the map have sensors to avoid collision?"

"My engineer can answer that question," Duris said.

The engineer was a small, graying human who looked as if the current stress might cost him his few remaining sprigs of hair. "Yes, the sensors are excellent."

"Tell me," Obi-Wan asked Duris, "what is known of the situation at this time?"

"A group of Five Family executives were kidnapped."

"This Desert Wind group we've heard of?"

"We do not know," she replied. "We've heard little from them in the past year, and considered their threat broken. Frankly, it doesn't seem like their style."

Obi-Wan closed his eyes and counted to five, and then opened them again, retaining his most serious expression. "Can you holomap the entire system?"

The engineer nodded. "Well, of course, but why?"

"In order to do something like this, to make the car disappear, they have to have removed it from the grid. The individual magcars should react to the absence of a moving object, slowing and speeding themselves in compensation. The degree of disruption will increase the closer we get to the point of departure."

"But they have clearly affected our computers. They left no trace—"

"They left no direct *data* trace. But can the phantom car influence proximity sensors on other system vehicles?"

"Well . . . ," the engineer's mouth suddenly widened as he grasped Obi-Wan's implication. "No. The safety system is off the main grid, a backup system to prevent a single mistake in central command from causing a systemwide catastrophe."

"Good," Obi-Wan said, as the complete system sprang to life in a floating web of glowing silver threads. "Now I want you to filter for proximity feedback from the cars themselves, showing their actual positions and their projected positions according to schedule."

The engineer blanched. "But . . . we are not on Coruscant,

sir. We have no computer fast enough to find the original point of departure—"

Obi-Wan raised his hand. "I am not searching for a thing. I need to sense something that is *not* there. Where computers falter, the Force may prevail. Please. Give me the images."

The engineer gawped at Obi-Wan. Then Duris nodded her head and waved her primary hands, and he performed as requested. Soon every image on the grid was doubled. "Make the projected images red, and the actual ones blue," Obi-Wan said, his voice dropping low.

Duris remembered stories of these mystic warriors, and fought to repress a tremor of almost supernatural awe. She nodded to the engineer, and a series of ghostly overlay images began to form. Impossibly complex, all of it, because as each car accelerated or decelerated to compensate for the missing car, they began to interfere with other cars on the tracks, causing them to slow or speed in a widening ripple effect.

Obi-Wan stood in the middle of the vast rippling maze, his eyes half lidded, arms outstretched as if actually feeling the entire web of motion. Then, slowly, he turned and pointed to a stretch of tunnel between one of the outer rings of luxury apartments and the central city. "This," he said, "is where the phantom car originated. It is therefore here that the real car went offline."

Duris glanced at the engineer, who hunched his shoulders. *Perhaps.*

The Jedi traced a line along a branching tunnel. "And it went here . . ." The tunnel branched again. He traced his finger along one of the paths, and then backtracked and took the other. "And then here, where it slowed and changed levels . . ."

The throne room was blindingly silent. The quiet heightened the impact of each word almost unendurably. "And then it began moving again, until . . ."

He cocked his head sideways. "This is strange. There is no track indicated here. Should there be?"

The engineer cleared his throat. In fact, he looked a little

frightened, regarding their guest with something halfway between dread and awe. "Well . . ." He consulted a holo rotating above his briefcase, and when he raised his head again a
moment later, that tense crease of his lips deepened. "There
is a utility corridor that was taken off the map because it was
in bad repair, and not up to recent safety standards."

Obi-Wan's eyes were still closed. "But?"

"But in fact, if it is still up to the former specifications, it
could take the load safely."

Again, silence. Obi-Wan nodded. "Here you will find your
missing car."

The engineer swallowed hard. "Regent Duris," he said.
"There remains the problem of reaching it. If we assume that
the kidnappers are tied into the central network, they'll see
anything we do to reroute a car. That reduces our options to
acting off the grid. It will take hours to position a strike
squad. Have we that much time?"

Obi-Wan looked at her. Duris chewed at her chitinous
lower lip. If this was Desert Wind, then there was little fear
for the lives of the Five Families. Desert Wind kidnapped,
but had never killed in cold blood. Not their style. But they
had doubtlessly made arrangements for their captives to be
spirited to some more secretive place—and from there, no
one could predict what might happen.

Of course, it was always possible that it was *not* Desert Wind. On Cestus, misinformation was simply a fact of
life . . .

Glancing back at Obi-Wan, she realized that she had not,
for even a moment, doubted that this amazing man had done
what all of Cestus's computers could not. That by power of
his mind and the mysterious Force, Obi-Wan Kenobi had
found their missing Family members. With all that had happened in the last day she felt dazed and confused as she had
not in all her time on the throne, as if suffering from a mild
form of shock.

"You might be right," she said. "We may have no time, and
the usual means will not serve. Master Jedi—have you a
plan?" Somehow, she knew he would.

"Tell your security people not to shoot until they've made an identification," Obi-Wan murmured.

"What are you going to do?"

Obi-Wan paused for dramatic effect, and then replied: "Something drastic."

38

Ore cars, equipment shuttles, passenger vehicles, mining machines, and repair droids all flowed through the same labyrinth of magrails and lev tracks, zipping past and moving around each other as if they were living, breathing things, individual tissue structures within a larger organism, cells in the body Cestus, drones in the technological hive.

And atop one of those cars, clinging to the surface with nerves and muscles honed by decades of training, crouched Jedi Knight Obi-Wan Kenobi. He compensated for impossibly swift and sharp turns, accelerations, and decelerations with a profound understanding of the rhythms of the universe and its invisible currents.

Sequestered in his rooms, Obi-Wan had privately absorbed the shuttle system patterns over the course of a long, sleepless night. In G'Mai's presence he'd spent no more than a few minutes updating that research. Even if they had watched him spend hours immersed in study, what he was about to attempt would still have been impressive to them. With the secret practice and knowledge, his next actions would appear miraculous, putting his hosts—especially the volatile Quill—off-balance emotionally.

But first he had to actually *do* it, knowing as he did that sensors on the various vehicles observed his every move.

The vehicle began to slow and veer to the left. Following instincts far beyond the level of conscious thought, he jumped even before he saw the next car.

For a moment Obi-Wan clung to the tunnel's wall, then felt a blast of air as the next magcar barreled toward him.

For a moment its transparisteel walls resembled the great glowing eyes of some subterranean creature. He glimpsed commuters who had been absorbed in their datapads or conversations suddenly stare at the man hanging upside down from the top of the tunnel, and they gasped as he dropped toward them. A yellow-skinned Xexto flailed her four arms in shock, screaming that the poor human was attempting some kind of bizarre suicide.

Sorry, Obi-Wan mouthed, then clutched the front of the car, catching it as it slowed to round the curve, but still, it rammed the breath out of him.

He clung with desperate strength. Eighteen seconds until they reached the next point, and he counted them off to himself, smiling inwardly at the civilians gawping up at this strange apparition.

Before any of them could react with anything but distress, he was gone again.

Obi-Wan wedged himself between the ceiling and the wall, bracing with hands and feet. A cargo tunnel intersected here, and it was only ten seconds before he could hear it howling on its way to him, and he saw the single eye glaring only moments before it was beneath him. He dropped down onto an ore car. The jagged heap of rock was so steep that he almost slid off onto the tracks below. He scrabbled for purchase, found it, lost it, then found it again. The artificial hurricane ripped Obi-Wan's legs out sideways, and he pulled them back in an instant too late. His right heel slammed into a wall, whipping him around and back, ripping at his grip, forcing him to release his hold and then to regain it a few chunks back.

The wind lashed him mercilessly, and there was nothing to be done about that, not now. He knew that Cestian computers had modeled his Force-based analysis of the system kinetics, and would have found it accurate. By now they might even have adapted their own programs to enable them to track his whereabouts by reckoning the presence of an undeclared body hopping from car to car throughout the system.

That, and the overhead monitors, made it clear that he was performing for an audience both critical and suspicious.

From car to car he migrated, until he reached a junction where he could finally hop free, landing on the metal track beneath. He breathed in short, sharp bursts, refusing to give in to the fear lurking just below the surface of his concentration.

Timing. Timing.

Obi-Wan bent down and felt the metal path that the magcar levitated along at cruising speed. The car was coming. Not long now, and it was also too late to make other plans. Nothing now but to carry through. A sudden flood of air pressure hit him like a tide, overriding his carefully constructed mental blocks.

Now. Obi-Wan turned and sprinted down the tunnel as fast as he could, fleeing the car barreling down on him; he could hear its warning siren. At the last instant he leapt forward, using the last strength in his body to accelerate himself, and spun in midair.

For an instant, his body propelled by superbly conditioned muscles and a nervous system in tune with the deepest currents of the Force, Obi-Wan's velocity came within five meters per second of the magcar's. He braced himself, exhaling perfectly in time with the impact, arms bent as shock absorbers. Breath smashed out of his body with a gigantic *huff,* but that very exhalation provided him with the cushioning that allowed him to survive the impact. If he hadn't almost matched the magcar's speed . . .

If he hadn't spun to grasp . . .

If the exhalation hadn't been perfectly timed . . .

He would have been smashed down, dragged under, ground into splinters. As it was, Obi-Wan struggled to pull himself up higher and higher on the car, until, scraped and panting, he lay above it and settled in for the rest of the ride.

In the council rooms, members of the Five Families fortunate enough not to be kidnapped were watching the entire display with shock. "What kind of creatures are these Jedi?"

Llitishi whispered, mopping perspiration from his crinkled blue brow.

"I don't know . . . but I am profoundly grateful to have them on our side," said the elder Debbikin, hoping for his son's safety. "I think that we must seriously reconsider our stance." There was much murmured agreement, followed by eager attempts to tap into the sensors for further data.

39

For more than an hour after the magcar's power had been cut and it had settled to the shaft floor, the mood in the diverted car continued to deteriorate. The captured leaders of the Five Families had watched with alarm as their solitary kidnapper was joined by three ruffians dressed in Desert Wind khakis. The intruders had exchanged a few quiet words, then gone about their plans. Clearly, they wished to separate their captives from the city grid as swiftly as possible.

"What do you intend to do with us?" Lady Por'Ten whispered.

"Wait," a masked Desert Wind soldier replied. "You'll see." The dark-eyed Nautolan said nothing.

At first they had hoped for rescue, but as they watched their kidnappers set up electronic scramblers to confuse the tunnel sensors and monitors, they realized their chances of being found were slight.

One man patrolled outside the car, leaving two within it with the Nautolan. Young Debbikin watched the one outside. He walked back and forth around the car . . . and then he was gone. For a moment there was confusion, and then the figure reappeared. Only . . . was it the same person? Had he been mistaken, or had the car's tinted windows revealed some kind of brief and violent struggle?

Hope was a luxury they dared not indulge in. And yet . . .

"And now—" the taller of the Desert Wind ruffians began. He never had a chance to finish the words. A black noose dropped down under his chin. The cord tightened, and the man was hauled up through an emergency door in the car's roof, kicking and screaming, scrabbling at his neck with hooked fingers. Instantly their Nautolan kidnapper wheeled, snarling.

Cloak fluttering around him like the plumage of some bird of prey, Obi-Wan Kenobi dropped down into the car. The tan-clad Desert Wind soldier was the first to reach him, and therefore the first to go down in a brief flicker of a lightsaber. He stumbled back, the shoulder of his jacket smoking and spitting sparks.

The Nautolan glared at his adversary, and for a moment the hostages were all but forgotten.

"Jedi!" the Nautolan snarled.

Obi-Wan's eyes narrowed to slits, his courtly manner a distant memory. In an instant he had transformed from ambassador into the deadliest of warriors. "Nemonus," he hissed, then added, "Not the first time you've tried blood diplomacy."

"Nor the last," the Nautolan growled. "But it *is* the last time I'll tolerate your meddling."

Without another word the two leapt toward each other and the fight was on.

As long as they lived, the men and women in that car would remember the next few moments. The Nautolan wielded his glowing whip in a sinuous blur, with demonic accuracy. It arced up and around, flexing and coiling like a living thing. Wherever it went and whatever he did, the Jedi was there first.

There had been much speculation as to why a Jedi would prefer a lightsaber to a blaster. All of the disadvantages of such a short-range weapon were obvious. But now, watching the drama unfold before them, another fact became obvious as well: Obi-Wan's lightsaber moved as if it were an extension of his body, a glowing arm or leg imbued with the mysterious power of the Force.

The two adversaries were almost perfectly matched. One might have expected the lightwhip's greater length to give advantage, but in the confined space that simply wasn't true. Strangely, while the Nautolan's lash splashed sparks here

and there, gouged hot metal from panels, and sent flecks of
fire floating down to where they huddled on the ground, none
of them was touched. The Nautolan was pure aggression.
His face narrowed to a fighting grimace, spitting curses in
strange languages, moving his torso with a boneless agility
that seemed impossible for any vertebrate.

Certainly the Jedi would cower. Would flee and save himself. Nothing could stand before such a bafflingly lethal onslaught—

But Master Kenobi stood firm. He wove through that
narrow space, his lightsaber flashing like desert lightning,
deflecting every flicker of the whip. The Nautolan's speed
and ferocity were matched by the Jedi's own cold and implacable determination. They leapt and tumbled, wheeling
through the confined space, somersaulting so that they were
virtually walking on the ceiling as they evaded and attacked,
achieving a level of hyperkinesis simultaneously balletic and
primal.

Master Kenobi was the first to penetrate the other's guard,
such that the lightwhip was barely able to enmesh the glowing energy blade in time to deflect. The cloth along the Nautolan's arm flared with brief, intense heat. They saw the
abrupt change in the kidnapper's demeanor. The Nautolan
snarled, and fear shone in his face. The Jedi was winning! In
another engagement, two at the most, Master Kenobi would
have solved the lightwhip's riddle, and go for the kill.

The Nautolan lashed this way and that as if gathering his
energies for renewed aggression. Then with a single smooth,
eye-baffling motion he scooped up the wounded Desert
Wind soldier as if he were a mere child. The Nautolan
bounded up through the roof, and was gone. They heard his
footsteps pattering down the tunnel. And then . . . nothing.

Master Kenobi turned to them, his face beginning to relax
back from its battle mask. If he had not chosen to speak,
there might have been no words voiced in that car for an
hour. "Are you hurt?" he asked.

Quill was reduced to mere babbling. "No! I—that was

amazing! I'd always heard stories of the Jedi, but never . . . I just want to say thank you! Thank you so much."

Master Kenobi ignored him and went from one of them to the other, checking to see that all were well. Then he examined, analyzed, and disconnected the override device. Within moments light returned to the car. The droid began to wheel and pivot as if awakening from drugged slumber. He looked at Kenobi. "Ah! Master Jedi! I assume it is you who has returned my function."

"That's true."

"And your orders?"

"Get these people back to the capital."

"At once, sir."

The droid fit his action to his words. The rescued hostages gave a ragged cheer—even Quill, whose faceted eyes shone with awe. Young Debbikin tugged at their savior's robes again. "Master Jedi," he asked. "How can I repay you?"

The Jedi smiled grimly. "Tell your father to remember his duty," he said.

40

Deep in the mountains a hundred klicks southeast of the capital raged a mighty celebration. There was much dancing and laughter, and more than a bit of drunken boasting.

Nate leaned back against a rock, deeply satisfied. The operation had indeed gone smoothly, without a single life lost. His throat was a bit sore from General Kenobi's lariat, but the support brace concealed in the neck of his cowl had worked perfectly. The extra padding in the shoulder of OnSon's "Desert Wind" uniform had protected him from the carefully judged swipe of General Kenobi's lightsaber. In every way, from obtaining the crucial intelligence from the criminal Trillot to transferring it, from evaluation to creation of a plan, from penetrating the transport security network to diverting the car, from impersonating the exhausted forces of Desert Wind to subduing resistance among the Five Families, from simulating combat with General Kenobi to effecting their eventual escape . . .

Every step had gone off without a hitch.

There was another, additional bonus: from his perch atop the roof of the car he had been able to witness the "duel" between the two Jedi. Nate had thought that he had seen and learned everything about unarmed combats. Now he knew that, in comparison, Kamino's most advanced martial sciences were mere back-alley thuggery.

Nate knew that the Jedi had something that would keep troopers alive, if he could only learn more about it.

But how? That thought burning in his mind, he sat back

and looked up at the stars, deliciously content to replay each motion of lightsaber and whip.

Sheeka Tull had landed *Spindragon* a safe distance away, and walked into camp under a burgeoning double moon. She had just completed a tiring run connecting three of Cestus's six major city nodes, delivering volatile cargo illegal to ship through the subterranean tunnels.

A familiar unhelmeted form in dark green fatigues approached her, waving his hand. "Ah, Sheeka. Good to see you."

From brown skin to tightly muscled body, everything was familiar, but still she looked at him askance. "You're not Nate," she said, although the trooper's casual dress lacked military insignia or other identifying marks.

Forry blinked then transformed into wide-eyed innocence. "Who else would I be?"

She grinned and pointed. "Nice try. He has a little scar right here on his jawline. You don't."

Sirty came up behind Forry, laughing at their brother's efforts to fool her.

Forry grinned ruefully. "All right. You're right. Just a little game we like to play." He jerked his thumb. "Nate's on the other side of camp."

"Nice try." She slapped him on the back and went to see her new . . . friend? Were they friends? She supposed that she could use that word for their relationship. Friends with her dead sweetheart's clone. It was a bit morbid, but also strangely exciting.

She found him leaning back against a rock, lost in his own thoughts. He smiled and raised a cup of Cestian spore-mead as he saw her.

"What do we celebrate?" she asked, suspecting that she already knew the answer.

"A little operation that went even better than expected. And no, no one is dead."

She searched his face. "Disappointed?"

He glared at her. "Absolutely. I was hoping for human bar-becue tonight."

She leaned back against the rock with him. "Touché. I shouldn't blame you simply for enjoying your work. It's what you were trained to do."

"Superbly," he agreed. She was relieved that these lethal, bottle-bred warriors had a sense of humor.

"And you've been fully trained in all matters of soldierly behavior?" she asked.

"Fully."

She paused, and looked at him more carefully. "And do soldiers dance?"

Now he seemed to lose that smile and become genuinely thoughtful. "Of course. The Jakelian knife-dance is a pri-mary tool for teaching distance, timing, and rhythm in en-gagement."

She groaned. Practicality again. "No. Dancing. You know: man, woman. Dancing?"

He shrugged. "The cohorts compete with each other in dance. Team and individual events."

Sheeka found herself fighting a growing sense of exas-peration. "Haven't you ever done it for fun?"

He squinted. "That *is* fun."

"You exhaust me," she said, and then held her arms out. "Come on."

He hesitated, and then came to her.

The musicians were playing some fast-paced number with flute and drum. Their jig steps were bouncy and light. The other recruits grinned, laughed, chattered, and swung their partners around with the kind of enthusiasm that suggested a serious need to blow off steam. The troopers watched, tap-ping their feet to the rhythm. From time to time one of them would perform a series of precise, martial movements to the music, spiced with tumbling floor gymnastics. The recruits approved, clapping along and cheering.

Just what happened today? She hesitated to ask. He had great coordination, but not much sense of moving in unity with a partner. Still, she liked it. She liked it a *lot*.

"I heard things on the scanner," she said, innocently enough.

"Really?" he asked. "What did they say?" He held her firmly and caught a half beat cleverly enough to spin her. Several of the other couples had as well, and the air filled with whoops of joy.

"Oh, something about a group of Five Family types being kidnapped and then rescued."

"Kidnapped? Rescued?" he said, wide-eyed. "Goodness. Sounds exciting."

So. He wasn't going to say anything. Need-to-know, she supposed. Still, from the number of people celebrating, she knew that the operation had been substantial, and she guessed that she might be able to pry the details out of a farmer or miner.

He must have noticed the thoughtful frown on her face, and misinterpreted its meaning a bit. "So," he said. "I get the sense that you don't approve of our mission."

"That wasn't what I was thinking."

"But you don't. Why do you help us?"

"Not voluntarily."

"Then why? What leverage does someone have?"

Her answering laugh was a bit tighter than she had intended. "Somewhere on Coruscant is a computer file listing every indiscretion ever committed in the galaxy. There was a need, my name came up, and doing a favor is better than spending a decade on a work planet."

"And your name is on this list?"

She nodded. "You're a quick study."

"I believe that's called sarcasm."

"Ooh," she squealed. "More human by the minute. Next we try irony."

He scowled ferociously, and she laughed. "So . . . what did you do?"

"My younger sister joined a religious sect on Devon Four. When they refused to pay taxes Coruscant slapped an embargo on them. When a plague struck the colony, they were going to die, every woman, man, and child. No one would do a thing. So . . ."

He nodded understanding. "So you got them their medicine. And your sister?"

She brightened. "Raising a squalling brood of brats somewhere in the Outer Rim. I'd do it all over again."

"Even though it brought you here."

Strangely enough, she was feeling more than just comfortable, and a thought drifted through her mind that *here* meant both the planet and his arms. *Hmmm.* "Even though."

"I notice you spend more time talking to me than my brothers," he said, his lips close to her ear. "Why is that?"

"You hold my interest."

"Why?"

"I don't know," she said honestly. "Perhaps because you are the only one trained for command. That makes you more like Jango."

His attention sharpened. "They say he was a loner."

"Yes," she said. "But a natural leader, too. At other times he could be invisible, as I understand quite a few people learned to their brief and painful regret."

Nate gave a hard, flat chuckle. Yes, indeed.

"But if he wanted, when he entered a room every head would turn." She paused a beat. "Especially mine." Her voice grew softer. "But that was all so long ago. I was eighteen years old, and Jango was twenty-five."

"Was he a bounty hunter then?"

She closed her eyes, dredging up old memories. "I think he was in transition. He'd only been free maybe two years, since the Mandalorians were wiped out. I met him in the Meridian sector. He'd lost his armor somehow, and was searching for it." A ruminative smile. "We had just about a year together. Then things got dangerous. We were raided by space pirates. Our ship got blown from the sky, and in the middle of a really nasty space battle we were forced to take separate evacuation pods. I never saw him again." She paused. "I heard he survived, and got his armor back. I don't know if he looked for me." Sheeka shrugged. "Life is like that, sometimes." Her voice had grown wistful.

Then she chuckled, and he drew back slightly and looked at her in puzzlement. "Why do you laugh?"

"You do remind me of Jango. He always locked his emotions away. But I can remember times when he let them out of their cage."

"Such as?"

Her sweeter, saucier side was bubbling to the fore, and she was happy to feel it. She'd feared she'd never feel that evanescence again. "If you're lucky, I might tell you sometime."

She knew he was curious now, and pardoned herself for the slight exaggeration. In truth, Jango was a man of few words who kept his feelings in check. In his life, and his chosen lifestyle, that reserve had been vital for survival.

Just from their few conversations, she knew that for all his practical and lethal knowledge, Nate hadn't the foggiest notion about ordinary human lives. Until this, until the moment that he had taken her in his arms, she could feel that he had treated her with a certain respect and distance, more like a sister than anything else. He probably knew only two types of women: civilians to be protected or perhaps obeyed, treated with courtesy at the least. On the other hand were the sorts of women who offered themselves to soldiers in exchange for credits or protection, to be used and discarded. It could be emotionally risky to break down such a simplistic worldview.

But she had to admit that she was interested in breaking through his reserve, wondering what she might find beneath it.

What would happen, how might he respond if she allowed the bond between them to deepen? And if she took it in a new direction? She drew him away from the dancing and laughter into the shadows. "What now?" she asked.

"We're off-duty until dawn, why?"

She took his hand. "Come," she said. "I'd like to show you something." Confusion darkened his face.

"I have to be available—"

"You said you were off-duty. Are you confined to base?"

"No—" He stopped. "If I'm called, I would need to be back within twenty minutes. Can you guarantee that?"

She calculated distances and velocities in her head. "Yes."

Five minutes of scrambling over broken rock took them to *Spindragon*. As he strapped in, Sheeka swiftly completed her predeparture checklist and lifted off. With a practiced touch she rocketed almost a hundred kilometers to the southeast in about twelve minutes. At first she skirted the ground to elude scanning. Then, when they were a sufficient distance away, she rose up into a standard transport lane, filled with commuter pods and double-length cargo ships transporting goods among clients reluctant to pay the orbital tax.

Nate watched the ground whirl beneath them, enjoying the ease and command with which Sheeka piloted the craft. Competence was something he could always appreciate. This woman was different from others he had known, and that difference disoriented him slightly. Curiously enough, he enjoyed the sensation. So Nate relaxed as she took him into a saw-toothed stretch of hills, and then set them down again gently, not eighteen minutes after they left the camp.

The camp was built into the hillsides, several different mine openings suggesting both natural and artificial breaches in the surface. As she landed, a dozen offworlders and two X'Ting emerged to meet them. All grinned, nodded, or waved at them in greeting.

"What is this place?"

"They are my extended family," she said. "Not by birth. By choice."

"Is this where you live?"

She smiled. "No. We don't know each other that well yet. But . . . my home is a lot like this."

Now he was able to make out more dwellings. They appeared to be camouflaged, the coloration perhaps designed to make them more difficult to see from the air. From the ground, though, they still tended to melt into the shadows and rock formations.

"Why do they hide?"

She laughed. "They don't. We just love the mountains, and enjoy blending with them as much as possible."

Again, the danger of seeing everything through a soldier's eyes.

High, sweet voices rang down from the slope. Nate turned to see several young human boys and girls up there playing some game of laughter and discovery. They dashed about calling names, squealing, enjoying the long shadows.

Down around the rock-colored dwellings swarmed older children. Some of them were graceful X'Ting, slender and huge-eyed, reminding him a bit of Kaminoans. Adolescents, he supposed, working with adults. Building, repairing tools perhaps.

He watched them, thinking, feeling. He found the environment a bit confusing. Or could it be Sheeka herself who troubled him? Whichever, he found himself remembering his own accelerated childhood, the learning games he had played . . .

Once again, Sheeka Tull seemed to have read his mind. "What were you like as a child?" Clever. Had she brought him here to see children, hoping that it would spark his own memories?

He shrugged. "Learning, growing, striving. Like all the others."

"I've visited a lot of planets. Most children's games help kids discover their individual strengths. How can you do this? Aren't you all supposed to be the same?"

Teasing him again? He realized, to his pleasure, that he hoped so. "Not really. There was a core curriculum that we all mastered, but after that we specialized, learned different things, prepared for different functions, went on different training exercises, fought in different wars. No two of us have ever had the same environment, and because of that we are stronger. In the aggregate, we have lived a million lives.

All of that experience grows within us. We are the GAR, and it is alive."

"Loosen up, will you?" she clucked, and stretched out her hand to him. He hesitated, and then after checking his com-link to make certain that he could be reached in case of any emergency, he followed her.

41

A southern wind nipping at their backs, Sheeka led Nate up a worn, dusty hillside trail into the mouth of one of the tunnels. The mouth was about four by six meters, and once inside, the trooper saw that the shielded buildings outside were not the living spaces he had supposed them to be. Toolsheds, perhaps. Within was a large communal area lit by glowing fungi arrayed along the walls, nurtured with liquid nutrients trickling from a pipe rigging. The fungi rippled in a luminescent rainbow. When he brought his hand close to a bank of it, his skin tingled.

"Most places on Cestus, the offworlders pretty much dominate the X'Ting. Consider them primitive even though they give lip service to respect. But there are a few little enclaves like this one, where we actually try to learn from them. They have a lot to offer, really, if we'd just give them a chance."

A variety of human and other offworlder children ran hither and thither with their little X'Ting friends, burning energy like exploding stars, flooding the entire cave with their exuberance. The day's major work had ended, but some of the adults were still fixing tools, laughing and joking in easy camaraderie.

They greeted Sheeka warmly as she approached, glancing at Nate with tentative acceptance. *After all,* their attitude seemed to say, *he's with Sheeka.* The air churned with luscious smells. In several nooks meals were being concocted from a variety of tangy and exotic ingredients. He found the jovial messiness oddly appealing.

But as soon as that thought sank in, conditioning rushed forward to yank it back out.

"What do you think?" Sheeka asked.

He strove to compose a answer both accurate and in alignment with his values and feelings. "This seems . . . a good life. An easy life. Not a soldier's life. It is not for me."

Nate had assumed that she would accept such an answer at face value, but instead Sheeka bristled. "You think this is easier? Raising children, loving, hoping. You?" A sharp, hard bark of laughter. "You're surrounded by the replaceable. Ships, equipment, people. A modular world. A piece breaks? Replace it." Her small strong hands had folded into fists. "You never leave home without expecting to die. What do you think it's like to actually care if your children survive? To *care*? What do you think the universe looks like to someone who cares? How strong would someone have to be just to preserve hope?"

Her outburst knocked him back on his emotional heels. "Perhaps . . . I see what you are saying."

She continued on as if she had prepared this speech for days. "And how much strength do you think it requires to keep your spirits high when everything you've spent a lifetime building . . . that your parents and grandparents spent a lifetime building . . . can be destroyed by the decision of someone too far away to touch?" She paused a moment. "And men like you."

It was his turn to bristle. "Men like me protect you."

"From other men like you."

He might have taken offense at that, but instead he felt a bit sad, realizing that Sheeka was not as different as he had thought. She was just another outsider after all. "No. Men like me don't start the wars. We just die in them. We've always died in them, and we always will. We don't expect any praise for it, no parades. No one knows our names. In fact, by your standards we have no names at all."

Something in his face, his voice, or his carriage reached through her anger, because suddenly she softened. "Nate . . ."

Sheeka reached out as if to take his hand, but he drew it

away. "No. Is that what you wanted to hear? Well it's true. We don't have names. And no one will ever know who we are. But *we* do. We always do." He felt his shoulders square as he said that simple truth. The troopers knew who they were, always. And always would. "We're the Grand Army of the Republic."

Sheeka shook her head. "Nate, I'm sorry. I didn't mean to judge you."

His stance did not soften. She had dropped her guard. It was unfair to attack now, but he could not stop the training that was, in the final analysis, all he knew. "I haven't had your choices. Every step of my life I've been told what to do."

"Yes," she said, her voice small now.

He took a step closer, looking down on her dark, lovely face. "And what do you know? We both ended up in the same place."

He paused. She had nothing to say.

"So what difference did all those decisions make?"

Sheeka looked up at him, their eyes meeting for a moment that was too intense. Then a child running between them broke the moment. She managed a rueful smile, said, "Come on," and led him back out of the cave.

The two of them sat on a hillside, watching the moons and listening to the happy sounds. Sheeka had spoken a bit of her life here on Cestus, of small pleasures and trials.

"So," she concluded, "sometimes all we could do was wait, and hope. Don't you think that requires endurance?"

"Is that what it was like?"

She gave no answer, just twisted a stalk of grass up and knotted it into a ball, throwing it downslope.

"I am sorry," Nate said. "I live only to defend the Republic. I regret if that defense brings misery to some, but I won't apologize for who and what I am."

Without saying a word, Sheeka slid closer to him. When she started speaking again, his own thoughts ended, and he found himself losing interest in anything save the sound and cadence of her voice. "All you have to lose is your life, and you hold that cheaply enough. Are you so strong, Nate? Are you really as strong as the least fungus farmer?"

Their eyes locked again, and he felt the beginnings of an emotion he had never before experienced: despair. She would never understand him.

Then Sheeka, swollen with anger, seemed to deflate a bit. "No," she said. "That's wrong of me. I know one of the problems—it's the whole name thing. I'm sorry. I'm used to calling droids by numbers and letters. People have *names*. You guys just have shorthand for your numbers."

"I'm sorry—" he began, but she held up her hand.

"Do troopers ever have real names?" she asked.

"Rarely."

"Would you mind if I gave you one?"

She was staring at him with such sincere intensity that he almost laughed. But couldn't. The whole thing was amusing, really.

"What name did you have in mind?"

"I was thinking Jangotat," she said quietly. "Mandalorian for 'Jango's brother.' "

He laughed, but found his voice catching a bit in mid-chuckle. *Jangotat*. "Sure," he said. "If that makes it easier. Fine."

Her answering smile burst with relief. "Thanks. Thanks, Jangotat. That's a good name, you know," she said, thumping him with her elbow. They both chuckled about that, until the mirth died away to a companionable silence.

Jangotat, he thought.

Jango's brother.

A smile.

That I am.

42

The armored cargo transport lay broken, flames gushing from its shattered innards, its treads curled back from their axles like shreds of skin from peeled fruit. The cargo itself was scavenged or burned, its load of credit chits looted: the cash would be useful for purchasing goods, buying silence, and providing for the widows and orphans of any Desert Wind fatalities.

Black oily smoke curled from the transport's ruptured belly and boiled to the clouds. Hands bound behind their backs, its crew had begun their twenty-kilometer trek back to ChikatLik. The message they carried would be heard loud and clear: *Chaos is coming.*

And as lovers of comfort and order, the Five Families would seek out a source of security. The Separatists had been shown to be too risky and dangerous, and possibly in collaboration with the forces of Desert Wind. The only option? A closer bond to the Republic.

"It goes well?" asked the newly christened "Jangotat."

"Well enough," Kit Fisto said, gazing through his electrobinoculars. "We strike, they grab at shadows, and we sever their limbs. Soon the Five Families will pray for order and safety." The words were confident, but something more unsure lurked behind them.

"You don't sound totally pleased, sir."

"I am not comfortable with such deception, even though I admit its value."

Jangotat concealed his pleasure. His perceptions were sharpening, something that kept soldiers alive. Maybe the whole "Jangotat" thing wasn't so bad. *Don't be afraid to take chances. Think odd thoughts. All right, then. Here's one this Jedi would never expect.* "May I say, sir, that such nonconventional warfare saves lives."

To his surprise, General Fisto's mouth twisted in a rare display of mirth. "Does it indeed?"

"Yes, sir."

The general put the electrobinoculars away. "Well. If a soldier of the Republic can find such a goal admirable, can a Jedi do less?"

He realized that this was, for the Nautolan, a joke, and smiled in return. The moment of shared levity gave Jangotat the courage to ask something that had been on his mind for two days now. "Sir?"

"Yes?"

"What you did with Master Kenobi . . . could an ordinary man learn that?"

General Fisto stared at him with those vast, unblinking eyes. "No."

"Some? Even a little?"

There was a long pause, and then the general nodded. "Well, perhaps. Yes. Some."

"Would you teach me?"

"Nate . . ."

"Sir . . ." Jangotat looked to either side swiftly, saw that they were alone and lowered his voice. "Please don't laugh at me . . ."

The Nautolan shook his head gravely. "Never."

"I'm thinking of taking a name."

General Fisto's teeth gleamed. "I've heard that some do. What name are you thinking? Be careful," he warned. "Names can be powerful."

The trooper nodded. "So . . . a friend suggested: Jangotat. Brother of Jango." He narrowed his eyes as if expecting rebuke. "Would that be . . . a good thing?"

Kit Fisto did him the respect of genuinely pondering the question. Then, after almost a minute, he answered, "Jango was a man of great strengths. A worthy foe. I would be proud to have his namesake at my side." He slapped the trooper's shoulder. "Jangotat."

"Would you inform General Kenobi? I've already told my brothers."

The Nautolan's eyebrow arched. "And what did they say?"

Jangotat laughed. "They wished they'd thought of it first."

Kit Fisto seemed to look at him a bit differently. "Among my people, the taking of a name is a serious thing," he said. "An occasion for gift giving."

"That isn't why I—"

The general held his hand up. "You asked what it might be possible for you to learn. I have a small thing you may . . . enjoy. I can teach you and your brothers some of the most basic exercises taught Force-sensitive children in the Jedi Temple."

"But I will never be as good as a Jedi, will I?" This was said without despair or resentment. Merely a question.

"No," the Jedi said. "You will not. But you will know yourself, and the universe, better than you ever have."

The two of them shared a smile. It was a moment of genuine openness between these two unlikely comrades, a precious thing between them.

"Then let's get started," Jangotat said.

The four troopers squatted in a circle outside their cave, crouching around Kit as he began his lesson. "There is a thing I can teach you," the Nautolan said, "a game taught to the very youngest Padawan learners. It is a thing called Jedi Flow." He paused. "Do all of you wish this?"

They were so attentive and open that Kit couldn't resist a smile.

"All right," he said, then paused, considering. "Jedi feel the Force as an ocean of energy in which they immerse themselves, floating with its currents, or directing its waves. For the average person, the subtle sensations of life are no ocean—but can still be a stream or river. Can you understand this?"

They nodded slowly.

"Your body holds memories of pain, anger, fear. It holds them in your tissues, conditioned responses that attempt to protect you from future injury."

"Like scar tissue?" Forry asked.

"Exactly like it," he said, approving. "Tight like a fist. It warps and twists you. When you collect enough of them, they are like armor. But Jedi wear no armor. Armor both protects and numbs. Jedi must expose themselves fully to the currents of the universe. I can teach you how to remove some of these wounds. Think of them as boulders, obstacles on the river of energy. Learn to flow around your fears and angers instead of crashing *against* them. Learn to do this well enough, and you can even direct the river to move the boulders for you, widening the riverbed, increasing the flow of energy."

"But *how*?"

He searched for some simple way to express his thoughts. "Physical action is the unity of breathing, motion, and alignment. In other words, breath is created by the motion of your diaphragm, and the movement of your spine. Motion is created by breathing and proper posture. And alignment is created by a unity of breath and motion. To keep this triplet in mind as you practice your combat arts is to take a martial technique or physical challenge and transform it into something more." Kit grinned his predatory, Nautolan smile. "Enough theory," he said. "It is time for practice."

For the next two hours Kit taught them exercises to refine their breathing, concentrating on exhalations only, allowing air pressure to fill their lungs passively as the rib cage expanded. He was gratified to see how rapidly they absorbed the lessons, and gave them more.

The Nautolan showed them how to turn two-dimensional calisthenics into three-dimensional gymnastics, moving static exercise positions through additional ranges of motion, turning poses into dynamic waveforms, and melding all with the triumverate of breathing, motion, and alignment. He also demonstrated how to take those exercises and combine them, flow in and out of them, creating their own combinations to address any specific fitness needs.

But always, always, preserving and attending to breathing, motion, and alignment.

When he was done they were sweaty but exhilarated, and begged for more.

"No," he said. "That is enough for one day. Just remember: the point, the value is not in the exercises, or not exclusively there. The greatest value is in transitioning *between* one exercise and the next. All life is movement between states, between moments. Work to make every moment a symphony of these three aspects. Evolve into your excellence. Use external tasks merely to test your integration and clarity. That is the road to becoming an exceptional warrior."

43

In the innermost chambers of ChikatLik city, negotiations had moved into new and higher gear. Few in the capital knew anything but rumors: Five Family executives had been kidnapped, payrolls hijacked, transports destroyed, power stations sabotaged. The general mood suggested change, and major change at that. Things had been quieter than usual in the public section of Trillot's lair, and back in her private chambers a pall had descended over the usual revelry.

It was late now, and barely a sound could be heard in the entire twisting, turning nest of catacombs.

Trillot rested on her couch, puffing from one of her pipes, attempting to self-medicate. Accelerating the shift from male to female was a touchy process: *this* fungus to relieve stress, and *that* leaf to eliminate fatigue. Another to stabilize her mood. However unpleasant, Trillot found this preferable to the monthlong fertility period as the cycle went from male to female. A time of almost overwhelmingly volatile emotions, X'Ting traditionally sealed themselves in their quarters for this period, preferably with a mate.

No such isolation for Trillot! She had been awake for four days now, and although her system would eventually crash, necessitating thirty hours of coma-like slumber, for now she managed to keep the worst of it at bay. Meanwhile, spies brought her information from all over the city. She filtered it, deciding what was actionable and what she should pass on to Ventress, who had her own mysterious sources. The holovid she had asked Trillot to pass to Quill, for instance . . .

Still, Snoil's discovery of the entire synthstone business

was disturbing. Even with their new information, this century-old folly was the ultimate wild card. Who knew what the Jedi might do with such leverage? The sooner Kenobi was dead, the better.

These musings might have been enough to disrupt her sleep cycle, but there was more: her growing need to lurk outside Ventress's bed chamber. Invariably, the experience left her trembling.

Trillot was grateful for the narcotic currents coursing through her blood. What might have been profoundly disturbing in a more sober mood seemed merely a matter of curiosity. Strange. When she chose, Ventress appeared able to shield herself from the most powerful Jedi. But she had such contempt for Trillot that she allowed her ugliest dreams to seep from her sleeping mind.

Trillot took another puff and closed her emerald eyes. Instead of darkness, a fantasy of fire and blood repeated itself again and again.

Warships rose.

Towers fell.

The Republic might dissolve, the Separatists trigger a wave of secession that washed through the entire galaxy. Consideration of profits, however enormous, might soon be moot. As might survival itself.

"Fire and blood," she whispered.

The council chambers had been locked in verbal turmoil for long hours when Obi-Wan entered. He very nearly smiled. Since the subterranean kidnapping and "battle," the major subject of conversation was not *whether* they should acquiesce to the Republic's request, but rather *how* they could most swiftly comply.

This he knew even though he had not been present. A Jedi had means. Especially a Jedi with solid Republic credits to spread around.

"Yes, I was called?"

Snoil sat at the circular conference table across from the executives, half a dozen holodocs floating around his head.

He gestured to Obi-Wan. "We've had a breakthrough. They've decided to meet the Chancellor's terms."

A vast relief. The sooner he put this distasteful situation behind him, the better. "Excellent."

The immense room was filled wall to circular wall with representatives of the Five Families. And not just the executives who claimed the top slots—there were three dozen or more lower-tier Cestus Cybernetics executives thronging the room, poring over their holodocs, arguing and proposing. They added signatures and thumbprints on the touch-screens for instant upload to legal computers all over Cestus, and from there broadcast to Coruscant for instant verification.

The air before Obi-Wan flickered, and a holodoc appeared. He turned to Snoil. "This meets your approval?"

He noticed the crinkles of exhaustion on the Vippit's stubby arms, and realized that Snoil must have found the past days of negotiation grueling. "Absolutely."

Obi-Wan signed as the Republic's representative, and felt vastly satisfied. He and Duris shared a smile. "I assume that when the Supreme Chancellor reads the contract, he will approve. But barring some problem on that end, I believe that we have come to an agreement."

"And not a moment too soon, Master Jedi," she said.

One of Duris's lawyers put a datapad in front of him. "And now, Master Kenobi, we need your signature on the following documents—"

Suddenly and without formal announcement Quill entered the chamber, waving a rectangular holocard above his head as if it contained the secrets of the universe. His faceted eyes gleamed.

"Wait! Hold the proceedings! Do *not* thumb that holodoc."

Duris stared at Quill with suspicion. "What is the meaning of this?"

"Better we ask the Jedi the meaning of *this*." He placed the card in a datapad, smirking with triumph. An instantly recognizable image sprang into the air. It was not taken from a standard security cam—those had all been disabled down

44

Initially Trillot was nervous as Ventress swept into her chambers, but as soon as she saw her visitor's mood, the X'Ting relaxed. "So. It is ended? The Jedi leaves?"

Despite her scathingly cold smile, Ventress shook her head. "He'll try to return. I know him."

"I tell you that my spies—"

"See with their eyes," she said with contempt. "The Families will make their move now. Quill has informed them that if Kenobi broadcasts his information to Palpatine, Cestus Cybernetics is done. I think we can trust them to be suitably . . . definitive in response."

Murdering a Jedi? What in the brood's name had Trillot gotten herself into? Too late to complain now . . . nothing to do but ride it out. Trillot cursed the day she had agreed to help the Confederacy, the day she had betrayed the Jedi. Bantha muck. While she was at it, why not simply curse the day she was hatched? That was, in the final analysis, more to the point.

45

No honor guard appeared at the spaceport to see Obi-Wan and Doolb Snoil away. Considering the hash he had made of his attempts at diplomacy, the Jedi was glad to be allowed to leave at all.

The guards who escorted him to the spaceport said not a word until they actually reached the site. One of them turned as if to speak, then paused, looking down at the ground. He walked away, shaking his head.

Obi-Wan walked up the landing ramp into the Republic transport ship. Behind him, Snoil shuffled along with only the slightest of slime trails on the track. "Obi-Wan," he said plaintively. "What happened?"

"I am not certain, my friend," he said, and as the door closed behind him, he strapped himself in. His mind was still far away. Something was wrong, *had* been wrong since his arrival. No. Not then. But things had disintegrated soon after. What had been the trigger? He did not know. Blast! If only he knew the source of the incriminating holo! He turned to the lawyer. "On Coruscant," he said, "tell all that you know. You performed well. Whatever fault exists is mine——" He paused, the vaguest of suspicions forming in the back of his mind. "Or perhaps——"

"What?"

Obi-Wan sighed. "I don't know, but I felt something. From the beginning, there have been factors beyond my understanding. I have missed something, and that blunder made all the difference."

"Oh dear," Snoil said. "All of that planning and work. I never dreamed things could go so wrong."

Obi-Wan shook his head, but said nothing. He had no words to comfort his distraught friend. This was, in every possible way, a complete disaster.

As soon as Xutoo made the basic preparations, the ship lifted off. As it rose, Obi-Wan turned to Snoil. "I've made my decision," he said. "It is no longer safe for you on Cestus. You will go, but I must stay. My job here isn't finished. I'm going to join Master Fisto."

Snoil's eyestalks trembled with amazement as the Jedi began a checklist of preparations for jettisoning an escape pod. "But you were told to leave! It was a direct request, and any deviation would be a violation of Code Four-Nine-Seven Point Eight—"

"I've gone a little too far to be worried about such niceties," he said. "We have other mynocks to slice." He managed a smile. "Good-bye, Doolb. You're a good friend. Go home now. There's no more work for a barrister here."

"But . . . sir!"

Obi-Wan turned to Xutoo and gripped his shoulder. "Get him home safely."

"Yes, sir."

And so saying, Obi-Wan pressed a series of switches, and the capsule sealed. It seemed to sink into the wall behind it. A moment later there was a light *shoosh* sound, and the Jedi was gone.

The ship had just crested the upper atmosphere, making the transition to vacuum. Ground-based and orbiting scanners tracked every ship exiting or leaving, but at this point, where the two sets of data overlapped, it was easiest to cloak activity.

A red warning light blinked in front of him, indicating that the emergency system was about to begin its instructional sequence. Obi-Wan disabled it: the computer voice would merely be a distraction. He intended to pilot the craft by skill and instinct. The escape capsule had both manual and automatic settings, and could maneuver its way to a ground beacon, but Obi-Wan dared not allow its repulsors to fire too quickly: their radiation would be too easily detected.

So he plummeted, counting on the capsule's heat shielding and primitive aerodynamics, tweaking the glide angle slightly as he headed down toward the Dashta Mountains.

He had to time this very, very carefully, waiting until he was low enough that his appearance on the scanner wouldn't be connected with a disgraced diplomat's transport. Let them think his capsule was merely an unlicensed pleasure craft.

As Obi-Wan counted off the seconds, the heat became more and more oppressive. Crash foam, doubling as insulation, billowed up shoulder-high in protection. As the temperature of the outermost layer of shielding climbed to thousands of degrees, he was sobered to realize that he was dropping blind, his fate entrusted to the unknown pod technicians. He hated that dependence even more than he disliked flying, far preferring to trust his own profound connection to the Force. But there was no avoiding it. This time, he had to trust.

It was time. His fingers found the repulsor button and . . .

Nothing happened.

As the ground raced toward him he watched the altimeter, fighting a surge of panic. Something was *wrong*. His metal tomb hurtled toward the ground at such speed that, if it struck, they wouldn't retrieve enough midi-chlorians to enlighten a Jedi amoeba.

Obi-Wan struggled to reach his lightsaber, the mushy thick foam filling the capsule making every effort a struggle. When he finally wrapped his hands around the silver handle, he angled it away from his body and triggered the blade. Foam smoldered. Sparks and smoke erupted in the narrow, cramped confines. The capsule juddered, wind beginning to peel away the external shielding beginning at the point where the lightsaber beam had damaged its aerodynamics. Critical seconds dragged past as the external layers sloughed away. But he'd achieved the desired effect: the repulsors' trigger circuits ran through the capsule's skin, very near his shoulder. If he couldn't send a signal by pushing a button, the lightsaber's energy field might power that circuit more directly.

Nothing happened. All right, then . . . a few centimeters to the left.

He tried again, burning a second hole in the capsule. More of the outer shielding peeled away, but luckily, this time the circuit fired.

One huge jolt, and then another. Blessedly, the damaged external shielding shucked away clean. The capsule parted like two halves of a nut shell, and Obi-Wan was in a thin, transparent, winged capsule. Wind whistled through the lightsaber holes, but the inner life-support capsule, constructed of a nearly indestructible cocooned monofilament, held together better than the external shell.

After the first few moments, air flowed freely. Watching pieces of metal flipping away around him, Obi-Wan held his breath as the automatic repulsor circuits took the capsule into a smooth glide path. A few rough moments, and then he was sailing in a long, shallow unpowered arc. His descent began to slow. The wind howled against the outside skin. Below him, the desert floor was an endless stretch of brown and dull green spots. Far ahead, visible only as darker wrinkles beneath the cloud cover, lay the Dashta Mountains. In minutes he'd be close enough to see ground detail. Minutes to think, and plan, and allow his disappointment to simmer into pure energy. Obi-Wan watched a chunk of pod skin flipping away around him. Other chunks turned end-over-end, tumbling away from him. It wouldn't be the end of the world if a blip showed up on a scanner. *Not necessarily a bad thing,* he thought. *If there is someone behind this, and if they damaged my escape pod, then they might be scanning the sky. If they see the metal debris, they might just conclude that their plot worked . . .*

Whoever they are. And whatever they want.

Doolb Snoil watched the display as their ship rose, freeing itself of Cestus's gravitational pull. Once free, it paused as the nav computers plotted their jump to hyperspace. He already missed his friend Obi-Wan, and was formulating an explanation to the Chancellor. What would he say? Was there any way to cast this disaster in a favorable light? He doubted it, but . . .

Xutoo's voice disturbed his reverie. "Ah, sir, we may have a problem." There was an edge of something Snoil understood all too well in that voice: controlled panic.

"Problem? Problem? Master Kenobi promised there would be no problem!"

"I don't think he took *that* into consideration, sir."

"What?"

From a point between Cestus's two moons, a small ship approached them, bearing in like a bird of prey. It was small and black, with an ominously spare design that said it was built for pure practicality. A war drone. A hunter-killer.

Mind working at fevered overdrive, Snoil managed to rationalize the ship's presence. *Perhaps it's just visiting Cestus, and has mistakenly aligned its flight path with our departure point—*

Then all such optimistic speculations were revealed as foolish. The new ship fired a probe droid at them. The intelligent weapon spiraled in, locked on target, and began to home in, a spinning ball of death. A salute from the Five Families?

The consummate professional, Xutoo managed to keep his voice calm at a moment when Snoil wanted to scream at the top of his lungs. "I've commenced evasive maneuvers, but I don't know. Sir, I would suggest that you follow General Kenobi's example and evacuate."

All Snoil could say was: "Aiyee!"

The ship began to make looping evasive maneuvers. More probe droids must have joined the first, because they rocked and juddered with blasts as Xutoo did his best.

"Sir," Xutoo repeated. "I suggest you go."

"No. I will stay here with you. Master Kenobi promised I would be safe."

"I can't make you go, sir, but in a moment I'll jettison the remaining escape pods in an attempt to distract the missile."

Listening to Xutoo's machinelike calm somehow penetrated Snoil's defensive mechanisms as even the explosions had not. No escape pods! He broke. "No! No! Wait for me!"

Pushing himself to emergency speed, Snoil moved as rapidly as a human being might stroll, wedging himself into the escape capsule. He pushed the automatic sequence button, and his eyestalks twined in anguish. Crash foam billowed up around him, and sight was lost. For a moment he could barely breathe. Then his lips found the emergency nozzle and air flowed into his lungs.

Then things went black as his pod sank back into and through the ship's walls. He felt a rush, and then a jolt . . . followed by sudden, deep quiet. Then a sensation of floating.

Snoil had no control at all—everything was managed by the automatic emergency program. A screen opened up before his eyes, some kind of computerized display showing the exterior of the ship as six other escape pods burst free.

Two of them attracted probe droids away from Snoil as he plummeted toward the atmosphere, but the screen showed the ship evading one . . . two . . . three of the droids, and he began to feel more optimistic.

Then the screen went very, very bright. When the light dimmed, only smoke and debris remained. Xutoo and the ship were gone, destroyed.

He stared, horrified but almost incapable of speech, watching as missiles streaked after the remaining pods.

Snoil was frozen with fear as the pod descended. The pods spun crazily as evasion programs began to kick in. One of the droids rushed past a spinning pod—and headed directly for him.

He watched as one pod after another was blown completely out of the sky, now beginning to turn blue as they skimmed deeper into the atmosphere. He heard something babbling in the background and became horribly aware that that sound was his own voice, raving out against the moment of expected pain and finality. "I'll sue! Or my, my heirs will sue! For damages and emotional distress . . ." A probe passed immediately close to him on the left, in pursuit of one of his capsule's programmed distractions. The resultant explosion painted the sky yellow and sent his pod juddering to the right, coincidentally forcing another droid to miss its target. "Oh my, that was close, and—" another horrendous explosion, and he made a bubbling, shrieking sound. "And oh my!"

He turned to look back up—once he managed to determine which direction "up" was—and saw another missile heading directly for him. "No, no, I was joking! I'll retract that complaint! I'll file a full admission of guilt or wrongdoing, or . . . *Aiyee!*"

And in the instant before discourse would have become terminally irrelevant, one of the other escape pods swooped back in, intercepting the offending missile.

As Snoil closed his eyes and offered his soul to the Broodmaster, a new explosion dwarfed all the others in both scope and effect on Snoil, who realized that his shell would certainly need washing after all *this*.

Then suddenly, there was nothing but silence from outside. To his wonder, he realized that he had survived the storm. Now there was just the little matter of the landing.

A red warning light flashed on the control panel, and the capsule requested a series of manual operations, warning him in a calm female voice that certain *"explosive impacts have damaged the capsule's automatic systems. Please do not worry, as the manual backup systems can perform perfectly well. Please perform the following functions in the sequence requested."*

And one after another he did perform the tasks as requested, while simultaneously watching the ground explode toward him. The altimeter shifted toward zero with nauseating rapidity. *"—Now disengage the external shields—"* A switch. *"—and now please, within five seconds, disengage each of the primary source nodes, routing all of their power to the secondary chamber—"* Which switch? The altimeter dizzied him, but he dared not look at it, nor glimpse the ground spinning up at him like a vast hand rising to swat him from the sky.

"And now please trigger the main repulsor."

Disaster was almost upon him now. Certainly nothing he did would make any difference. Surely this next moment would be his last. Surely—

A violent whip sideways almost made Snoil's stomach roll. The capsule bobbed as the repulsors fired, and the air outside flamed pink. Snoil managed to breathe again, his eyestalks ceasing their wild and frantic dance as he drifted toward the ground below.

Far below him and to the west, Obi-Wan Kenobi rolled his escape pod into shadows and heaped sand and rocks atop it. Instinct made him gaze up at the sky, where streaks of red and white blossomed against the clouds. He frowned, trying to make out the shapes, and then recognized them for what they were: shattered chunks of the ship reentering the atmosphere. His heart was heavy, fearing that his bungled mission had cost the lives of Xutoo and the harmless, brilliant Snoil. How had this happened? What secret forces opposed them here . . . ?

Then he saw the purple glow of repulsor fire, and relaxed just a bit. Someone *had* escaped the ship. And Snoil was nothing if not lucky. There was more than a chance that his old friend remained alive.

And that would be good. If anything on Cestus could be considered certain, it was this: they would need every strong hand and agile mind in the hours ahead.

46

Obi-Wan disguised his distress signal with narrow-burst encoded messages. Less than two hours later, Thak Val Zsing and Sirty reached him with a dozen recruits. He sent half of them after Snoil and followed the others back to camp, where he rejoined Kit Fisto and the clone troopers.

There he was heartened to see all that had been accomplished. They fed him, listened to the short version of his narrow escape, and then settled down for serious conversation. "The least of our problems," he concluded, "is that negotiations with G'Mai Duris and the leadership of Cestus have failed."

"I agree," Kit said. His black eyes gleamed. "There are other forces at play here. From the beginning, we have been manipulated. It is time the next phase of our operation went into effect. Nate?"

He said this raising his voice and nodding toward the clones, who one by one rose and gave their reports.

As the food worked its way through his system, Obi-Wan was comforted by the troopers' measured, military cadences. On occasion he'd found that emotionless precision irritating, but now it calmed him. The value of such competency could not be underestimated. Here, it might save all their lives, and the plan as well.

All in all, he was pleasantly surprised by the commandos' accurate, perceptive, and entirely admirable reports.

When they were complete, Kit Fisto leaned forward, resting his elbows on his knees. "Your thoughts?" he asked after Obi-Wan had remained quiet for almost a full minute.

"Impressive," he said. "It makes my own blundering seem all the more childish in comparison."

Obi-Wan stood, slapping his palms against his legs. "The situation has changed," he said. "Our resources have changed, and the nature of our adversaries has changed. Gentlemen"— He scanned the assembled. "—an unknown person or persons destroyed our transport ship and killed one of your brothers. This was an unspeakable act, and must be addressed as such."

The recruits, their new and improved "Desert Wind," were hard now. Their grueling training had weeded out the weaklings and transformed them into a band capable of following orders, of marching courageously into danger. Still, a vital question remained: were they really willing to kill or die? It was never possible to determine who would cower under fire. Only combat itself could answer the questions burning in every raw recruit's breast:

Will I? Can I?

He saw that question now. Saw also that his brush with catastrophe had not diminished him in their eyes. In fact, it seemed the surviving members of Desert Wind now accepted him as they had not before, saw him as an ally, one who might now be willing to go beyond his stated parameters into something more radically dangerous.

Someone had attempted to *murder* him. Someone had betrayed and manipulated him. Duris? The Five Families? Trillot?

Someone. But who? Who stood to gain by his death?

He pulled his mind back to the task at hand. "We will continue on," he said. "And we will finish what we started together. You do not know me, but through the glowing reports of my associates, I know *you*." He had their eyes and minds. What he needed was their hearts. "In the coming days, the nature of our new situation will become clear to you, and I trust that none of you will falter at the grim task ahead. This is no longer a charade. Justified it may be, but I ask that you control your rage. I ask you to follow the path of least violence for the damage that we are called upon to do. To be merciful when possible, and courageous in action when not."

He paused, and gathered himself. "We journeyed to Cestus seeking a diplomatic solution. It would seem that that option is no longer available to us. Ladies. Gentlemen." He locked eyes with each of them in turn. "We must consider ourselves at hazard."

47

For hours G'Mai Duris had pored over her advisers' reports and suggestions, seeking to better understand her current position. The Republic had attempted to influence her decisions by deception. The Jedi had won her the leadership of the hive council. Had given her a piece of information that could destroy Cestus Cybernetics, or offer her people a new beginning.

But by perpetrating a fraud, Obi-Wan had plunged her into a nightmare. She could not support the Jedi, or accept his support. The information in her hands could not be used to manipulate Cestus Cybernetics. Without support from the Republic, the information would do little save ensure her own assassination.

Another question remained as well, one she was having a more difficult time answering. How *exactly* had the Jedi been foiled? She didn't believe for an instant that the scheming Quill had trapped Obi-Wan in such a fashion. No. She had seen too much of her cousin's past power-grubbing to think her rival capable of such a coup. Quill had received serious assistance. But from whom?

There was another force at work here, and one that might prove far more dangerous.

Her assistant Shar Shar rolled into the room, blue skin gleaming splotchily in alarm. "Regent Duris!" she cried. "We have terrible news!" Shar Shar extruded an arm and punched a code into the machine, waving her stubby hands through the reading stream until the images changed. "This just came through a minute ago."

The view was from orbit, one of the drone satellites used to monitor and protect the entire planetary system, everything from the moons to the mines. They watched Obi-Wan's ship rising up through the atmosphere. "We lost the image for a moment as the shift between the ground monitors and the orbiters was disrupted. Perhaps by this drone ship—"

Something appeared from the direction of a moon. It was black and configured strangely, and Duris thought her eyes deceived her. For a moment she imagined it to be some great bird of prey, but then she saw it to be no manner of living thing, but a ship of an unfamiliar design.

But was it really unfamiliar? Hadn't she seen such a ship design among a series of craft purchased by Cestus Cybernetics security just last year? It appeared from nowhere, swooped out of frame until another satellite caught it, and then it and the Jedi's ship were both in the viewing field at the same time. The black ship spat something out toward the Jedi ship, which promptly commenced corkscrewing maneuvers. "Who is in the escape pod?" G'Mai asked.

"Let me see." Her assistant manipulated the field. "Not much shielding on a pod. We might be able to—ah! Not human . . . it was the Vippit barrister."

"Then the Jedi is still piloting the ship?"

"Perhaps, and—" Suddenly the entire visual field flooded with light, enough to wash the shadows from the room and temporarily render them all dazed and nearly blind.

"What was *that*?" Duris asked, instantly comprehending the horrid absurdity of the question. She knew *precisely* what it was. Even more important, she understood what it meant.

Some unknown force or person had destroyed the Republican ship and, with it, the Jedi personally appointed by Supreme Chancellor Palpatine to negotiate with Cestus. She groaned. Things had been horrendous enough. The discovery of Obi-Wan's perfidy, and its public disclosure, had tied her hands. But this went so far beyond *bad* that she would have to find new descriptions, and those new words would have to wait until she ceased feeling too nauseated to think.

For all her current anger, she suspected Obi-Wan had acted from a desire to bring Cestus back into the Republic's sheltering fold. With respect and deep relief she noted that no one had actually been harmed during the fraudulent kidnapping. In her heart she believed that this suggested genuine concern for the lives and welfare of even the lowliest security people, let alone the Families themselves. But who or whatever had acted *against* the Jedi had displayed no such scruples. Beyond doubt Cestus would be blamed, and she would have no option but to throw her support to the Confederacy.

And although she could not fully grasp the intents of all sides in this matter, she knew that for all of his deception she preferred Obi-Wan to these shadowy assassins.

"What do we do?" asked Shar Shar, bouncing in agitation.

"There is only one thing we can do," she replied. "And that is to safely retrieve any survivors. Snoil, at least, may be alive. Search for a rescue beacon!"

48

Jangotat and the rest of the rescue party had traveled most of the way to the location indicated by Barrister Snoil's homing beacon, zipping along close to the ground on speeder bikes. They were less than three klicks away when they picked up the first signals from ChikatLik's approaching rescue craft.

"We have a problem, Captain," Sirty said.

"Agreed, Sergeant." Obi-Wan's escape from the ship had been anticipated, and had gone off without a hitch. His capsule had been all but invisible to the scanners. Snoil's unanticipated exit was another matter altogether. The Vippit's rescue beacon would be seen by anyone with a scanner tuned to the emergency frequencies. The troopers had their orders: to retrieve Snoil. There was no telling the nature or inclination of those who now rushed to find them. Was it still important not to expose the presence of trained Republic forces on Cestus? What to do?

He made his decision from among a handful of equally bad options. "Forry and Desert Wind travel north to intercept. Dig in and do what you can to make yourselves look like a larger force. They won't be anticipating hostile fire, and *should* retreat."

"Yes, sir."

"On it!"

Two of the speeder bikes peeled off to head north. He sent a coded message to those remaining with him. "Follow me. Increase to maximum velocity."

* * *

The Republic transport drama had attracted attention from members of the Five Families. A seething Quill had already returned to Duris's throne room, and Llitishi was said to be on his way. Quill radiated both hatred and triumph. How long would it be before he found a way to kill her? A month? A week? A few days?

"Regent Duris," said Shar Shar, rolling side-to-side with dismay. "Our security force approaches the beacon location for the escape capsule, but there is a problem."

"And what is that?"

The little blue ball frowned. "Look." On the projection field, a few small dots zipped from the direction of the Dashta Mountains, heading for the capsule.

"What is that?"

"Ordinarily I'd guess aboriginal nomads, ma'am. But they're moving kind of fast."

Quill sneered, his wings fluttering with repressed rage. "We know that Desert Wind was cooperating with the Jedi. We are simply seeing the weapons that bought such cooperation, *Regent*."

"And now they intend to rescue the Vippit?" Her head spun.

"They may even be responsible for the attack."

"They have no such weaponry." Duris bit her tongue. These waters were deepening. Could Desert Wind have been involved? But if they had other allies, allies who might have supplied the technology for such an assassination, then were the anarchists playing both sides against the middle, supporting anyone who would provide them with weaponry? Then what of her intuition that Quill had obtained the holovid from complicit sources? And if he had—*Whose trap is this, really? And who has been caught in it?*

Duris was beginning to think that Obi-Wan might have been more truthful than she thought. Why, then, had he not proclaimed innocence in some way? If security considerations were involved, why had he not asked for a private audience? No, she had seen his face: surprise, shock, consternation . . . and shame.

"Ma'am!" Shar Shar called out. "The rescue force is under fire!"

Duris manipulated her chair-arm sensor, momentarily unable to find the feed. "Any visual contact?"

Shar Shar tried to manipulate the drone satellite but couldn't get magnification powerful enough to show anything but a few specks and flashes in the desert. "No," the Zeetsa said. "But they are using weapons similar to those known to be possessed by Desert Wind."

Of course. That meant nothing. And everything. Her head hurt. "Tell them to pull back. Put a smaller security team into the area."

The other dots were moving. Had they reached the capsule and extracted the survivor?

"They're leaving!" Shar Shar bubbled. The dots on the map bleeped out. "And they must have reached the mountains. Our drone satellite can't see anything at all now."

Had Snoil been rescued? Kidnapped? Murdered? Tortured for information? Welcomed as a friend? It was impossible to say from this vantage point. But the differences among those possibilities might cost G'Mai Duris her cloak of office.

More important, they might cost the life of every being on Cestus.

49

With anarchists attacking on multiple fronts, there was little time for rest in ChikatLik. The attacks were always
carried out with laser precision, and inevitably involved minimal structural damage and no loss of life. Still, with every
strike an industrial complex was damaged, production
slowed or stopped. Mines were rendered too dangerous for
workers to enter, vehicles were sabotaged, and security
forces were humiliated and enraged. And behind it all, behind every mark on the map that meant another blown
bridge, another crippled skyport, another central processing
by-station rendered useless, Duris thought she sensed the
mind of Obi-Wan Kenobi: brilliant, ferocious, tactically di-
verse, and respectful of life in all its forms.

Could the Jedi still be alive?

If the majority of production loci were jammed, if those
critical production lines were slowed to a crawl, her hands
would be tied. She would have to either sue for peace or call
in Confederacy forces to protect their interests, throwing
Cestus onto the path of destruction. Because if Cestus declared for the Confederacy, then the Republic would consider her an enemy planet producing lethal arms. Cestus had
no fleet capable of resisting *either* juggernaut. Politically,
economically, and personally she would be torn to pieces,
and Cestus would end as a minor footnote in dull academic
histories detailing failed attempts at secession.

During those days the Regent slept little. It seemed that
every five hours or so there was another report, bearing
new embedded images of flaming refineries, fleeing security

forces, stories of commando teams—perhaps Desert Wind, perhaps something else—striking from silence and shadows, destroying only equipment, and then fading away again. Just dissolving into thin air.

Then in the middle of a night, Shar Shar's cries roused her from uneasy dreams. "We've trapped Desert Wind!" she called. "Please, come now."

G'Mai Duris wrapped a robe around her ample body and hurried to follow her assistant's spherical blue form as it ricocheted down the hall toward the observation room.

She recognized the location in the holos: the Kibo geothermal station west of the Zantay Hills. Kibo had appeared on a high-priority list of possible targets and thus been allotted additional security teams. Apparently those precautions had borne fruit.

"What do we have?"

"A Desert Wind unit. No more than ten. They were sabotaging one of the towers, and a secondary sweep picked them up. We swooped in before they could escape. Seemed to have cut off their retreat."

"Good, good," Duris said. "Then there is a chance for capture, and then interrogation." Perhaps now they would finally learn a bit of the truth. Perhaps.

50

Obi-Wan Kenobi was pinned down in a bunker at the rock-tumbled edge of Kibo Lake, just outside the power station's white duracrete dome. For the last hour a slow wind had been building. The air was clouded with sand and dust, reducing the accuracy of defensive fire. Their enemies seemed less encumbered: one of his recruits was already wounded by sniper blasts. The surprise and the accurate return fire had dispirited the others.

The clone troopers were still disguised as Desert Wind fighters. Even though Obi-Wan knew that the incriminating holovid existed, if there were no additional witnesses, and no obvious clone trooper involvement, it would be easier for Coruscant to deny allegations.

Kibo Lake's fifty-kilometer-wide volcanic crater was the fourth largest on the planet. Active vents at the bottom transformed this, one of Cestus's largest bodies of groundwater, into a hypermineralized geothermal soup pot, home to a collection of odd primitive aquatic forms, and a power source for many of the outlying mines.

The geothermal stations tapped those volcanic vents, concentrating the heat and ultimately powering a series of steam turbines. The power was sold in a dozen forms planetwide.

Both stealth and courage had been required to move into position for the assault: they'd skimmed silently across Kibo Lake's simmering alkaline soup and simultaneously crawled over the crater wall from the desert, in a precision pincer operation.

Explosive charges had been carefully placed, guards neutralized without fatality. If all had gone well they would have faded back into the desert an hour before the first explosion's false dawn illuminated the night sky.

It was not to be. The problem had been an accident, really. Thirty hours before their attack, Kibo's security system had malfunctioned. The entire security network had been quietly taken offline for repair, and it was impossible for Obi-Wan to test their attempts at a bypass. Worse still, there was no way to know when the system might come back online.

Perfect opportunity? Or perfect trap?

For half an hour Desert Wind had watched and waited and sweated before deciding to go on with the plan. So half of them entered the refinery while the others remained behind, hoping that when the alarm system switched itself back on it would not reveal their intrusion. Failing that, they hoped to disarm it completely.

Their plan might have worked, except that the plant security wasn't testing the old alarm system at all. The power station staff were installing a completely *new* system, one that did not show up on any of the plans provided by the ever-bribable Trillot.

Obi-Wan had walked directly into an unintentional trap.

"We're surrounded!" Thak Val Zsing hissed.

"No," Obi-Wan said calmly. Val Zsing stuck his head up and was immediately driven back by accurate blasterfire.

"We're pinned," Obi-Wan corrected, "but not surrounded. Right over there—" He pointed at a series of ceramic spirals near the main dome. "—heat extraction coils run boiling water to the turbines." He spoke as calmly as he could, but knew that his companions' patience would not last indefinitely. "Jangotat?"

Jangotat had been patiently watching his quadrant since the ambush was discovered, and now responded evenly. "Yes, sir?"

"I want you to draw them for me. I'll provide covering fire—" Jangotat knelt down as Obi-Wan traced in the dust with his fingertip.

The trooper grasped the implications instantly, but Thak

Val Zsing was still uncertain. "I don't understand," the old man said.

"Watch, and learn," Obi-Wan said. "But now we need covering fire."

"A *lot* of covering fire," Jangotat added. "Are you Jedi as good with blasters as you are with lightsabers?"

"Better," Obi-Wan joked. "We only use lightsabers to make fights more . . . equitable."

The ARC grinned. "Let's do it, then."

Obi-Wan chuckled to himself. Gaining a new name seemed to have given Jangotat more personality as well.

Obi-Wan and his forces began a flurry of counterblasting that temporarily tied down the guards crouching just beyond the dome. Taking that opportunity, Jangotat dashed out from the hiding place and, firing by instinct, managed to hit one of the security guards on the fly. A fatality. No way around it, now. Obi-Wan had known that this action might cost lives, but he'd allowed himself to hope—

His thoughts were interrupted as Jangotat dashed from the side and zigzagged across the wharf, drawing a blistering stream of fire. Blaster bolts ripped around his feet as Jangotat made a high, clean dive into the volcanic pit. Obi-Wan flinched. That water had to be *hot*!

As he had suspected, the forces pinning them down changed locations slightly to get a better view of the steaming surface. In that moment, Obi-Wan aimed carefully and blew a hole in the heat condenser coil.

Live steam billowed from the burst coil and the security men screamed, for a moment forgetting all plans and intentions. A good scalding could do that.

He glanced behind himself long enough to be certain that a speeder bike swooped in to fish Jangotat out to safety. Then Obi-Wan led the charge toward the disorganized security forces.

Forty meters separated them. If Obi-Wan could just steal a few seconds, aggression could compensate for superior numbers. One of the blind, scalded men turned his weapon on the charging intruders, too late to keep them from closing the gap.

One of the Desert Wind recruits went down hard, his chest transformed into a smoking husk. The clash was joined.

Obi-Wan's lightsaber flashed, and guards fell. Steam gushed from the damaged coil. While it stung his eyes, he was not nearly so close to it as those first men had been. That must have been brutal.

The air around Obi-Wan blurred with lightsaber slashes. Speeder bikes screamed in from above now, and Obi-Wan glimpsed Kit Fisto's speeder streak past as the Nautolan plunged into the fray, lightsaber flashing left and right, deflecting laser blasts and severing blasters at the barrel. Fortunate guards scrambled back to safety. Unfortunate ones fell clutching wounds, and a few would never move again.

They had been trapped, and tricked; disaster had been averted only because Jangotat had been willing to do *exactly* as ordered, even though those orders seemed insane. Disaster had been reversed, become a rout that might devolve into a slaughter if he didn't stop this. He waved the withdrawal signal to the Nautolan, and their troops went into retreat. They had done more damage than their original plan had called for. When the explosives detonated, this entire facility would be a splintered mass of rubble.

And yet, try as he might, he felt no pride at all.

Lives had been lost. The door to chaos had just been opened, and it stretched wider by the moment.

51

In the days since the Jedi had been expelled from ChikatLik, Desert Wind had destroyed three refineries, an energy facility, and a manufacturing plant.

And this, Duris knew, was only the beginning.

She didn't know where to turn. All she could do was issue security orders. Although they would be carried out without fail, she was no longer certain how much difference it would make.

Duris no longer knew who to trust. The Five Families constantly lied. It was their nature, fed to them along with their first food. Every few hours the Cestus map sprouted another red blotch. And that meant that time was running out. Already, she knew, the Five Families were making their own plans. Either to find a way to remove her from office, or worse.

And the devil of it was that what she wanted most of all was to speak with Obi-Wan one more time. To ask him to explain. Perhaps if it had been just the two of them, that might have been possible. But now . . .

"Your orders, ma'am?" Shar Shar burbled.

"Keep gathering information, Shar Shar," she said. "And hope for a miracle."

On the most secretive of occasions, those executives known as the Five Families met in their most private facility, a bunker complex seventy kilometers south of ChikatLik. The bunker was officially called an "entertainment complex," and was complete with sufficient communications gear to

monitor the entire planet, as well as enough food and water
to supply ten people for six months. The outer facility was
complete with a holoatrium, exercise and dining rooms, luxurious suites, and lounging areas. An inner room was even
more secure, with walls thick enough to resist even glazion
energy torches for a standard day.

Despite her relation to the X'Ting clan, Trillot had never
before entered the bunker, and doubted she ever would
again. At the moment she was hosted by her distant cousin
Quill, who owed her favors. Still, nervousness hung in the air
like a pall of smoke. The ambience did not improve when,
from a darkened corridor, a tall shaven-headed woman entered the room, the pale skin at her temples scribed with tattoos. Ventress wore a skintight suit of black Sullust leather
that emphasized the disturbingly boneless quality of her
movement.

Trillot stood to make the introductions. "I present to you
Asajj Ventress."

Those present stood politely. Then they sat again and
awaited her comments.

"I am Commander Asajj Ventress." Her tattooed scalp
held their eyes as if the static inkings were animated. "I represent Count Dooku. Our new venture, the JK droids, will
give you wealth and power beyond limit. But make no mistake: my master has greater concern than profit. If you conduct fair trade, you will be rewarded." The representatives
whispered to each other, nodding enthusiastically, and Ventress had to raise her voice slightly to get their attention
again. "Attempt to deal with this as mere commerce," she
warned, "and you will die to regret it."

Dame Por'Ten raised a thin, blue-veined hand. "No need
for such talk, Commander. There may have been some confusion recently, but with the . . . *departure* of Obi-Wan Kenobi,
I can assure you we are back on track."

Ventress inclined her head. "Well then," she said, her lips
curled in a cold smile. "Let's discuss particulars."

There was a bit of polite agreement before someone had

the honesty to actually speak her mind. "What is it you request?"

Ventress focused her gaze upon the speaker, then dropped her eyes politely. "That you continue to serve your best interests."

The answer seemed to please them. "And what might those be?"

Ventress raised her eyes. They burned like coals. "Survival. And you would *not* be alive, any of you, if you had yielded to the Jedi. Now then, I know at least one escape capsule survived. I believe both Kenobi and his allies are still alive. I *feel* it. They will attempt to disrupt our commerce."

Lady Por'Ten recoiled before Ventress's ferocity. "Wha-what should we do?"

The slightest of smiles curled those thin lips. "Obey me," Ventress said. "And provide me with your data, data you can project on a map."

"Why?"

Her eyes hardened. "Do not ask for answers that you cannot understand," she said. "Let us merely say I intend to prove Kenobi my inferior. His lies are my reality."

All the data had been gathered and then input to the computers. It included every sighting, every act of sabotage, everything that was known, including the escape pod's disappearance.

Everything.

Asajj Ventress walked through the midst of the projection field, eyes closed and fingers outstretched, resembling a blind girl mapping an unfamiliar room.

Or so it might have seemed to one of mundane mind. To others, she seemed a strange and terrible siren wandering through a sea of living energy, gliding along lines of intention.

Trillot thought Ventress the most beautiful, frightening sight she had ever beheld.

Finally, Ventress turned and faced them. Her hand stretched

out, one quavering finger touching a point in the midst of all the glowing lines. "Here," she said. "They are in *this* place."

"Are you certain?" Lady Por'Ten asked. "You can be so sure of their location?"

The others held their breath, not wishing to contemplate the potential danger of questioning this woman in any way, shape, or form.

Her chest heaved slowly as she replied. "You of the Family are dead to the Force. But Obi-Wan. Yes . . . he is alive with it. He and . . . yes . . ." She closed her eyes. "One other." She inhaled, as if scenting something in the air. "The Nautolan. Yes. He is Jedi, too. I feel it. I can feel their ripples in the Force."

She smiled at them. "If you see ripples in water, do you not know where the stone was dropped? If these maps and this information are good, my analysis will be true."

As Ventress spoke with the others, Trillot felt the pressure mount. If this operation failed, the gang lady might bear the brunt of anger from both sides. But if she succeeded . . .

Quill leaned close to her. "You have done well. Continue your support, cousin. If the Five Families profit, you will be rewarded beyond your dreams."

"My dreams are quite expansive," Trillot said, turning to look at them. "What is it you offer?"

"For three hundred years," Quill said, circling Trillot seductively, "there have been Five Families. Mining, fabrication, sales and distribution, research, and energy. But mining has always understood that labor was an integral part of our process."

"So?"

"So . . . after Duris is dead, there will be room in the hive council for Trillot."

Trillot's eyes glowed.

"Think of it. Your grubs would no longer crawl in the shadows."

"Invited to the balls?"

Quill smiled. "Dining at the head table. Trillot, my friend. My sister. It is high time for you and your family to emerge from the darkness and take your rightful place."

Quill had found Trillot's weakness. "What must I do?" she said.

Ventress watched it all without speaking. Her hands were still outstretched, as if she could feed through her fingertips. Trillot had heard that Obi-Wan Kenobi had faked a fantastic demonstration only days before. Could Ventress actually do such an incredible thing? And if she could, did that not imply that she was superior to the Jedi . . . ?

"Remember who is your friend and ally in these matters. Not Duris, certainly."

"No."

"Nor Kenobi," he said quietly, glancing to be certain their deadly ally was out of hearing, "who uses our planet as a pawn on the galactic game board."

"Yes." Trillot was shaking.

"Do you fear Kenobi?"

Trillot nodded.

"Do not. Our ally, the great Asajj Ventress, will destroy him. You must supply her with whatever she asks, whenever she asks, without question. Kenobi may still trust you, and come to you for help. If he does, you must act without hesitation. The moment will come, and when it does, you may emerge into the sun."

"We must act," Ventress said, turning to them.

"What have you in mind?" Lady Por'Ten asked.

Ventress stalked the chamber almost as if she were oblivious to the others. "I have in mind a test for your JK droids."

The members of the Five Families glanced at each other nervously. "They are not lethal until their Gabonna crystals are replaced, ma'am."

"No matter. Captives can be profitably questioned. But one other thing is necessary: months ago Count Dooku designed and ordered special infiltration droids. According to your reports these droids are complete, and ready for testing."

"Yes, that is correct," one of the technicians agreed.

"Then they, and the JKs together, will follow my commands," Ventress said, and she smiled. And that smile was so unfeeling that it made a snarl look warm and welcoming in comparison.

52

They were not alive, but they crawled through the darkness. They had no minds, but dreamed of death. They had no bodily needs, yet were ravenously hungry.

At the moment the four droids in the lead were little more than clear sacs of jelly. Dull lights embedded in their semi-solid bodies revealed clumps of metallic shapes suspended within.

Those in the rear were more solid, golden, hourglass-shaped droids. Their small, pointed legs crawled easily along the path blazed by their larger brothers. JKs.

The four infiltration droids used their indeterminate shape to squeeze through the smallest passageways, finding purchase wherever they could, then taking whatever shape best served their needs. Laser nodes along their surfaces scalded the rock, melting it and grinding it to widen the passageway.

For kilometers they traveled like this, becoming more solid when they needed to push an obstruction aside, more fluid when they needed to explore, making the way for the JKs.

The lethal procession whispered beneath the ground, below every sensor, beneath any potential observer. And they traveled in near silence. When they met an obstacle they burrowed or burned through it.

One meter at a time, they simply approached their prey. Without fatigue or trepidation, without mercy or living intent they moved forward, motivated by nothing save a programmed appetite.

One that would shortly be satisfied.

53

For hundreds of years the Dashta Mountains' deep shadows had provided protection for smugglers, runaways, thieves, political malcontents, and young sweethearts. No one knew all the paths that led into the chambers, and likely enough no one ever would. Therefore it was the depths of the caves themselves that were selected as the best place for a celebration.

After all, the initial strategy may have gone awry, but their secondary plans had gone swimmingly. If the Jedi regretted the loss of life, the rejuvenated forces of Desert Wind felt that they had finally struck a telling blow against the Five Families.

After six of those raids, Sirty's communications skills combined with Doolb Snoil's phenomenal mind for research, tapping into ChikatLik's holovid network to extract a vital and telling piece of data: droid production had dropped by more than 30 percent. If they could but maintain the current pace of action, the Five Families and the government would be forced to the bargaining table, where all desires could be met.

And while Obi-Wan wasn't nearly so certain that their current course would indeed take them to the desired land of plenty, there had been much violent action, many hairbreadth escapes, and three lost comrades to honor. Tensions were building to a killing point, and a bit of celebration would do them good.

So the revel had been building for hours, guards posted at the cave mouth. While alert status remained high, Desert

Wind's heightened appetites were simultaneously slaked with food, drink, games, bragging and boasting, and dancing.

Resta Shug Hai spent most of her time by herself, sipping mead, a drink that had similar effects on human and Cestian. Since the very first days of training she had been an outsider, the lone X'Ting among human recruits. The barrier had gone both ways: after a lifetime of fighting for her land and identity, there was little love lost for the offworlders. Even as the troops began to enjoy victories, and the normal camaraderie bound them all together more tightly, she had remained somewhat apart. But she finally stepped forward, swaying slightly as if her tongue had been loosened by the mead. "I sing song," she said.

Doolb Snoil happily clapped his chubby hands together, cheering her on.

"X'Ting songs like Thak Val Zsing's history lessons," she explained. "Every clan have own song. Tell people's story. When song die, people die. Resta last to know her clan song."

And she sang it. Obi-Wan didn't speak the language, but he didn't need to. He understood the emotions behind the alien words. And if emotion held true, the song spoke of courage, and toil, of love and hope and dreams.

What struck Obi-Wan most was her evident pride and courage. If Resta and G'Mai Duris were typical of their people, the X'Ting were incredibly strong folk. Despite the plagues, despite their lands being stolen from under them, despite no external evidence at all, they dreamed on.

When she finished, the rock walls rang with applause.

Jangotat made his rounds of the outer caves, taking a few moments to speak to each of his brothers, all of whom declined intoxicants. Then he checked in with the recruits who were taking guard positions among the rocks or monitoring the scanners. No matter how well hidden they believed themselves to be, it was inevitable that eventually their lair would be discovered. Still, considering that the mountains themselves could shield them from enemy bombardment, it would take hours for enemy troops to ascend the slopes under fire, and all rear exits were either well guarded or sealed off.

In the world of field operations, this was about as secure as life could get.

Making his third rounds, a sense of ease descended over Jangotat. General Kenobi's initial plot had failed, but this new operation seemed to be working fine: breaking energy lines, crippling water plants, and looting payrolls for their growing war chest. The local troops had performed well under pressure.

Unknown enemies had doomed their initial ruse. Jangotat now considered the entire world of diplomatic subterfuge unfit for a soldier, or, he now believed, those strange and fascinating creatures called Jedi. Odd. He thought of the Jedi not merely with respect, but with the sort of fraternalism ordinarily reserved for members of the GAR. In the unchanging order of things they were high above him, but were fighters, leaders extraordinaire. The most recent adventure proved that perfection eluded them, as it did all beings. Even diving into the scalding water had been only a temporary, if intense, pain. A liberal application of synthflesh from their first-aid kits had covered wounds and reduced redness and swelling in a few hours.

Most important, they had won.

Jangotat found himself entering a state of contentment rarely experienced by one of his station. He was fulfilling his primary function, enjoying an opportunity to learn from two superlative teachers. There were other . . . interesting factors as well.

He cast about, hoping to find Sheeka Tull, but did not. Doubtless she was ferrying in another load of supplies. The thought gave him a warm feeling.

In the last moments before he lost his honor, old Thak Val Zsing was thankful and content. For years he had struggled to bring advantage to his people, and those hard times had taken their toll even before the last few disastrous years, when betrayals and murderously ruthless security reprisals had reduced Desert Wind to a shadow of its former strength.

But despite his early reservations, it looked as if the Jedi were actually the answer to his prayers; perhaps his grandchildren would not have to eat the dust for as many long, painful years as had Val Zsing before them.

He had watched the revelry, noted with sober approval that the two Jedi maintained a slight and leaderly aloofness from the proceedings, polite but not intrusive.

These Jedi were responsible and respectful. Strange, all of 'em. The human, the clones, the Nautolan . . . and that Vippit was the strangest. All fluttery fear when the retrieval team found his capsule, but as soon as they'd brought the mollusk into camp, he'd instantly found work coordinating intelligence. Sharp as a laser scalpel, that one.

In the final analysis, Thak Val Zsing had lost leadership of Desert Wind, but was winning the war. Not a bad trade. Not a bad final chapter in the long, strange life of a murderer's great-grandson, a history teacher turned miner and anarchist leader.

So Thak Val Zsing found himself a fine bottle of Chandrilan brandy and wandered back to one of the rear caves to enjoy it—a taste of a homeworld he might never see again. There were only two things that Thak Val Zsing enjoyed: fighting and drinking.

The bottle was three-quarters empty when he momentarily blacked out, leaning back against the cave wall to watch the stalactites spin. And spin they did, in a happy blur that made him cry out in pleasure as he finished the bottle. He was down to the dregs, sliding down a warm dark tunnel toward blissful slumber, when he heard a cracking sound. Another. Then the ground beneath him began to heave.

He looked at it curiously, finding it amusing. Distantly, the tinkle and burr of dance music echoed through the caves. Although he could not hear the happy voices, Val Zsing knew that they were there. He could feel it: after an uncertain start, with the Jedi attempting to pull off some kind of elaborate con operation, the plan was back on track, with the program of harassment and sabotage that Desert Wind had begun so long ago. And now it would succeed.

He was basking in that thought when the cracking sound came again. Thak Val Zsing rolled over onto his hard round belly so that the cave was right-side up again, and blinked his bleary eyes.

A rock rolled to the side, revealing a fissure in the ground. Perhaps it was one of the myriad micro-tunnels running through every bit of these mountains. Most were too small for a human, so there was no need to be concerned about the safety. What was this, then, some kind of volcanic activity? Perhaps a burrowing male chitlik . . . ?

And then the first shadowed, amorphous shape emerged.

The four plastidroids and their JK companions had traveled a hundred kilometers at an average rate of just under ten kilometers per hour. It had taken them half a day to reach their target. Tirelessly they crawled through the dusty tunnels, edging toward their prey. The droids did not always travel in a straight line: when tunnels branched, some of them took alternate paths, either burrowing or climbing back to maintain a rough sense of direction. When they reached an obstacle that they could not easily push or burrow through, they backed up and went around. When the sensors at their surface detected the sounds of music, they began to converge, all of the fractally mapped alternative pathways canceled. Machines could not sigh with relief, but one prone to fancy might have attributed a certain eagerness to the manner in which they seemed to accelerate as they emerged from the cave floor.

The plastoid infiltration droid pushed its way through, melting and crushing rock as it went. Then a second, third, and fourth followed it.

After them appeared the JKs, until all hunched quivering in that empty cave—empty save for a single intoxicated human who watched dazedly, assuming that the drink that dulled his pain had also clouded his sight with hallucinations.

The four plastidroids looked like gigantic protozoans, studded with shadowy mechanical puzzle pieces in place of nuclei or organelles. Once reaching the desired destination, magnetically encoded pieces suspended within each bag wormed their way toward each other and began snapping together. Slowly, as the lengths of metal and plastine found each other, the newly formed limbs created nightmarish silhouettes beneath the transluscent skins, stretching them.

The JKs seemed to watch as the four bags of plastine and metal heaved and quivered. In turn, each was distorted by the assembling metallic pieces within it, until there stood not four amorphous shapes but four fully formed infiltrator droids, treaded monstrosities as tall as three humans with heavy armored bodies and long, flexible necks.

Thak Val Zsing watched, not understanding what he was seeing, laughing at the hallucination's oddness. Intoxication had caused stranger visions in the past, but not many. It was all terribly amusing. He continued to chuckle until the first infiltrator machine was almost completely formed. Its outline, suddenly and horribly familiar, began to resemble that of a killer droid that had shattered a mining union strike five years earlier.

That outline burned its way through the chemical fog, the realization that death had just, impossibly, oozed up from the very ground below him. He stood and staggered back against the wall. Then a moment came when he realized that he was wrong, that what he saw was no hallucination at all, but something real and appalling.

There are defining moments in a being's life, moments when actions are taken—or not taken. Once done, certain things cannot be undone. Thak Val Zsing was drunk, so perhaps he could be excused. He was also old, and the veteran of more Desert Wind raids than he could count. Perhaps life gave every person a specific allotment of nerve, and when that allotment was expended, there was simply no more.

Until the end of his days, Thak Val Zsing struggled to explain, to himself if not others, why he did nothing except crawl back beneath a shelf of rock. And there he trembled, sobbing his fear and misery.

And did not raise the alarm that would have turned the murder machines' attention to him.

It is a choice no one should have to make: to save life, at the cost of the soul.

As the JKs waited patiently, lubricant drained from the plastine skins still tightly stretched over the now fully assembled bodies of the infiltrators. One at a time, the skins stretched around the metal frames, then ruptured, like birth membranes rupturing around metal infants.

The JKs sniffed the air like living things, as if hungry to fulfill their function.

And in their mechanical way, perhaps they were.

54

Kit Fisto leaned back against the uneven rock wall, his tentacles twitching in sympathetic rhythm with the music. Although his face did not change, he was amused to find himself responding to these primitive melodies. Like most Jedi, Kit had been raised not on his homeworld, but in the halls of the Temple. However, to amuse himself, he had made a study of Glee Anselm's customs, becoming especially fond of its music. On Glee Anselm, no one would be gauche enough to play songs with less than three different rhythms, and far more complex melodies than this. Still, there was something attractive about it, and he finally raised a hand and said: "Hold! I would join you."

The musicians paused, surprised that the normally taciturn Nautolan had spoken, let alone that he wished to participate. Nervously, they offered the various instruments at their disposal. Kit scanned them before choosing one that combined string and wind. "This will suffice."

He noted that Obi-Wan and Doolb Snoil were watching and decided to make a special effort. Obi-Wan had proven himself one of the ablest warriors of Kit Fisto's experience. And while some might have considered it an unworthy urge, he wished to impress his companion with his native music.

So, taking the instrument in hand, he began to blow and strum simultaneously, each action reinforcing the other. It took him a few moments to find his way, and despite his extreme dexterity there were notes that he could not hit, chords that he could not play. It mattered not. As had his forebears, Kit had mastered the art of performing music underwater, and although he was comfortable in the air, sound took on a different character when transmitted through the thinner medium. Adjustments had to be made, and his nimble mind and fingers made them within moments. As his tones grew smoother and more pleasuring, the other musicians began to accompany him on string and wind instruments. Then voices crooned in wordless song, in a fashion that almost made him homesick. Despite the aridity of their world, these Cestians were a good lot.

Then came the ultimate compliment: some of the more daring attendees rose and actually began to dance. At first they had difficulty finding the beat and rhythm. With Nautolan music it was more important to listen to the pauses *between* notes than to the notes themselves, which were sustained in irregular bits. They seemed to find their groove, and were beginning to really enjoy themselves. Snoil's long, fleshy neck traced the beat in the air, his eyestalks keeping counterpoint.

Then Kit stiffened, his dark eyes narrowing before his conscious mind comprehended the threat.

The rough cavern floor trembled, as if sections of the mountain had wrenched their way free and now crawled toward them in the darkness.

A bearded miner from the Clandes region sprinted out of the back caves. "We're invaded!" came a scream. Then a light flashed, and the miner hit the ground like a bag of smoking rags, no longer screaming at all.

"What in space is that?" Skot OnSon yelled, shoulder-length blond hair flagging.

"This shouldn't be possible," Fisto said, surprise momentarily fixing him in his tracks.

Something appeared in the passageway leading to the back caves. Its neck was serpentine but mechanical, supporting a head that was both weapon and sensory probe. The body it was attached to was as tall as two humans at the shoulder, but composed of more individual pieces than he would have thought possible for something of its size, almost as if it were constructed from baubles found in a child's toy chest. It rolled on treads. A thin sheaf of plastine was stretched about the frame, and his mind searched frantically, some part of him sure he already knew what this thing was.

Whirring around its feet were one . . . two . . . three . . . four of the golden JK droids.

"Run!" Skot cried. That single word accomplished what the appearance of horror had not: spurred them into action.

Revelers fled toward the exit. The general chaos spoiled the sight lines for targeting, made the soldiers of Desert Wind fear to fire for risk of hitting their own people. The infiltration droid's blaster fired again, catching two more Desert Wind fighters.

When the soldiers tried to help their friends, the smaller JKs swooped in. They could not be stopped, reasoned with, blasted, or evaded. Shock tentacles, electrified netting, stun darts, and blaster bolts erupted with dizzying variety.

It was impossible to predict their moves, or escape them. The JKs restrained and cocooned one miner after another, moving on to their next victim with mechanical dispassion.

"What *are* they?" Skot screamed, fleeing toward the entrance. "It's not possible!"

Kit raised his lightsaber, triggering its emerald blade. His every nerve tingled. Obi-Wan had been right. From the very beginning this entire operation had been a disaster.

"Not possible? No one told *them*!" Sirty yelled tightly. The battlefield sarcasm disappeared almost as swiftly as it had blossomed. "What do we do, sir?"

Kit looked around quickly, trying to spy Obi-Wan. If the other Jedi was in a good position, it was possible—

No more time for thought. One of the droids had trapped a family of four at the edge of the pit. Its blaster tendril pivoted to face them.

"Cover me!" Kit called, and dashed out. He felt the tingle before the beam struck, and skittered aside. He weaved wildly, fiercely, Form I–style improvisation applied to pure evasion. He dodged and dashed, covering ground toward the crouching family with blistering speed.

Sizzling bolts missed him by bare centimeters. Where

they struck, rock shattered and smoked. He felt a brief, intense electric jolt as a bolt grazed his hip, splashing against the ground. The Nautolan had begun to dodge even before the beam arced in his direction. Kit thanked his Jedi skills, and knew that his only hope was to stay out of range. These were personal security droids: apparently the tactical chips hadn't been swapped. That would limit their effectiveness as instruments of aggresssion, but still . . .

Now he was close to the infiltration droid, and his lightsaber seared the air, slicing through the treads with a flash. The intruder droid staggered and toppled toward the others. Another droid was nicked but managed to stay erect as it pivoted to target Kit.

Finally, he located Obi-Wan. The Jedi had clung to the shadows, and approached the droids from the rear, grim and determined, two clones at his back. Their sidearms were inadequate to stop the invading machines, but proved excellent distraction. Obi-Wan was able to approach from another angle. His lightsaber flashed, slicing treads. As one of the droids fell to the ground, Obi-Wan closed the gap and slit its mechanical underbelly. Gears and plastine coils bulged out.

Oily smoke flooded the cave. Miners, troopers, and Jedi were engulfed in vile thin vapor. While not actually poisonous, the caves soon echoed with hacking and retching sounds. Through it all, the JKs captured one miner after another. Nothing stopped them. Nothing slowed them. They seemed to aim where a person would be in a moment, rather than where he or she was *now*. The infiltration droids had weaknesses, but the JKs seemed to have none at all.

Obi-Wan's senses tingled and he whirled barely in time to see one of the infiltration droids fixing him in its sights. There was no place, no time to move, only time to raise his lightsaber, awaiting the deadly flash.

With an eye-numbing blast, the droid was struck from the other side. It staggered, long enough for Obi-Wan to close the gap and sever its treads. The mechanical monster reared back and then fell sideways, crushing segments of stalactite as it did.

He looked over at the spot where the saving blasts had been launched—and saw Doolb Snoil waving back, stubby arms bracing one of the portable cannons against his shell.

Despite their desperate straits Obi-Wan could not repress a smile. After all this time, Snoil had repaid his debt to the Jedi several times over, even if it meant disobeying orders—

Then a *crack*ing sound drew his attention to the ceiling. One of the stalactites had been weakened when the droid reared up. It separated from the ceiling and began to fall. "Snoil!" Obi-Wan cried out, but it was already too late. The barrister looked up just as the rock spear hit his shell, lancing through the outer toughness into the vulnerable flesh beneath.

Within seconds Obi-Wan was at his side. As he cradled Snoil's heavy, fleshy head in his arms, the Vippit's rapidly declining body temperature confirmed Obi-Wan's worst fears. His friend was dying. Snoil's eyestalks weaved up toward him. "I did it, didn't I?"

"Yes, you did." Obi-Wan had never noticed the little flecks of color along Snoil's neck. They were bright green and blue against the browning flesh, and they were growing dull even as he watched.

"If there is any combat bonus, make certain that my broodmates receive full measure . . . and . . ." His stalk-tip eyes grew dim and glazed. "And see that it isn't taxed. The agreement we signed with the Republic, which my grandfather negotiated . . . ," he said proudly. He coughed a green bubble, and even before it burst he went still.

Obi-Wan laid Snoil's head gently on the ground. "A great barrister, from a great line," he said.

Then he returned to the fight.

Jangotat found himself trapped between a press of miners and an onrushing JK. Escape through the front cave seemed to be unimpeded, although instinct told him that enemy troops would be stationed in line of sight of the cave mouth, ready to pick off fleeing anarchists.

How had this disaster happened? General Kenobi had been correct: there was more here than met the eye.

Still, it was his duty to follow orders, and his inclination to protect unarmed and innocent civilians.

From a hiding point behind a massive stalagmite he fired at the droids again and again with his blaster rifle. The blue laser bolts sang off the outer casing, doing no damage. Resta and another Desert Wind fighter fired at it. The JK went at them, ensnaring the man in stun-cable as Resta sprang to the side with surprising agility.

Was that the only way to escape one of these demonic things? Sacrifice a friend?

A terrible crash shook the cave as another of the infiltration droids fell, and he took heart. The cave entrance rocked with another flash, followed by more screams. Bodies and wreckage flew back into the cavern, and smoke rolled. Screams and moans filtered out from beneath the rubble.

There. The trap had closed, and the pressure was crushing. "Side caves!" someone yelled. The miners, farmers, and soldiers of Desert Wind scrambled back and away from the main action. Jangotat stood with his back against the wall as the miners fled into the side cavern. This entire mountain was honeycombed with such tunnels. There was no way an enemy could cover all of them. Many of his compatriots could escape to fight again another day . . . he hoped.

Another droid toppled and fell. Was that the third infiltration droid down? How many remained? If the blasts from outside stopped, they might have a chance. But they didn't, and that meant they were dead in the water.

The sight of green fluid bubbling from Doolb Snoil's crushed shell triggered a deep, hot wave of regret. The barrister had been a true asset. In his own way, the Vippit had even displayed courage.

He glimpsed the Jedi, magnificent and fearless in battle, leading others by word and example. Glimpses were all he could catch: they moved so swiftly from one hiding place or

ambush spot to another, darting out to slash at a leg or protect an innocent farmer. His spirits soared. Perhaps—

Then to his dismay Jangotat spotted Sheeka Tull. When
had *she* entered the cave? Why hadn't he seen her? He knew
that he should leave the main cave with the others, but
Sheeka was cut off. She cowered behind a boulder, perhaps
uncertain where to go.

"Sheeka!" he called to her. In the tumult his voice could
not be heard. Only one thing to do—he dashed out and
grabbed her, pulling them both behind a boulder as the last
infiltration droid blasted in his direction. He heard himself
scream, watched the world turn white, and then all sight and
sound and sensation died away to darkness.

55

Sheeka Tull had argued with herself about coming to the celebration, not entirely comfortable with the deepening of her relationship with the clone trooper she now called Jangotat. It was all too possible that if she went to the camp, their relationship would grow more entangling still. But despite her misgivings she had gone, and now she was both horrified and glad of her decision.

The unexpected droid intrusion had overwhelmed her. She still shook almost uncontrollably. The droids were creatures of nightmare, and she felt her mind trying to shut down on her, attempting to surrender consciousness to save her the horror of painful death. Her feet froze to the ground as the giant droid locked its sights upon her. Her wind *whuff*ed out of her as something collided with her from the right side, and she was pulled down behind a boulder by none other than Jangotat himself. There was no doubt but that he had risked his life to save hers, shielding her body with his own. When a blaster chipped rock behind her it grazed Jangotat: his face contorted in agony and he bit through his own lip. His clothes peeled away in smoking scraps, exposing a badly scalded back. He rolled off her, unconscious, shirt and pants smoking. Dead?

No. She checked. Merely stunned. Even half conscious, Jangotat's hands cast about, as if searching for his rifle. She found it and placed it in his palms. His fingers curled around it, and he trembled, as if trying to awaken himself.

As if war was all he knew, or ever could know.

The yelling and screaming intensified to a ghastly peak,

then died away. Another wall-shaking explosion followed, but she risked a peek.

Several of the recruits were engaged in heroic combat against a killer droid tall enough to graze the ceiling. Their combined blasts actually drove it back a step. To her left, a golden hourglass-shaped droid absorbed a similar volley with little apparent effect, tentacles casting about and bringing down one miner after another.

The side caves still looked clear. She dragged Jangotat over in their direction and was met halfway by a tall, thin, blond miner, Skot OnSon. She barely knew him. Yesterday he was a boy. Now his eyes were an old man's.

"Can I help you get him out of here?" OnSon asked her, keeping one eye on the battle. The air was rent with eye-searing energy bolts.

"Okay."

OnSon's calm facade seemed to crack a bit. Was it the sight of Jangotat's seared face? Was that what had unnerved the boy, even as he struggled to find courage? Or was he using this excuse to get out of the charnel house?

Together they pulled Jangotat toward safety and darkness. The tunnels behind them flashed with light. Screams echoed in the caves, even as they lost themselves in the labyrinthine twists and turns of the side tunnels, winding their way toward a dubious safety.

56

Obi-Wan led a group of six refugees into a side cave, shepherding them across the uneven floor through the darkness. Behind them, he heard the clank of a pursuing droid. His group had only three blasters. Two of its members were children. If they were lucky, the cave would narrow, such that the larger droids couldn't pursue. Would one of the JKs spot them? If it did, they were most likely dead.

He brushed past webbing as he ran. Old? New? A few hand-size winged reptiles were suspended in one of them, and he remembered something that Kit had told him about the ARC's first day in the caves. What was that?

"Gen' Kenobi!" Resta called, jerking him out of his desperate memory scan. It took only a moment to see the threat: the cave had indeed narrowed, and blocking the exit were four gigantic cave spiders, staring at them with glowing red eyes.

How could he have forgotten! Kit may have driven the spiders out of the main caves, kept them away with sensors and proximity mines, but in fleeing, these unlucky humans had jumped from the griddle to the grave.

The spiders hissed, and Obi-Wan triggered his lightsaber. Spiders ahead. Droids behind. They were trapped, and perhaps all he could do now was sell his life dearly . . .

Then he realized that *the spiders weren't hissing at them. No.* They were hissing at the approaching JK droid, and he understood why. It was behaving as it had in the arena, half a lifetime ago: dividing into segments that then gripped the ground like the limbs of a thick-legged, small-bodied spider. Perhaps they'd watched a JK cast a web at a fleeing human, and must have thought the droids to be some strange kind of arachnid, more natural competition than the offworlders.

The arachnid defense of their territory was automatic and devastating.

And the JKs seemed to accept the challenge. They cast tentacles, stunning several spiders, but others shot silk in cascades as the offworlders retreated to the shadows.

It was one of the most bizarre spectacles Obi-Wan had ever seen. The spiders could not stop the JK, but they could slow it with their silk, and by swarming it with smaller spiders. The air clouded with silk and stunned, smoking spiders but they came on and on. Obi-Wan managed to get his people out, but turned to watch the spiders as they made their stand.

The JK fired, pumping juice into the spiders until . . .

It's running out of power! Obi-Wan realized. It had probably defeated the equivilent of a hundred warriors, but was running out of power! Now the spiders rained more silk on it, and Obi-Wan screamed to his people to fire at the stalactites above the JK, burying it in rock and sticky strands. Even then, the JK trembled against the rock. Exhausted but refusing to give up, still trying to reach its enemies.

Unbelievable.

Obi-Wan faced the cave spider clan. An immense red female stepped slowly forward, sheltering her young. Obi-Wan and the female stared at each other, and in her eyes he saw awareness. They were not friends, not allies, but had faced a common enemy.

The matron bent her forward legs, bowing. Obi-Wan raised his lightsaber in salute. The matron backed away into the shadows with her brood.

"You're letting them go?" one of the farmers breathed.

"We're letting each other go," he corrected. "No favors. Just respect." The shadows had claimed the spider clan. One day soon the offworlders would be gone, and the caves would belong to the spiders. What then? Was there any way for the eight-legged folk to ever walk in the sun again?

Perhaps. There might be a way to finesse such an outcome. First, of course, he had to survive.

"Come on," he said. "We've got to find a way out."

57

Navigating twisting side tunnels, it took another exhausting hour for Sheeka to make her way back to the surface. For the first ten minutes, they heard distant explosions and screams. Then . . . nothing. The golden-haired young miner stayed with her the entire time, but as soon as he saw that she was in the clear, OnSon said, "I've got to go back."

"No." She clutched at his arm. "You'll be killed."

"Maybe. Maybe." OnSon examined the wounded clone. "Take care of him. He fought well." And he disappeared back down the tunnel.

Sheeka wiped her face, gritty with the rock dust that seemed to have ground its way into her body's every crevice. It took her a few moments to orient herself. She was on the far side of the ridge. Good. This was where she had hidden *Spindragon*. An arc of light split the southern sky—the cave battle was continuing. The distant thunder of security assault ships filled her ears.

In the depths of those caves, sheer chaos had clawed its way into the living world. For a moment she was torn. Was there anything she could do? Were her friends being maimed and slaughtered, friends who might survive if she went to their aid? Then Jangotat groaned, and all options were reduced to one: find the trooper medical assistance immediately. Get help for the man who had protected her at the cost of his own flesh. She dragged him down over the rocks. Jangotat was semiconscious now. He shuddered with pain for a few minutes, and then fumbled with something at his belt. Almost immediately, his body relaxed. She panicked as he became a deadweight, but when he began to struggle to his feet she figured he had self-administered some kind of pain-killer that left him dreamy but still able to walk.

She supported his shoulder, trying not to touch any of the spots seared by the droid's blast. He stumbled along beside her, knees buckling and ankles turning. Then he began to carry some of his own weight, and for that she was grateful.

They stumbled down the side of the defile. There, hidden in a maze of shadows, was *Spindragon*. Although by now the muscles in her legs and back screamed for release, Sheeka ignored them and hauled Jangotat toward the ship, and safety.

"Leave . . . me . . . ," she heard him whisper, and it alarmed her that some part of her silently agreed, wanted to give up. But Sheevis Tull, the same man who had taught her to fly, had taught her to ignore the weak and traitorous voices in her head. She disregarded them and bent to the task at hand. *Breathe, pull, rest. Breathe, pull, rest . . .*

She lost count of the cycles of pulling and breathing, but a moment came when *Spindragon*'s autopilot sensed her proximity and automatically extended the ramp, a sensible, albeit costly modification. She climbed up the incline, Jangotat gripping at her with a weakening hand. With every minor jolt, he grunted as if the pain stripped his nerves raw.

A few more staggering steps brought them into the ship's interior. Sheeka loaded Jangotat into a crash seat, and initi-ated the ship's warm-up sequence.

"Don't worry," she called back to him. "We're getting out of here."

He seemed to smile at her weakly, and made a closed-fist gesture she had seen him make to other clones. She thought that it meant "good to go." Gritting her teeth, Sheeka turned back to her controls. She would have to deal with him, of course, but the first task was to get out of the mountains in one piece.

Her scanners indicated that a quartet of enemy ships was sweeping toward her from the north. Time to move.

All systems flushed and ready, Sheeka started her engines

and lifted *Spindragon* from the ground, whirling her in place as the first of the pursuit ships appeared over the broken stone horizon.

Their intentions were announced with the first bolt that sizzled in her direction, striking sparks and splashing slag from the rocks.

Her face tightened in a fighting snarl: the daughter of Sheevis Tull was not so easily killed. She had made low-altitude runs through the mountain passes more times than she wanted to remember, every one of them wickedly dangerous. Always in the past she had risked arrest, imprisonment, revocation of her flying privileges. This was different. This time, it was life and death.

Without further delay, Sheeka accelerated her ship toward the south, scrambling her transponder beacon so that it would broadcast no identifying signals. Now the only thing she had to worry about was being shot down in a blazing fireball.

Of course, that was a pretty big *only.*

If only she had armament! But *Spindragon* went in and out of cities too frequently, was scanned on a weekly basis. The Five Families were terrified of another uprising, and forbade suborbital craft from carrying mounted weapons.

The pursuit craft were two-person security units, built for long-range recon and pursuit of . . . well, of suborbital ships like hers. All muscle and brain. But it just might be possible to meet their challenge . . .

Unlike her pursuers, Sheeka Tull knew the mines.

She rose up, flipped, and dived into an opening that was little more than an angry gash in the desert floor. With stomach-wrenching speed she dropped straight down. At the last moment she straightened out, making a sharp right turn.

The security ships were only seconds behind her. Her task was to get far enough ahead of them to break visual contact. The heavy mineral deposits would reduce scanner efficiency. Given that, there was an excellent chance they'd be confused by the tunnels, and confusion shifted the odds in her favor.

But first—

A flash bright enough to stun the eye washed the tunnel from wall to wall. Sheeka screamed and threw a hand in front of her face in a reflexive motion that almost cost her her pitch and yawl control. She spun *Spindragon* sideways to slip between two enormous underground pillars, then zipped around a corner and sank to the cave floor swiftly, killing all lights.

She could hear them, but they could not hear her. Distant searchlights splashed around the broken rock walls as they slowed to a crawl.

"Where . . . are we?" Jangotat gasped.

Sheeka slipped out of her captain's chair and walked quietly to him. "Shhh," she said. "They can find us with sound."

"That may be a problem," he gasped.

"Why?"

"Because I think I'm going to scream." Despite the pain his lips curled in a bitter, self-mocking smile. "I'm out of pain meds."

She wanted to hug him. Instead she said: "I think we'll make it. Hold on."

Sheeka had a few tricks up her sleeve, and one of them was specifically designed to misdirect scanners: a trick that would blind her and the pursuing security ships as well.

The difference was that she had been down here before, and they had not.

She hoped.

"I'm going to try something," she said. "If it doesn't work, then—"

"Try it," he said, and closed his eyes against another fit of shakes.

"For luck," she said. She bent and, wiping the blood from his chin, kissed him firmly on the lips. His eyes widened in pleased surprise, then she gave a crooked grin and went back to her captain's chair.

No way to prevent this next part from being dangerous. She could see a searchlight off in the distance, reflected between a pair of stalactites, and figured that this would be her best chance. Sheeka enriched the fuel mixture absurdly, until the unburned hydrocarbons gushed from *Spindragon*'s rear as dense, black smoke.

Within seconds the lights had turned in her direction, and she struggled against a surge of panic. Then she calmed her breathing and lifted off from the ground a meter or two—much more was impossible because of the low ceiling. But she moved. Yes . . . even without her running lights, the reflected illumination revealed a turn up ahead. It was just as she remembered. If only the rest of it conformed to memory as well . . .

She turned the corner just in time: a sizzling energy bolt slagged the wall just behind her. The passageway churned with dense, oily smoke. The pursuing ship slid past them, right through the murk, and collided with the wall in a flame-blossom that temporarily turned a smoky night into day.

Just as she thought: the ships were maneuverable and fast, but not well armored, and with no crash shields. The entire cavern glowed fiercely as the ship exploded.

Her chance. Spewing more smoke, Sheeka took the opportunity to cruise low, knowing that the other ships would home in on the destruction.

And there came one now, prowling like some kind of predator. Smoke belched from *Spindragon*'s rear as the engine labored on its absurdly rich mix, but she knew that the cloud was large enough to conceal her.

The approaching ship had twin beacons in the fore, so that it looked like some kind of lurking predator. An energy bolt ripped through the smoke and slammed against the wall, causing a rock slide she could hear and feel but not see. She tensed as another bolt sizzled by, but didn't move. The search ship was just questing about. It didn't know where she was.

But Sheeka did. Just barely, but she did. She lifted up and pivoted her ship about. She knew where another exit lay, and if she was careful, she just might make it.

Both front and rear viewscreens showed nothing as she crept away. Occasionally she caught the barest glimmer of a headlight, but then as she turned the corner once and then twice she left that behind and moved as quickly as she could toward the exit, trying not to think of the deadly search behind her, or wonder what had become of the Jedi and their proud plans.

58

Obi-Wan surveyed the small group of stragglers who had survived the cave slaughter. They huddled in a rocky defile, invisible to any ship overhead, but of course also invisible to other survivors or potential allies. If there were any who had not fled into the desert.

All in all, he estimated that half their force had been killed or captured, and most of the rest scattered. He did not look forward to making his next report to the Supreme Chancellor.

That, of course, assumed there would *be* another report.

He climbed back up to the top of the ridge without exposing himself to enemy fire, looking down to where they had left their new transport, a cargo craft purchased from a small farming community southwest of the capital.

The ship was now a smoking crater. Much of the communications gear, and their astromech unit . . . gone. Doolb Snoil . . . slain while heroically saving Obi-Wan's life. At least two clones had made it out—he did not know if there was a third. He had seen one ARC go down protecting the woman Tull, but no more than that.

Unless something changed drastically, this mission was shaping into the greatest disaster of his career.

Kit Fisto came up behind him. Although it was not in Kit's way to offer a comforting gesture, Obi-Wan knew his companion's hearts. Everything that could go wrong had gone wrong, but none of it had been the Nautolan's fault. Perhaps, just perhaps, it was not his fault, either. G'Mai Duris had warned him that sinister forces were at work. That they were never meant to succeed . . . could that be true? And if so, what did it mean?

"I do not understand." Kit said. "Each individual move we have made has been without stain."

Obi-Wan rotated those words in his mind, seeking to put the lie to them. To his sad relief, he could not. They had done everything right. "And yet we've been outmaneuvered at every turn," he said, finishing his thought aloud. "Almost as if we've been playing the wrong game all along."

All along. Obi-Wan remembered the moment in the throne room when he had pretended to locate the car by sensing its influence on the rest of the system. Well, he had only thought of that because of similar, less complex exercises taught long ago by Qui-Gon Jinn. He'd felt that same part of himself triggering, rising as from slumber. He needed to see something. To notice something. *Look at all the pieces. Which ones have been disturbed? What do you* not *see, as well as see? Not* sense, *as well as sense? Where should there have been a ripple where there was not? If something has caused each of your plans to disrupt . . . if someone attempted to kill you . . . was that Duris's way? And do any of the Five Families have the power to cause such catastrophe? And if they do not, then what possibility does that leave?*

"Obi-Wan?" Kit asked, and suddenly Obi-Wan realized that he had been staring trancelike into the distance. Kit was studying him, and worry creased the Nautolan's normally impassive face.

He whispered his reply. "There is another player. Another *major* participant in this tragedy, and has been from the beginning. Somewhere in all of this."

"But where?"

Obi-Wan shook his head. "I don't know. But I fear that before this is complete, we will know the answer to that question. And will wish we didn't."

One of the clones approached from behind him. He cursed his self-pity. If *he* was confused, how much more so were these poor creatures, raised since before birth to operate within an immutable chain of command? He had to shake off this malaise, be worthy of their trust.

"Your orders, sir?" Sirty asked.

"Collect the equipment," he said. "Round up the survivors. We're moving to the secondary location. I don't know who betrayed us. But this time, we keep the loop closed."

Sirty nodded tightly. "Very good, sir."

"Casualties?"

"Sixteen dead or captured that we know of, sir."

Obi-Wan noticed that a few more stragglers had joined them without attracting the hunters. Good. Where there was discipline, courage, and creativity, hope still remained. "Casualties?"

"Captain A-Nine-Eight, Nate, is missing and presumed dead."

That hit Obi-Wan hard. Strange. Hundreds of thousands of clones, all cut from the same cloth. And yet hearing about that particular trooper caused him a special pain, and he wasn't entirely certain why.

59

Sheeka Tull made very, very certain her pursuers were thrown off the track before continuing. She traveled south to the commercial air corridors, and then slipped along those, changing directions several times to be absolutely sure that *Spindragon* was not followed.

Once certain, she zigzagged 200 kilometers into a stretch of rolling brown mounds 180 klicks east of the Dashta Mountains. A river channeled snowmelt from the Yal-Noy's whitecapped peak to their north, so the hills were greener than much of Cestus's surface, pleasing to the eye even from a distance. Still, the water supply was adequate rather than generous, so the population remained relatively low.

Most called them the Zantay Hills. Sheeka Tull called them home. Sheeka went into a landing pattern, and breathed a sigh of relief as the engines slowed and stopped.

At first there was no sign of habitation. Then an X'Ting cloaked in a brown robe emerged from one of the metal buildings. As Sheeka Tull walked Jangotat down the ramp, he hailed her, the customary smile of greeting gone thin and tight.

"Brother Fate," she said.

"Sheeka," he said. His faceted eyes peered more carefully at the burned uniform, and the unhappy expression deepened. "Bringing this soldier here is *dangerous*."

Sheeka tightened her grip around Jangotat's waist. "He was injured in *our* cause. Help him, Brother Fate. Please."

The old gray-tufted X'Ting examined the wound, rubbing the singed cloth between his fingers. "Blaster?"

"What difference does that make?" she said urgently. "Help him!"

Brother Fate let out a long, slow sigh. His faceted emerald eyes were filled with pity. "For you, my child," he said, and then raised his voice to the others. Slowly, a few other people, and then a stream, emerged from their shelters and, smiling, approached.

Three children emerged, came running toward her, crying, *"Nana!"* and hugging her leather skirts.

"Tarl!" she cried, hugging the boy child. "Tonoté," the girl. "Where is Mithail?" One youngster hung back a bit, but then she gathered him into her arms and kissed his mop of unruly red hair. "How have you all been?" she asked. As she distributed hugs and kisses to them she watched from the corner of her eye while Jangotat was carted away by several X'Tings in dark cloaks.

"Who is the man?" Mithail, the youngest, asked.

"A friend," she replied, and then ruffled their hair. "A friend. Now. Tell me everything that's happened in the last week."

60

Groaning with pain, Jangotat pulled himself into wakefulness. Everything inside him hurt, which he found alarming. Was this how it felt to die?

He tried to open his eyes. He felt his lids slide up, but was still unable to see. Global pain combined with blindness triggered an unexpected and quite unwelcome panic response. He sat up, as he did so experiencing a tearing sensation in the skin along his waist. Agony forced an oath from his lips, and he thrashed his arms about, trying to discover the extent of his . . .

Prison?

"Now, now, calm down." A pleasant male X'Ting voice. "Everything is all right. It is imperative that you rest."

Absolutely nothing in that voice triggered any sense of threat, but Jangotat couldn't dampen his reaction. Danger flared over his entire nervous system, as if his every sense had triggered simultaneously. And yet . . .

And yet . . .

His conscious mind knew that he was *not* in danger. In the oddest paradox, the flood of pain and the sense of danger existed simultaneously with a sense of peace, and this he found confusing.

"What . . . what are you doing?" he gasped, alarmed at his own weakness as they took his arms gently. Tenderly, perhaps. He wanted to sink back into those sheltering, supporting arms and find peace and release. Wanted it so abruptly that the very depth of his desire frightened him. "Stop. I have to report—"

"You must heal," a familiar voice said.

It was the robed X'Ting who had met Sheeka outside her ship. Yes. The ship. He knew this creature. Where had Jangotat seen him before . . . ? "Who are you?"

"Call me Brother Fate," he said.

"Where is Sheeka?" Jangotat gasped.

"With her children," the robed X'Ting replied. A burr of other voices filled the room around him.

"Her . . . children?"

"Yes. She makes her home here, among us."

"Is this where her husband lived?"

"Yes." Brother Fate paused. "Before she left this last time, she asked us to take special care of her children. I believe she suspected herself to be in danger." The voice paused again. "It seems she was correct."

"Yes. But it was . . . in a good cause."

"Yes," the voice said. "So were they all."

"I have to go," Jangotat gasped. "Or at least report."

"Not yet. You will interrupt the healing process. You could die."

"The first duty of a trooper is to protect the safety of the whole. We live but a few days, the GAR lives on forever . . ." His mouth seemed to be moving without his mind being engaged, and in that automatic state he momentarily seemed his old, fierce self. Then his strength ebbed, and he sank back down again.

"Forever?" Brother Fate clucked. "You won't last an hour if you don't stay quiet and let me treat this wound."

Jangotat groaned. Then something minty and cool was pressed against his nose, and sleep claimed him.

Under ordinary circumstances, the only time Jangotat remembered his dreams was when sleep-learning vast quantities of tactical data. Then events in the external world might trigger the memory of an odd dream or two. Aside from that, nothing.

But then he'd spent his entire life surrounded by troopers and the tools of war. This place was different. This was all new and unknown. Here in this alien place the darkness swarmed with odd images: places he'd never been, people he'd never seen. It was all so strange, and even while sleeping he seemed to grasp its oddness.

Twice . . . perhaps three times he rose toward the surface of his mind like a cork bobbing up in an inky sea. Neither time could he see anything, but once he felt something, as if something heavy and oblong lay on his chest. When he began to move beneath it, it slithered away, and once again he slipped from consciousness.

Jangotat awakened from a dream of a rising sun, and once again felt a squishy, flat weight upon his chest, a resistence against inhalation. This time, his skin no longer felt tender. It was a rather gauzy feeling, if that made sense, as if he were filtering all sensation through some kind of thin filter.

But the weight was there. He moved his hand much more slowly this time, just a bare centimeter at a time.

Whatever lay on his chest pulsed more rapidly, but didn't move. His fingertips probed at a solid but gelatinous mass. Cool, but not cold. It felt rather like a piece of rubbery fruit. He moved his hands in both directions. It was about half a meter long, and . . .

But that was all the strength he had. His hands dropped away, arm gone numb. He tried to call out, to ask someone to remove the thing from his chest, but some instinct told him that it was this thing that kept the pain from searing his mind. So he said nothing and settled back again. Beneath the sheltering bandages his eyes closed, and then relaxed. There was nothing he could do right now. That much was true. So he could heal. *Would* heal, if such capacity remained.

Jangotat remembered the cave debacle. He remembered watching their recruits scattering, mowed down by the killer droids, captured by the JKs, or fleeing from the cave to be slain by enemy blasters.

Xutoo had perished in orbit. All right. And men and women who had trusted him died in the caves. And that meant there was a debt to repay. And troopers knew how to repay debts. Yes, that was one thing they understood quite well.

In the darkness, Jangotat's burned mouth twisted into a cold and lethal smile.

61

Jangotat flowed through endless cycles of sleep and wakefulness. Sometimes the cool, moist animal was on his chest, and sometimes not. Sometimes he heard voices and sometimes he didn't.

When he awakened hungry, Jangotat was fed some kind of fruity mushroom mash. The texture was vile and slippery but the taste was incredible, fresh, as if made by hand.

From time to time he was massaged, and afterward felt someone peeling dead flesh away from his back. The hands managing him were the softest and most caring he had ever known. He was alarmed to realize that there was a part of him that craved that, loved that, and wanted more if he could have it.

No. This is not my life. Not a trooper's life . . .

He could not be certain but it seemed days later when the last twist of gauze was finally unwrapped from his eyes. He reached up and gripped his nurse's wrist. A thin wrist, like a stick, really. He could have snapped the bone with a single wrench. By touch, he knew his caregiver to be a male X'Ting. *Brother Fate.* He heard breathing, but no words. "Where is Sheeka Tull?" he asked.

"Right here," she answered from nearby. He swore that he could hear the smile in her voice.

Layer upon layer of gauze was unwound, and as it was, light began to stream into his famished optic nerves. "We've turned the lights down. Your eyes may still be sensitive."

And so they were. When he opened them slowly, blinking hard, the light in the room struck like a physical blow.

He held up one hand in front of his eyes.

"Are you all right?"

He blinked and lowered his hand again.

As images began to resolve, he saw he was recuperating in another of Cestus's endless cave formations. Sheets and blankets covered the walls, and simple furnishings divided the floor space into living quarters. There was a fair amount of equipment that he didn't recognize but guessed to be medical materials of some kind. A makeshift hospital?

"Why did you bring me down here?" Jangotat asked.

The brown-robed ones glanced at each other in amusement.

"Who are you? Are you medics or mentops or something?"

"No, not exactly," Fate said. "It's a little hard to explain." Although he declined further explanation, Jangotat felt no harm from the X'Ting, and managed to relax.

"It's time for us to look at those wounds," he said. They helped Jangotat to a sitting position and peeled away the leaves that had been placed—

Leaves?

He hadn't looked more closely, merely felt them on his body. What he had assumed to be cloth was actually some kind of broad, pale, fleshy thin fungus.

They peeled the fungus away one sheaf at a time. They were dead, that much was certain. In peeling them away, a thin film of mushroom remained behind, clinging to his skin.

His skin . . .

The light in the room was dim, but there was enough to look down at his body. He remembered when the killer droid's blast struck him, searing away skin. He feared muscle and bone might be damaged as well. Looking at his body now, he saw a pale shininess between knee and hip, but nothing else to indicate that a burn had ever existed at all.

This . . . this is better than synthflesh, he thought, comparing the fungus to the healing compound included in ARC first-aid kits. This discovery would have to go in his report. To see such results from a healing chamber was one thing entirely. To see its equivalent achieved with a few leaves was simply astounding. This was X'Ting biotechnology? Certainly, on the galactic market these plants would be precious.

Nicos Fate was joined by a human male and an elderly X'Ting woman, and the three checked him from foot to follicle. Sheeka stood watching, and averted her eyes as they peeled the sheet back.

At least, he *thought* she turned her head.

Finally they seemed satisfied with the general trend of his healing, replaced the bed covers, and turned to Sheeka. "We've done what we can. Now it's up to you."

And the three physicians filed out of the room, leaving Sheeka and Jangotat behind.

For a long time Sheeka just looked at him, and then finally she sighed. "I've endangered these people by bringing you here."

With a groan, he pushed himself up to a seated position. "Then I should leave."

"It's not as simple as that," she said. "What you've brought to this planet can't be unbrought."

Jangotat frowned. "I'm sorry things seem to have turned out so badly."

"I thought," she said, "I really thought I might be able to avoid all this. That never again would I have to watch people I love die." Her face twisted with sudden sharp anger.

"You must hate me," he said. "I'm sorry."

Sheeka raised a reasoning hand. "I hate what you represent. I hate the purpose for which you were made. But you?" She paused before speaking again, and he filled that pause with a thousand hurtful comments. *I hate you most of all . . .*

But what she said was the one thing he would never have expected. "I pity you, Jangotat," she said. There was genuine compassion in her voice. He looked up at her wonderingly, barely comprehending her words at all.

*   *   *

A day later Sheeka and the insectile Brother Fate took him out of the cave. This was a simple community, although what exactly they traded in, he was not certain. Medicines, perhaps? They seemed to have a fungus for all occasions: some were tough enough for shoe leather; others said to be edible in a variety of tastes and textures. Brother Fate pointed out a dozen medicinal varieties. The cave fungi seemed the center of this village's activity. But was that all there was to this place? He sensed something more.

"Why are you here?" he asked Brother Fate.

"Everyone needs a hive," the X'Ting said.

"But . . . I'd heard X'Ting didn't mix much with offworlders."

"No," Brother Fate said. "Strange, is it not? G'Mai Duris is Regent, but the X'Ting are the lowest of the low."

"The offworlders did that to you, and you help them?"

He shrugged. "My ancestors were healers in the hive. Bring any injury to us, and we want to heal. It is our instinct, and there are no limits. Five hundred years of history doesn't change a million years of evolution."

Jangotat bore in, disbelieving. "You help your oppressors?"

Brother Fate smiled. "No one here ever oppressed me. Many here ran from Cestus Cybernetics, from the cities, looking for a better way. How are they different from X'Ting?"

If that was really Brother Fate's attitude, then there was hope for this planet after all. The X'Ting medications alone were a potential spice mine.

There was so much to see here, so much that didn't perfectly reflect his own worldview. There were many children in the community, so whatever this village was, it was no mere sterile medical enclave. No.

"I need to communicate to my men," he said to Sheeka on the first day he was able to walk outside. Well, more accurately, she and Brother Fate walked while he hobbled along between them. Children wound their way around them, laughing up at him, aware that he was an offworlder, certainly, but perhaps not completely understanding exactly what the term *offworlder* meant.

"I can't take the risk of a message being intercepted," she said. "But I'll figure something out."

Although his wounds were healing with abnormal speed, Jangotat's impatience burgeoned. This was not where he belonged. Not here in the mountains, where the air was clear and clean, the scenery lushly beautiful.

This was not where he belonged, although Sheeka's stepchildren Tonoté, Tarl, and Mithail asked him a thousand questions about the world outside Cestus: "What other planets have you been to?" "What's the Chancellor like?" "Have you ever seen a Podrace?" He found to his pleasure that he enjoyed answering them.

This was not his world, although two days after he arrived he was well enough to be taken to Sheeka's round, neat, thatch-roofed home.

And there in the house that her dead love Yander had built for her, he saw another side of the formidable pilot who had saved his life in the caves. Here he saw an aproned woman managing a houseful of happy children. She merrily produced great heaps of bread and vegetables and strange, fishy-tasting fungi. Jangotat liked his fresh steaks and chops—but had to admit that his belly groaned with satisfaction from the thick, chewy mushrooms alone.

He inquired about that, and little Mithail said: "The Guides tell us that—"

Sheeka's soft, warning smile was enough to get the child to be quiet, and Jangotat noticed that the conversation swiftly and sneakily was turned to other things, and he was coaxed into discussing battles and campaigns on far-off worlds. He was amused when childhood imagination transformed grinding fatigue and constant terror into something romantic and exciting.

He chuckled, and then let the amusement die, asking himself if he wouldn't have responded the same way, given the same life and the same stimuli.

And there at the table, his mouth filled with hot bread,

he watched the siblings' easy camaraderie. Not so different from his own brethren. Not every clone trooper joke, jest, trick, or game was somehow related to the arts of death.

Just 95 percent of them.

Here, there was also farming, and gathering, the setting of traps and the repulsion of predators. The entire community seemed to be enthralled with the very process of living. The intensity of the work seemed joyous, and he could appreciate that as well.

And he wondered . . . what would *he* have been here?

And the thought was so sudden, and so achingly strong that for a few moments he stopped chewing, eyes unfocused on the wall, thoughts previously unknown to him unreeling in his mind.

He turned and looked down at Sheeka's end of the table, and realized that he was sitting where her former husband might have sat, and that these might have been his children. Something very like a tide of sorrow washed over him, one swiftly stemmed, but real nonetheless . . .

This is not my world . . .

Jangotat was sleeping when Sheeka Tull entered the cave infirmary, and for this she was glad. Even with the healing fungus, his body had suffered terrible insult, needing constant monitoring and care to ensure that no infections set in.

She conferred quietly with Brother Fate, who reassured her that all would be well.

She left Brother Fate's little cubicle and went back to the sleeping area, looking down on Jangotat. He slept flat on his back, as Jango had. His brawny chest rose and fell slowly, and he made the same little sleep sounds that Jango had once made. That she had grown accustomed to. That, once upon a time, she had foolishly allowed herself to hope might be sounds that accompanied her own sleep, all the days of her life.

She closed her eyes, trying not to think the thoughts tumbling into her mind. *Another chance,* she thought. *You know what Jango was. You know how it felt to be with him. You never thought you'd feel love like that again.*

The most devastating male animal she had ever known. Was that an insult to the memory of her dead husband? Yander had been good, and kind, and . . .

And not Jango Fett. And now, here was Jangotat . . .

Another chance.

"No," she whispered. It would be wrong. It would be selfish.

It would be human.

The next day he felt well enough for walking in the hills, and accompanied burly little stepson Tarl and red-haired stepdaughter Tonoté as they went to check chitlik traps up in the tree-line caves above their fungus farm. The orange-striped, cave-dwelling marsupials' mammary glands exuded a cheesy substance called kista that helped offworlders cope with the toxins and microorganisms in Cestus's soil.

They sang to him a tune he had heard before:

One, one, chitliks basking in the sun.
Two, two, chitlik kista in the stew.
Three, three, leave a little bit for me.
Four, four, can I have a little more?
Five, five, set the traps to catch alive.
Six, six . . .

So the children could augment the community by capturing and "milking" the creatures of kista, then releasing them again—usually without damage.

Set the traps to catch alive . . .

He'd seen few dead animals since arriving. No furs, no curing meat. All he had eaten was the satisfying, hearty fungus. These folk "hunted" without harm.

Who were they, and what had made them that way?

Jangotat watched the children as they checked the slat-walled deadfalls. The chitliks hissed from behind the barriers, but struggled less than he would have expected as they were milked, almost as if playing a game of some kind with their captors. The creatures seemed aware that the humans meant them no harm. Later, he found himself helping the kids design traps and snares based on his own survival training—although of course they needed to be modified to ensure that chitliks were caught alive.

He rolled over on his back on the grass, looking up at the sun and relishing the simplicity of his present life. Soon enough he would be back in combat, but for right now, the most important thing was the capture of a few small, furry creatures that would provide vital antitoxins for the village meals, with enough surplus to supplement trade in fungi.

The children were fascinated by his nimble fingers, and he amused them with simple skills he had been taught in his own "childhood": knife juggling, rope escapes, silent stalking, sign reading, a dozen other tricks that he had learned as normal children learned counting games or skipping rope.

And although there was laughter in his eyes as they came down together from the mountains into the hills, Jangotat's heart was heavy. And that night at the collective meals . . . so similar, yet so different from the communal meals he had enjoyed with his brethren on Kamino, he thought . . .

This is not my world.

And then: *But it could have been.*

62

To Obi-Wan Kenobi's way of thinking, what could be done had been done. Every mistake that could possibly have been anticipated had been corrected. This time, only a fraction of the surviving recruits knew exactly where the central headquarters lay. The forty-eight survivors were organized into cells of five or six, with only the other members of the cells knowing their names. The outlying farms and mines had suffered a wave of arrests. Many who had been unwise enough to indulge in a bit of tavern-boasting about their recent exploits were now languishing in prisons—or had been slain trying to escape.

Who knew where the captives had been taken? There was little those captured by the JKs in the mines could tell, but together with the holovid they could make a convincing case for Jedi perfidy, perhaps sufficient to induce more planets to leave the Republic.

In the last days Obi-Wan and Kit had set up camp in an abandoned tricopper mine, one with an entrance through a sheltered overhang that could not be seen by flybys or drone satellites. One known to none of the captured recruits. One free of cave spider nests, with multiple exits that could be taken at a moment's notice. Obi-Wan was determined that the previous slaughter would not happen again. They could not *afford* another such catastrophe.

Forry approached. "Jangotat is still unaccounted for," he said.

Skot OnSon, their youngest recruit, had been brought blindfolded to the new cave, and now stood at what he considered attention. "Some of our guys tried to get him out," he said. "We found their bodies, but—"

"So you don't really know what happened to him," Obi-Wan said.

"No, General Kenobi."

Obi-Wan hunched over his hands, trying to make sense of the data. "We may have been betrayed," he said quietly.

There was utter silence in the cave. Then Sirty spoke up. "You suggest that Jangotat has broken Code?" He said that with the air of a man informed that gravity has abruptly ceased to work.

Seefor looked at Obi-Wan with something close to anger. "It has never happened."

Obi-Wan was angry with himself that he had allowed such a speculation to creep into his mind. The troopers were as loyal as mortal flesh could be. Seefor had rightfully found his implication offensive. "I do not mean to insult you. I merely state a fact: Jangotat was behaving oddly before the attack."

Kit Fisto chose this moment to speak. "I believe that he was killed. An energy blast could have fried his comlink. Tons of rock were dislodged. He may be buried."

Another pause. The clone troopers did not like this idea, but greatly preferred it to the alternative. "There's another possibility. We haven't been able to raise Sheeka Tull by comlink. It's possible that he's with her . . . they were seen together."

Kit clapped his hands. "From now on, security is watertight," he said. "No messages out of our camp. This cannot happen again."

"Agreed, sir."

"Then we have to move to step three," Obi-Wan said harshly. "Intensified sabotage. Kit?"

Kit examined the floating hologram, and then spoke. "It might be possible to determine the most critical parts of the fabrication and distribution system, and halt or slow production without damage to the physical plant itself."

"And this selectiveness is important because . . . ?"

"Cestus cannot survive without a cash stream. To disrupt it other than temporarily would kill thousands."

"So?"

"So I have a plan . . ."

63

Strictly speaking, the thousand-square-kilometer sprawl of Clandes Industrial's complex was not a city at all. It would most accurately be considered a starburst-shaped collection of manufacturing facilities located three hundred kilometers south of ChikatLik, seventy-five kilometers southeast of the Dashta Mountains. Clandes's twenty-four underground levels bristled with employee barracks and support structures for the merchants, cantinas, personal service corps, and the transportation agents who enabled them. Much of the complex was based on the hive cluster that had once occupied the location. Once, before the plagues.

As the surviving X'Ting moved out, offworlders of a dozen species moved in. In time barracks had sprung up, and then support systems for those dormitories, transport pads, and the other jobs that accompanied them. Eventually what had grown here would dwarf all of the outlying farming and mining settlements, and become its own entity.

But the heart of it was the manufacturing complex that still accounted for 60 percent of Cestus's economy. And in this very special case, was responsible for something else as well:

The JK droids.

Obi-Wan and his anarchists had spent all of a long and stressful night analyzing the various routes into and out of Clandes, all the trade that went in, and all the resources that it controlled . . . and controlled it. It took hours to find a single line that seemed to be the most critical.

Every day millions of liters of water were used for agriculture and machining, for drinking and recreation. Cestus's water was perfect for its native life-forms, but the micro-organisms were lethal for offworlders, and demanded thorough processing before even ordinary industrial uses, let alone consumption. Whereas most of the water for ChikatLik was piped in from northern glaciers, water for Clandes flowed from two sources: snowmelt from the Dashta Mountains and the Clandes aquifer, a geological formation holding water deep in layers of underground rock and sand, under sufficient pressure to discharge to the surface with minimal effort.

The nerve center was the main plant processing the aquifer water for consumption in the city. If it could be destroyed, the plant would have to be repaired, or within days Clandes's residents would be drinking their own sweat. That shutdown would cause a serious reshifting of priorities as the plant was repaired, and once again the Five Families might be coerced to the bargaining table.

Obi-Wan thought about it from every angle. Out of the dozen or so possibilities, it was probably the best. There was an additional advantage: whoever planned the counterassault against Desert Wind had clearly authorized the use of deadly force. Was it Regent Duris? He had to assume so, and to assume that she would expect a similar level of lethal escalation. Attacking the aquifer station, on the other hand, was more roundabout, and respectful of life—the kind of attack unlikely to be made by a desperate enemy with limited resources. And therefore less easy to anticipate.

Obi-Wan had other concerns as well: it had been four days since his ship had been blown from the sky, and with it their only long-range communications gear. Four days since any sort of message had been sent back to the Supreme Chancellor and the Jedi Council. Soon Coruscant would assume that the mission had failed. That meant naval bombardment. And bombardment meant disaster.

Clandes attracted merchants of all kinds, from interstellar cargo barges to aboriginal caravans crossing the deserts at night seeking Clandes's gates and landing pads.

And that day the guards at the gates studied the flow more carefully than usual. Although the guards had to expect additional assaults, there was little they could do to prepare for one.

The attack had to operate in two different sites and with two different intents. The locations: the pumping station at the foot of the Dashta Mountains, and the purification plant in the town itself. Disabling both simultaneously might confuse the security force, giving their people time to slip away. If the attempt to sabotage the stations failed, Desert Wind forces would plant targeting beacons to guide the inevitable bombardment. With such pinpoint targeting, even if disaster struck, the bombing fatalities might be limited to dozens rather than thousands.

So while Obi-Wan Kenobi and half the forces entered the city in a variety of guises, Kit and his followers approached the aquifer station from the mountains, landing five kilometers away and then moving over and through rough broken terrain to approach the station from shadow.

"Alarms?" Seefor asked soberly.

Kit examined the flat hand-size viewscreen. It displayed the outline of the physical plant, plus shadowy, floating images representing the security fields around the plant. "They're there, as of a week ago."

"I'll be surprised if they haven't been enhanced," Seefor said.

"So we have to wait." But not for long. He felt exposed here. Since things had started souring, he had the uneasy sense that every move he made was anticipated. Kit hated to admit it, but he and Obi-Wan were running out of moves. The first time they repeated themselves, they were all as dead as the hopes for a diplomatic solution.

Timing was everything. Obi-Wan Kenobi shuffled along with the caravan Thak Val Zsing had arranged for them, bringing a variety of luxury items to the tent-city open market on the surface above Clandes.

They carried a dozen types of dried and shredded mushrooms, perfumes and toys, rare spices from the desert caves, scented oils for bath or bedchamber, carvings made from the petrified bones of long-dead creatures that had walked Cestus's deserts when the soil had been fertile and moist.

The bearded, pale-skinned human guard examined the offerings and laughed. "Not much market for this nonsense today. Everyone's on alert right now. Maybe you'd better turn around, come back later."

A ridiculous notion. The guards knew quite well that the caravan would have traversed a hundred kilometers to reach the tent city's gated entrance. They would lack water, and food, and would long for rest beneath a sheltering roof. He wondered if the guard was weak-minded as well as venal? It might be worth a try to—

But before he could implement his planned bit of mind control, Resta stepped forward. " 'Cuse me," she said. " 'Fore we go, sell goods otherwise, we want give you first look. You, me, done business afore." And here Resta's red-ringed secondary hands raised her robes to show a series of copper bands on her belt, each one representing another journey into Clandes. The belt dangled with them. "We make credit, you make credit. Business better wit' friends. What say?"

The guard watched them both. One of his pale shaggy eyebrows raised as he extended his hand. Resta placed a small jangling bag into it, and the guard peered within. A smile split the fleshy expanse beneath his unkempt yellow beard, and he stepped aside.

The caravan entered, and Obi-Wan was immediately glad that his face and form were mostly concealed: a probe droid floated by them, imaging the group, no doubt relaying it to live or computerized security databases. This was the ground-level open market entrance, and the entire area was filled with booths, selling thousands of different wares to Clandes residents who ventured to the storm-swept surface in search of bargains and exotica.

After half an hour helping his companions erect their own booth, Obi-Wan pretended to sort carvings before he caught a nod from Resta, and was forced to pay a bit more attention to the next customer, a yellowish Glymphid whose long, slender head matched his skinny body.

"Have you a carved bantha?" the Glymphid asked. "I long for home."

Those were the appointed code words, and after a brisk bit of bargaining, Obi-Wan sold him a carved walking stick. "This is just fine," the creature from Ploo II said. "I might be willing to have some more of this work. Custom work. Would you be interested?" Obi-Wan nodded.

The Glymphid turned and led Obi-Wan and Resta toward the duracrete dome marking a city entrance. The guard paid minimal attention, and they descended a turbolift tube into the heart of Clandes.

Obi-Wan had expected Clandes to resemble the capital. He was both right and wrong. At ChikatLik the hive had made a home in a cavern created by natural water erosion. Here the walls glistened, fused to glass, and he realized that the entire cavern had been formed by some kind of underground volcanic activity: they'd probably moved in a million years after the molten bubble had cooled. Its new offworlder masters had built on top of the X'Ting architecture.

Resta had not spoken since they entered, but now she whispered under her breath, "See low rocky building behind spire?"

Obi-Wan nodded.

"That power station. Cut my farm off, so sell power to some Five Fam' place. See building next to it?" A three-story brownish rectangle. The purification plant.

"That where you go. Resta no take you farther. Unnerstan'?"

Obi-Wan nodded again. "I thank you for everything."

Resta snorted, anger reddening her face and bristling the slits at the sides of her neck. She gestured at the bustling pedestrians. "Think Resta risk life for you?" She spit on the ground. "Resta no care 'bout her life. Her people almost gone. Just want to take as many wit' Resta as can." And without shaking hands or giving any other sign, the golden-carapaced woman turned and left.

The city bustled like a nest of sea-prigs. About a third of the citizens wore uniforms in orange-and-gold cloth. Obi-Wan knew these to be the factory's corporate colors, and was sobered to realize the extent of the damage he was about to create.

The streets had been laid out along the original hive structure, with the mathematical precision of a computer-generated maze. Therefore it was easy for Obi-Wan to find his way through the color-coded labyrinth until he found himself three stories deeper down at the outskirts of the three-story brown building.

He slipped into an alley, examining the building from the side. He had seen the schematic, but given any opportunity preferred to trust his own eyes. Three stories. According to his information the third floor held the most vital controls, so that was where he went.

Obi-Wan floated from the shadow on the wall, ascending using even the narrowest of handholds, using his sensitivity to balance on footholds where a reptile might have fallen to its death. Once at the window he looked back down at the street. The alley was narrow, so that it wasn't easy to see him, but if anyone looked directly up, there would be a problem he would rather not deal with. So far, so good. The lock was not as easy. It was complicated and beyond his ability to pick. Security alarm? He felt around the edge, trying to sense the presence of a protective energy field. Yes. He could sense the conduits, but the power wasn't pulsing with any intensity. So the alarm circuit existed, but wasn't on during the day, when the purification plant probably swarmed with guards.

Obi-Wan triggered his lightsaber and burned a hole through the lock and window. When sparks ceased to spit and the window cooled, he reached through and opened it.

He slid through and was in. The room was empty, but not for long—the door slid open.

He spun across the room and was in hiding before the door opened. A man walked in, and Obi-Wan rendered him unconscious before he was even aware of a threat. His victim wore an uncoweled uniform, one that would expose Obi-Wan's face. All he could do was hope that there were enough employees that he wouldn't be immediately detected.

Fewer would die that way, and that was to be hoped for. Their original mission had gone awry. Hopefully, things were beginning to get on the right track . . .

He stepped out into the control room, scanning swiftly. Smaller than he might have thought, with banks of control computers along the walls. This part of the operation was simple enough to be run by one or two attendants, and perhaps, just perhaps, he'd already taken out his opposition.

Then optimism died. There, in the middle of the room, squatted the deceptively beautiful golden hourglass of a JK droid.

Obi-Wan groaned. Any fool could have anticipated that Cestus would continue to make use of its own security droids. Still, hope is a terrible addiction to overcome. No way through it now, though. He had limited time, and it was all too possible that his companions were already selling their lives dearly.

The glittering, elegant form would seem oh, so innocent to one who had never seen the droid in action. He approached it gingerly. What to do? Once it recognized him as an intruder he would have only moments to act. In all probability it was already too late. Disaster loomed if the JK raised an alarm. Only an idiot would relish the prospect of simultaneous duels with droid and guards.

What was the JK's alarm perimeter? He was surprised that it wasn't the room itself, then realized that it might be possible for maintenance workers to enter a room as long as they kept a certain distance, behaved in a specific way, or carried electronic identification of some kind. Did the JK trigger on sound? Proximity? Was he even now being scanned for secu-

rity codes embedded in badges or clothing? Were there spoken code words that might disarm the mechanism?

Two things he was certain of. One, he didn't have those
code words. Two, if he attempted to reach the controls it
would attack.

What to do?

He had faced the JKs in the caves, and had little taste for
another encounter.

Speed. He needed speed. Gambling everything, Obi-Wan
Kenobi drew his lightsaber and triggered it to life. He hurled
it at the control panel at the same time that he threw himself
directly at the JK.

Its attention was split between orders to protect the equipment and those to apprehend the attacker. Tentacles extended
rapidly from its side, snapping after the tumbling lightsaber,
and might have caught it if not for the beam severing two of
its arms.

As the lightsaber hit the panel, the JK hissed as if it were
alive. The energy blade sliced through the control paneling.
Coils of wire bulged free, and sparks showered from the
smoking metal; automatic shutdown went into effect. The JK
seemed to realize it had been tricked into splitting attention,
and turned itself fully back to Obi-Wan.

Obi-Wan called to his lightsaber, but he saw at that moment that it was tangled in the panel's wiring. There was
not another full second for thought—the JK was closing
fast. Making a snap decision he raced toward the biodroid,
pulling the lightwhip at his side as he did. The biodroid was
on him, wrapping its arms around his legs.

Pain. The mechanical arms surged with energy. The hair
on Obi-Wan's head flared away from his scalp and he fought
shock as the charge threatened to shut down his nervous system and paralyze his diaphragm. As it pulled him closer, attempting a retinal scan, Obi-Wan triggered the lightwhip,
and it spun out at an angle, ensnaring an entire quadrant of
arms in a single instant. Sparks sprayed from the torn durasteel. He threw his hands in front of his eyes as the spray

splashed across his face. He heard, but did not see, the mechanical arms as they tumbled to the ground, severed by the strands. But now he had lost *both* tools.

The droid seemed to realize that it, too, had been wounded, and actually rolled back a step. Obi-Wan made a snap decision and lunged in, deciding that it would be least prepared to deal with an aggressive forward motion. It attempted to respond, but this time with a noticeable time lag in response. Stumps twitched as the JK attempted to strike him with phantom severed limbs, but the remaining arm lashed across his face, tearing skin and shocking with a sizzling jolt of pain—but by then he had moved to close quarters.

His vision was still blurry, but the Force was strong in Obi-Wan. He could sense the place where the lightwhip had struck, weakening the JK's sparkling case. *There.* Obi-Wan closed his traitorous eyes, inhaled, finding the place within himself where there was no fear or doubt. Dwelling there. Every muscle in his hand was perfectly coordinated as it flashed down, gaining acceleration as it struck, a perfect transference of force to the already damaged surface. He heard the *crack!* and folded his arm, striking again and again with his elbow at the same spot. The injured droid tumbled over backward, sparks spraying all about them.

He didn't know how many times he struck, only that when he was finished, the JK lay thrashing weakly on its side. Obi-Wan stood, feeling similarly weakened. He looked down at the droid with newfound respect. It had required two energy weapons and bruising hand-to-tentacle combat to stop the thing. His heart thundered in his chest, but he focused and continued about the business at hand.

Obi-Wan had only to plant his explosives, and all was done. If they were disarmed before detonation, then he hoped Desert Wind had done its job, planting beacons to guide a bombardment that *would* destroy the purification plant.

Obi-Wan plucked his lightsaber from the ground, and then

the lightwhip. He triggered it; the narrow luminescent thread flared for a moment and then died. Its power cell was exhausted, and regretfully he tossed it away. The device had served its master well, but now there were other concerns. No more time for toys.

64

Twenty-five kilometers away, Kit Fisto crouched in the shadows of the aquifer station's bleached white rectangular walls, waiting. The security sweeps revolved once every twenty seconds, invisible, undetectable to anyone without superb apparatus—or profound Force sensitivity. He moved them through the energy maze one level at a time, until they were completely within the shadow of the station's walls. "I have to leave you now. If you manage to cut the power, make your way inside."

"And you?" Thak Val Zsing asked.

"I'll meet you there," he said. Kit peered down into a flat-bottomed duracrete riverbed outside the walls. Without another word he jumped and slid down its rough, slanted side toward the bed. He was able to slow his sliding descent, but knew that he wouldn't be able to get back out up the wall. If the plan went wrong, there would be trouble indeed.

According to their information, water from the Dashta dam sluiced through the trench in hourly currents. There was no way around this next part, and he prepared himself. He heard the rumbling before he saw it, a great pounding wave that shook the duracrete and swept around the corner like a raging wall. Kit rolled into a ball as it struck him, allowing it to carry him along with it down the channel and to the mouth of the drop-off. Within moments he was flipping through the current as if he had never left Glee Anselm at all. *Bang.* The tide slammed Kit into the wall, but he relaxed with the force, riding it, feeling the pressures and intensities of the raging flow. A grid up ahead, metal bars twisted together to make fist-size holes. Kit's lightsaber flashed, foaming the water with clouds of gas bubbles. A circular swipe, and the bars parted as Kit's head slammed into the severed section, knocking it ahead of him. He eeled through, kicked himself away from another wall, and found himself in an even narrower channel, water pressure increasing the speed and intensity of the flow.

Ahead the water was passing through a flash-heating ray, boiling it for a few seconds before passing the heated water on to another system of pipes.

The ray brushed his skin, and Kit's nerves screamed with shock. *No!*

He swam upcurrent, caught between icy flow and the boiling heat ray. *Fire and ice,* he thought, suddenly aware that the cold had leached strength from his body.

The current pushed him back toward the boiling water, and he pulled at the sides of the channel, trying to lift himself out. No purchase.

The first thread of panic wormed its way into his mind, and Kit Fisto clamped down on it instantly, concentrating on each stroke, centering himself, allowing the Force to find his way between the onrushing currents one meter at a time, until he reached a ladder, only two meters overhead. Kit concentrated, dived down in a fast loop, and burst up out of the water to grab the bottom rung and lift himself out. He shivered: the snow runoff was as cold as the cauldron had been torrid. It took a moment before his body adjusted and the shaking diminished. Here on the far side of the scanners, he could climb the wall safely, make his way to a juncture box on the second level. Clinging to the wall, he waited.

And waited.

Something was wrong. Val Zsing and his people should have gotten through by now. He checked his chrono—

And then suddenly the water flow beneath him died to a trickle. The power had been cut! A backup alarm began to ring. Distant shouts echoed in the corridor. There would be only a few moments before the power would come back on, but his men had heard those shouts or the alarm, and would make their move. It was his job to clear the way.

Kit crawled along a ledge until he found a barred window, and used his lightsaber to slice through it, letting himself in.

He heard the sound of racing feet just outside the door. A secondary alarm rang insistently, perhaps announcing the appearance of Desert Wind. He waited until the feet had passed, then made his way along the corridor.

The pumping station's ground floor was some ten thousand square meters, with a ceiling that arched four stories overhead. The artificial streambed ran through the center of it, where every bit of water trickled past heat rays and the crackling arc of a flux light, the first line of purification. While not filtering the water as thoroughly as the station in town, it was the first line of defense, killing 80 percent of microorganisms and neutralizing many toxins.

The floor bucked as an explosion shook the complex. This blast originated near one of the outer doors. Kit Fisto smiled grimly as more guards ran in that direction.

With the present limited lighting and a distracting attack going on at the front, it would be easier for him to complete his mission. Not easy, perhaps, but easier. Clinging to the underside of the catwalk, breathing into the strain in his fingers and shoulders, Kit hand-walked around the room's perimeter and dropped fifteen meters down to the deck, landing silently.

He slipped into the room, and the single guard didn't even have time to turn around before Kit hurled himself forward. The guard managed to level his sidearm as Kit sliced it from his hand. The Nautolan continued the motion into a kick to the head, disabling the hapless Cestian before he could make a sound.

He whirled, examining the control panel, shutting down the water flow to Clandes. The next phase was easy: destroying the panel to freeze the setting. Kit's lightsaber flashed, and within seconds the panel was a smoking ruin.

He surveyed the damage swiftly: it would take days to get

this station working again. The floor beneath his feet shook as an explosion ripped through the building.

Good. More confusion, more damage. Hopefully, not more loss of life.

Time to make good his escape.

Kit Fisto left the room and instantly ran into the returning security team. He was a beat ahead of them, his lightsaber flashing as he was forced to defend himself without restraint. He tried to avoid lethal maneuvers. *They are just trying to do their jobs.* There came a time when such restraint was of no use at all, and after a whirlwind engagement, two men fell. A third brought his weapon to bear and the Jedi leapt over the railing, falling two stories to land in a crouch.

More guards. His lightsaber seemed to move of its own accord, before the blasts were launched, and he blocked two, three, four . . . and then was among them, tight-lipped and narrow-eyed.

Guards screamed, dying there.

This Cestus affair grows uglier by the moment, Kit Fisto thought bitterly. Then regrets and second guesses dissolved as a web of lightsaber light filled the air around him, and guards crumpled to the ground. He flirted with battle fever, the howling demon in his mind trapped behind the bars of discipline, but guiding him as he slid down Form I's razor edge.

He heard the siren before he stopped, but just before, making him think that the sound had simply not impressed itself on his consciousness; his focus had been so tight that everything external had simply failed to register.

Eight guards lay around him, moaning. Kit's mouth twisted in an oath he would have been ashamed for the Jedi Counsel to hear. This was exactly the sort of carnage he'd hoped to avoid.

Out.

On the way a huge technician swung a pry-bar at him. Sick at heart, the Jedi spun to the inside of the aggressive spiral and twisted it out of his hand. He shifted his attacker against the wall as his eyes rolled up, voluntary nervous system paralyzed by a strike to the nerve plexus beneath his arm. "Sleep," Kit Fisto whispered as the technician slumped. "All life is a dream."

Or a nightmare, he thought. One from which more and more Cestians would never awaken.

65

Nothing even vaguely resembling good cheer lived in ChikatLik's halls of power. The word from the Clandes manufacturing facility was that the water flow was reduced by three-quarters, and it would take days if not weeks to get everything back online. In the meantime, if drinking water was not shipped into the city, Clandes risked an unprecedented humanitarian disaster.

G'Mai Duris's three stomachs felt variously heavy, sour, and leaden. Who was doing all of this? The Jedi? Might Obi-Wan still live? After his ship had been blown from the sky, they had detected only a single escape capsule, containing the barrister. Who then? And in another sense it hardly mattered. It was obvious to her where all of this would ultimately end. There would be a naval bombardment, and the Republic's war would leave Cestus a smoking husk.

And the worst thing of all was that she was about to meet a complication. Oh, yes, Quill had smirked, claiming that the person about to enter the throne room represented an answer to their problems, but Duris had been a political animal long enough to know that most solutions were just future problems in a pretty cocoon.

Nonetheless she straightened her back, expanding to her full height and breadth in her throne chair, and nodded to her assistant to allow the guest entrance.

Her heart beat faster, although there was nothing on her painted face to betray it. And she knew that the newcomer would feel her heartbeat, even from a distance.

She was afraid.

The woman who entered the room walked like a military officer, but with that same unnatural lightness Duris had noted in Kenobi. It bespoke severe physical and mental training, a sinuous quality simultaneously enviable and somehow terrifying. The Jedi had displayed the same refined motion, the same absolute and intimidating focus, but through it had also projected decency and wisdom, a profound respect for life and spirit.

Those qualities were missing from this creature. Her dark eyes peered out of her pale, shaven, tattooed skull and saw . . . what? What deep, cold spaces between the stars did *this* one call home?

The woman made the deepest, most arrogant bow Duris had ever seen in her life. "Commander Asajj Ventress, at your service," she said. "I crave but a single minute of your valuable time."

"No more?"

"No more. I am no politician. My business is with your manufacturing concerns."

"The business of Cestus is business," Duris replied.

Ventress might not have heard her at all. "I am trade ambassador from Count Dooku and your allies in the Confederacy of Independent Systems."

"Allies?" Duris asked with mock surprise. "We have no political aspirations. We do have *customers,* of course, whom we cherish highly." She tried to filter the stress from her voice, and was not completely successful.

Ventress cocked her head slightly sideways, her pale lips curling into a contemptuous smile. "You do not entirely welcome my presence."

Duris forced her own lips into her most formal, neutral expression, and her voice to do the same. "Of late, I have had reason to be cautious whom I trust. But I wouldn't want you to think I number you among the untrustworthy."

Ventress's mouth twisted. Duris sensed that the offworlder had not merely detected the evasion, but actually enjoyed it.

"I see. Yes." Ventress lowered her head, and remained silent. At first Duris assumed that Ventress would speak.

After a full minute passed the Regent realized that the woman was waiting for her. Whoever spoke next would be in the weaker position, but Duris could see no polite way to avoid it.

"Tell me, Commander Ventress," she said carefully. "I understand that you have been here on Cestus for a number of days."

"Do you?" she said without raising her eyes.

"Perhaps you were enjoying our fabled hospitality."

Stepping softly, Ventress circled the throne, until she stood behind Duris. "Was I?" The other eyes in the chamber were glued to this woman who walked among them with such authority, such apparent disregard for their protocol. Yet none dared show offense.

The tattooed woman leaned forward from behind Duris. Her face was just at the Regent's velvet-padded shoulder. Duris could smell the woman's breath. It was cloyingly sweet, like cake batter.

"I fear I have little time for entertainments. There are mighty deeds to be done. The galaxy is in foment."

"What brings you here?" Duris asked.

"I wish merely to ensure that our orders progress smoothly. I understand that the Clandes factory will be shut down for some days."

"I assure you we can accelerate the repair process. Perhaps seventy-two hours . . ."

"Yes, yes," Ventress whispered, and then continued to circle. "My Master and I would appreciate that greatly. But there is another matter. You may think that you have information that would cripple Cestus Cybernetics. Some small matter of a two-hundred-year-old contract, obtained under false pretenses. Might this be true?"

Duris dared not lie. "Perhaps."

"Yes. A two-edged sword, that. If you bring this before the Senate, I promise the Supreme Chancellor would use it to shut down the factories as fully as any bombardment. Your hive would suffer, I promise you. And more than that—you, *personally,* would bear the brunt of Count Dooku's wrath."

Duris nodded silently.

"I'm certain threats are superfluous," Ventress continued. "But Lady Duris . . . if there is anything that I can do to help, please do not hesitate. Count Dooku and General Grievous have powerful resources, and empathize with your struggle against a corrupt, repressive Republic. Together, we can do great things." She paused. "Great . . . things." She smiled. "That is, for now, my only message. With your permission, I leave."

Commander Asajj Ventress backed out of the chamber, bowing, her eyes half lidded, almost reptilian.

When the doors closed behind her, Duris exhaled a long, sour, infinitely relieved breath. Her entire body felt like a coiled spring. The woman made her flesh crawl. Clearly, Asajj Ventress was more lethal than Master Kenobi. Duris was certain deceit had not come naturally to the Jedi. This creature had no such compunctions. No shame, no fear. No mercy, either.

In fact, as little mercy as the ship that had blown Obi-Wan from the sky.

With painful clarity Duris could visualize, actually *see,* five generations of Cestian social progress sliding into oblivion, and there seemed nothing she could do about it.

Her assistant Shar Shar rolled closer. "The rest of the council is ready to meet, ma'am. Are you . . ."

Duris was still lost in her speculations. The timing of this woman's arrival was no accident. Had Ventress landed before or after Obi-Wan? And were their efforts coordinated or mutually antagonistic? Surely she was aware of Kenobi's presence, but had he been aware of *her* . . . ?

"Ma'am?" asked Shar Shar, her skin purpling in anxiety.

"Yes?"

"Are you ready?"

Duris nodded. In the air around her, a dozen holoscreens blossomed. Smooth-pated marketing and sales executive Lli-tishi spoke first. "Regent Duris. The fraudulent kidnapping is clear evidence of the Republic's intention to interfere in Cestus's sovereign affairs. It is time for us to strike. We must find these rebels and their collaborators, and show the Republic that we will never bend the knee."

Duris ached for his naïveté. "And who then will our friends be? Can you imagine that the Confederacy sent its spies to help us only? We stand in the shadows of two giants, each of whom uses honeyed words to attract us. Each of whom would destroy us rather than see us fall into the other camp."

Executive Llitishi seemed reluctant to agree. "That is not necessarily true—"

"Ah," G'Mai Duris said. "And with which of our sons and daughters are you willing to gamble?"

And to that question, he had no answer at all.

The rest of the meeting did not go well, although there were stories of rebels caught, and sabotage averted. But the death toll had now passed thirty. The fires of wrath generally proved easier to ignite than extinguish. Cestus's security forces would hunt these saboteurs down, but a sinking sensation deep within her bones told Duris that this would hardly be the end of her troubles.

Too clearly, she remembered her experiences with Obi-Wan Kenobi. It seemed a lifetime ago that she had first opined that there might be no solution to her problems. With every passing hour, she began to believe that she had been more prescient than she could ever have imagined.

66

As G'Mai Duris's court and cabinet were disturbed by the goings-on, both hive and criminal contingent were in similar turmoil. Gambling and drug revenues dried up as ChikatLik, fearing the coming of war, began to hoard resources. All of Trillot's varied businesses were at risk, and she had begun to feel the pinch.

But it was more than a pinch that she felt as Ventress returned to her den and presented herself. As always, the offworlder carried herself as if her humanoid form were a mask. This was pure predator in every word and action. This one lived to kill.

"I am a simple woman," Trillot said, "who cannot claim to understand all of the meanings and machinations. But it seems to me that no one can truly say how this will end. Begging your pardon, of course, Commander."

"For once, you are correct," Ventress said. "No one can know how this ends—with one exception." When she spoke there was an odd passion in her voice that Trillot had not heard before.

"And who, or what, is that?"

Ventress narrowed her eyes, and her pale cheeks colored. "Count Dooku foretold it, and I have seen it. Whatever else happens, Obi-Wan Kenobi and I will meet again. On Queyta I promised Kenobi I would kill him. My Master wants him alive. So: he will leave Cestus in bondage, or he will rest beneath its sands."

There was a flush in her face that Trillot recognized. It was lust. No mere physical passion, although a nameless, fleshly hunger burned within her. It was like lust turned inside out, and it burned inside this strange woman like a fire she could not extinguish.

The two strange and powerful offworlders were on a collision course, and she prayed not to be between them. When such giants clashed, small folk such as Trillot could be utterly destroyed.

On the other hand, however, in times such as this even small people could make large profits . . .

67

"Where are you taking me?"

"Shhh," Sheeka Tull replied.

For most of an hour they had trod uneven ground. Jango-tat had long since lost track of direction, so many twists and turns had they taken. Two thicknesses of cloth covered his eyes, then a sack was pulled down over his head. Triple protection. Why was a blindfold so critically important? He had been promised a surprise, then told that he could only enjoy it if he allowed himself to be blindfolded. *A secret, you see.*

He had accepted the blindfold, then Sheeka and Brother Fate spun him in a circle. When he stopped he felt the wind blowing against his skin and made an educated guess as to the direction he now faced. When they began to lead him up the side of a hill, he had to forget such thoughts and concentrate on not taking a bone-breaking spill.

After perhaps fifteen minutes of climbing, the air chilled, the ground leveled, and he guessed that they had entered a cave. Even then the blindfold did not come off: they twisted and turned through the cave, over treacherous footing and with strange watery echoes tinkling in the distance.

For almost another hour they walked over uneven ground. Twice he heard falling water, and cool misty sprays moistened the backs of his hands. Then they began to climb down a series of steps chipped into the stone.

For a long moment he merely stood there, wondering what it was that she wanted him to do. But she didn't say anything at all. Finally, feeling a bit frustrated in his solitary darkness, he said "What?," immediately embarrassed by the single syl-lable's inadequacy.

His hands fumbled at his blindfold.

"No," Sheeka said. Her own cool fingers took his, moved them down.

"Why not?"

"I don't want you to use your ordinary senses," she said. "Your eyes, or your ears."

Confusion warred with a powerful and unaccustomed urge to please her. Not so odd, perhaps. She had saved his life and proven a stout comrade. ·

"What do you expect me to do?"

"Use your heart," she said. "Tell me, what do you feel?"

He stopped, and thought. Despite the warnings, he con-centrated on ambient sound and sensation. He heard the faint *shush* of rippling water, and the distant sound of falling droplets echoing in the darkness. He felt the uneven ground beneath his feet, and . . .

"Air, moving against my skin," he said.

Her voice sounded a bit frustrated, but still calm. "No. Deeper. Not your senses. Your *heart*."

"I hear water—"

"No! Stop using your ears. What do you *feel*? In here." She placed her hand over his heart. He sighed deeply, feeling her palm's warmth as if it seeped into and beneath his ribs.

Suddenly he had the urge to believe that she was not merely playing some kind of game with him. There was something there, if only he could find it.

"I feel . . . warm."

"Where?"

"Inside," he answered. He tried to follow up with more words, but they wouldn't form. Then he noticed that the blindfold-induced false midnight was no longer totally black. Inchoate shapes formed within it, as if faces watched him, judging him. He couldn't quite distinguish them, but they seemed not like pictures, even dimensional pictures. They were more like squirming shapes pushing through a flat elastic surface. Rounded faces, with empty eyes. He had the sense that he knew this form, knew this creature, but couldn't be certain where he had come to know it, or under what circumstances . . .

"It feels like floating on a golden current," he heard himself say. "I'm half asleep, but totally awake at the same time."

"Yes."

"I . . . oh!" He had started to speak again, but then his throat seemed filled with dust. Now speckles of light twinkled in the darkness. They were followed by shadowy forms flowing together, then separating, then together again . . .

His legs wavered, buckled. A remnant of his injuries? He went down to his hands and knees, then felt her hands on his shoulders. It took a few moments to catch his breath. Then he stood again and dropped his arms to his sides, fingers flexing and unflexing, breathing shallow and high. Trembling, feeling as if he were about to burst, he raised his hands to the blindfold, then hesitated. "Sheeka?" he asked unsteadily.

"Yes," she said. Not a question. The single word was calming. He removed the sack from his head and untied the blindfold.

The cave roof was low but glowed with warmth and dull orange light. The radiance originated beneath the surface of a water pool that rippled with a steady heartbeat rhythm.

The ceiling dripped with stalactites, and the walls glowed as if they had been polished by hand. The very ground beneath them pulsed with a soft and persistent radiance, reflected back from waterfalls of frozen stone.

He coughed, realizing that he had momentarily forgotten to breathe.

A dozen eels floated at the surface, vast milky eyes studying them. That strange light seemed to come from *within* them, so that from time to time their skin appeared almost translucent. Jangotat could actually see the bones and organs suspended within.

Blind.

"What is this place?" he asked, realizing that some part of him already knew the answer to that question.

"This is where the eels come to meet us."

"The dashta eels?" He knew little of them save the briefings of the Jedi. He knew that they were integral to the JK machines. "The living component of the bio-droids? We thought they came from the Dashta Mountains."

"No," she said quietly. "Both mountains and eels are named for Kilaphor Dashta, the first explorer to map both mountains and the Zantay caves, four centuries ago. They were holy to the X'Ting for thousands of years, but withdrew to the caves when the hive began its conquest of Cestus."

"These look larger than the eels we've seen," he protested.

"Those are the young, prior to sexual differentiation."

The water rippled with their gentle wavering. One of them swam in a lazy circle and then returned. Their blind eyes studied him. Why?

Sheeka was still talking, although she must have realized that his mind had been captured by the sight before him. "Cestus is honeycombed with passages, underwater rivers, and pools. Not even the X'Ting know the location of the dashta eels' home nest. As far as we know this is the last remaining place where they interact with other species. It was here that they brought us the first fungus spores."

"The medicine?"

"Yes. And the meatless meals."

"How can these be dashtas? According to my reseach, they are much too large. They . . . these creatures are intelligent . . ." How did he know that? So far they had done nothing but float. But something about those blind eyes. They made gentle sounds, cooing, calling, comforting . . .

"Yes," Sheeka agreed.

He shook his head. "I've read the reports. Dashtas are nonsentient."

"Not nonsentient. Call it a form of sleep. A gift from the Guides—a lifetime of dreams. Even unconscious, their nervous systems supply the Force sensitivity. I don't understand all of it. I'm just grateful it works."

He paused for a moment, digesting information. "What are you saying?"

"Female dashtas lay millions of eggs," Sheeka said to him. "The males fertilize only a few thousand. Unfertilized eggs produce young who never mature."

"The eels gave you their children?"

She nodded. "Those who would have died in competition with their fertilized brothers and sisters. They lived on, and in living gave life to we who befriended them."

"Why would they do such a thing?"

"Long ago," Sheeka said, "this planet was more fertile, and there were more sentient species. They died out in competition with each other as the sand ate the forest. The struggle for survival was distasteful to the dashtas, who retreated deep into the planet's core. We've been their first new friends in millennia."

"You."

"Yes. The eels offered us their unfertile eggs, knowing that the JKs would bring Cestus more fully into the community of worlds."

"There is conflict in that world, as well."

"Yes. As long as there are eaters and eaten, there will be conflict. But the dashtas hold the potential for sentient creatures to meet their needs without slaughtering one another. This is our potential, not our present."

Need rarely triggers war, Jangotat thought. *Desire is far more deadly.* The X'Ting had driven the spiders into the mountains. If the plagues had been no accident, then Cestus Cybernetics had all but destroyed the hive. The Separatists and the Republic might well destroy Cestus Cybernetics . . .

An endless chain of domination and destruction. And he was one of its strongest links.

Jangotat kept his thoughts to himself. There was something more important here than philosophical discourse. He desired understanding more than he yearned for his next two minutes of air. "They have no eyes. Why do they glow?"

"For us," she said, and sat on the rock to gaze more closely at the eels. "For you, and me. I come here sometimes. Not too often, but occasionally, when I need to renew myself."

Her words were true. He could feel it, and had for some minutes now. It was a sensation not of warmth, nor of cold . . . but of something else. Something that was an . . . aliveness. He felt a compressed lifetime of murderous lessons dissolve, as if he was not any of the things he had been trained to be. But if he was not those things, then what was he? "I'm a soldier," he whispered.

"No," she said. "That is your programming."

His spine straightened. "I am a mighty warrior's clone brother."

"No," Sheeka said. And there was no mocking in her voice. There was, instead, some other emotion he could not name. "That is your body, your genetics. We're more than that. You are not your 'brothers' and they are not you."

Jangotat's sight began to blur, and he wiped at his eyes with his hand. Looked at the moisture collected there on his fingers, dumbfounded. He could not remember ever shedding tears before. He knew what they were, but had never seen them from his own eyes. And if he could do one thing that he had never done . . . perhaps there were others as well?

What *was* this place? One part of him wanted to flee as swiftly as possible. And another wanted to lie down here and be bathed in eel-light for the rest of his days.

"What do you feel?"

He closed his eyes again. A marrow-numbing tingle flowed through him, lifting him up, seemingly above himself. He heard himself speak without recognizing the words, and realized it was possible he had never really known himself at all. "What do I feel?" he asked. His voice shook with emotion. "What have you done to me? I feel everything. Everything I never knew I lacked." She had taken his hand. Her fingers were small and warm and cool. "I . . . see myself, back to infancy, out to old age." It was true.

Child.

Infant floating in a decanter, the spawn of endless night.

His body torn and war-ravaged, dying, the light of combat still glowing in his eyes.

Then other flesh, aged Jangotats, ravaged and worn not by war but by time, time he would never have. A wrinkled Jangotat, sight dimming, but smiling, surrounded by . . .

"Yes?"

For an instant he saw children he would never sire, grandchildren he would never hold, and the sudden, wrenching sense of the path denied was so devastating that he felt himself implode. It was as if all he had experienced on Cestus had awakened some deep and irresistible genetic memory within him. The memory of what his life *should* have been. Could have been, had he been a child of love and not war. He saw those children, but then, in their eyes he gained the strength to go backward, back to his own infancy, back to . . .

Jangotat sagged to his knees. The tears he'd spent a lifetime repressing welled up once again. "It's wrong," he whispered. "All wrong." He gazed up at her with haunted, hollow eyes. "I never heard my mother's heart. Never felt her emotions while I slept, safe in her womb."

"No," Sheeka said gently. "You didn't."

Hands shaking, he sank his face against his palms. On any other day of his life the heat and wetness would have shamed him, but Jangotat was beyond shame now. "No one ever cradled me," he said. "No one will miss me when I'm gone."

He paused, and into that pause he heard a voice within him whisper, *Please, Sheeka. Say that you'll miss me when I'm gone. When I've performed that single function I have practiced to perfection.*

Die.

Here on this planet. Or the next. Or the next. *Tell me that some memory of me will stay with you. That you will dream of me. Remember my smile. Praise my courage. My honor. Please. Something. Anything.*

But she said nothing, and he realized that it was best that way, that he had come to a place in his life where lived the core conundrums that no outside entity could resolve for him. This was *his* loneliness, *his* grim and inexorable destiny. And in this terrible moment, all the fine words about the immortality of the GAR rang as hollow as a Sarlacc's belly.

"Jangotat?"

Despite his horrific realization, he couldn't stop another clumsily disguised plea: "No one ever said they love me." He turned and looked up at her. It was as if tearing his gaze away from the pool required a physical effort. "Am I such an ugly thing?"

"No."

No. He was not an abomination of nature. He could feel everything that she was not saying, knew why she had brought him to this place: to experience the fear and loneliness he had hidden away from himself. It was mind numbing. And necessary.

His next words were a whisper. "Why would anyone ever leave this place, once they had found it?"

And now for the first time in minutes, she spoke in complete sentences. "Jangotat, it's not one or the other. We don't live either a life of action and adventure, or one of spiritual contemplation. True, the brothers and sisters come here to meditate. But then they return to the world."

"The world?"

"The world outside. Farms, mines, the city. The world needs us to be active, but to also contemplate the consequences of our actions. To obey orders is good, Jangotat. We all live within a society with reciprocal obligations. But to obey them without question is to be a machine, not a living being. Are you alive, Jangotat?"

His mouth worked without producing words.

"I think you are. Wake up before it's too late. You're not just a number, you're a man, a living, breathing man. You were born dreaming that you're some kind of machine, an expendable programmed device. You're not."

"Then what am I?" He blinked hard, shivering. "What is this feeling? I've never known it." He paused, mouth opening in astonishment. *"Loneliness,"* he said finally, answering his own question. "I feel so alone. I've never felt alone before. How could I? I was always surrounded by my brothers."

"I've felt lonely in a crowd," Sheeka said. "Only one thing really cures loneliness."

"What is that?" Another plea, but this one did not shame him.

"The sense that the universe knows that we're here."

Confusion warred with clarity. "But how can it see me among so many brothers? We're all the same."

"No," she said, her voice carrying a new sharpness. "You're not. As you told me, no two of you have ever had the same experiences. So no two of you can be the same."

"I lied," he said, the words twisted with anguish. "There's no *me* inside. It's all *us*. The GAR. My brothers. The Code. But where am I? Who am I?"

"Listen to your heart." Her palm and fingers rested against his chest. He felt the warmth, so deeply that for a moment he feared its cessation, feared that if she drew her hand away he would become a man of ice.

Again.

"Your heartbeat says it all. It says we are all completely unique."

She paused.

"And that, in that very uniqueness, we are all the same."

We are all the same . . . because we are all unique. The words echoed through the chamber, but he heard them not merely with his ears. He knew now why she had asked him to cease listening to the sounds. Cease using his *outer* ears, so that the inner voices could whisper their secrets. "Unique, as every star is unique. As every particle of the universe is unique."

And in that uniqueness, we are all the same. Every being. Every particle. Every planet. Every star.

He was speaking to himself. She spoke to him. The dashta eels spoke to him. His wrinkled, bearded, and beloved future self, the Jangotat who would never be, spoke to him. The child he had never been, who had known a mother's love and a happy home, a mother who would nurture him that he might one day make his own choices in the world . . .

All of these spoke to him. Each in its own voice, but to-

gether they blended into a single chorus, a single blended
sentiment, overwhelming in its simplicity and abiding love.

He sagged from his knees onto his side. All false strength,
all bravado drained from him like water squeezed from a
sponge. In its place remained a sense of lightness rather than
power. He had always felt himself to be a man of iron, if not
durasteel. What need had durasteel for air or water or love?

Jangotat heard a wet slippery sound, then another and yet
another. He looked up. The legless eels wriggled cooing
from the pool, surrounding him. Very tentatively, he bent and
reached out, touched the nearest. Its blind, eyeless face observed him with a vast and aching intelligence. Its touch was
Love itself.

"What did you see?" Sheeka asked from behind him.

"Another life," he said.

"Another life?"

He nodded. "I might have been born to a mother and father. Had brothers and sisters. Played with my pets."

That last seemed to surprise her. "Pets?"

Absurdly gentle emotions flooded him. "I saw a Corosian
phoenix once. The most beautiful thing I ever saw. I wanted
one. As a pet." He laughed at himself. "Not at that station.
Not at any post I know of. A burden to the army, you see?"

"Strange," she said, voice troubled. "Strange. Usually the
Guides are a healing influence."

"They are." His bruised lips turned up in a smile. "For
given that other option, I choose *my* life. However and for
whatever purpose I was given life, still I choose everything
that led me to this moment."

He paused again, the world spinning around him. Within
him. "I choose everything that led me to this place, and to
you."

She sank down beside him, the eels parting to make room.
Although they could not see, they saw all.

She pressed her full warm lips against his, setting her
hands against his cheeks to draw him even closer. Although
he had shared kisses with other women, this was different, an
unfolding in his heart.

Sheeka Tull placed her cheek against his, and whispered something that he could not quite hear.

"What?" he asked, afraid to know. "What did you say?"

"That thing you've never heard," she answered. Then paused again before speaking the words he had waited a full, brief lifetime to hear. "I love you."

Sheeka Tull's beautiful dark face rippled with reflected light. Jangotat knew that his existence had contained no greater peace and fulfillment than this. They kissed again, her lips warm against his.

68

The next days seemed a sort of dream, a phantasmal passage from which he would inevitably awaken. The village accepted the fact that he had moved into Sheeka's house, her children that he had moved into her guest room.

As Jangotat sat sunning himself, Sheeka's son Tarl came to sit with him on the porch. They talked for a time, and then Jangotat began to use his knife to carve the yellow-haired lad a toy.

He knew that they were welcoming him to become one of them. That while such a choice was impossible, Sheeka was inviting him to stay. These were peaceful folk who prayed Cestus would not be pulled into a conflict beyond their understanding. He now comprehended so much more. The eels had given their beloved friends permission to use the sterile young, but for defensive purposes only. Only to give the humans a means of income, to save the economy of the planet that gave them life. Modifying security droids for the battlefield was an abomination that might destroy them all. Just another level of confusion.

But despite the problems, without really saying a specific word, the Zantay Hills fungus farmers were offering Jangotat something he had never really had: not merely a bunk, but a home. Sheeka's stepdaughter Tonoté came to sit at his other side, her red hair ruffled by the noon breeze blowing in off the desert.

"Where will you go after?" Tonoté asked in her disarmingly fragile voice.

"After what?"

"After you stop being a soldier. Where will you go? Where is your home?"

"The GAR is my home."

She leaned her small head against his shoulder. "But when you stop fighting. Where will you go?" Strangely, those words seemed to resonate in his mind. *Where will you go . . . ?*

You're not intended to "go" anywhere. You will die where you are told.

"I don't know what you mean." Why had he lied? *The greatest wish of a trooper is to die in service.*

Isn't it? The possibility of another fate had never really occurred to him. The clones hadn't existed long enough for any of them to wither in their premature fashion, or retire . . . whatever *that* might mean to a being with such a truncated life span.

There was simply no precedent.

Tarl looked up at him adoringly, and Tonoté bent her long graceful neck to lean her little head against Jangotat's shoulder. Sheeka watched from the window, smiled secretively, then closed the shutters again.

69

Sandstorms raged the next day, followed by one of Cestus's brief, violent rains. It tamped down the dust but also created a canopy of dark, heavy clouds. Time seemed to stretch endlessly, and through much of the morning Jangotat wandered the muddy streets alone, seeking he knew not what. Something. Some understanding of these people that continued to elude him. They watched him as they flowed among the stone houses, and were friendly enough, but treated him as what he was: someone who was just passing through. Just on his way to somewhere else. The deepest smiles and sweetest laughter were confined to those who would stay, or might return.

He was neither.

Late that evening, news reached Sheeka that contact had been made with Desert Wind. Jangotat made his tearful goodbyes with the village, and Sheeka's children. He longed to return to the dashta cave to make another, equally difficult farewell, but intuition told him the request would be presumptuous. It was he who had been presented to the dashtas, not they to him. Their lair was a secret, and a risk had been taken even bringing him there. He could not, would not, ask for more.

Sheeka took him to a neutral landing site, where a few minutes later a two-person speeder bike appeared, piloted by Desert Wind's youngest member.

"How are things going, Skot?" Sheeka asked.

OnSon's mouth managed to twist into the vestige of a smile.

"We're regrouped, and that's more than I would have expected a week ago. It's all right, except for Thak Val Zsing."

She started. "What of him?"

OnSon sneered. "He betrayed us. I'm not sure what happened, but the old man lost it. He knew those killer droids were coming. Instead of warning us, he saved his own hide. Pretty messed up." He looked at Jangotat. "Well. I didn't really expect to see you up and around so soon."

Jangotat shrugged. "I've had a lot of help from . . ." He glanced at Sheeka, who shook her head subtly. "Friends."

"Friends are good to have," OnSon said.

Sheeka Tull's beautiful dark face was calm and impassive. "Will I see you again?" she asked Jangotat quietly.

"I don't know." Finally, the truth.

She rested her head against his chest and pounded it softly with closed fists. "I don't know why I do this to myself," she said in a small voice. "I just have this soft place in my head for you strong, quiet, self-contained types."

His arms, arms that could not protect her, enfolded her small, wiry frame. "Don't you mean *a soft place in my heart*?" he whispered into her hair.

She glanced up at him, a hint of mischief lightening her face. "I meant exactly what I said."

Then Jangotat surprised himself, leaning down to kiss her thoroughly, without any concern for what OnSon or anyone else might see or think.

And then he left. As the speeder bike raced on, he looked back at the dwindling, dust-blown figure of Sheeka Tull, intuiting that he would never see her again, but not knowing exactly what that might mean for either of them.

70

By roundabout routes young OnSon brought Jangotat back to the new camp. It was set up in an abandoned mine in a tumbled range of hills, completely overgrown and impossible to approach without being seen. He immediately approved of the location, and wished that they had found one as good before their first disaster. Such foresight might have spared some of the spider clan.

After hiding the speeder they moved through rocky overhangs—mindful of the possibility of spy satellites—and he was led into the cave.

His surviving brothers welcomed him, of course. Memory of what had happened just prior to his injury was muzzy, but according to all accounts he had acquitted himself well.

Crouching in the rocks at the outskirts of the camp lurked old Thak Val Zsing. Where before he seemed merely gray-bearded and a bit tired, now he was elderly. Derelict. Broken, a shadow of the boastful and boisterous man he had been just days before. The other members of Desert Wind avoided him like the plague, and twice he saw men spit into the dust at his feet. In a single unthinking instant, Thak Val Zsing had obliterated a lifetime of courage.

Honor. Such a fragile thing.

Jangotat spent hours exploring the new environs, familiarizing himself with the escape routes, and getting caught up on all the logistics. He was briefed on Obi-Wan's JK encounter and the Clandes plant's temporary closing.

All those losses, and the near death of General Kenobi,

and all that had been accomplished was a *temporary* shutdown. This was 10 percent.

"What have you heard?" he asked Forry.

"Word is General Kenobi still hasn't got an uplink. Must be ready to pop."

"So . . . no news on the Clone Wars?"

"None. Anything could be happening up there. Out there." Forry shook his head. "This is about as ten percent as it gets."

Late that night a shuttle landed at the western pad, disgorging the two Jedi without fanfare or fuss. Obi-Wan and Kit slipped through the camouflaged cave mouth and were immediately briefed by the clone commandos and brought up to date on all that had happened in their absence. Then the Jedi went off to a small side cave they had taken as their own lodging, and made preparations for sleep.

Kit noticed an odd quietude about Obi-Wan, but his companion decided to speak before the Nautolan could inquire into his mood. "I remember her words, Kit."

"Whose words?"

"G'Mai Duris. She warned me that this could turn into a no-win scenario, one where I might well fail to prevent the destruction of an entire, peaceful people."

Kit stirred the fire with his stick. Sparks circled up into the air. "Then we mustn't fail. By the Thousand Tides, there must be a way."

"Yes," Obi-Wan said, and managed a smile. "But knowing it, and saying it, is not the same as finding it."

71

Anxious but loath to reveal the extent of his anxiety, Obi-Wan watched as Sirty struggled to repair their damaged equipment. After heroic exertions the trooper had managed to conceal a message on a tight-beamed commercial fertilizer order from Resta's Kibo Lake farm, but he doubted they would be able to use *that* particular trick again. The forces arrayed against them were powerful, and clever indeed. The only safe thing to do was assume that no more than a single message could be sent or received in any single route.

Sirty's comlink squawked to life. "We have it, sir!"

"Luck?" Obi-Wan asked.

"Perseverance. I was able to tap into one of the backup circuits. Military equipment has built-in redundancy."

"Splendid."

Obi-Wan took his position as the communications equipment fired up. Within seconds he received an image of a male Falleen tech at a distant relay station.

The high-collared, emerald-skinned hologram image raised an eyebrow. "I do not recognize your communications protocols."

"Automatic authentication has been damaged," he said, and then provided a coded series of words, concluding with: "—This is Obi-Wan Kenobi, Jedi Knight, on Republic business. Provide a link and you will be rewarded."

"Very well."

After six minutes of static Obi-Wan learned that his first choice, Master Yoda, was unavailable, in the field supervising an operation. He made a swift decision, changed his access codes, and Palpatine himself appeared. "Chancellor?"

The politician's wise and weathered face creased with pleasure. "Master Kenobi. The Council and I had begun to worry."

"There is cause," the Jedi admitted. "Not all has gone well."

"Explain, please."

Obi-Wan took a deep breath and then proceeded. "Cestus is not an obscure planet producing a dangerous machine. It seems to be at the center of an invisible game board. Count Dooku has infiltrated deeply, focusing unforeseen resources here."

"To what end?" The Chancellor's deep, resonant voice was calming.

"To the end that my mission was compromised, and that we are forced to hide. We strike at the infrastructure when possible."

The Chancellor brooded before answering. "Do you expect this tactic to be successful?"

"I do not know. But I request more time to try."

The Chancellor shook his head. "We need results, General Kenobi. I intend to assign a supercruiser to assist you."

Obi-Wan's heart sped up. "But sir, don't you think—"

"I think that a warship positioned in orbit around Cestus would make them a bit more mindful, don't you?"

"But the Confederacy will use it as an excuse to counterattack with their own ships, and claim that they were merely protecting an innocent planet against Republic aggression."

"Well then, you had better resolve the situation before those ships arrive, hadn't you?"

The Chancellor terminated the transmission.

Obi-Wan seethed. There it was. First "a ship" and then "before the *ships* arrive." The Chancellor was sending a not-so-subtle message: if Count Dooku interfered, Palpatine would be happy to humble him. In fact, considering their problem in getting Confederacy forces to expose themselves, Obi-Wan wondered if this entire affair might not have been a feint, a mere drawing thrust, designed specifically to provoke an aggressive response.

But no. If he thought that, the next thought, the very next thought was to wonder if Palpatine was capable of sacrificing all of their lives in exchange for victory . . .

Despite his distrust of politicians, he did not, could not believe this.

But if he did, what then?

And if he could not resolve this, death could come in any of a dozen ways: slain by friendly fire, by security guards, by military bombardment . . .

Or even at the unseen hands of their mysterious adversary.

By sunrise the next day it was once again time to organize themselves into a cohesive unit. With Nate's return, Obi-Wan sensed a chance to increase their efficiency.

Plus . . . Obi-Wan sensed that *something* had happened to the soldier. While he had certainly healed his flesh and bone, even more interesting were the apparent changes in his psyche.

"Jangotat, where exactly were you?" he asked the prodigal trooper when he first gave his abbreviated report.

"I don't know the exact location, sir, and I'd rather not convey that data." A pause, followed by a swiftly added, "Unless the general insists, of course. Are you insisting, sir?"

"No," Obi-Wan said, after thinking carefully. "I assume you would relate anything of interest or concern to this operation."

"Affirmative, sir," Jangotat answered, and returned to cleaning his weapons.

That had been almost twenty hours earlier. Now Obi-Wan watched the troopers practicing unarmed combat among themselves, throws and holds and short, chopping blows with the side of the fist. Nothing fancy, but all with professional form and intensity, combined with an adequate knowledge of the interior targets. This was not merely demonstration, although recruits were watching. Nor was it merely exercise, although by the time they were finished all were sopping with sweat.

No, he intuited that this was a diagnostic activity, a way for the troopers to assure themselves that every member of their ranks was up to Code in every conceivable manner.

And he detected something else, as well—a sense of fluidity and grace in motion a little surprising to see from a mass-produced warrior. If he was not mistaken . . .

Yes. There was a hip feint flowing into a heel kick, a storing of elastic energy in the muscles and tendons that bespoke some small amount of more advanced training. In fact, he guessed that he knew exactly where they had obtained such knowledge.

"Excuse me," he said when they had finished an intense engagement. "I seem to recognize some elements of Jedi Flow drills. Has Master Fisto been instructing you?"

They looked both pleased and embarrassed, and Obi-Wan realized they had been showing off for him.

"Yes. A little. Just some basics, of course," Forry added hurriedly, as if worried Obi-Wan might be offended.

He laughed. "No, please. That's fine. But . . . with your permission, might I join for a few falls?"

Sputtering their delight, the troopers spread out as Obi-Wan stepped into the ring and faced off with Jangotat.

He knew that the man would be strong, quick, and well trained. The additional flow was a beautiful thing to feel, and Obi-Wan allowed the engagement to continue for several minutes. It was just a game, of course, with the intent to shift and adjust dynamic balance, not merely overwhelm the opponent. What he hadn't anticipated was the clone's capacity for subtlety and improvisation. And his sensitivity to slight changes in pressure and speed was excellent.

Obi-Wan tested his theory, playing with the other commandos, one after another. They were skilled, and fluid, but . . . Jangotat had something else. Emotional empathy. Insight. More of an ability to imagine what his opponent might have been thinking or feeling. It was hard to believe that the man had been wounded only a few days before. Where had he gone? What had he done?

Obi-Wan faced Jangotat. "Let's take this up a notch. First fall?"

Jangotat nodded, setting himself.

The two engaged, with Jangotat making the first aggressive move. Obi-Wan balanced the incoming force with a finely judged sidestep and pivot. When the dust cleared the captain was on the ground, neatly confined in a Juzzian armlock, nerve-pincered at wrist and elbow. Obi-Wan stood with one foot on Jangotat's shoulder, twisting and stimulating the nerves until Jangotat slapped the ground in surrender.

He thanked them for the exercise, and had turned to walk away when the trooper hailed him. "Master Kenobi!"

Obi-Wan stopped and waited for the soldier to catch up with him. "Yes?"

"I—" He was about to say something, but then withheld it at the last moment. "We are greatly inferior to you."

That wasn't what he had been about to say. Nonetheless, Obi-Wan responded to it. The last minutes of combat had taught him valuable things about the ARC trooper, all of them positive. "No! No! You are courageous, coordinated, tenacious . . . qualities anyone would admire." He smiled. "Qualities *I* admire." Obi-Wan sighed in exasperation. *Something* had awakened within the ARC trooper. Where ordinarily Obi-Wan would have celebrated that awakening of individual spirit, however, if the trooper sensed that Obi-Wan might be an ally in finding his individual truth, that revelation could hardly have been more inopportune than it was now.

In another week they might all be dead. Still, it made no sense not to do what he could to comfort a troubled soul. Finally, he asked the question he had long thought, and knew the official answer to, but had never dwelled upon. "I know that troopers are obedient to a fault. But in your heart, do you ever question orders?"

Jangotat's shoulders squared so swiftly that the posture could only have been a programmed response. "Soldiers do not question. Soldiers obey." He paused, and Obi-Wan had the sense that the trooper's mask had been dropped. This was a different man from the one who had originally taken ship with them. "Don't they?"

There was a question *behind* the question. And another behind *that* one as well. Obi-Wan walked for a few minutes, secure in the knowledge that Jangotat would follow. He found a small clearing and sat on a rock, inviting the trooper to sit beside him. "Many volunteer for the military life. Others are conscripted for a time, then after the alarm bells have died away return to their farms or families. But what of a man born for war, trained for war? I can sense your ambivalence, Jangotat. There are answers you would like to have. Considering how carefully your mind has been shaped, I'm impressed that you can even formulate your queries." Obi-Wan sighed and scratched at one of the abrasions won during his recent struggle with the JK. "You cannot be free. You were born to fight in other men's wars with no hope of gain or glory."

He closed his mouth, certain that he had said too much. Obi-Wan had never commented on this matter of clones and freeborn people. It was not his affair. Perhaps even now Jangotat regretted his inquiry.

Surprisingly, Jangotat was not put off by Obi-Wan's words or tones. "What about feelings?" he asked. "The Jedi are the best fighters I've ever seen. But you've got feelings."

Obi-Wan chuckled. "If not, we wouldn't strive to keep them under control." Obi-Wan feared that he, like so many others, assumed that every trooper had his place, an infinite array of identical laser cannon fodder regressing like a hall of mirrors until it not only filled but defined the horizon.

But Jangotat put the lie to that assumption. "Do you have a home?" he asked, almost shyly.

"The Jedi Temple is my home. And has been since childhood."

"And you *chose* to become a Jedi?"

"Yes. I was raised from infancy within the Temple's walls. There was certainly a moment when I made a formal decision to become a Jedi Knight, but in fact my feet were placed on that path before I could walk."

"Weren't you too young to make a decision like that?"

Obi-Wan considered the question carefully. Was there any way that the boy he had been could have known what his present life would be? All of the dangers, the travails? Or the wonders? What would that boy have thought, had he known?

He answered with deliberation. "If I had made that choice with my head, perhaps."

"Your heart?"

"Some might say," Obi-Wan replied. "But truth is that we sense the Force with our whole bodies. Every part of me knew that this would be my destiny. I knew I would not have the joys and comforts accorded normal folk. Even at that early age, I accepted that fact." Obi-Wan reached a hand out to the clone, clasped his shoulder. "I made that choice."

"That choice was made for me," Jangotat said.

So they were on opposite sides of a divide: one a man who had forsaken all the normal trappings of life for an existence of service and adventure. The other, a replaceable cog in a faceless army, chosen before birth, poured into a mold that he was uniquely suited to fill.

Had Obi-Wan made the choice, or had his midi-chlorians? In the final analysis had either he or Jangotat had any real choice at all . . . ?

Did anyone?

72

Shadows arced in silent pantomime against the cave wall, fueled by a roaring scrap-wood fire. As Obi-Wan scanned the assembled members of Desert Wind, he thought that all over the galaxy, throughout all ages past, courageous beings of a thousand breeds had held conclave in such caves, before such fires, for similar reasons.

"We face tremendous obstacles," he began.

"But we done all right," Resta said.

"It's true. And at a cost. And the cost is rising. We cannot afford it."

"How did this happen?" OnSon brushed his long blond hair back from his forehead, exposing a crescent moon of a scar. "We've worked so hard . . ."

Obi-Wan was troubled to hear the pain in that young voice. "It's true," he replied. "And the fault is not in you. You have given your blood and sweat to us in full measure. We've failed you." Kit Fisto stared into the embers impassively. Obi-Wan wished he could guess what his friend was thinking.

The men and women, perhaps thinking that the Jedi was preparing to leave them, protested vocally. "No!" OnSon said. "Without you we would never have struck so hard and deep. This hasn't been for nothing!"

"No," Kit Fisto said. "It has not. But we have been thwarted at every turn, and we believe that there are additional factors of which we are unaware."

"What factors?" Resta growled.

"Information has reached the government, gathered either

through spies or devices, or traitors, or . . ." And here his voice trailed off as he sank deeper into his thoughts.

"Or what?"

"Or someone who is both knowledgeable and ruthless. Someone who is able to . . ." His voice trailed off again. The spark of an intuitive flash stirred in his mind. That flash had first arisen during a deep meditation early that morning, while the rest of the camp was asleep. During his trance, he had sensed that there was a connection. During his stay on Cestus he had brushed auras with someone . . . or *something* . . . that had become a vital factor in this whole situation. But he had been behind the curve continuously since he had arrived. Everything had been perfect, and yet . . .

He shook himself out of his self-induced trance and continued. "Everything that has happened has thrown our plans out of sequence, and as a result we are fairly certain that Supreme Chancellor Palpatine will soon have a supercruiser here to threaten Duris. If the situation has not progressed by that time, there is a very real possibility that they will begin a bombardment that leads to total war." He paused to give time for his words to sink in. "If that happens *everyone* loses."

"What can we do?" Skot OnSon asked.

"I have an idea," the Jedi replied, "that might end this conflict without another shot fired, and without crashing the entire economy. It's dangerous, but it just might work."

73

In the days since Fizzik had joined his sister Trillot's organization, advancement had been rapid. It seemed that the gangster trusted nothing so much as blood relations. Fizzik found himself carrying out missions of greater and greater importance, but never allowed himself to forget how quickly his shift in fortunes could change. So when Fizzik was sent east to the Jantos trading post to meet with the Jedi, he was understandably anxious.

"So," Fizzik said, "what do you want?" His nerves twitched in this place. If his sister had wished him assassinated, the mission profile might have looked very similar.

"I seek to make a purchase," Obi-Wan said.

"And what precisely is it that you desire?"

"A class six Baktoid radiation suit."

"And to what use would you put such a suit?"

"That is my affair."

Fizzik peered into the bearded Jedi's blue eyes, wishing he were better at reading human facial expressions. This was a dangerous piece of information to carry. He knew that the Jedi were causing chaos in the industrial complexes, and anyone who aided or abetted sabotage could be executed.

A radiation suit. Had he once heard rumor of a control system protected by a reactor? Possibly, but one never knew how trustworthy such rumors were. What was this Jedi up to?

But Fizzik kept his thoughts to himself, stood, and bowed. His was not to reason why. His was merely to serve his sister until he found a more desirable berth.

Which, considering the deteriorating conditions here-about, might not be found on Cestus at all.

"And you trust this Trillot?" Kit asked after Obi-Wan returned.

"She's given me everything I asked. Spoken truthfully in every way I can check. Our sources on Coruscant trust her." He sighed.

"I notice you don't say that *you* trust her," Kit observed.

"I have a plan," Obi-Wan said. "And it needs Trillot. And I am willing to take the risk. Trillot once spoke of a hidden control station, protected by a radiation field. It would be very expensive to obtain protection, but if I had it, I could enter the Cestus reactor complex and shut down Clandes's entire production line without causing extreme damage to the infrastructure. I think that that might do it."

"And then, sir?" Forry asked.

"We could call off the bombardment, and negotiate."

"But how much money have we raised from our raids?" OnSon asked. "Wasn't it supposed to be a survivors' fund?"

"If this doesn't work, there won't be enough survivors left to divide a credit," he said. "Our priorities have changed."

The worst part was the waiting. For a signal from Trillot. For a signal from the fleet. From the outlying farms, vulnerable to reprisals from the Cestian security forces.

Waiting was always bad, but Obi-Wan used some of that time to spar with Jangotat. The trooper seemed to have an insatiable appetite for Jedi combat, and as long as he remembered the ARC's limitations, Obi-Wan was inclined to share a bit more knowledge with him.

With Obi-Wan's permission, Jangotat demonstrated his understanding of the Jedi Flow drills until he was sopping with sweat.

"Well?" Jangotat said, and then added, "General?"

Obi-Wan tilted his head sideways, realizing that they had somehow wandered into a very odd relationship. "You're doing well. Remember when you find a knot of tension in your body—don't power through it. Relax, let it melt. Breathe into it. Your flesh remembers every pain, emotional or physical, you have ever suffered," Obi-Wan said. "It is trying to protect you. Pain and fear compete with skill and awareness."

"General Fisto said that thoughts and fears are like boulders, and the Force is the river rushing between them. Most people grow so clogged with pains and regrets that the water can no longer flow from the mountain to the sea."

Obi-Wan laughed. "Very good. Much of Jedi training is designed to remove those obstructions."

"But General Fisto warned that I could never learn to be as good as a Jedi," Jangotat said.

Obi-Wan's voice was gentle. "The joy in life comes not from surpassing another's gifts, but in fully manifesting our own."

Jangotat weighed those words, then apparently decided that practice was better than analysis and spent another grueling hour wrenching his body into exotic shapes and surges, finding the deep wells of fear, and resentment, and loneliness locked in his muscles, releasing them. One meter, one moment at a time, Jangotat was finding his way to the sea.

74

Admiral Arikakon Baraka was in a foul mood. He had been forced to take part in the clone training exercise, and now he followed orders that were taking him far afield from the Separatist hunt, bringing the *Nexu* to a planet called Cestus. By the time he finished threatening this Rim world, the rest of the fleet would have already engaged in some major battle, and the glory would belong to others.

This was no way to gain promotion, or the approval of his ancestors, which he craved even more.

Nonetheless, Baraka monitored the navigation routes, commanded his men, ran drills on all critical systems, and prepared to do his job. He would grind these Cestians to dust, then head back for the major battle sure to take place somewhere in the Borleias drift.

Only one thing stood between him and glory.

And soon, there would be nothing at all.

The speeder bikes purred to Obi-Wan's touch, ready for the last leg of this adventure. Kit addressed the clone commandos as he finished packing his bags.

"Suspend all operations," the Nautolan said. "There must be no chance that any of you fall into enemy hands. Your bodies would be incontrovertible evidence against the Republic, paraded to the Thousand Worlds as evidence of Palpatine's treachery. Unless you hear directly from us, if we do not return, try beaming another message through Resta's farm. Signal Admiral Baraka to pick you up. Unless you receive a direct order do *not* leave this camp. Is that understood?"

The troopers glanced at each other uneasily. "Isn't it possible that we could launch a rescue if you run into trouble, General Kenobi?"

Obi-Wan managed a confident nod. "Do not leave this camp except under direct orders, am I clear?"

The troopers nodded, and the Jedi headed out into a strong headwind. The sandstorm continued to build as they traveled north toward ChikatLik. At times Obi-Wan looked behind him and couldn't see Kit's speeder; he had to trust that his companion was there.

Just as he could see no sure solution to the situation at hand, but needed to have faith that such an answer did, indeed, exist.

"We have the credits you requested. Where is our suit?" It had taken an entire day to make their way back into ChikatLik, and Obi-Wan's nerves were badly frayed. This was an unforeseen additional complication.

Trillot tittered. "There is nothing on this planet more highly protected than those suits. My nest is raided periodically—if it was found here, no legal defense or explanation would suffice."

Plausible enough, but . . .

Obi-Wan noted her discomfort, and suddenly he sensed danger around him. "Well then, where is it?" What was wrong? All the words were right, and yet . . . and yet . . .

"Follow me to my personal turbolift," Trillot said. "I will take you to the dock myself. Where are the credits?"

"Half now," Kit said, laying a satchel on the table before him. His dark, unblinking eyes never left their hostess. "And half after we have our suit. Fair?"

"Of course," Trillot replied.

Obi-Wan and Kit followed Trillot to the lift platform. They entered and the door closed behind them. As they descended, Kit turned to Trillot, his huge dark eyes reflecting the dim light. "I have heard of you, and am glad for this opportunity to meet. If there is difficulty, I promise you we'll never meet again."

"I think we will have no further business" was the gangster's pious reply.

When the lift stopped, they were in a freighter-size hive cavern beneath the main city. As far as the eye could see, thousands upon thousands of deserted hive cubicles stretched around the walls. Obi-Wan smelled water: a subterranean lake, perhaps a river. The dock was surrounded with stacks of unopened crates. *A hive converted to a smuggler's lair,* Obi-Wan thought. *Smuggling goods through subterranean rivers? Ingenious. But . . .*

"Be cautious," Obi-Wan said as they stepped out.

"An unneeded warning," Kit replied.

A third voice entered the conversation. "And a belated one." Instantly, a shimmering circle of light sizzled the air around Obi-Wan. He recognized it instantly: a Xythan force shield. *A snare.*

"A new security device created by Cestus Cybernetics. It absorbs and returns all energy. Feel free to use your lightsaber."

Obi-Wan knew that last voice. Suddenly, and with shocking clarity, all that had happened in the last days made terrible, and possibly terminal, sense. "Asajj Ventress," he said.

She appeared out of the shadows, but it was not shadows alone that had protected her. In each hand she held a glowing red lightsaber with a curved handle.

A dozen young X'Ting emerged from the boxes around her. Males, barely out of their adolescence, judging by the light rings of fur around their necks. They swaggered and postured, but they were callow.

"You have perfected the Quy'Tek meditations, Adept," he said. "You can shield your Force."

"From fools, yes," she said, and smiled. "Go ahead—use your lightsabers. The field will draw power from them."

"And those?"

Trillot crept around the edge of the energy field. She

seemed like a vex caught between two reeks. "They are loyal to the hive," she said.

"She has no love for you, Trillot," Obi-Wan said.

"And even less for you, I think." The gangster tittered.

Ventress turned to the gangster. "You may leave now, Trillot. Your protocol droid will translate my orders to the X'Ting."

Trillot went back up the turbolift as swiftly as it would move her.

Ventress smiled. "I knew, in the end, I would defeat you."

"You call this a fair fight?" The acid in Obi-Wan's voice did nothing to mask the lethal fury building within him. Now he understood all the death, all the critical failures since his arrival on Cestus. All attempts to bring this matter to a peaceful conclusion had been thwarted by this bald-pated witch, and the confusion he had felt until this moment was wiped away completely.

"No," she said calmly. "I call it victory."

Commander Baraka's supercruiser emerged from hyperspace and moved into position over Cestus. A swift scan revealed no defenses capable of resisting a ship of the *Nexu*'s class, so he approached without haste, taking this opportunity to put his crew through a series of attack drills.

Until ten hours passed, or they received a coded message, there was little to be done.

Cestus lay before them, a world of wealth without warriors to protect it. They now needed only a message from the surface, or one from the Supreme Chancellor. It was just a matter of time.

When the cruiser entered the system, alarm ripped through ChikatLik like a whirlwind. Everyone knew someone who had heard the rumor that the city was to be destroyed. Thousands left the city in the first three hours, a stream of refugees that clotted the skylanes and roadways.

G'Mai Duris went on the air, promising her citizens that the vessel was only there to protect the Republic's interests.

Since Cestus was a friend of the Republic, how could anyone think harm would come to them? The fact that this broadcast was also sent to every major star system along the Rim missed no one.

Quietly, leaders of the Five Families made excuses and slipped away to their private haven beneath Kibo Lake. To most Cestians, it seemed their planet was trapped between the Republic and the Confederacy, and they hoped to ride it out, survival temporarily transformed into a more urgent motivation than profit.

To the Five Families, a game was being played out that could end with their power broken, or raised to the highest levels. Palpatine might win. Count Dooku might win. No matter which, they intended to survive.

True, a storm had been unleashed upon Cestus, but as long as they survived, Confederacy contracts might yet be honored. After all, the entire galaxy was watching, and this would be a perfect time for Count Dooku to provide an objective example of the advantages to be found in trading the Separatists.

There were other factors, of course, factors discussed only among the Families, or by those who had reviewed very private evaluations distributed solely to the top families. But those factors, and their implications, would be meaningless if they did not survive the next few days . . .

"This will end in . . . perhaps twenty hours." Ventress glanced at the two Jedi, still trapped within the energy shield. "I regret that I will not have the opportunity to match lightsabers with you again, Obi-Wan Kenobi. Count Dooku wants you alive," she said, prowling at the edge of the shield. So intense was her hunger that the tips of her twin sabers trembled. "But mightn't he forgive me if I simply slew you in single combat?"

"Please." Obi-Wan locked eyes with her. "Try me."

"I'd rather that honor be mine," Kit said.

"Ohhh," she breathed. "Oh, yes, you and I. It will happen, Obi-Wan Kenobi. But I must remember that the operation is more important than my individual satisfaction or advancement. Surely you can understand this."

She looked up at the craggy ceiling above him. "The Supreme Chancellor will humble Cestus as an example to other breakaway planets. The fate of this one small planet will push hundreds of star systems into the Confederacy's arms. Mission accomplished."

"What of the biodroids? Don't you want them?"

She smiled. "It would be good, but volume production will require cloning, and our efforts to clone the dashta tissue will require another year, at least. For the time being, that is a dead end. A bluff."

She smiled and came closer, so close that her face almost touched the wall of shimmering energy. "Those beacons you planted in Clandes. Very nice. You could not enter the actual plant, so you triangulated three external signals. A good plan. But one easily countered. What a shame that the coordinates have been recalibrated," she said.

"What are you talking about?" Obi-Wan said, fearing that he understood her meaning precisely.

"You planned to destroy the filtration and power plants with minimal loss of life." She *tsk*ed. "I'm afraid that that won't do. Our plans require a more . . . dramatic event."

"What have you done?" he whispered.

"No . . . better you should ask what is it *you* have done," she said. "And why would you have a cruiser deliberately strike a cave fault, destroying the entire industrial complex and its millions? Yes, I think that a slaughter like that will polarize the galaxy, don't you?"

His head spun. And Count Dooku had no way of cloning or mass-producing dashta tissue for at least a year? "Then your droid order was a sham?"

"Intended to frighten Palpatine and your precious Jedi Council into an overreaction. I would say our plan worked, wouldn't you?" Her laughter was as warm as dry ice. "The resulting slaughter will tip the galaxy in our favor. Then once we do clone the tissues, who needs Cestus?"

"You're a monster," Kit said, voice calm as a dead sea.

At that moment the vast energies within Obi-Wan swirled and stilled. As hopeless as the situation seemed, he believed to his core that this was not over. Somewhere, Ventress had made a mistake. And when that single mistake manifested, he would be ready to take advantage . . .

75

Still under direct order, the four surviving clone troopers remained confined to base. They were fully aware of the forces struggling around them, and also of the nightmare about to descend on Ord Cestus.

Jangotat's mind swam with visions and possibilities. He more than anyone knew the ARC mission mandate. It was engraved on his brain like his own number. *Stop the production of JKs. Preserve the social order.*

Preserve the order? But the order was corrupt! The Five Families were willing to murder countless civilians to make a profit. If that was not the very definition of *betrayal,* what was? Even worse, only a fool couldn't see that they had already allied themselves with the Separatists, and the Jedi were no fools, that much was certain.

They, then, were caught in events, controlled by their programming. *Just like a clone,* he thought.

The *Nexu* hovered in orbit above them. Any minute now a message might come from General Kenobi to begin bombing. If not, within a few hours the ship would take out the beacon-marked targets without additional authorization.

These people were going to die. Ordinary citizens with roots couldn't just throw their homes in a rucksack and ship off when danger came. They railed against the darkness, they fought on for their loved ones, they prayed in silence.

The troopers waited, but the longed-for communication with the generals did not come. Dead? Captured? Time was running out. In a few hours the bombardment would begin, and that was all to the good, wasn't it?

Jangotat stalked the camp's perimeters, chewing on a nerve-stick while acid boiled his gut. *Something is wrong.*

When he circled back around to the others, Seefor was talking. "What do we do now?"

Forry shrugged. "If he doesn't come back, it didn't work. Then the bombardment begins, we call in transport, and we go home. Nothing to do but wait."

Jangotat wandered away, mind racing, hoping against hope that their Jedi commanders would call in, that the word would come that the line was shut down without the vast damage of an orbiting strike.

He was a bit surprised when old Thak Val Zsing and the X'Ting woman Resta approached him. Val Zsing had seemed broken, but now there was something alive and almost aflame about him. "I know things," he said. "Please. Listen to me."

Jangotat, remembering what he had learned in the cave, opened his senses. He saw the man's wounds as well as his strength. He believed that this miserable wretch needed, deserved, one chance to redeem himself.

We are more than our actions. More than our deeds, or programming.

"What is it?" he asked.

"No one talk to Resta. No one talk to Thak Val Zsing," she said. "So we two talk. Talk about the old days. What Gramps say 'bout the prisons, how Resta's hive forced to dig in them. I remember things about them." She tapped her finger against her temple. "I see I know things about 'Secutive 're-sort.' " She snorted. "You know, the one they rip away power away to build? The one that kill my man?"

The X'Ting leaned closer, her thick red eyebrows arched and erect. "I look at 'puter map."

"Our computers?"

Thak Val Zsing nodded. The old man's eyes were piercingly hot. "Same routing map you used to get through the tunnels, when the Jedi put on their little show, remember, star-boy?"

Jangotat agreed that he did, still not seeing the point.

"That program charts energy usage, utilty bills, all kindsa real-time routing information on the major systems." Val Zsing's voice hushed to an excited whisper. "And we saw something. Oh, brother, did I ever see something."

"In last five hours, since big ship pull into orbit, 'resort' light glow." Resta leaned forward, so excited she could barely contain herself. *"That where Five Families hide!"*

"I want to discuss a possibility with you," Jangotat said to his brothers. He struggled to conceal his excitement.

"Possibility?" Seefor asked. "What kind of possibility?"

"The Families may have made a critical mistake. If this intel is good, for the first time we know where they are. They've powered up their resort facilty, which we believe to be a shelter. Considering the present emergency, I'd say there's a high level of confidence that they'll be there. If we grab them, we can *force* them to make a deal. If they capitulate, we can end this and stop the bombing."

For a long moment no one spoke. Sirty was the first to break the silence, and was shocked. "But you'd be counter-manding direct orders!"

Jangotat slammed his fist on the table. "We could win the day!"

"Brother," Seefor said, "under the Kamino Accords I am compelled to warn you that your suggestion is not to Code."

Forry glared. "You don't do this," he said. "Besides—" He gave an ugly laugh. "—the old man's a coward. Probably a liar, too."

Against Code? Seefor's accusation struck Jangotat like a physical blow, but he didn't allow himself to cower. Even the idea filled him with physical nausea. No clone had ever broken Code or disobeyed an instruction of any kind. He felt an energy wall slam down in his mind, and his every muscle trembled as he even contemplated the forbidden. "I believe him," he said, and had to grit his teeth for a moment to stop them from clattering. "Ask yourselves: if you'd lost your honor, wouldn't you do *anything* to regain it? Wouldn't you want someone to give you that chance?" He knew that he had scored with that one: a clone commando had nothing if not his reputation. Seefor flinched in sympathetic pain at the very concept.

And yet at the same moment that he mentioned such a thing, he realized that he had drawn a line between himself and the others. There was something different about him, and they could feel it, but had yet to comment. By mentioning the unmentionable, however, he had given a focus to their instincts.

He was no longer completely one of them. He was something else, and his brothers were on guard.

"It is not Code, Jangotat," Seefor said, and stared at him. He knew he could take it no farther.

Jangotat returned to his bedroll. He knew what he contemplated, and why. He knew it was forbidden but he believed, believed with everything inside him, that if the generals knew what he knew, they would approve of his actions.

And yet . . .

He would be breaking Code.

His chest muscles constricted, and he felt a cold sweat dampen his armpits. What was right? What was truly Code? Was it the letter, or was it doing what he believed his commanders would do if they had his information?

Jangotat wrestled with that for hours before he made up his mind and slipped out of his bedroll. He had almost made it back out to the open when Forry caught up with him.

"Where are you going?"

"You know I have to do this," Jangotat said.

Forry nodded. "And you know I can't let you."

"Then stop me if you can," Jangotat replied. All things being equal, Jangotat and Forry should have been roughly equivalent fighters.

But things were no longer equal. Jangotat was fighting for everything Forry fought for, plus just a little bit more.

Sheeka. Tonoté. Mithail. Tarl.

The Guides.

It's not what a man fights with. It's what he fights for.

The two moved toward each other, paused for an instant

just as they reached critical distance, judging. In the next instant there followed an eye-baffling flurry of punches and kicks. Forry was stronger and faster . . .

But it didn't make a difference. Jangotat saw more clearly now, more than he ever had in his life, as if the entire moment were frozen in invisible ice. He saw Forry's patterned responses, the programmed blows and chops. Jangotat felt outside this somehow, watching the motion without being involved in it. Forry might as well have sat down and detailed his every intended motion in advance. Moving slowly, with greater calm than he had ever experienced in combat, Jangotat simply slid between Forry's movements. As he strove to keep the balance between them he contracted his stance, and Jangotat's natural flinch response moved his elbow into perfect position to clip his brother's jaw.

Forry slid to the ground, and was still. Jangotat stood there for a moment, shocked. Was that what it felt like to be a Jedi? Was that even a *fraction* of how it felt?

Or was this just how it felt to be free? He didn't know what door had been opened in his head, what training and . . . and . . .

And *love* had done for him.

He felt a deep excitement. He might be heading into death, but he was more alive than he had ever been, than *any* of his kind had ever been.

He could, he *would,* succeed. There was no other option.

He met with Thak Val Zsing and Resta by the speeder bikes. It took them only a few minutes to sabotage the other speeders—it would take his brothers an hour to fix them, by which time he would be long gone.

For fifty minutes they rode to the northwest. The air riffled his hair, and the new sun flared to his left as dawn breached the darkness. He enjoyed the solitude, the sense of being beyond it all. Of knowing, for the first time in his life, that he had chosen his fate.

A new, precious day. Perhaps his last.

He grinned ferociously. Best not waste a moment of it.

*   *   *

Fifteen kilometers north of Resta's farm a lava tube gaped in the middle of a mud plain. That is where they entered, carrying with them knapsacks filled with ordnance. For ninety minutes they crawled through darkness, bruising and slicing their knees on the glassy surface. Thak Val Zsing led the way, and from time to time he called back to them. "The prison was to the east now, and we're in one of the escape tunnels." He laughed with self-mockery. "Escape tunnels. What a joke: the whole planet was a prison—there was nowhere to escape *to*. But the central computers say that the Five Family resort was built in one of the wings of the old prison after it was abandoned."

They reached a larger section, crawling out into a cave tall enough for them to stand. More than tall enough: this was part of an old mine, with smaller shafts twisting off in all directions.

"This is as far as I know," the old man said. "This is where my grandfather escaped." Cestus Penitentiary's deepest pits were now bunkers for the Five Families. A savage irony, that.

"Let's go," Resta said, and tried to shoulder her way ahead.

Jangotat stood in her path. "You must live," he said.

"Got nothing live for. Lost mate. Lost farm."

Jangotat shook his head. "What happened here, to your people, shouldn't have happened. What you have done here will not go unnoticed. When this is over, file a report using the phrase *A-Nine-Eight tac code twelve*." He held her eyes. "That means that you performed extraordinary service for me during official business. You are a friend of the Republic, and the Republic looks after its own."

She glared at him, unwilling to believe. To trust that there was any way for her save revenge and death. "No. Go with you."

"Someone must sing your hive's song," Jangotat said. "Find a new mate. Make strong children. Never stop fighting."

She was so astonished that she didn't react when Jangotat

spun her and placed her in a sleeper hold. Resta struggled to free herself, and she was strong—stronger than most human males. But he had the right angle and position. No matter how she struggled, he hung on. She ran him back against a wall, but he hung on. A hundred different alien physiologies flashed through his mind, then he remembered the Geonosians. They were also insectile, and air strangles were considered worthless. But there were nerve clusters—

There, at the base of the skull. He disengaged one of his arms and leaned in with his elbow, pressing from both sides, gambling everything. Impact could prove fatal, but pressure alone . . .

Resta went limp and rolled over, unconscious.

Jangotat stared down at her, panting. What a fighter! What had it taken to sap the will of these people? "What are their *men* like?" he whispered to Thak Val Zsing.

"You don't want to know," Val Zsing replied.

Jangotat took a few moments to calm himself. Then Thak Val Zsing pointed out the last tunnel, and together they descended into darkness.

76

Another hour's crawling brought him to the wall of the outer chamber. A swift scan revealed that the wall was only one-centimeter durasteel, and Jangotat knew that he could handle it. The armor-piercing mines were designed for use against battle droids, but they would work here as well. Pulling out two of the round, flat disks, Jangotat attached them to the wall with their adhesive bands and set the timer. He and Thak Val Zsing had barely had time to retreat back around the bend when the sharply focused blast detonated with a clap that knocked both men onto their backs.

Dazed, Jangotat grabbed his rifle and rushed into the next room as red and yellow lights flashed warning. Through the smoke he glimpsed a bank of communications equipment and stacks of food supplies. He swiveled in time to glimpse a human and a Wroonian rushing into a dome-shaped durasteel bunker, slamming the door.

He got there too late, banging against the door with the butt of his rifle. The door was at least five centimeters thick. Nothing in his sack would get them through *that*.

The shelter hummed, vibrated, then settled down as the doors sealed shut.

"What now, star-boy?" Thak Val Zsing asked, coming up behind him.

"Let's check the room out," Jangotat said. "There might be something."

The room was an atrium, a hothouse designed to fit in with the rest of the shelter. It was as dense as a rain forest, unlike any terrain Jangotat had seen on Cestus. They moved through it slowly, watching for any movement.

He turned to see the Jedi Killer coming for them. He did not think, he acted.

He remembered the JKs all too well. Their speed, power, and versatility were beyond intimidating. There was no time to think, little even to move. He managed to step backward as its tentacles reached for him, and barely heard Thak Val Zsing scream "Look out!" as the floor beneath him rippled. A disguised tentacle, reaching, changing colors for camouflage as it did!

Amazing. One of the tentacles touched him, and he felt the shock for but an instant as he leapt back. One instant was long enough to send the hair exploding away from his scalp, but he was able to trigger a rifle blast at close range, severing the tentacle.

Thak Val Zsing was firing from the side, but the energy bolts glanced harmlessly off the JK's golden casing.

Val Zsing scrambled back screaming, just in time to avoid another tentacle. Jangotat threw himself to the rear, firing as he did, riding it out and rolling backward, coming to his feet in a single smooth motion, turning in the same motion, switching his rifle to maximal energy pulses.

Too fast!

The JK was a marvel, zigging this way and that, its narrow treads blurring far too quickly to track. Three shots, four. The rifle's barrel pulsed white as its blasts furrowed walls and floor, always missing the skittering machine. The rifle's power core was overheating, about to shut down. Jangotat gave ground, leaping back the way they had come.

Thak Val Zsing was already crouching there in the shadows, trembling and silent. The JK moved a meter toward them, then stopped and floated backward. Clearly, it wasn't going to be lured out of position.

"We can't stop it!" Thak Val Zsing said, shaking.

Jangotat grabbed him by the shoulders, shook him hard. "Get yourself together, man! Thousands will die if that cruiser fires."

But whatever emotional bones Thak Val Zsing had fractured back in the caves were still unable to carry the weight of his fear. Thak Val Zsing retreated.

Jangotat cursed and made a decision. Perhaps he couldn't stop the thing with gun blasts. *Let's see what bringing down the ceiling on it will do.*

He jumped through the hole, rolling and blasting at the ceiling as he did. Chunks of rock fell massively, glancing off the duracrete shelter dome and burying the JK, almost killing Jangotat at the same time. He lay gasping, leg shattered, as the rock began to roll away and the JK emerged.

"Thak Val Zsing!" he screamed as the thing came toward him. "Blast you, Val Zsing! Coward!" His frustration was complete, as was his failure.

The JK pulled him close, until he was almost touching it. It shone a beam of light into his eyes, perhaps attempting to match a retinal scan to its data bank. Then, unable to identify, it sent a jolt out along its tentacles.

Jangotat fell onto his side. Crackling blue flames danced up and down his body. He could see them. Feel them. Hear them.

What he couldn't do was move. At all.

"Thak Val Zsing! Coward!"

The former leader of Desert Wind was beyond fear, beyond shame. There are moments that define a human being, and once those moments occur it is impossible to undo them.

But sometimes, one could create a new fate.

Val Zsing peeled the adhesive off the mounting strip and slapped one of the armor-piercing mines to his chest. He had observed Jangotat, and was familiar enough with explosives to figure out the directions.

He entered the shelter and went straight at the droid. Its arms grabbed him so swiftly that he barely had time to trigger the timer.

The JK hesitated for a moment, as if trying to figure out why Thak Val Zsing hadn't attempted to escape. *Come on. A little closer* . . . It drew him in, to within a meter, and a tentacle rose to face level and flashed a light in his eyes.

Now, he thought. *Let it be now.*

Thak Val Zsing heard a last sound. *Ding.* Light flared, dwindled swiftly to black, and then there was nothing at all.

The detonation sent a wave of energy through the room, jolting Jangotat's nervous system. The little blue crackles rippling over his body died out, shaking him out of paralysis. Groggily, he checked his leg: broken, punctuated with shrapnel. A few bits of cloth told him what had happened to his companion.

So. No coward after all, Thak Val Zsing.

The JK was spattered with blood and dust, sooty, but began to right itself, its case undented. The thing was indestructible. A mixed curse: its case had shielded him from the blast.

Jangotat groaned. It was over. There was no hope after all . . .

But then the JK began to thrash about. As Jangotat watched in stunned amazement, it pushed itself upright, then fell over, then spun in a circle, stood, and shook, making an ear-grating keening sound.

And suddenly Jangotat guessed the truth. What a great joke! The best ever. He could only hope that he could tell it to someone, that his companions might one day laugh at the big freaking joke the whole business on Cestus had become. Jangotat laughed hysterically as he took a painful glance over at the bunker door. Nothing. The Five Family executives were sealed safely inside.

No one is safe, he snarled. *Time for a little lesson.*

Would this be right? Wrong? These people had sentenced an entire planet to death, and there was no one to stop them.

The JK ignored him, running back and forth and then banging itself into a corner, shuddering and bumping back and forth.

Jangotat thought that that was the funniest thing he'd ever seen.

He managed to drag himself over to the shelter door, wedging it shut with the blaster rifle. There. The weapon was good for something after all.

Now he couldn't get in, but neither could they escape.

Pain fogged his mind. What were the coordinates? He couldn't remember. What a joke. What an enormous joke. Then he remembered: why, the coordinates were *him*. He was the coordinate.

He fished for his comlink and pulled it out . . . smashed and useless.

Then he began laughing at himself again. This was a fully stocked shelter, from which the Five Families had evidently thought to ride out any revolt or attack. Their own communications gear would work just fine.

On board the *Nexu,* the communications tech, a veteran named CT-9/85, detected a signal. "Sir," he said to the officer in charge. "We have an ARC targeting code coming in over the radio, priority frequency."

Commander Baraka crossed to the comm station, face suddenly intent. "And the message?"

"To change initial bombardment coordinates to . . . somewhere a little east of Kibo Lake. Then to stand by for further instructions."

"Does this look legitimate?"

"One hundred percent. Trooper's calling the load in right on top of himself. Can't get more serious than that."

Baraka snorted his discomfort. What kind of brainless machines were these creatures? "What is that location?"

"We show it as a blip on the power grid. Might be some kind of secret base."

"Then let's get on with it," Baraka said, and gave the order.

Jangotat lay half across one of the chairs in the atrium, his shattered leg splaying out to the side. He busied himself with another message for ten minutes, and hit the transmission button just seconds before the bunker began to hum and shake.

The entire time Jangotat waited, he was surprised to find himself humming a tune.

One, one, chitliks basking in the sun.
Two, two, chitlik kista in the stew.
Three, three, leave a little bit for me . . .

What was the name of that tune? When had he learned it? Oh, yes: he remembered that he had heard Tarl and Mithail and sweet little Tonoté singing it, in the Zantay Hills. He hoped they would be safe.

The next explosion was shattering, and very close.

"From water we're born, in fire we die," he whispered. "We seed the stars."

77

Moments after the *Nexu* released the full fury of her primary energy weapons, the dome above the mysterious target had become a flame-scarred concavity. The groundquake fault that should have destroyed Clandes instead sent a minor tremor throughout the Kibo Plateau. There were no fatalities and few injuries, although the shock was measured as far south as Barrens. In Clandes a few walls cracked and alarms sounded citywide. To the north, toward ChikatLik, there was another, more immediate effect.

The underground lake's surface reflected flashes of red and yellow lightning as the energy field confining Obi-Wan and Kit Fisto lessened for an instant. Kit felt pain and fire as he lunged through, his lightsaber absorbing enough of the energy to keep the shield from frying him. It snapped back on swiftly enough to singe Kit's left heel as the Nautolan jumped free.

The protocol droid barked an order, and all of Ventress's allies laid their weapons down.

"Surely they're not surrendering," Kit said.

Ventress laughed. "By no means. I told them they don't stand a chance against you with blasters."

"And . . ."

"And now," she said, "defend yourselves, Jedi."

The young X'Ting thugs moved in. Obi-Wan groaned. He couldn't simply cut them down. Young and foolish, they believed they were acting for the good of the hive.

"I know what you're thinking," Ventress grinned. "You wish you could talk to them. A pity you don't speak X'Ting."

"Obi-Wan?" Kit asked.

"Well, we can't just slaughter them."

No . . ? Kit seemed to want to ask. "They're hardly innocent." The Nautolan radiated urgency, the pull of Form I strong as he prepared for battle. Ventress was the key. They had to stop her. And if these idiots put themselves between them and Dooku's minion, the woman who might be the salvation of millions, that was their misfortune.

But . . . it would be a massacre. Obi-Wan searched his conscience, and made a hard decision. "We must do this without our lightsabers."

Kit seemed to struggle with the idea, and then finally sighed. "A bit of exercise, then," he said, and reluctantly extinguished his blade.

Obi-Wan dampened his as well, and as if on cue, Ventress's foolish young X'Ting allies attacked from every angle. Obi-Wan leaned away from the swipe of a durasteel crowbar, the edge of his foot cracking the X'Ting's knee as he did. A second youth jumped on him from behind. Obi-Wan gripped a primary right hand, a secondary left hand, and torqued: The X'Ting corkscrewed through the air and shattered a pile of boxes.

Kit Fisto snarled, surrendering to the pull of Form I's unarmed techniques. His attack was absolute fluidity, one motion flowing into the next without a wasted effort. Heads cracked, limbs twisted against their joints, and X'Ting flipped howling into the lake.

Ventress stood back, her eyes watching, and Obi-Wan knew she was waiting, learning about her opponents.

The cavern was awash with whirling bodies. These were lackeys, and Ventress would sacrifice every one of them to learn what she wished to know. She knew the Jedi wouldn't just cut them down. She was watching, and studying, and saving the moment for herself. The Jedi's unarmed tactics would reveal their lightsaber technique: there was nothing they could do to prevent it.

Obi-Wan's opponents had enthusiasm, but little technique. The Force blossomed within him, and time perception distended, slowing reality to a crawl. He had all the time he needed to slide out of the way of the blows, retaliating with perfect economy.

From the corner of his eye he saw that Kit had made his way almost to Ventress, and what he saw as the Nautolan increased his efforts almost broke Obi-Wan's concentration. His companion was a living, martial hurricane, his body moving in two and three directions at once, joints flexing, unlimited by human vertebral restraints.

Who he touched went down. And those who went down, stayed down. Ventress might have gathered a rabble, but the youthful X'Ting were fearless, and fought as if for their lives.

Such an onslaught left no time for thought or planning, no room for pretty moves. There was only attack and defense, and precious little time for defense.

Obi-Wan himself could only attack and attack, taking the battle to them, creating his own timing and distancing, smashing his way toward Ventress.

Stingers bared, the young X'Ting came at them in waves. Obi-Wan calmed himself, using them as shields against each other, moving continuously and ferociously as he went.

Now . . . a blow from the upper left quadrant. Obi-Wan was just a hair slow defending there, and a wicked knife slit his cloak. Again and again, he narrowly skirted disaster. *She's watching?* Obi-Wan thought. *Let her.*

Obi-Wan missed the moment, but Kit finally won his way through to Ventress. She raised her hand, and the X'Ting who had harried the Nautolan turned to attack Obi-Wan, leaving her to face Kit alone.

Now, finally, Kit drew his lightsaber. Ventress drew a pair of blazing, red blades. She inclined her head, breathing more quickly, lips curling into a smile.

"Finally," she said.

"Your pleasure," Kit hissed, and went at her. He was like

fire, Ventress like smoke. The dance had substance but not form, a blur of light that seemed impossibly fast, unbelievably deadly. The two leapt and swerved, collided and bounced away. Single against double lightblades. Hands, knees, feet, all in a mind-numbing blur.

Obi-Wan would have given his right hand to join. Or even to watch such a display. But he had his own worries, his own battle to fight.

He struggled with the urge to simply draw his lightsaber and slaughter the X'Ting. His enemies came on and on, struck quickly but clumsily, got in each other's way. Obi-Wan was direct in attack, and as elusive as a breeze.

He'd missed the engagement, but suddenly—*Kit was down!* Wounded and groggy from a kick in the jaw, for the first time Ventress had pierced his guard. Her left-hand saber sliced his arm but as sparks flew he dove away from her left blade, leaning into a glancing blow from her right.

Obi-Wan heard the scream but couldn't see the wound's severity. Kit rolled as Ventress came at him, splashing down into the lake. Ventress stood on the dock smiling hugely, arms and legs spread in triumph, laughing in that arctic voice.

The Jedi tore his way through the X'Ting, breaking arms and legs as he went, then drew his lightsaber.

"This is between me and Ventress," he screamed. Enough of this play! "Anyone who stands between us, dies. Translate it, Ventress!"

"Why?" She snarled.

"What?" he said scornfully. "Haven't you learned what you wanted to learn? Seen what you wanted to see? What is the point in sending these children to their death? They only die because they trust you. Is there nothing left inside you? If not goodness, then loyalty?"

Her eyes flickered for a moment, and he knew that something he'd said had struck a nerve. She nodded. "Tell them to leave," she said, and the protocol droid spat out its translation.

He covered the distance between them with a single somersaulting leap. Asajj Ventress was extraordinarily quick, but her very ferocity gave Obi-Wan a hairline opening, a moment when he had the better leverage. He blocked Ventress's lightsabers, and managed to pin her blades down.

Ventress was surprised, but in the next moment disengaged her right-hand blade and slashed at his neck, attempting to behead him.

There was no time for conscious thought, no time for anything but response as Obi-Wan ducked and spun back. Ventress drew his attention to the left and leapt into the air in a spinning kick that slammed Obi-Wan down into the dock. Once down, he never had a chance to get up again, found himself fighting from his back, wiggling and edging backwards, movement so limited that he knew the confrontation might be over within seconds. The first touch of desperation wormed its way through his emotional shields.

Obi-Wan bared his teeth. As Master Yoda had often said these days, *The dark side has clouded the Galaxy. Difficult to see, the future is.*

Floating below the dock, Kit Fisto could still hardly move. He had barely evaded death from a lightsaber wound to the head, and his senses still were far away. But some deep instinct had warned him that his compatriot Obi-Wan was in trouble, fighting to protect both their lives. He woke up enough to reach for his lightsaber.

He triggered it, and sliced the pilings supporting the dock. Ventress howled in surprise as she and Obi-Wan tumbled into the water. Kit wanted desperately to help, but had exhausted his supply of strength. Surrendering to his wounds, he lost consciousness.

Obi-Wan had but a moment to snatch his rebreather and jam it into his mouth, and in the next instant realized that Ventress couldn't! She clutched a lightsaber in *each* of her lethal hands!

He went at her savagely, never giving her a moment to sheathe one lightsaber, to slip in her own rebreather.

The Jedi Knight could move in three dimensions, attacking from under the water and from all angles, and Ventress's desperate defense forced her to gulp air when her head cleared the water.

Nearing panic, Ventress dropped one of her lightsabers, and lunged at Obi-Wan, surprising him. She flipped back away, taking that moment to don her own rebreather.

Then, eyes burning with hatred, she came at him.

The two circled each other like some kind of aquatic predators, but both were out of their elements. The question was which would adapt most swiftly.

Lure her. Leave an opening for a stroke in the upper left. I will block more slowly, as she expects. Then I will flinch, as I did with the X'Ting, and she will think she's aggravated an injury, and that I will back up. She saw me do it twice.

The water was murky, and he realized that he was wrong to trust his eyes. *Stop. Defocus. Feel the water pressure as she makes her moves. Trust the Force.*

Obi-Wan felt the water surge at him, and he let that surge carry him in its natural arc. His lightsaber flashed in, and for the first time, he cut her.

The wound was low on the ribs on her right side, and her eyes widened in pain and sudden fear.

Instead of moving back, Obi-Wan moved in. She butted him in the mouth, ripping out his rebreather. But the movement stunned her, and he tore hers out in the same instant.

So. There they were, the two of them, beneath the water. The first to bolt for the surface would be exposed and vulnerable. The first one to break loses.

Well, then, Ventress. Which of us can hold our breath longer?

This would be as good a place as any to die. If this was his end, how better than to take a creature like Ventress with him?

And she saw his face. *Yes. Like Duris. I'm ready to die here and now, and for these reasons. I'm willing to die to kill you. Can you say the same?*

In the same instant, Obi-Wan threw caution to the winds,

and went at her. His blade was here, there, at all angles, and her wound slowed her . . .

She wielded her single remaining blade, eyes wide and staring.

Then something broke inside Ventress. She shrieked a mouthful of bubbles, and triggered something at her belt. The water around her churned into an expanding onyx cloud, as if she had emptied an ink-sack into it.

And in a flurry of bubbles and blackness, Asajj Ventress was gone.

78

Dripping and limping, Obi-Wan and Kit helped each other from the lake.

"Are you all right?" Obi-Wan asked.

"I will be soon enough," the Nautolan replied. "She may have underestimated me."

Obi-Wan remembered the severing of the dock, and shook his head in delighted disbelief. "I would say so, my friend. Come."

They followed a stairway cut into the rock, climbing up almost twenty stories before reaching the hives' surface, some two kilometers south of ChikatLik. Obi-Wan and Kit watched as, on the southern horizon, lightning seemed to flash. The distant thunder of massive bombardment wafted to them.

"The destruction has begun," Obi-Wan said. "We have failed."

"Strange."

"What?"

"I would have expected the attack more to the southwest."

"You're right," Obi-Wan murmured. "It seems to be near Kibo."

He took out a pair of range-finding macrobinoculars and focused in.

Through the closer view a column of smoke and fire spiraled into the air. There were dark shapes raining from the clouds, as well as energy beams. A lethal, blazing conflagration.

"Well?" Kit asked.

Obi-Wan's eyes narrowed in confusion. "Strange indeed. Come."

When they finally reached their ship, a blinking control light attracted their attention.

"A message," Obi-Wan said.

"We should claim it."

"I should get you medical attention."

"I will survive," Kit insisted. "Take the message."

Obi-Wan manipulated the keypad, and the hologram image of an ARC officer appeared.

"Jangotat," Kit murmured.

The strong brown face had been battered, his left eye closed, but the trooper was smiling slightly. "Greetings to General Kenobi, General Fisto. This is A-Nine-Eight, he whom you have been kind enough to call Jangotat. If you receive this message, then at least one of you is still alive. In all likelihood, I'm using a stepladder to pick sunblossoms." Beat. "Contrary to Code, I disobeyed your direct commands, and take full responsibility for all that may have happened as a result. Not my brothers, who did everything they could to stop me. I went to the Five Families' bunker at Kibo, with the intention of capturing them. You were limited in your actions, and because of that, thousands of innocent people were going to die. Things didn't work out the way I'd hoped, but there was an answer, and as you probably know by now, the Five Families are dead—"

Kit whispered, "They . . . what?"

"—I used a priority signal to reset the bombardment coordinates to the Five Families' bomb shelter. Not long now."

So . . . the smoke . . .

"What does this mean?" the Nautolan said.

"That depends on the kind of woman G'Mai Duris is," Obi-Wan said.

He closed his eyes. "Duris is Regent and head of the hive council. With the Families in chaos, she is the most powerful woman on the planet . . . and I believe we can negotiate with her. Call Admiral Baraka."

"Thousands?" Kit asked in disbelief. "Jangotat saved *millions.*"

"But he didn't know. He had no idea that Ventress had changed the targeting codes. He had no idea just how important his choice was."

Obi-Wan and Kit shared a moment of silence. Then Obi-Wan reached out and put in the call to the *Nexu.*

The following day in the Zantay Hills, as Jangotat had requested in this, his last will and testament, the Jedi showed the message to Sheeka Tull.

"Don't worry about the JK droids," Jangotat continued. "They'd never have functioned on a battlefield. Anyone who has ever met a dashta would know they are healers, not killers. When Thak Val Zsing died violently in its arms, *the dashta inside the JK went insane.* I know, I'm no tech guy. Don't ask me how I know, I just do. Nonlethal security application? That's one thing. Killing thinking people was just beyond them. Even a *sleeping* Guide was driven crazy. The Guides are simple, good creatures. They brought the X'Ting and the offworlders together. The X'Ting brought fungi to farmers dying of poor soil. They brought back some of the old ways.

"I believe the Five Families knew the truth, and lied to Count Dooku. Perhaps they planned to take the first payment, then disappear before the Confederacy mounted the JKs in combat, leaving Cestus to pay the price if the Republic fell."

Obi-Wan and Kit stared at each other, dumbfounded. Had *anyone* in this entire matter told the truth? Astounding! Nothing but lies, top to bottom.

"I will not be returning, which grieves me, because I wished to. For the first time in my life I actually dreamed of a future." Jangotat paused, lost for a moment in a private thought. Then he went on. "This is hard for me. I am not a person of words. Until I met you, I was not certain I was a man at all. I was the vows, the uniform, the rank. No. You showed me I was more than that, more than one of a million soldiers stamped out of a murderer like pieces on an assembly line. There is value in knowing your place in the universe, but there is also something else, and you helped me discover that."

The three regarded each other uneasily.

"There is something that you need to know: if I had lived through this, if I had returned with my duty done, I would still have returned to the GAR. As hard as it might be for you to understand, it is still a great and good thing to fight for what you believe is right. Sheeka, if I were another man, I could think of no greater joy than to stay with you. If and when my days as a trooper were done, I would have wanted to come to you, if you would have me. I am sorry I'm not the man you once knew—"

She had known Jango? Quite a bit made sense now.

"—I'm sorry that you and I had neither past, nor future."

Sheeka made no sound, but her lowered eyes spoke volumes.

"Know that more than anything else in the world, I was a soldier. And that you, and no one else in all the galaxy, held this soldier's heart in your hands."

Save for Sheeka's gentle weeping against Obi-Wan's shoulder, there was no sound in that room for a long, long time.

79

ChikatLik swarmed beneath them. It was now easier for Obi-Wan to detect the original architecture, and see where offworlders had made their mark. The hive still lived. It could grow and change, like any living thing. It had been ground almost into the dust, but the hive lived.

He, Kit, and G'Mai Duris stood on a bridge, peering down as the city seethed beneath them. Synthetic air currents rippled her gown.

"Strange how they go about their lives as if nothing has happened," she said.

"Has it?"

"Debbikin, the Por'Tens, my cousin Quill, half the Llitishi clan. Wiped out. What remains of the Families is in chaos, fighting over scraps. As they fight, the hive council has taken power. The surviving officers of Cestus Cybernetics will have to deal with us fairly now. The rule of three hundred years just ended," she said, "and no one seems to know it. No one seems to care, to feel, to grasp that they are free."

"Are they?" Kit asked.

"Yes, Master Fisto. As free as they have the strength to be."

"A different thing." Obi-Wan paused. "But they have a leader worthy of admiration. In this whole sordid affair, you are the only one who told the truth, even to your enemies. You, G'Mai Duris, are an extraordinary woman."

She lowered her eyes shyly. "You are too kind. Well, Master Kenobi, I suppose that you win here after all. You are generous to allow us the Supreme Chancellor's initial terms. I am surprised you are not harsher. We are hardly in a bargaining position."

"Nor am I a bargainer," Obi-Wan said. "This role is not comfortable for me, and I will be glad to put it down. Regent, I regret that my duty bound me to deceive you."

"We were not friends, Master Kenobi. Your actions bore the weight of necessity. In the world of politics, truth is merely another thing to be bartered."

"Then I wish to spend the rest of my life among friends."

They shared a smile. "I hope you know that I will always think of you as our friend," she said. "My friend." A pause. "So, then," she said, returning them to business. "The Republic guarantees us service droid contracts for its army. This will give Cestus a chance to establish networks of service and instruction on every world in the Republic." She paused. "But no more JKs. If the Chancellor keeps his word, then we will still be safe."

"I think that your current situation might reasonably be described as a running start."

"Thank you, Master Kenobi."

He had a thought. "I need a favor from you," Obi-Wan said.

"Yes?"

"Many people sacrificed themselves in this fight," he said. "Many of them died. I wish an amnesty for the survivors, and those you captured. No black marks against them. Let them go back to their lives. Let this be a new beginning. And one more thing . . ."

"Yes?"

"Let the spiders have their caves. They have little enough."

"I am sorry for the endless cycles of misery on Cestus. Our hive made many mistakes—but I will do what I can to correct them."

80

The time had come for the Jedi to say their good-byes. The remaining forces of Desert Wind filled the caves a final time. Resta sang them a song of Thak Val Zsing's courage. They shook hands, saluted, shared hugs and strong, warm words as the surviving troopers packed their equipment on the shuttle dropped down at the personal request of Admiral Baraka.

"Master Kenobi?" Sheeka Tull said during a quiet moment.

"Yes?"

She couldn't meet his eyes. "Did I do a bad thing," she said, "an evil, selfish thing?"

"What do you mean?"

"I wanted to bring back something I thought I missed from my life. Something . . . someone I knew a long time ago."

"You tried to bring him back?"

She nodded. "For all my talk of living for today, I see now . . . that I was the worst kind of hypocrite."

"How?"

"I woke him up, Master Kenobi. He could have gone his whole life feeling complete, and finished, and at peace with his path."

Obi-Wan folded his fingers together. "He sounded complete to me. He sounded much like a man who has traveled the galaxy's rim only to find himself at home."

"But don't you see? He knew what to say. He knew I would see that vid, that he wasn't coming back. And he said that to set my mind at ease." She wagged her head side to side. "I know, I know, I sound crazy, and maybe I am, just a little, right now."

She looked at him with desperation. "Tell me. Tell me, Jedi. Did I wake him up, convince him he had a life that was precious, just in time for him to lose it? And what does that make me?"

"A woman who once loved a man, and then tried to love him again."

Tears streaked her face as she gazed at him.

"None of us is completely in control of our heart," Obi-Wan said. "We do what we can, what we will, what we must . . . guided by our ethics and responsibilities. It can be lonely."

"Have you ever . . . ?" she began, unable to finish.

"Yes," he said, and offered nothing more.

For Sheeka Tull, that single word was enough.

"So," Obi-Wan said. "You must be strong. For Jangotat, who, I think, would have thanked you for however many days of clarity you were able to afford him. For yourself, whose only sin was love."

He came closer. He rested his hand on her flat stomach. "And for the child you carry."

She blinked. "You know?"

Obi-Wan smiled. "A strong one, I think. And he'll have a name, not a number."

"Not a number."

"No."

They stood in an empty cavern. The eels had gone. What had driven them away? Groundquakes? Rumors of war? No one knew. Perhaps they would return. Perhaps not. But humans had abused their precious gifts, and humans and X'Ting alike could wait for the Guides to make up their own minds. Here, for a hundred years and more, in love they had offered the greatest gift imaginable: their own children, that their new friends might prosper. And that gift had almost killed them all.

Best they be gone.

*   *   *

Among the rocks outside their second camp, Obi-Wan and Kit witnessed the death ceremony of an ARC for one of their own. It was as simple as could be imagined.

The three dug a shallow trench and gently placed Jango-tat's body within. Each added a handful of sand and dirt. Then Forry said, "From water we're born, in fire we die. We seed the stars."

When they were done the Jedi helped the commandos build a rock cairn, taller than it was wide, like a single declamatory finger pointing to the stars. They stood for a time, looking at the cave, the rocks, the sky, absorbing a bit of this place that had cost them so dearly.

Then they were done, and there was nothing left to do.

And so they left.

81

Trillot tossed and turned in her bed, deep in a recurring vision of blood and destruction. *Mountains fell. Planets exploded. The space between the stars ran black with blood.*

She awakened suddenly, relieved. It was only a nightmare. Just another of an endless stream of horrid sleep-fantasies . . .

Her vision cleared, and her sense of relief evaporated. More substantial than any nightmare, Asajj Ventress stood over her.

"You strode my dreams," Ventress said. "And as you did, I saw you."

Her single lightsaber descended.

At a spot only thirty kilometers from ChikatLik, two guards lay broken in the shadow of Ventress's ship. She tucked her lightsaber back into her belt, mounted the ramp, and began to check her instruments, preparing for takeoff.

"Obi-Wan," she said quietly. She wished to see him dead. But in the water, when she could have followed him down into death, he had remained firm. He was . . .

She focused on her hands. Why did they shake? This was not like her. She knew who she was. She had made her bed long ago, and was more than prepared to lie within it.

Asajj Ventress turned her mind to the hundred small preparations necessary for flight. Halfway through the preparations, she realized that her hands had stopped shaking. Action. That was what was needed. That was what she hungered for. She would accept Count Dooku's scathing approbation, then volunteer for the most dangerous assignment General Grievous could devise, and on whatever planet that was, in whatever maelstrom of wrack and ruin she could immerse herself, she would find cleansing, and peace.

Ventress lifted off into the clouds above ChikatLik, and was gone.

From behind a rock on the slope just beyond Ventress's landing zone, Fizzik crawled out, trembling uncontrollably. It was time to leave Cestus. This planet had suddenly become an insanely dangerous place. If only he could get back into Trillot's nest, perhaps he could get his hands on some of his sister's credits before her corpse was found.

Of course, if the body was discovered before Fizzik could escape, it might not go well.

What to do, what to do?

Lack of courage meant poverty.

Fizzik decided: he had been poor before, but he had never been dead, and he wished to keep it that way for a very long time.

82

Night had come to the Dashta Mountains. Sheeka Tull had waited for the Jedi and the ARCs and everyone else to leave, then knelt at Jangotat's cairn, saying her own very personal good-bye.

She looked up, watching twin streaks of light in the sky, where two very different ships headed in very different directions.

Sheeka touched her belly, still flat but nestling her child. *Their* child. Hers and Jango's.

No, not Jango. Jango would never have died to save strangers. Jangotat was a different man. A better man.

Her man.

A name, not a number, Jangotat. A-Nine-Eight.
I swear.

AFTERWORD

In 1977, when I first saw that Star Destroyer cross the screen, I had never published a single word of fiction, never written an episode of television. To think that thirty years and two million words later I would make my own contribution to the canon would have boggled my young mind.

Serious thanks to the folks at Lucasfilm with whom I spent two glorious days at Skywalker Ranch hashing out the details. To Sue Rostoni of Lucas Licensing. To Shelly Shapiro of Del Rey, for being the kind of editor who trusts her writers, giving them the space to spin their dreams.

To Betsy Mitchell, for giving me this opportunity. Appreciations also to my wife, novelist Tananarive Due, for constantly reminding me of my responsibilities, and to my daughter, Nicki, for empowering me to fulfill them.

To my niece Sharlene Chiyako Higa, for letting Unk borrow her nickname for a certain little blue ball.

To my new son Jason Kai Due-Barnes: thank you more than you can ever know.

To all of the *Star Wars* fans who contacted me over the months, offering encouragement and enthusiasm. Especially Andrew Liptak. You helped remind me what this was all about. And Adam Daggy, for his excellent Jar Jar impression.

There are other people to acknowledge, and many other pieces of the puzzle called *writing a book,* but one contributor it would be criminal to forget is Mr. Scott Sonnon, who created the wonderful Body-Flow technique I "borrowed" as a Jedi institution. If there is a Force-sensitive art on this planet, it is this man's work. His technique can be found at www.rmax.tv.

In 1983, during the crew party for *Return of the Jedi,* I briefly met George Lucas. Tongue-tied, I managed to stammer out how much I loved his work. There are so many other things I might have said, and on the chance Mr. Lucas might read these words, I would like to add:

Thank you, for creating this vast and flexible playground. Thank you for creating one of the twentieth century's most popular myths, a gift that has brought billions of happy viewing hours at a critical time in world history, a time when, perhaps, we need more than ever to believe in honor, sacrifice, heart, and that special magic called *life itself.*

As long as I live, I will never forget The Moment when Luke Skywalker flew so desperately down the Death Star's trench, John Williams's score soaring magnificently, and the audience overwhelmed by Industrial Light and Magic's mind-bending inaugural. At that pulse-pounding moment, a moment when it seemed the individual human being could have no point or purpose, no meaning in a universe so vast and cybernetic, we heard Obi-Wan Kenobi whisper that we should *trust our feelings.*

The Force flows through us. It controls us. We control it. Life creates it. It is more powerful than any Death Star.

Hundreds of millions of people said *yes,* and sighed, and applauded, and went home or turned off their videos feeling just a little more empowered than they did before the lights went down and the Twentieth Century–Fox fanfare came up.

No small feat.

May the Force be with you, Mr. Lucas.

And with us all. Always.

Steven Barnes
Longview, Washington
www.lifewrite.com
January 13, 2004

THE HIVE

by STEVEN BARNES

FOR NICKI, STEVEN AND SHARLEEN CHIYEKO

Happy birthday, kids!

1

G'Mai Duris, Regent of the planet Ord Cestus, formally folded the fingers of her primary and secondary hands. She was an X'Ting, of segmented, oval, dull gold body and gentle manner, one of the insectoids who had once ruled this planet. Before the coming of Cestus Cybernetics, X'Ting hives had thronged this world, but now the soulless industrial giant not only dominated the planet but also threatened the safety of the Republic itself.

Obi-Wan Kenobi watched as Duris prepared to address the hive council, the last humble remnant of X'Ting power. Like the offworlder capital of ChikatLik, some hundreds of meters above their heads, the council room was nestled in a natural lava bubble. The walls of the egg-shaped, fifteen-meter-high chamber had been glazed burnt sienna, but most of that original color was covered with handwoven tapestries. Three doorways, each guarded by two members of the X'Ting warrior clans, led out of the room—one to the surface, the others to deeper, less traveled places within the hive.

The twelve councilors seated at the curved stone table were a mix of relatively youthful X'Ting, their carapaces still brilliant, and elders showing gray and white splotches amid their bristling thoracic hair. Their vestigial wings fluttered in distress. From time to time their primary or secondary hands would smooth their ivory ceremonial robes. Every red or green faceted eye studied her carefully; every auditory antenna was tuned to her words.

Duris hunched her thorax and cleared her throat, perhaps

gathering her thoughts. She was almost as tall as Obi-Wan, and her broad, segmented, pale gold shell and swollen egg sac gave her considerable gravitas.

At this moment, G'Mai Duris needed every bit of it.

"My peers and elders," she said. "My dear friend Master Kenobi has told me an astonishing thing. For centuries we have known that our ancestors were cheated out of their land—land purchased with worthless baubles we believed were legal tender.

"For years we had no means of redress, save to accept whatever sops Cestus Cybernetics threw our way. But that has changed." Her eyes gleamed like cut emeralds. "Master Kenobi brought with him one of Coruscant's finest barristers, a Vippit who knows their laws well. And according to the central authority, if we should choose to press our suit, we can *destroy* Cestus Cybernetics. If we own the land beneath their factories, we can charge them whatever we wish for land usage, possibly even take the facilities themselves."

"What?" exclaimed Kosta, the council's eldest member. All X'Ting cycled between the male and female genders every three years, and Kosta was currently female. Although too old for egg bearing, her sac was still swollen to impressive size. She looked shocked. "Is this true?"

"You would do nothing except destroy the planet!" Caiza Quill sputtered. Only minutes earlier Duris had deposed him as head of the council. His rage and surrender pheromones still spiced the air. "Destroy Cestus Cybernetics, and you destroy our economy!"

Kosta's expression bristled with naked contempt for Quill's transparent half-truths. "The hive was here before Cestus Cybernetics. It is not the hive that will suffer if this company changes hands . . . or even if it dies. It will be those who have sold themselves to offworlders for a promise of power."

"But my lords," Duris said, drawing their attention back to her once again. "I have obligations to the offworlders, people who came to Cestus with skills and heart, wanting only to build a life here. We cannot use this opportunity to destroy. We must use it to build, and heal."

The X'Ting hive council members nodded, perhaps pleased by her empathy. Although she was new to their ranks, they seemed satisfied with her grasp of the responsibilities.

But Quill was in no way mollified by her words. His stubby wings quivered with rage. "You have won nothing, Duris! I will block you, I swear. Regardless of what you think you have, what you think you know . . . this isn't over yet." He stormed out, humiliated and enraged.

Obi-Wan had watched the proceedings, withholding comment, but now he had to speak. "Can he do that?"

"Perhaps," Kosta replied. "Any member of the Families can veto any specific business deal." She was referring to the Five Families, who ran the mines and factories that fed the droid works. Once there had only been four, but Quill had wormed his way into their midst by delivering labor contracts and quelling dissent, selling out his own people in the process. "If he believes it is in his best interest, or just for the sake of hatred, he will try." An alarming thought seemed to occur to her. "He might try to keep you from sending the Supreme Chancellor this information. Perhaps you should send it immediately."

Reluctantly, Obi-Wan shook his head. "The Chancellor will use it as legal pretext to shut down Cestus Cybernetics. In that case, no one wins. Your best bet is to use this information as emergency leverage."

Only days before, Obi-Wan had arrived on Cestus to stop the planet from selling its deadly bio-droids to the Confederacy. By means of a unique "living circuit" design, the droid works had created a machine that could actually anticipate an attacker's moves. Understanding their potential, Count Dooku had ordered thousands of the devices—originally designed for small-scale security work—with every intention of converting them to battle droids.

The thought of such an army, marching in the thousands, chilled Obi-Wan's blood. In the face of such a juggernaut, both the Jedi and the Grand Army of the Republic might fall. The spread of such lethal devices must be stopped at all costs!

The favored means of deterrence was negotiation, but bombardment was not out of the question. Initial contacts had not been promising: Cestus Cybernetics was loath to cease production of such a valuable commodity, and believed Chancellor Palpatine would never order the destruction of a peaceful planet selling a legal product. With the X'Ting as allies, Obi-Wan's assignment would be far simpler.

Over the last days he had gained the trust of G'Mai Duris, Cestus's puppet Regent, and taken the first steps to furnish her with real political authority. If he could win over the hive council, as well, there might be serious cause for optimism.

The council members listened to him speak of politics and finances, swiftly comprehending the reasons it might profit them to side with Coruscant. But after expressing confidence in his assessment, they swiftly changed the subject. "There is another matter to discuss, Master Jedi."

He glanced at Duris, seeking a clue about the new concern. The Regent turned to face him, moving one portion of her segmented body at a time. Her primary and secondary arms spread, empty palms extended, X'Ting body language indicating confusion. "I know nothing of this," she said.

Kosta drummed the fingers of her secondary hands against the table. She consulted with the other members of the council, speaking in clicks and pops, and then addressed Obi-Wan. "It is possible, Master Jedi, that you can perform a great service for us this day."

"In what fashion?" he asked.

Again the council members glanced at one another, as if measuring the wisdom of speech. Then, after a brief conference, Kosta began.

"There is one other way that Quill might hurt us, if he decides that the hive is no longer deserving of his loyalty."

That was a possibility. Certainly, Quill's addiction to power and naked self-interest might trigger betrayal.

Obi-Wan felt an emotional charge building in the chamber. He knew that sense: fear of approaching a threshold. The hive council was about to do something that could make the X'Ting deeply vulnerable.

Kosta continued. "What we are about to tell you is known only to members of the council, and to elite members of the hive's warrior clan. Even G'Mai Duris did not know this, although her partner, Filian, did." She bowed respectfully. "Filian was forced to conceal this knowledge from you, by oath."

It was clear this revelation was painful to Duris. Until now, she had clung to the illusion that she had known her deceased mate completely. "What is it?"

"There is much about the history of our planet that you could not know, Master Jedi. Much that is not in the fabled archives of Coruscant."

"Regrettable, but always true," Obi-Wan said. "Please illuminate."

"Once," Kosta explained, "the hive was strong. We had defeated the spider people in a great war, and brought the entire planet under the rule of the hive and our queen, who was wise and just. We believed that it was time for us to enter the galactic community. But this was not merely a matter of gaining political recognition. We coveted the role of trading partner, but what resources might we offer to become so?

"What products could we produce? What minerals might we have? We searched, and found nothing that was not available on worlds nearer the galaxy's central hub. Nothing that would give us the advantage we sought.

"Then we heard a rumor that Coruscant was planning to expand its prison system, and was looking for host worlds on the Rim that might be willing to lease or sell land for such facilities. Land was one thing Cestus had in plenty, and it seemed an admirable opportunity. Overtures were made, and we won a contract."

She sighed. "At first, all seemed well. Several facilities were constructed, and the scum of the galaxy were safely quartered in reconstructed caverns beneath our sands."

All of this Obi-Wan knew, of course.

"Once the deal was struck, we swallowed our pride and accepted a position on the Republic's bottom rung. Many of our workers were hired for the mines and factories. We learned to negotiate, so that future leasings and sales were more favorable. We were paid our rental fees, with which we hired surveyors to more carefully examine our resources with a mind to expanding trade.

"Then something completely unexpected happened. Executives from Cybot Galactica were convicted of fraud and gross negligence and sentenced to prison here. These former beings of power were forced to dig in the depths of the caverns. Some of the work was useful: enlarging their living spaces, building shops and offices. Some of it was mere make-work, the time-honored prison task of turning big rocks into little ones. But during the digging, the executives discovered minerals used in advanced droid fabrication. A treasure, floating unsuspected in the Outer Rim!

"The executives hatched a plan to free themselves. In meetings with the prison authorities, they proposed to make the guards and warden wealthy beyond their dreams. The essence of the proposal was that the pooled talents and contacts of the various prisoners might well create an endless stream of first-class droids. Here on Ord Cestus there was labor aplenty, mountains of raw material, skill, and savvy. They needed only permission.

"The deal was struck, the stage set for the creation of Cestus Cybernetics. The executives put out the word to former customers and employees, and immigration to Ord Cestus began in earnest. The first factory was in operation within a standard year, producing a modest repair droid that received favorable reviews and respectable orders. They were up and running."

Kosta raised her voice. "But as the fledgling company grew in power and wealth, it came into conflict with the queen and king. First, managers purchased additional land with worthless synthetic gems. The royals were forced to swallow this humiliation, but they did attempt to negotiate larger shares of wealth for the hive, for the education of our people, for healthcare."

"Healthcare?"

"A necessity. Since the founding of the prison there had been numerous strange and damaging ailments spreading through our population. The inmates, from every corner of the galaxy, brought countless diseases with them, creating wave after wave of illness. We sickened by the thousands.

"The negotiations were fierce. Our rulers threatened to withhold X'Ting labor and to refuse to allow Cestus Cybernetics to expand its mining operation.

"Then the Great Plague hit us." Kosta leaned forward, emerald eyes gleaming. "I know that it cannot be proved, but we knew, *knew* that this plague was no accident. It was unleashed upon us to destroy the royal family, to splinter the hive so that there would be no effective opposition. Perhaps even to exterminate us."

Obi-Wan flinched at the passion in those words. Was such villainy possible? Foolish to ask: of course it was. Coruscant knew little of what happened on the Outer Rim. And since Cestus Cybernetics controlled the official information stream, any conceivable perfidy might have been concealed.

"And this genocide almost worked. But as the plague swept through the hive, a frantic plan was put into action: to place several healthy eggs in suspended animation and to hide them in a special vault deep below Cestus's surface, where only a chosen few would know the truth, the path, and the method of opening.

"The vault was constructed by Toong'l Security Systems— a company in competition with Cestus Cybernetics, and known to be trustworthy. The workers were blind-shuttled to the site and never knew the location. When it was completed, we knew that whatever happened to the rest of the royals, there would be at least one fertilized egg pair that was safe— royals, who could mate and create a new line."

Instantly, Obi-Wan grasped the significance. After the plague, the surviving X'Ting had scattered across the surface of Ord Cestus. But a new royal line might draw them back together again, unite them. G'Mai Duris was but Regent, holding the power until the return of a new royal pair. Under her capable hands the power transfer might rejuvenate this unhappy planet. A promising idea!

Obi-Wan organized his thoughts carefully, and then spoke. "So . . . with this news about the ownership of the land beneath Cestus Cybernetics, a pair of royals to unite the planet might give you greater voice on Coruscant, and build your people a better future?"

"Yes," Kosta agreed, eyes sparkling. "There are problems, though. First, the plague was deadlier than we expected. After the royals died, several X'Ting clans chose to stay deep below the surface, to seal off all contact with offworlders. They became almost a separate hive: there has been virtually no contact with those clans for a century. Worse still, every X'Ting who knew the secret of the vault died in the plague. All that remain are keys to open the outer door. Lastly, Toong'l Security Systems was destroyed when its planet was struck by a comet. Its leaders might have told us how to open the vault, but . . ." Kosta made a resigned shrugging motion.

Obi-Wan squinted. "But certainly you can still use other means to retrieve the eggs."

The old X'Ting female sighed, nervously knotting the fingers of primary and secondary hands. "You don't understand the status of royals. By breeding and culture, every X'Ting must obey them. It is our way, and it is in our blood. Therefore, they are both the greatest treasure, and the greatest threat. An X'Ting royal pair in the hands of Cestus Cybernetics would reduce every X'Ting on this planet to slavery. Rather than have that happen, a tamper detector was built into the vault. We are not certain as to its details, but we have reason to believe that after three unsuccessful attempts to open the chamber, the eggs will be destroyed."

By the stars! These people had been so desperate?

"So . . . ," he began cautiously. "What service do you wish of me?"

"Twice in the past we tried to regain the precious eggs. Twice our bravest have tried to reach the vault. Twice they perished before they could reach it." A pause. "There is a story whispered among our people. It is said that a hundred and fifty years ago a visitor came from the center of the galaxy. A warrior with powers beyond any the X'Ting had ever seen. He called himself a Jedi. It is said his courage and wisdom saved our people. I think it no mere coincidence that now, in our hour of need, another Jedi has appeared."

Obi-Wan felt a thrill of alarm. He had not anticipated such a situation. "Madam," he said, "it is a great weight you wish me to carry."

"We believe you capable of withstanding it."

He had heard no story in the Jedi archives about a visit to Ord Cestus, but it was certainly possible. Many Jedi avoided acclaim; they were capable of stunning feats of valor, followed by such modesty that they might decline even to give their names. "And you fear that Quill, angry with the Regent, might betray these secret eggs to the Five Families. And that they might launch their own effort to recover them, and use them against you."

"You see our situation, yes."

He did. Coruscant wanted something: the cessation of droid production. The X'Ting, indeed all beings on this planet, were more or less dependent on a continued income stream from Cestus Cybernetics. Obi-Wan was asking them to side with him, to trust him. He had thought to do this through diplomacy, but providence had given him a means of winning their trust more directly, had he sufficient courage. "I accept your request. I will attempt to recover your eggs," he said.

Kosta sighed in relief. "You will need a guide. A small cluster of X'Ting warriors have studied the original maps through the deep hive. Originally there were five broodmates. Only one survives." She turned to the others. "Call Jesson."

The council members leaned their heads together, touching antennae as they buzzed and clicked in X'Tingian. After a few moments a small male left the table and scuttled off into a side tunnel.

"G'Mai, I am in your hands," Obi-Wan said quietly. The elders had carried themselves well, but the Regent was the only X'Ting he could claim to know. If anyone here could be relied upon for full disclosure, it was she. "Is there anything else that I should know before setting out on this mission?"

"Jedi," Duris said. "I know only the whispered rumors about the visit of a Jedi Master. I'd never heard of the royal eggs before this day."

The council members turned as the small male councilor returned. Behind him, in a gray tunic with a diagonal red stripe, marched a larger male bristling with red thoracic fur. His red, faceted eyes took in the entire room at a glance, scanning Obi-Wan and making an instant, positive threat assessment. The newcomer's primary and secondary arms bore numerous pale scars: this was an experienced warrior, probably a member of some elite hive security unit. A triple-sectioned staff hewn of some clear material lay diagonally across his back.

The newcomer put the palms of his primary and secondary hands together, then spoke in a series of clicks and pops.

Kosta raised her left primary hand. "It is requested that you speak in Basic when in this human's presence."

The X'Ting soldier turned to regard Obi-Wan. His first scan had taken a fraction of a second. The second took longer, long enough for Obi-Wan to sense the intense disdain in the X'Ting's eyes. "My pardon to our *honored* guest. My words were: 'First Rank Jesson is present and ready for duty.'"

"I should go with you," Duris offered. "This is my job, my planet. If we fail, and Quill betrays us, we are all undone."

"But you are your people's leader," Obi-Wan said. "You are needed here."

Duris protested, but the other council members voted her down. She seemed as distressed as Obi-Wan had ever seen. "You came here as a friend, and helped me more than words can say," she said, taking his two hands in her four. "I hope that I have not brought you to your death."

"Jedi are not so easily killed," he said.

"If you are half the warrior Master Yoda is said to be, you will prevail," she said.

Jesson's eyes narrowed at that. If Obi-Wan had felt more confident in reading X'Ting facial expressions, he would have said the soldier's dominating mood was one of contempt.

"Well, let us begin." Obi-Wan turned to his guide. "We descend into the bowels of the planet together," he said. "Will you tell me your full name?"

"First Rank Jesson Di Blinth," the other said, and bowed formally. "Of the volcano Di Blinths."

"Well met, Jesson," the Jedi replied. "Obi-Wan Kenobi, of Coruscant. Are we ready to leave?"

Jesson conferred swiftly with the other members of the council. Two members touched scent glands at the sides of their necks, and with damp fingers made a series of dots on the table before them. Jesson made moist markings of his own in a similar fashion.

Obi-Wan raised an eyebrow, and Duris explained: "Much of our information is stored in scents."

"These contain most of what we currently know or remember about the path," Kosta said. "No one has taken it in so long . . ."

"I thought you said that four of your number tried, and were slain in the process," Obi-Wan said.

"Not completely accurate," Jesson said, studying the tabletop. "The first attempt was through the direct opening to the egg chamber, which buttresses a lava tube. My brother never returned, and we know that defensive mechanisms were triggered. A backup entrance was tried next. My second brother never returned, and the door was jammed."

"Did you attempt to open it?"

Jesson regarded him with scorn. "Whatever happened

there cost the life of a brave warrior. We will not disrespect him by assuming we can succeed where he failed."

"What, then?"

"There is another way down, through the old tunnels."

The mention of that word quieted the room for a long moment, and again G'Mai Duris raised an objection. "I should go. Obi-Wan risks his life because of me."

"Later, perhaps, when you have shifted back to male," Kosta said, her emerald eyes flashing with compassion. "But now you are not as strong and light as you will be. We cannot risk you. You are our face with the offworlders."

Duris took Obi-Wan's hands in hers. "Then go with luck," she said.

Obi-Wan nodded. "The Force is what we will need." He turned to Jesson. "Well, if it is to be done, it is best done swiftly."

And together they left the chamber.

2

Above them stood Ord Cestus's capital city of ChikatLik, a metropolis of six million citizens built into a natural lava bubble modified by the hive. The bubble's natural gray glaze was a rainbow of reflected colors from the city lights and holoboards. ChikatLik boasted the architecture of a hundred cultures, was a forest of twisting spires and elevated tramways, airways filled with droid shuttles, taxis, personal transportation and trams of all kinds. The bubble walls concealed a network of transport systems within the ground itself: subways and magrails and lev tracks, technological wonders ferrying workers, executives, ore, and equipment.

But down here, far below ChikatLik's streets, there was only the hive. Generations of hive builders had chewed and burrowed through the ground. The texture of the walls had a chewed duracrete appearance that Obi-Wan had noted elsewhere in ChikatLik, clear evidence of X'Ting construction.

Down in the lowest tunnels the walls were coated with rectangular patches of manicured white fungus that emitted a steady bluish glow. "Is this your form of illumination?" Obi-Wan asked.

Jesson nodded. "The fungus is well maintained here, fed and trimmed. Farther back it grows wild, and the fungus eats into the walls, slowly widening the tunnels."

The fungus had etched the rock until it seemed like the surface of some ancient sculpture. Obi-Wan ran his fingers over it as they walked, felt that he was reading an ancient book of X'Ting secret history. "How many outsiders have been here?" he asked.

"You are the first," Jesson told him.

Obi-Wan sighed. Jesson's tone had been flat and cold. He and the X'Ting would have to come to an understanding, but he hoped to delay it until they had spent a bit more time together. "Where does this come out?"

Jesson turned to him, sneering. "Listen, Jedi. I will follow my orders and take you along with me, but I don't have to like it. You offworlders ruined our planet. You cheated and brainwashed us and corrupted our leaders—"

"If you're thinking of Quill, I believe he's been removed from the council."

"And replaced with Duris," Jesson said. "I doubt she's much better."

"If you think so little of your leaders, why do you obey them?"

Jesson drew himself up to full height. "I obey my training, and the rules of my clan. I am loyal to the hive, not merely the council. And now the council wishes the return of the royals. This I will help them do." His wings fluttered a bit. In the glow of the fungus they seemed like sheets of pale blue ice. "Make no mistake, Jedi. I will take you with me. But fantasies about your great powers won't save you in the deep hive. Maybe Duris believes that some sorcerer from Coruscant once saved the poor ignorant X'Ting, but I am no mewling grub, to believe such tales."

"Fair enough," Obi-Wan said as they continued down the tunnel. "I'd never heard of it myself, so I'm not asking you to believe."

Jesson shrugged, although he seemed satisfied that Obi-Wan was not trying to convince him. "It is typical for a colonized people to identify with their oppressors. This yearning for an alien rescuer is pitiable. It is hive-hatred."

Obi-Wan was about to speak when Jesson raised his primary arms. "Be very quiet." The X'Ting brushed past a curtain of hanging moss. Curiously, once on the other side Obi-Wan heard a steady droning sound. The moss seemed to have functioned as some kind of damper.

Then Obi-Wan gasped. He felt he had walked into a fantasy realm, where gravity itself was suspended.

Hanging from the ceiling was a series of swollen blue spheres attached as if by an invisible adhesive. No legs or arms or anything resembling faces were visible. He reckoned that these creatures were the same species as Regent Duris's assistant Shar Shar, but much larger. They were vaguely translucent, with thin blue veins. By the dim fungal light he could see organs pulsing slowly, as well as some kind of distended stomach or bladder.

"What are these creatures?" Obi-Wan asked.

"Their species are Zeetsa. We feed them, and they produce a food called Lifemilk. Once our people depended upon them, and we lived together. But over time they developed more mind and will. Those who wish to join our society are allowed to do so, while those who choose a more peaceful, quiet existence can have that, as well."

He sighed, and for a moment seemed to forget his antipathy toward Obi-Wan. "Lifemilk is a great delicacy." He turned to the Jedi. "As an offworlder, you can afford it more readily than most X'Ting."

The bluish surfaces of the Lifemilk creatures gave off a calming, peaceful radiance, but even had Jesson been more sanguine, Obi-Wan would not have chosen to sample at this time. One never knew the effects of alien foods, even benign, and he had to rely upon all of his senses in the coming hours.

The room was warm, almost uncomfortably so, and Obi-Wan swiftly determined that the heat emanated from the many bodies crowded together.

As he watched, the smooth surface of one of the globes began to roil. A bulge recognizable as a nose appeared, followed by two eyeholes, emerging from the surface almost like a creature floating up through a pool of oil. Obi-Wan blinked, startled, as similar faces grew on two of the other spheres. Generalized faces, something between an X'Ting and a human, almost as if the Zeetsa had no real form of its own, instead borrowing appearance from its neighbors.

The three spheres with faces pivoted to watch the intruders who had awakened them from their long, productive slumber.

He heard something gurgle in the room, and thought that it was the Zeetsa version of speech. They were speaking to each other, wondering, perhaps, who this offworlder was . . .

No . . . not who, but *what*. If Jesson was accurate, no other offworlder had ever come this way, and that meant that in all probability they had never seen a human being at all.

The room was the size of a star cruiser docking bay: immense, and silent save for that constant murmuring. Obi-Wan had the feeling he was walking through a room of sleeping children, except for the disquieting faces that appeared on the smooth surface of the dangling, gravity-defying bulbs. One of them formed lips and a recognizable mouth, and he stopped for a moment, transfixed. As he watched, his own face appeared, complete with beard, etched into the surface of the blue sphere.

And then the corners of the mouth lifted. "It's trying to communicate," he whispered, astonished.

"It is dreaming," Jesson said. "And you are a part of the dream."

The bulb pivoted to follow them as they reached the far side of the cavern. The tunnel there was darker than the Lifemilk creatures' place of resting, and Obi-Wan took that final image, the smile of a sleeping, mindless creature, with him into the darkness.

3

The tunnel leading away from the Zeetsa chamber was narrower. If he had wished, Obi-Wan could have scooped blue-white fungus off both walls with his elbows as they walked. The mold here grew in wild patches, some of them slippery splotches underfoot, slick enough to make an unwary explorer turn an ankle. The wild moss gave a fainter light here, and from time to time Jesson used a glowlight to lead the way. The air itself felt musty and close. Obi-Wan guessed no one had been here for years.

"Where are we now?" he asked.

"Beyond where I have gone," Jesson replied. "But I know what lies ahead."

"And that is?"

"The Hall of Heroes," Jesson said. "This is where the greatest leaders of our people were honored, long ago, before the clans split after the plague. In that world, every warrior strove to perform great service for the hive, that his image might one day appear in the hall."

"And what of the people who remained down there?" Obi-Wan asked.

"They are the true X'Ting," he said, a hint of pride entering his voice for the first time. "Perhaps when this is over, I will stay with them. It is said they believe we 'surface' X'Ting have forgotten the old ways. This is truth."

"Will they try to stop us?"

"I think not. They, even more than those on the surface, have awaited the return of the royals. In fact," he added, "once we have opened the vault, I can think of no safer hands in which to place the eggs."

Obi-Wan stopped. "The eggs are to be taken to the council, Jesson."

The X'Ting's eyes sparked. "Yes. Of course."

Obi-Wan didn't trust that answer. Might Jesson turn the eggs over to the X'Ting who lurked in the lower hive? And if he did, how should he, Obi-Wan, respond?

One step at a time, he thought. They had much to overcome before that became an issue.

The tunnel came to an end at a massive metal door, bolted and barred, and so rusted that it seemed almost a part of the natural wall.

Jesson traced his hands over its surface. "This is the back way into the vault. We must go through the Hall of Heroes, where the old X'Ting still live. Many years ago they erected this door to seal out the plague. To seal us out of their lives." He looked back at Obi-Wan. "We will have to open the door."

"This I can do," Obi-Wan said. He drew his lightsaber and triggered its emerald beam. Then he took a deep breath and slowly began to press his blade into the door. The hissing sound filled the darkness. Liquid metal sizzled into steam. Within a few moments he'd burned a fist-size hole in the door. Obi-Wan stopped and peered through. Nothing but darkness beyond. He listened. Nothing.

No. Not nothing. *Something* scuttled on the other side of the door. But it was something distant. Claws on metal and stone. Other than that, silence.

The fingers of Jesson's secondary arms twined with tension.

"Is there anything you're not telling me?" Obi-Wan asked.

"There are stories," Jesson admitted. "Five years ago when we tried to free the eggs, one of my brothers went through another opening. I know he made it as far as the Hall of Heroes. But after that . . ." He shrugged. "We lost communication."

"I see." Obi-Wan didn't like the sound of that. It could imply entirely too many things.

He widened the hole, then waited for the metal to cool so that they could wiggle through. "I'll go first," he said. The mold in the next chamber was just barely bright enough to reveal a large empty space with a rock floor. The room was perhaps twenty meters across, with gently convex walls. "Looks clear," he said, and then slipped through, instantly alert.

By the glow of his lightsaber he saw that the floor of the roughly spherical chamber was of level stone. In the center was a descending stone stairway. Obi-Wan supposed that it led to another chamber below them.

Jesson crawled through the burned hole nimbly and stood, holding up his glowlight.

"You've never been in here?" Obi-Wan asked.

"Never. And neither has any living member of the upper hive," he said. "I believe we are now inside the largest statue in the X'Ting Hall of Heroes."

They began down the stairs, turning in a spiral as they descended around a single rock column in the midst of a chamber hewn from stone. Hewn? *Chewed,* Obi-Wan thought.

"Something is wrong," Jesson said. Caution had crept into the X'Ting warrior's voice.

"What?"

"I smell much death," he said.

The silence itself was so oppressive that it was impossible for Obi-Wan not to agree with him. Something was wrong—he could sense it as well. Halfway down the stairs, Jesson aimed his light at the floor below them.

For a moment Obi-Wan couldn't believe what he was seeing. The entire floor of the chamber was covered with empty, shattered carapaces. Countless heaps of them, scattered about like bones in some large predator's lair.

"What happened here?" Jesson whispered.

"What would you think?"

The exoskeleton fragments, the skulls and legs and chestpieces, seemed to stare back at them, simultaneously mocking and warning. "Either they crawled into here by the thousands and died, or . . ."

"Or what?" Obi-Wan asked.

"Or something dragged them in here."

Obi-Wan crouched, running his fingers along the broken edges of a carapace. There was no moisture in the remaining flesh at all. This had happened years ago.

He rose and led the way to the descending stone stairway in the room's center. The twisting exit had no guardrails, and it would be a nasty spill if taken unexpectedly. The dusty smell of old, forgotten death rose up to enfold them.

When they reached the bottom, his foot crunched on a leg carapace. "Light," he said simply, and took it from Jesson's hand.

The carapaces had been cracked open. No withered flesh remained to be seen. Devoured? Everywhere he looked, there was nothing but the cracked, violated exoskeletons of dead X'Ting.

Jesson went to his knees behind Obi-Wan, examining the remains. "I . . . I don't understand," he said as Obi-Wan returned the glowlight.

Something in his voice chilled the Jedi. "What is it?" Obi-Wan asked.

"Look at these bite marks."

Obi-Wan inspected. The carapaces had indeed been *chewed* open, not pried apart with tools. "Yes. Savage."

"You don't understand," Jesson said. "These are *X'Ting* tooth marks."

And suddenly the horror that had gripped Jesson brushed against Obi-Wan's spine. Here in the depths, where X'Ting had tried to maintain the old ways, *something* had happened. Clan turning against clan? War? However it had begun, what was clear was the way it had ended:

Cannibalism. These X'Ting had eaten their own. There was no lower behavior, no more loathsome foe. The fear of being slain by an opponent was always present, a natural part of a warrior's life. But the idea of being killed and then *devoured* . . . that was something different.

"I suggest we keep moving," he said.

"I agree," Jesson said, biting at the words. And they continued across the room.

Something moved. Obi-Wan couldn't see it, or hear it—he *felt* it, a displacement of the air around them, a perturbation in the Force.

"I don't think we're alone," he said.

Jesson reached for the three-sectioned staff slung across his back. The sections were of clear crystal or acrylic, connected by short lengths of chain. A club and a flail in one, Obi-Wan thought. He hoped the X'Ting used it superbly.

"That door," Jesson said, indicating an opening on the far side of the room. This room, like the one above it, had a concave wall, but less sharply angled.

"Let us make our way there," Obi-Wan said. "Swiftly. But I suspect that that is where our company awaits."

Jesson's lips pulled back from his teeth, displaying small, sharp, multiple rows. Obi-Wan would not care to have his arm caught in those jaws. "Let them come," the X'Ting said.

Step by step they progressed across the floor. They were almost to the doorway when the air's scent changed. Just a bit, a nose-wrinkling aroma drifting to them on the weakest of breezes. Something that dried tongue and throat, an acid tang reminiscent of stomach gases. Before he could consciously identify the smell, the first glowing eyes appeared. Glittering. Faceted, blinking at them from the darkness.

Then they were under attack.

Jesson dropped his lamp almost at once, and although it didn't extinguish on hitting the ground, the light it gave was slanted and partial. The sparkle of Obi-Wan's lightsaber was more brilliant, increasing with the hum and flash when he met an opponent's weapon or body.

These were X'Ting—the Jedi was sure of that—but X'Ting of a different variety than those he had seen until now. These were not specialized for combat: they were diggers, workers. The oversize jaws implied that they might have been the ones who produced the chewed substance that characterized the hive.

Most of them carried hefty metal pry bars. Weapons? Tools? For whatever purpose they had originally been intended, the bars would crack any bone they struck.

There was no more time for thought. The song of Obi-Wan's lightsaber was long and sour. X'Ting diggers fell before him like scythed grain. They hissed and came on, howling.

Obi-Wan measured his response, allowing them to come to him, then taking the aggressive posture when advantageous. Ferociously fast, the cannibal X'Ting attacked in a frightening wave, simply wading in swinging their metal bars, trusting in numbers to carry the day.

Against a Jedi, that was not enough.

The air around Obi-Wan hissed as his lightsaber swooped and twisted. After the first few moments he had adjusted to the pace and style of attack, and was able to determine a bit more about their adversaries. The first thing he realized was that they were nearly blind from years of groping in darkness, doubtless hunting by smell or hearing. His lightsaber's flare frightened some of them, freezing them in place, making some hesitant to attack. Those who did not hesitate died hissing their hatred and fear.

Between strokes, between breaths, Obi-Wan spared fragments of attention to see how Jesson was faring.

The X'Ting warrior needed no assistance. He performed with a fearless, aggressive, almost weightless agility, kicking and punching in all directions with all six limbs. His weapon whirled like a propeller, almost invisibly fast. He held the three-sectioned staff first by one end, then by the middle, then by the other, swinging it and twisting it into defensive and attacking positions, and every time he moved, one of his enemies fell to rise no more.

He crouched, sweeping the feet of several creatures from underneath them, and when he came up, Jesson coiled into a ferocious attack position that mimicked a spider stalking the strands of its web.

Their attackers circled them, hissing and coiling as Obi-Wan and Jesson put their backs together and surveyed the horde.

"We can't kill them all," Jesson said.

"No," Obi-Wan agreed. "But we don't have to. Follow me!"

Without another word the Jedi plunged into the mass of cannibals, plowing toward the door. He struggled not to think about what would happen to them—or to Jesson, at least—if they were overwhelmed. It was better to stay in the realm of Form III, the lightsaber combat he had practiced for so long. It was better, and no less effective, for one who understood that defense and attack were two sides of the same coin.

Left, right, left—he deflected blows, shattered weapons, and severed limbs in a blinding, dazzling display that singed blazing lines in the darkness. Their enemies, though ferocious, were hampered by their near blindness; only an unnatural hunger drove them forward.

They seemed to be awakening in waves, crawling out of whatever dark holes they had entered. Had these things scavenged in the darkness, on the waste and garbage that every great city produces? Even Coruscant had its ghouls, gangsters, and homeless creatures who had abandoned the light to live in the fissures between social tissues. But the creatures swarming them now matched the worst that great world-city could offer.

"Run!" Jesson called, and they sprinted toward the doorway. The passage narrowed, and it was a bit harder for the cannibals to reach them, making defense that much easier. He could see the stairway now, only a dozen meters farther away.

Obi-Wan whirled 360 degrees; he glimpsed Jesson as he deflected and attacked, his three-sectioned staff cracking heads and sending their enemies scurrying for safety.

But then a mass of wriggling bodies threw themselves at Jesson all at once, and the warrior went down. Obi-Wan arrived just in time to stop a jagged spear from descending into his guide; his lightsaber flashed, leaving the attacker howling with a missing limb. Using the Force to hurl another aside, the Jedi Knight bent swiftly, helping Jesson up from the ground.

He did not know what fear looked like on the face of an X'Ting, but he was fairly certain that that was the dominant emotion in those faceted red eyes. Fear and certainty of death, and perhaps something else.

Obi-Wan released his grip and Jesson ran at the enemy, leaving his triple staff behind. At first Obi-Wan's heart sank; then, as the Jedi watched, the X'Ting warrior disarmed the first cannibal who struck at him, wrenching a spear from the creature's hands. Jesson whirled the javelin until it was nothing but a lethal blur, sending cannibals howling and scrambling into the shadows. He kicked and punched, feinted with his stinger, and then broke heads with his spear. Soon he had broken free and he and Obi-Wan were heading down a ladder, down a long narrow tube, into darkness.

4

Hand over hand, Obi-Wan and Jesson climbed down a hollow stone tube barely as wide as their shoulders. As he gripped each rung of the ladder in turn, Obi-Wan wondered: what would they do if the bottom was sealed? Or blocked? In such a terribly constricted space, there was no room to maneuver. The cannibals could simply drop rocks down on them until—

Then his foot touched the ground. Jesson reached the bottom a moment later, and they were out in a large rocky chamber.

Using his captured spear as a staff, Jesson led Obi-Wan away from the ladder, across a chamber as broad as a Chin-Bret playing field. Dim wreaths of mold illuminated some of the walls: immense statues lined the room, images of gigantic, regal X'Ting in various imperious poses, each of them at least thirty meters in height, some twice that size. He could just barely make out the insectoid features. Most were built into one of the walls in apparently endless array. A few were freestanding.

Despite the spear, Jesson was limping, the Jedi noticed, and seemed winded. "We can rest, if you need to," Obi-Wan said.

"No," Jesson gasped. "I want to get as far away from the entrance as possible."

Obi-Wan looked back. "They don't seemed to be following us," he said.

Jesson stopped, his brow furrowed. "You're right. I wonder why?"

Obi-Wan considered the possibilities, and didn't like what came to mind. Under what circumstances did predators fail to pursue fresh meat into the open? "Are these other statues hollow?"

"Perhaps." Jesson paused. "I think I have heard of this, yes."

"Perhaps they live there. They could be watching us now."

"But why don't they pursue us?"

"Fear. Of us, or . . ." Suddenly, the cavern's open floor seemed far too exposed and vulnerable for Obi-Wan's taste. "Let's keep moving, shall we?"

Jesson nodded agreement and led the way across the wide-open space between the ladder and their destination, a cavern wall some hundreds of meters distant. The ground beneath their feet was spongy, more like farm loam than rocky cave soil.

"This way," Jesson said, and when they had crossed the cavern, he leaned against the wall, gasping for air.

As they took a breather, Obi-Wan looked back the way they had come. The vast statues were so shrouded in darkness that he could barely make them out. What a sight this chamber must be with full illumination! The one statue that had led them down into the chamber was largest of all, its outline fading into shadow. Was this an image of some great leader or warrior, perhaps the last, great queen who had swallowed her pride to bring her people into the Republic's arms . . . ?

Jesson paused, taking a sip from a small flask of water. He shook his head, and drops of water flicked from the tuft of fur at his thorax.

"Are you all right?" Obi-Wan asked.

"No," Jesson replied. He paused, then added, "Thank you for saving me." He said it grudgingly, as if the words hurt his mouth.

"We are companions," Obi-Wan replied simply. "Which way, now?"

"Well . . . the other entrance, the one that became sealed after a failed attempt, would be through these tunnels." He pushed himself away from the wall, and they walked along the cavern's far edge. Obi-Wan's feet sank into the flaky soil with each step, a not entirely pleasant sensation. The soil grew harder, and suddenly they were on a meter-wide strip of rock climbing along the wall.

Obi-Wan was happy to be away from the soft cave floor. Something about it disturbed him. What exactly had happened here? His puzzle-solving mind worried at the problem from varied directions as the ground beneath them began to tilt up into a steeper incline.

They climbed along the ascending path for several minutes, finally reaching a tumble of rocks that buried the footpath. There was no way around it. Obi-Wan peered over the side: they were now so far above the ground that his glow rod's beam simply dissolved into darkness. Jesson poked and prodded at the rocks with the spear. "My brother must have tripped a deadfall here," he said. A miniature avalanche, designed to protect the secret path. Jesson's brother had followed a faulty map, or perhaps just made a mistake. Obi-Wan and the X'Ting scrambled up over the rocks and gazed down the other side. Jesson pointed up along the path. "That's where the other door is. From here, everything looks all right."

"I hope so," Obi-Wan said soberly. "I don't relish the idea of going back up through the statue."

"Nor do I. All right. Good. We have our path of retreat secure . . . I think. Let's follow the map."

They went back down over the rock tumble, and then farther down the ramp. Gleaming in the lamplight were more statues of various X'Ting in heroic poses. Jesson studied them carefully.

"This is what we need," he said. Then he began muttering to himself in his people's clicking, popping speech.

Several of the engraved images depicted X'Ting with primary and secondary arms crossed, legs spread. Some were in male mode, and some in female. Around the heads of these full-size images were clusters of miniature engravings of similar design.

Suddenly Obi-Wan realized what he was looking at: hiero-glyphs, images extracted from pictographs of X'Ting and Cestian environments. This was very old, the beginnings of written language. Jesson was reading the wall.

"Sounds and smells," Jesson said. "Our culture is based on both. There is a code at work here, and if I can only re-member my Old X'Tingian will we be able to find the next passage."

He sniffed along the wall, studied, backed up almost to the edge of the ramp. Obi-Wan looked down into an inky void. They were fifty meters from the ground below. A bad fall.

"Shine the light higher," Jesson whispered.

Obi-Wan did. There was another level of images up above the lower, and Jesson smiled. "Do you see these images? This says: *We are not individuals, but of the hive. We are not to struggle alone, but shoulder to shoulder, and upon the shoulders of past hive heroes.*"

Obi-Wan nodded. A fine sentiment.

"Please. Elevate me," Jesson asked, setting his spear aside.

For a moment Obi-Wan assumed that this was a request for enlightenment, but then realized Jesson was being quite literal. He cupped his hands, and the X'Ting climbed up, bal-ancing himself with all four hands spread against the wall, feeling around. Then his fingers found their objectives, and Obi-Wan heard a sharp clicking sound.

The wall slid back, and an opening appeared. Jesson boosted himself up and disappeared into the hole. For a mo-ment Obi-Wan was worried; then Jesson's head reappeared. "It's all clear. A passage between chambers." He held an arm down, and Obi-Wan passed him the spear. Jesson gripped its shaft as Obi-Wan gathered the Force around him and leaped up to the opening. Then the X'Ting disappeared into the hole.

The hole was less than a meter wide, just large enough for crawling, but not much more. Darkness swallowed them completely, but Jesson shuffled ahead of him, and Obi-Wan had no option but to follow.

They were deep in the hive. The walls and ceiling were all of chewed stone. The roughly pentagonal tube branched off into numerous side tunnels. Again and again Jesson sniffed the path and found an old scent marker telling the way.

The roughness of the chewed surface threatened to abrade Obi-Wan's hands, and the strain of staying up on his toes as they crawled was slowly burning the muscles in his calves and shoulders. The rasp of his breathing echoed in the tube, making the close spaces seem closer still.

Then Jesson sighed, a long, low sound. The X'Ting warrior was outlined by a dim radiance coming from somewhere ahead of them. He made a contented *click-pop* mutter, and dropped from sight.

5

Cautiously, Obi-Wan crawled forward until he reached the end of the tube, and looked out.

"Come down," Jesson whispered.

There was no need to whisper. Nothing lived in this chamber. Its walls were crowded floor to ceiling with empty little pentagonal chambers, each just under a meter in diameter. An X'Ting larva hatchery? Obi-Wan crawled out and jumped down to another inclined ledge.

Jesson's faceted eyes shimmered with tears. "This is one of the old breeding chambers," he said. "We changed in so many ways after the Republic came. The hive was never the same. But this is as it used to be."

Here the luminescent fungus was bright enough to give a misty view of the floor twenty meters beneath them. It was covered with broken chrysalis shells, some of which might have lain there for a thousand standard years. Had this place ever known brightness or the shining of a star? As Obi-Wan's eyes adjusted to the light, he could see spires of rock that rose up irregularly through the soil beneath the cast-off X'Ting shells. Stalactites descended from the cavern's roof.

"Is this the chamber?" Obi-Wan asked.

"The other side," Jesson said, pointing across the way. "Through the next wall."

Astounding. Clearly, only an X'Ting could find his way through this labyrinth. The royal eggs had indeed found safe haven.

The chamber was similar to that of the Hall of Heroes: created by water erosion rather than by machines or the flow of lava. Despite its origin, the cubicles chewed in the rock walls implied that it had been modified by countless eons of hive activity, countless millions of willing workers. A thin, milky fog wreathed the floor, but through it he saw vast heaps and furrows of plowed dirt.

"How was the soil deposited here?" he asked. Usually soil was the result of plant and animal action degrading rock over time. Obi-Wan was surprised to find so much of it underground, away from a nurturing sun.

"Remember," Jesson said, pointing at the walls with his spear, "thousands of generations of us lived down here. Just as we had builders, and warriors, and leaders, there were also those who chewed rock, their digestive systems creating soil in which we could grow our crops. For eons we lived here, and the interior of Cestus was kinder to us than the surface."

Thousands of generations. A planet whose surface was sand and chewed rock, its interior rich soil.

Truly, the galaxy was beyond imagination in its variety.

They descended along this second ramp, and Obi-Wan found himself lost in thoughts of what all of this might have been like, back before the time of the Republic. He imagined the hive swarming with life, the royal pair presiding over . . .

Then Obi-Wan's skin tingled, and he became instantly alert. A ripple in the Force, warning him. "On your guard," he whispered.

Jesson's primary and secondary right hands gripped his spear fiercely. "What is it?"

Obi-Wan held up his right hand, demanding quiet. He felt something, a tremor in the soft soil beneath their feet.

Soft. As it had been in the previous chamber.

Soft. As if it were constantly plowed up.

"I've got a bad feeling about this," Jesson said.

"Let's go on to the other side," Obi-Wan said.

"I don't think we'll make it."

The ground trembled. A quake? "What is it?" the Jedi asked.

"Worms," Jesson said, his shoulders quivering, his four hands knotting into fists. "I should have known. They were thought to have retreated deep into the ground since the time of . . ." He seemed reluctant to speak. "Well, that supposed Jedi, at least."

"Was that the service this Jedi Master performed for your royals?" Obi-Wan asked, drawing his lightsaber. The soil beneath them continued to heave.

"I don't know," Jesson said, then added, "Perhaps. No offense, Master Jedi. You are indeed a mighty warrior, but if I know politicians, nothing much actually happened—he was just honored for being from Coruscant."

Despite their danger, Obi-Wan had to chuckle. "My opinion of politicians is much like yours," he confessed. "But I must say that G'Mai Duris seems better than most."

An abrupt tingle in the Force—and Obi-Wan grabbed Jesson and jumped back just in time. The soil beneath them burst, and the mouth of the first worm appeared. It was dark brown, its skin covered with countless small spikes, every three or four meters marked off with a segmented ring. If the proportions were similar to other such beasts that Obi-Wan had seen, then it was thirty meters long at the least.

And the worm was not alone. Two more burst from the ground, their mouths gaping hungrily. It was too late for Obi-Wan and Jesson to run back to the ledge, and too far make it all the way to their destination. All they could do was find a place to make their stand.

Obi-Wan spotted the first of several limestone spurs poking up through the soil. "Get to the rocks!" he shouted, and they dashed for the only visible safety. One of the worms humped along right behind them, moving almost as fast as a human could run.

Obi-Wan took the rear guard, letting his companion reach safety. The Jedi scrambled up the rock with barely a moment to spare. One of the worms tried to crawl up after them, but now Obi-Wan turned and fought. His lightsaber flashed, and the worm screamed. He couldn't actually *hear* the sound, but he felt it clearly through the Force.

Jesson's grip slipped. The spear rattled to the dirt, and Jesson slid down the rock toward the worm's cilia-ringed mouth hole. Its razor teeth clamped down on the X'Ting's right leg, sawing. Obi-Wan was there in an instant, and sliced the creature's head off. Severed, the head flopped back to the sand . . . the remaining body still alive and writhing.

Jesson scrambled up, leg lacerated but still functional.

"Thank you, Master Jedi," he said, shivering. Obi-Wan inspected the wound: the chitinous shell was splintered, exposing the tender pink muscle beneath. He bound it as best he could, and to his credit Jesson made not a single sound of pain, although it had to be brutal. When he was done, Obi-Wan looked down below them. Four worms crawled atop and beneath the soil now, and they showed no signs of abandoning pursuit.

So. *This* was what had happened to the "true" X'Ting, those who had remained behind. The soil they had built up over ages to grow their crops—burying their dead, fertilizing with their wastes—had finally become deep enough to conceal predators. The X'Ting in that first cavern had been caught unawares, driven into the hollow statues. And once there, they had been unable to open the sealed metal doors. There in the darkness, they had become desperate enough to resort to cannibalism. There they had been trapped.

As Obi-Wan and Jesson were trapped, here on one of the few rock spurs on the floor of this second cavern. Obi-Wan felt the first tiny whisper of despair and bared his teeth. He would not fail. Not die. Not here in the dark. He had a job to do; he would find a way to do it.

The worms hissed at them, their cilia wavering back and forth with a chilling, unnatural appetite.

Jesson grimaced and climbed a little higher as another worm tried to ascend the spur. Obi-Wan seared it with the lightsaber, and it retreated without a sound. Again Obi-Wan could sense its shriek through the Force.

The soil humped up in furrows. From both far ends of the cave additional worms appeared, plowing up the ground and gnashing at them. There had to be ten or fifteen in all by now. Some larger, some smaller, all deadly.

"Maybe they smell us. Or hear us. Or they're calling each

other to dinner." He shone his light up above them. "What's that? There's something up there."

Favoring his injured foot, Jesson climbed higher on the spur, shining his light as he did.

There was indeed something clinging atop the spur. *No,* Obi-Wan realized as they climbed. *Not something. Someone. And not clinging.*

Strapped to the rock by a length of rope was the desiccated corpse of an X'Ting male. Little was left but carapace and dried flesh.

"What happened here?" Jesson whispered. "This was my broodmate Tesser. He made it this far, and no farther." He climbed higher to touch his own forehead to his dead brother's withered brow. "He climbed up here to escape the worms. Strapped himself so that he wouldn't slide back down if he lost consciousness. If he became weak. And here he died." So. Now they knew what had happened to two of those who had tried to reach the egg chamber.

"We will die," Jesson said, his voice flat and drained of emotion.

"That's defeatist thinking," Obi-Wan said. "After all, Tesser made it farther than the other. Perhaps we can make it farther still."

Something like hope blossomed in Jesson's eyes. "You have a plan, Jedi?"

"Not yet, but I will."

What distance to the far wall? Obi-Wan measured it with his eyes: sixty meters. Too far to run. The worms would overwhelm the wounded Jesson, and perhaps Obi-Wan, as well. And there was no point in reaching the egg chamber without his X'Ting companion. Without Jesson's specialized knowledge, he had no chance at all of accessing the vault.

"What equipment do you have?"

"My spear is gone. I have the glowlight, and a grapnel line."

A grapnel line? *That* might come in useful. "Let me see it," Obi-Wan said.

Jesson showed him the gun. It was about the size of a hand

blaster, with a filament reel nestled beneath. Fairly standard
GAR surplus.

"How much line?" Obi-Wan asked.

"Twenty meters?"

So. They had twenty meters of grapnel cable as standard
equipment, but that wasn't enough to get them over . . .

To their left jutted another rock spur, this one about fifteen
meters from their destination: the far wall. The spur was
about thirty meters away. Could they make it that far? No,
not with Jesson's wounded leg.

All right. What, then?

Obi-Wan looked up above their heads and noted a ten-
meter stalactite above them, halfway between their current
position and that rock spur. A plan began to evolve. It would
depend on the strength of that stalactite, but it might just
work.

"I'm going to try something," Obi-Wan said. "If you trust
me, we might make it through this."

"All right, Jedi," Jesson said. "I have no choice. Let's hear
your idea."

"You'll see," Obi-Wan said, and climbed higher up the
spur. The worms humped around the base. From time to time
one or two tried to crawl up, but they couldn't get good purchase on the rock and slipped back down.

Obi-Wan took Jesson's grapnel and aimed carefully, firing
it at the protruding stalactite. The line flew true, its claw-
tip anchoring deeply into the rock. He yanked hard, and it
seemed firm enough.

"All right," he said. "Hold on to my waist."

Jesson looked at him dubiously, then his strong, thin arms
encircled Obi-Wan's waist.

Obi-Wan braced himself and swung off the rock spur.
They flew in a long, shallow glide, the radius of their arc taking them so close to the soil that the worms hungrily snapped
at them, cilia weaving as if in starvation or anger.

Jesson clung to him, faceted red eyes wide in wonder as
they flew . . .

Then the X'Ting uttered a shrill series of terrified clicks

as the stalactite above them broke. They were on the upswing of the arc when it happened. A huge chunk of rock snapped free and fell, sabotaging their arc. They flew up, then the rock smacked down into the soil, jerking them back down hard, so that they whuffed into the soil a moment later, the impact slamming the breath from Obi-Wan's lungs.

He scrambled up as fast as he could, winded but unwilling to die a meal for the worms.

"Run!" he screamed as the creatures streaked toward him. He had the presence of mind to trigger the grapnel's release mechanism and jerk the line free. The reel pulled in the filament as he sprinted toward the next rock, feet pounding puffs of dirt from the ground. Jesson was limping too slowly. Obi-Wan closed his mind to pain, grabbed with his right arm, and, ignoring the strain, forcing himself to greater effort, heaved the X'Ting soldier up on the rock then leapt up himself as one of the worms grabbed his left boot. He reached out, scrabbling for the rock and failing to find purchase as the worm struggled to drag him back down. But Jesson had regained his senses, and reached down for Obi-Wan's wrist with primary and secondary hands. He braced his spindly legs and pulled for dear life.

Obi-Wan managed to brace his knee against the rock and pushed, forcing himself up as the worm lost its grip. He scrabbled up a bit higher and then, bracing himself, turned with lightsaber in hand and cut his attacker in half. The severed portion dropped to the ground and writhed, ichors oozing from the end, then disappeared into the ground and was gone.

The Jedi gulped air and breathed a sigh of relief. He looked up at Jesson. "Thank you," he said.

"We're even now," Jesson said. He scanned the wall ahead. "Well, we're better than halfway there."

"That might be enough, if we're clever," Obi-Wan said. He climbed up the limestone spur, measuring the distance to the far wall, hoping that he had been correct. Otherwise, it was all too possible that their skeletons might, one distant day, be found here on the rock.

"Where is the far opening?" he asked, shading his eyes with his hands. "I can't see it."

"There is a rock ledge, about five meters above the ground," Jesson said, pointing.

Obi-Wan squinted until he could make it out. "Yes."

"And beyond that is the entrance to the chamber. I can get us in. After that . . ." The X'Ting shrugged. "I do not know."

"All right." Obi-Wan measured the distance between the far wall and the rock spur, and found a surface that looked suitable.

He fired the grapnel. Once again the line flew true, anchoring itself in the rock. He anchored the other end to their spur. He hated to leave the gun behind, but either there were additional resources available on the other side, or all attempts at survival might be futile.

"Give me the light," Obi-Wan said. He turned Jesson's glowlight up to full radiance and shone it directly in the worms' eyes.

For many years the worms had been in the caves beneath ChikatLik. But it was possible they hadn't been down here long enough to grow blind—that, in fact, brilliant light might actually be painful and confusing to them.

And clearly it was. Already they were scurrying away, their pain echoing through Obi-Wan's Force-sense. "Let's go!" he yelled. And he began moving out over the soil, hand over hand along the line.

Twenty meters, give or take. The worms seemed to have recovered from the light: they were humping back in the direction of their quarry. Obi-Wan swung his feet up and crossed them over the line for support, then triggered the lamp again beneath them. The worms gave their soundless squeal and retreated—

But not as far. Obi-Wan extended his senses through Force, sensing the hissing, coiling creatures as they crept back. He unhooked his feet from the line and moved hand over hand again, increasing his speed.

The line cut into his fingers. Pain like the slice of a frozen razor raced down his arm to his elbow. He bit back a scream, refusing to give up their position.

Could the worms see them? He wasn't certain, but Obi-Wan considered it unlikely the creatures had evolved to hunt prey dangling over their heads.

Still, the vibration of the falling rock, and perhaps the scream of the wounded worm, had summoned additional creatures from deeper in the caves. By the fungal glow along the walls, he could see that the soil beneath them *teemed* with worms, boiled with them, hundreds, thousands of them— finger-size to meters in length. They jostled and snapped at each other, reaching up for Obi-Wan and Jesson.

One of the severed segments actually managed to leap free of the soil, gnashing at Obi-Wan's pant leg, missing the calf muscle but enmeshing itself in the cloth. It whipped its tail this way and that, trying to find purchase.

Swaying, trying to shake the thing free, Obi-Wan lost hold with his right hand. Behind him, Jesson emitted a sour, frightened wisp of air.

Dangling by his left hand, Obi-Wan called his lightsaber to his right hand, triggered it, and cut at the thing hanging from his leg. Severed, the worm fell in halves to the ground below them.

Hand over hand. Hand over hand. The grapnel line sliced his palms, but he shut the pain away in a small dark room in his mind and concentrated on the task at hand.

When finally his feet were over the ledge, he dropped down and pivoted. Jesson was almost there, swinging back and forth like a pendulum. The X'Ting warrior jumped down and almost missed the ledge; he battled for balance, Obi-Wan snatching at his hand.

Then they were both safe on the ledge, far above the snapping mouths of the worms.

Breathing a sigh of relief, Obi-Wan turned toward the wall. Viewed from the far side, shadow had disguised a shallow tunnel, but the mouth was easy to see now. At the end of the tunnel was a sealed durasteel door inset with some manner of electronic reader device. "How do we open this?"

Jesson pressed his face up close to the door. "It is said that any X'Ting can open this door. It is what awaits within—"

As if it had been listening to his speech and timing its own response, the door sighed open. Obi-Wan and Jesson stepped inside.

6

The chamber within was roughly egg-shaped, constructed of some kind of white, curved tile, probably something produced offworld. There were two other doors: one on the far side of the chamber, and the other directly to the right of them, with another sensor housed against it.

Obi-Wan walked to the door across the way. A monitor screen was set into the middle, and he manipulated its finger-pad until a sharp little holo appeared. It seemed to be an image taken right outside this very portal. When it focused, he turned away again: huddled on the far side of the door was a body. Another X'Ting brother who had tried and failed to reach the egg chamber. Obi-Wan could not see what had killed the warrior, but his body looked as if the exoskeleton had been partially . . . *dissolved.*

He shuddered. Without whatever specific instructions had been destroyed by plague or supernova, could anyone have been expected to survive such a gauntlet?

Jesson was at the silver door, touching sensors and manipulating the controls. Obi-Wan waited while he attempted several different patterns, but then the young X'Ting warrior hit the wall with a balled fist in frustration. "I can't open it!"

"How many times did you try?" Obi-Wan asked, alarmed. "Don't you only have three attempts?"

"Not here," Jesson said. "Once we are inside, the challenge truly begins."

"I can try my lightsaber if you wish."

Jesson laughed. "I think not. This door was designed to resist any known torch. Just give me a bit of time, and—"

But Obi-Wan had already triggered his weapon and was forcing the glowing blade into the door. "Turn your head away," he warned. Jesson complied.

Within a few moments, Obi-Wan knew Jesson was right: this door was certainly tougher than the previous one. Regardless, the Jedi weapon blistered the durasteel, sending sparks flying and globules of glowing metal dribbling down to the floor.

The door was sandwiched with energy-absorbing circuits that slowed, but never stopped him. Finally the door twisted free, metal droplets spraying as it clattered down. They stepped through the smoking entrance.

Within was another egg-shaped chamber with a three-meter pentagonal gold seal emblazoned on the floor. On the far side, a single molded chair sat before an array of . . . what? Nozzles and beam projectors pointed menacingly at the chair, clear warning for anyone who would brave the challenge.

Rows of readouts and meters blinked to life as they entered, and Obi-Wan inspected them swiftly. Most of the controls were labeled in both Basic and X'Tingian. One of the most provocative labels read: WORM CALL/WORM SENSOR.

Worm call? Then one of his questions was more or less answered. The worms had not been natural to the cave. The security company had brought them here as a passive guarding device. But had something gone horribly wrong? Had the worms found a way into the Hall of Heroes, where so many X'Ting still lived?

That would explain much. What a moment of horror that must have been, when the mindless creatures appointed to guard their most precious treasure burrowed or found a way through the rock wall separating the egg chamber from the living settlement, and chaos reigned.

A hologrammic display caught his eye. A sonic gauge of some kind, labeled HYPERSONIC REPEL. So . . . the worms were called by sound, and could be repelled the same way. A simple answer, but one unknown to the X'Ting.

Jesson had already eased his way into the command seat.

Obi-Wan smelled the change in the room and guessed that the X'Ting was calming down, preparing to perform a task for which he had long prepared.

Jesson's four sets of fingers interlaced, and there was a *BRRRRAKK!* sound as sixteen knuckles cracked in a whiplash.

The X'Ting began his sequence, first speaking in X'Tingian, then switching to Basic, perhaps in respect for Obi-Wan. "The start-up sequence is on record," he said, his six limbs moving with insectlike precision as he manipulated the controls.

"What is all of this?" Obi-Wan asked, indicating the nozzles and ray projectors surrounding the seat in a halo. Was it possible that the legend, the fragmentary information available to Jesson, was incorrect, and it wasn't the eggs that would be destroyed if three wrong answers were given—but the questioner himself?

For the first few minutes Jesson's efforts were unrewarded; then a hologram blossomed before them. The glowing image was a schematic of the entire room, the chamber itself. They could see a narrow shaft beneath the gold seal, and at the bottom of that shaft, behind a thick shield, lay two precious eggs surrounded by a laser array. Tentatively, he reached out through the Force . . . but the mechanism controlling the array was too complex for his understanding. His heart sank. There was little question that the array would defeat any efforts he might make to circumvent it. How he wished that Anakin were here! His Padawan learner was an intuitive genius with all things mechanical, and might well have devised a means of defeating this apparatus. Obi-Wan felt helpless.

Thankfully, his X'Ting companion had survived to enter the capsule. Their only hope of success lay in Jesson's four capable hands.

Jesson took the controls as if he were playing some kind of complex musical instrument. Obi-Wan could hear varying sighs and squeaks, and the X'Ting warrior answered the calls in a blur of finger-play across the control board.

Finally the schematic floated to the left. A spherical target shape appeared, its three layers rotating above a core resembling the egg chamber.

Three concentric layers. Obi-Wan's mouth felt dry.

He glanced at his wrist chrono and was astounded. Had only an hour elapsed since they had first entered the catacombs? Since they had left the X'Ting council chamber? It felt like days!

An X'Ting voice with an interrogative intonation sounded, followed by a voice speaking in Basic. *"Answer the following question: What is in the hive but not of the hive? What nurtures but is nurtured, what dreams but never sleeps?"*

Jesson took a deep breath. From a belt pod he extracted a flat rectangle. "This is the last remaining key chip," he said. "I have only three chances, but I think that we will succeed."

"Do you know the answer to the riddle?" Obi-Wan asked.

"Yes," Jesson said confidently. "It is the Zeetsa. They live in the hive but are not X'Ting. They give to us, but in turn receive nourishment and care. They dream but are aware." His certainty increasing with every motion, Jesson placed the card in its slot.

There was a soft blur, and the voiced of the scanner said: *"Your answer?"*

"The Zeetsa," Jesson said.

There was a pause. The sphere began to rotate more swiftly and the outer third began to peel away, the pieces dissolving as they did. Jesson sat, astounded, as the voice said, first in X'Tingian and then in Basic:

"Incorrect."

Jesson stood from the chair, eyes wide and disbelieving. The voice said: *"Sit down, or the session is terminated."*

Jesson looked back at Obi-Wan. The nozzles at the edges of the room opened like sunblossoms welcoming the dawn. Obi-Wan suspected—no, he *knew* that if the session was terminated, so were they. And so were the eggs.

"Sit down," he said quietly. And Jesson did. The nozzles seemed to track their motion. Obi-Wan had no interest in discovering what might flow through them at a moment's notice.

"Do you wish to continue the sequence?" the machine asked.

"Do I have a choice?" Jesson said miserably.

"Yes. You may choose personal termination. If you choose this option, the eggs will not be damaged."

"I'll try again," he said, and swallowed hard.

"Very well." A pause. The pause lasted for so long that Obi-Wan wondered if it was going to speak again, but then it did.

"Who lived and now stand still? Who cared not for acclaim, but are idolized by all? Who carried weight and now ring hollow?"

"You speak Basic and X'Tingian," Obi-Wan said to Jesson. "Are the words accurately translated?"

The warrior's serrated teeth clattered. "I think so. There is a certain poetry missing from the Basic translation."

" 'Who lived and stand still,' " Obi-Wan went on. "That could have two meanings: to be motionless, or to persist, to 'still stand,' if you get my meaning. Do you understand this one?"

"I believe so," Jesson said, but he no longer seemed so confident.

"Then do you think you know the answer?"

Jesson stared at the spilling sphere. Just two layers left. "I think so."

"Then answer," Obi-Wan said, trying to give the X'Ting confidence that he himself did not entirely feel.

Jesson took a deep breath. "I am ready to proceed," he said.

"Answer," the machine said.

"The heroes of the hive. The Hall of Heroes."

The seconds ticked past, and nothing happened. Then the sphere began to rotate more swiftly, and the second, orange layer peeled away and vanished.

"Incorrect," the voice said.

Jesson shivered in the seat, and Obi-Wan detected a sharp, sour odor in the air. *Fear?* "They should not have sent me," the X'Ting said.

Self-pity? Jesson did not seem the type, but . . . Then the warrior went on, haltingly, "I can't do this. Because of me, the eggs will be destroyed."

There it was. The reaction hadn't been self-pity at all. It was concern for the eggs Obi-Wan had heard in Jesson's voice, seen in his body, smelled in the air.

The warrior was on the edge, about to give up. Obi-Wan had seen this before. It was not fear, as most beings knew it, because for most, fear was a matter of personal loss: loss of self-image, loss of health, loss of life. But even without being able to directly interpret the pheromones now flooding the air, he knew that these were not the source of Jesson's anguish. The X'Ting warrior loved the hive, and was now terribly afraid of letting it down. He had been well chosen. He would be more than happy to die in the accomplishment of this task, die anonymously and in great pain if need be, if the hive could only survive and thrive, and be raised up to its rightful glory.

Jesson was locked almost in paralysis, his hands hovering over the controls. Every muscle in his body seemed to be stiffened in unyielding contraction, all of the cockiness drained from him by the reality of the tests he had already failed. "How?" he said. "How could it be? What answers were they looking for?"

"We can't know," Obi-Wan said, and laid a hand on the X'Ting's shoulder. "All we can do, all we can *ever* do, is the best we can. The rest is controlled by the Force."

"The Force!" Jesson spat. "I've heard so much about you precious Jedi and your Force."

"It is not *our* Force," Obi-Wan said, trying to comfort him. "It owns us. And you. It creates all of us, but is also created by us."

"Riddles!" Jesson screamed. "Nothing but riddles. I've had enough!"

He leapt up from the seat and ran across the room, hammering at the door, screaming, "Let me out! Let me *out*!"

"Return to the seat, or the session will be terminated," the machine said calmly.

Obi-Wan gazed at Jesson and then made a snap decision. He went to sit in the chair.

"You are not the original participant," the machine said in its androgynous, synthesized voice. *"It is necessary that the original participant finish the process."*

Obi-Wan looked back over his shoulder at the wounded, broken X'Ting warrior. How proud and confident he had seemed only an hour before! How obvious now that all of that pride had been a thin shield against the fear of failing his people, a support against the terrible weight of that responsibility.

"He is unable to continue," Obi-Wan said.

"In one hundred seconds this test is terminated," the voice said. *"Ninety-nine, ninety-eight . . ."*

"Ask *me* the questions!" Desperation crept into Obi-Wan's voice. "Please. Ask me the—"

"Ninety-three, ninety-two . . ."

Obi-Wan jumped out of the chair and went to Jesson, still huddled on the floor, primary and secondary arms wrapped around his knees.

"Jesson," he said in his calmest voice. "You must try again."

"I can't."

"You must. There is no one else."

The X'Ting sank his head against his knees and shivered.

"All your life," Obi-Wan said, "you have prepared yourself for a great challenge. As all warriors do."

No response.

"Do not think I don't know how you feel. Your warrior clan could not protect the hive from Cestus Cybernetics. They have power beyond anything your people can match. And so you feel that even your death cannot free your people. Even the best effort you can manage is not enough to fill the need. So deep in your heart you feel that there is nothing."

Jesson finally looked up. "You understand this?"

"It is the same on planets all over the galaxy," the Jedi said. "Whenever there are conquered species, the warriors are the first to be oppressed. Because they are the most dangerous."

"Seventy . . . sixty-nine . . . sixty-eight . . ."

"All my life," Jesson said, "all I've wanted is to fulfill the function I was appointed at birth. As my ancestors did. When female, to bear healthy eggs, to learn and heal and teach. When male, to fight for my hive, to keep it safe. Perhaps to die."

Jesson looked up at Obi-Wan, faceted eyes glimmering with hope. If the offworlder could understand his misery, then perhaps, just perhaps there was a way out. There was an answer.

"And then when G'Mai Duris regained leadership of the hive council, you had hope."

"Yes!"

"Fifty-four, fifty-three . . ."

Obi-Wan fought to keep his voice calm, although he felt the urgency boiling within him. "And when you were chosen to be the one to find and bring back the royals, you thought that this was your chance. This was your opportunity to serve the hive. This was the moment of glory!"

"Yes!"

"It still is," Obi-Wan said. "All warriors dream of conquest, of glorious victory or glorious death. But none of us knows the price of our lives. None of us knows the worth of our deaths. That is for others to decide, after we are gone. All we can do is struggle, to fight with both courage and compassion, to sell our lives dearly. And later, after the battle is over, others will be able to decide if that sacrifice was in vain, or whether it was the deciding factor. Some of us must place our lives on the altar of sacrifice. Others on our dreams of victory."

Jesson gazed up at him, some small measure of hope and understanding creeping in. "And if I fail, and the royal eggs die?"

"Then you will have done all that you could, serving the hive with all your strength."

"And if my failure costs your life as well as my own, Jedi?"

Obi-Wan spoke as kindly as he could. "My life was forfeit the moment I set myself on this path. Tread not the path to war seeking to preserve life. That is a fool's dream. Seek to live your days honoring whatever principles you hold dear. Work to gain the highest skills of which you are capable. Sell your life dearly."

"Be true to the hive," Jesson said.

"Yes."

"How can a human understand so well?"

Obi-Wan smiled. "We all have a hive," he said.

"Twenty-seven, twenty-six . . ."

"Stand, X'Ting warrior," Obi-Wan said, putting durasteel into his voice.

Jesson stood.

"Fifteen, fourteen . . ."

He made his way back to the chair and sat down. The countdown ceased.

"Are you prepared to continue?" the voice asked in Basic, after a series of X'Tingian pops.

Jesson answered in affirmative clicks.

There was a pause. The rotating hologrammic sphere was moving more swiftly now. But a single layer remained over the egg chamber.

"Answer," the machine said. *"Who ate our eggs and now hide their young? Whose web of fear ensnares them? Who stole the sun but now live in shadow?"*

"It's too simple," Jesson whispered.

"Sometimes simplicity is the best disguise," Obi-Wan said. "Don't try to be tricky. Answer with truth."

"But that is what I did before," Jesson said. "And both times I was wrong."

"This was created by your own people," Obi-Wan said. "They would not make it impossible for you to succeed. Trust your forebears."

But Obi-Wan felt a slight prickle at the back of his neck. Something. A warning? A clue? Something. What was it?

Something about the array of weapons around the chair? The nozzles. The questions. Apparently simple for an X'Ting . . .

But the answers were wrong.

Obi-Wan's instinct was screaming at him, but he couldn't put his finger on what, exactly, it was trying to say. Couldn't, but had to. This was the last chance, and if he couldn't help his X'Ting companion, all was lost, and his cause was set back irreparably.

Still, in the depths of his heart, he felt a simple answer, heard it echoing with the truth of the Force.

"Answer truthfully," he said again. "Don't try to be clever. Don't try to second-guess. Give it the answer that you know to be true."

Jesson nodded. "The spider people," he said. "Once, they were the lords of this planet. Once, they drove us from the surface. We sent them to the shadows."

His hands splayed out on the control panel, and his eyes were locked on the rotating sphere. *What? What . . . ?*

It rotated more rapidly, and a thin whining sound arose in the room, seemed to envelop them. Then the sphere accelerated faster still, and the segments fragmented and flew away.

"Answer incorrect," the voice said. *"Egg termination has begun."*

Obi-Wan stared, shocked. How wrong could he have been? Rarely had his insights been proven so horribly wrong. Perhaps he could burn through the floor with his lightsaber and save the royal pair . . .

He triggered his weapon and blazed it into the floor's pentagonal gold seal. Beneath it, he imagined, was a case-hardened durasteel vault door. The hologrammic image was melting, blazing, even as the first sparks leapt from the floor and the room filled with smoke. Jesson sat stunned in the chair, unable to move. "No," he said. "I did everything right. I did everything. No, please."

"Vaporization fifty percent complete—"

The chamber lights flashed on and off in dizzying bursts, and nozzles at the corners of the rooms began to hiss, expelling a thin greenish gas. Obi-Wan snapped his rebreather into his mouth, sorry that he didn't have one for Jesson, as well. But if he could just get through this lock, if he could just get to the egg vault, even if his companion perished, the mission would still . . .

"Vaporization complete."

He felt numb.

Jesson leaned over the controls, sobbing. "Kill me, kill me," he said, speaking to no one in particular, and the universe in general.

The weapons array around Jesson began to glow, and the mist filling the air was sucked toward it. In a few minutes the room was cleared of mist, and Jesson lay still. Obi-Wan looked at his companion's limp body, feeling a sense of despair and failure that he had rarely known.

Then . . . *Jesson moved.*

He sat up and looked around, as torpidly as if he had been drugged. "Why am I still alive?" he asked.

"Look at the holo," Obi-Wan said quietly.

Without any fuss, the schematic had reappeared on the display. In miniature form, the egg chamber was rising up through the shaft.

"What . . . what is this?" Jesson said.

The computer began a series of clicks and pops.

"What does it say?" Obi-Wan asked.

Jesson listened carefully. "It says . . . *'Congratulations, X'Ting warrior. You have succeeded.'* "

Obi-Wan was staggered. What was this?

He looked more carefully at the weapons array around the chair and realized that he had been wrong. It wasn't a weapons array at all. They were *sensors.* And the gas? It had been some kind of analytic compound that combined with Jesson's pheromones, the smells that X'Ting emitted under stress. The resultant cocktail had been reabsorbed and analyzed by the sensor array . . .

Clarity struck like lightning. "You were never intended to answer the questions successfully," Obi-Wan exclaimed. "Your answers were probably correct. Answering them proved that you knew X'Ting history. The sensors proved you were X'Ting. But it needed to know how you would react to failure."

"To . . . failure? But I don't understand."

"You might have sought the egg from a wish to destroy it. Or to control all the X'Ting. It might have been for lust of power, or from greed. But when you came from love of hive, and failed, and saw your failure as killing the last king and queen, you felt not anger, but anguish. The test was not for your mind. It was for your heart."

"It smelled my grief," Jesson said, comprehending.

The burned gold seal rose up, exposing a durasteel column of the same shape. The column rose until it was Jesson's height, revealing a chamber. Thick transparent crystal windows slid open, showing a disk half a meter high. Around the edge of the disk blinked the red-white lights of an activated antigrav ring. With the greatest delicacy, Jesson pulled the disk out. The antigrav ring reduced its effective weight to no more than a few grams. Holding it in hovering position with the touch of their fingers, X'Ting and Jedi checked the little readout meter blinking at the top.

"They are alive," he whispered. "I will take them to the council. Our medical clan will know what to do."

"Yes," Obi-Wan said.

The walls were blinking more rapidly. A speaker squealed a deep, booming vibration that rattled Obi-Wan's spine.

"What's that?" Jesson asked.

Obi-Wan inspected the controls. "I think it's a worm repellent," he said. "The room is letting us leave."

The doors unsealed. They examined the far door. The dead X'Ting lay limp and half melted. "What killed him?" Jesson asked.

"I don't know. And I don't want to take the risk. We know the hazards behind us. We'll go back the way we came."

7

The egg cask was relatively easy to take through the door leading to the worm chamber. They stood on the ledge and gazed down on the floor beneath them. Artificial lights had triggered along the ceiling and, in combination with the fungus, illuminated the plowed soil where the worms had fled the shrill, painful sounds. Obi-Wan extended his senses into Force: nothing. The cave was deserted.

They moved the disk down to the dirt floor. With the help of the antigrav unit, the carbonite disk virtually floated across the cavern. The rock walls seemed so huge and majestic now. Obi-Wan hadn't been able to appreciate it, but as artificial lights switched on in the ceiling, the sight of cascading stalactites and vast arched walls took his breath away.

What sort of celebratory scene had the builders pictured for this moment? Were thousands of X'Ting expected to be gathered now, cheering this ceremony as a new queen and king entered the world?

How strangely and sorrowfully it had all worked out.

There would be such celebration eventually, of course, but not now. Now there was silence and shadows.

The egg cask slid easily through the pentagonal openings on the far side of the cavern. Jesson seemed drained but exultant, a different being from the cocky young warrior who had accompanied Obi-Wan from the council chamber less than two hours before.

Truly, Obi-Wan thought, transformation was not a matter of time. It happened in a blink, or not at all.

They crawled through the darkness, pulling the precious cargo between them. Jesson found his way through the labyrinth more easily this time, and their steady shuffling was not really laborious—it was filled with a sense of purpose.

"You know, Jedi," Jesson said back over his shoulder, "I may have been wrong about you."

"It's possible," Obi-Wan said, smiling.

A few moments passed, during which they proceeded in darkness, Jesson scenting his way and perhaps organizing his thoughts.

"I've seen what you can do, and who and what you are." He paused. "It is even possible that Duris wasn't lying about that Jedi Master. Maybe he really did visit, and maybe he really did do something worth remembering."

Obi-Wan chuckled. He himself might never know. At least, not until he returned to Coruscant. Then he might make polite inquiries, just to satisfy his curiosity.

On the other hand, some of the greatest Jedi were notoriously reticent to speak of their deeds. His questions might well be carefully deflected, his curiosity never satisfied.

They reached the next chamber, the hall of statues where they had first entered. Jesson climbed out and down onto the ledge. Obi-Wan gently pushed the egg cask out. Suspended by its antigrav unit, it floated down to Jesson as gently as a chunk of tilewood settling through water.

Obi-Wan jumped down lightly. There was a choice to make: to go back the way they had come, to reenter that first hollow statue and brave the cannibals again, or . . .

"I'm in no mood for an unnecessary battle," the Jedi said. "Let's climb the rocks and see if the door up on the far side will open."

"Agreed," Jesson said. Fatigue blurred his voice. The last hours had to have been the most taxing of the X'Ting warrior's life. A frantic battle, a climb through darkness, pursuit by carnivorous cave worms, dooming and then saving his species' royal heirs . . .

Obi-Wan wondered: would an X'Ting deal with this stress by celebrating, or by hibernating?

When they were both safely on the stone ledge, they guided the egg cask up the incline toward what Jesson said was a door.

It took several nerve-racking minutes to get the egg cask over the rockfall. On the far side they found something ghastly: the corpse of another of Jesson's broodmates, his lower body jutting from beneath a boulder. His withered secondary arm still clutched a lamp.

So much death, in service to their hive. Any species that produced both a G'Mai Duris and a Jesson Di Blinth was formidable indeed.

Obi-Wan picked up the lamp. It was of industrial design, heavier and more powerful than the GAR-surplus model Jesson had brought down into the labyrinth. When he triggered it, an eye-searing beam splayed out against the wall.

Pity it hadn't helped Jesson's brother.

Just a few meters up the ramp was the door that would take them back to the main hive. A droid mechanism had barred the door. In all probability, the same booby trap had triggered the deadfall.

"I think my question is answered," Jesson said behind Obi-Wan, voice deep and respectful.

"What question is that?" Obi-Wan asked, triggering his lightsaber's energy beam. He examined the door more closely, judging the best angle for the initial cut.

"Look. Please," Jesson said.

Obi-Wan turned around, allowing his eyes to follow Jesson's beam of light. It played out along the cavern, illuminating in turn image after gigantic image of the kings and queens of the X'Ting, their greatest leaders in colossal array. Rendered in chewed stone was a veritable forest of noble, insectoid titans. Some male, some female, some tall and young, some stooped and old, their four hands variously held in postures of beseeching, imploring, protecting, comforting, teaching, healing.

A hall of heroes, indeed, Obi-Wan thought. "What is it?"

"There," Jesson replied. "Where we first came in." And he focused the beam on the largest statue.

Now Obi-Wan could see the stooped, aged figure far more clearly. The narrow ladder tube they had descended had been a cane. The chamber in which they had fought so desperately against the cannibal X'Ting was, from without, seen to be a muscularly rounded torso. Their point of initial entry, the very first chamber, was a head with flared, triangular ears. The statue stood at least seventy meters high, taller than any other in the X'Ting Hall of Heroes.

Indeed, many questions were answered, but more remained, questions that Obi-Wan might never satisfy. For there, robed arm outstretched in greeting, gigantic and benevolent in the lamplight of a valiant, long-dead X'Ting soldier, loomed the hollow, chewed-stone statue of a smiling Master Yoda.

Read on for an excerpt
from the exciting prequel to
Star Wars: Episode III
Revenge of the Sith

LABYRINTH
OF EVIL

by James Luceno

CAPTURING TRADE FEDERATION VICEROY—AND SEPARATIST
Councilmember—Nute Gunray is the mission that brings
Jedi Knights Obi-Wan Kenobi and Anakin Skywalker, with a
squad of clones in tow, to Neimoidia. But the treacherous
ally of the Sith proves as slippery as ever, evading his Jedi
pursuers even as they narrowly avoid deadly disaster. Still,
their daring efforts yield an unexpected prize: a unique holo-
transceiver that bears intelligence capable of leading the Republic forces to their ultimate quarry, the ever-elusive Darth
Sidious.

Swiftly taking up the chase, Anakin and Obi-Wan follow
clues from the droid factories of Charros IV to the far-flung
worlds of the Outer Rim . . . every step bringing them closer
to pinpointing the location of the Sith Lord—whom they
suspect has been manipulating every aspect of the Separatist

rebellion. Yet somehow, in the escalating galaxy-wide chess game of strikes, counterstrikes, ambushes, sabotage, and retaliations, Sidious stays constantly one move ahead.

Then the trail takes a shocking turn. For Sidious and his minions have set in motion a ruthlessly orchestrated campaign to divide and overwhelm the Jedi forces—and bring the Republic to its knees.

CHAPTER 1

DARKNESS WAS ENCROACHING ON CATO NEIMOIDIA'S WESTERN hemisphere, though exchanges of coherent light high above the beleaguered world ripped looming night to shreds. Well under the fractured sky, in an orchard of manax trees that studded the lower ramparts of Viceroy Gunray's majestic redoubt, companies of clone troopers and battle droids were slaughtering one another with bloodless precision.

A flashing fan of blue energy lit the undersides of a cluster of trees: the lightsaber of Obi-Wan Kenobi.

Attacked by two sentry droids, Obi-Wan stood his ground, twisting his upraised blade right and left to swat blaster bolts back at his enemies. Caught midsection by their own salvos, both droids came apart, with a scattering of alloy limbs.

Obi-Wan moved again.

Tumbling under the segmented thorax of a Neimoidian harvester beetle, he sprang to his feet and raced forward. Explosive light shunted from the citadel's deflector shield dappled the loamy ground between the trees, casting long shadows of their buttressed trunks. Oblivious to the chaos occurring in their midst, columns of the five-meter-long harvesters continued their stalwart march toward a mound that supported the fortress. In their cutting jaws or on their upsweeping backs they carried cargoes of pruned foliage. The crushing sounds of their ceaseless gnawing provided an eerie cadence to the rumbling detonations and the hiss and whine of blaster bolts.

From off to Obi-Wan's left came a sudden click of servos; to his right, a hushed cry of warning.

"Down, Master!"

He dropped into a crouch even before Anakin's lips formed the final word, lightsaber aimed to the ground to keep from impaling his onrushing former Padawan. A blur of thrumming blue energy sizzled through the humid air, followed by a sharp smell of cauterized circuitry, the tang of ozone. A blaster discharged into soft soil, then the stalked, elongated head of a battle droid struck the ground not a meter from Obi-Wan's feet, sparking as it bounced and rolled out of sight, repeating: *"Copy, copy . . . Copy, copy . . ."*

In a tuck, Obi-Wan pivoted on his right foot in time to see the droid's spindly body collapse. The fact that Anakin had saved his life was nothing new, but Anakin's blade had passed a little too close for comfort. Eyes somewhat wide with surprise, he came to his feet.

"You nearly took my head off."

Anakin held his blade to one side. In the strobing light of battle his blue eyes shone with wry amusement. "Sorry, Master, but your head was where my lightsaber needed to go."

Master.

Anakin used the honorific not as learner to teacher, but as Jedi Knight to Jedi Council member. The braid that had defined his earlier status had been ritually severed after his audacious actions at Praesitlyn. His tunic, knee-high boots, and tight-fitting trousers were as black as the night. His face scarred from a contest with Dooku-trained Asajj Ventress. His mechanical right hand sheathed in a tight-fitting glove. He had let his hair grow long the past few months, falling almost to his shoulders now. His face he kept clean-shaven, unlike Obi-Wan's, whose strong jaw was defined by a short beard.

"I suppose I should be grateful your lightsaber *needed* to go there, rather than desired to."

Anakin's grin blossomed into a full-fledged smile. "Last time I checked we were on the same side, Master."

"Still, if I'd been a moment slower . . ."

Anakin booted the battle droid's blaster aside. "Your fears are only in your mind."

Obi-Wan scowled. "Without a head I wouldn't have much mind left, now, would I?" He swept his lightsaber in a flourishing pass, nodding up the alley of manax trees. "After you."

They resumed their charge, moving with the supernatural speed and grace afforded by the Force, Obi-Wan's brown cloak swirling behind him. Victims of the initial bombardment, scores of battle droids lay sprawled on the ground. Others dangled like broken marionettes from the branches of the trees into which they had been hurled.

Areas of the leafy canopy were in flames.

Two scorched droids little more than arms and torsos lifted their weapons as the Jedi approached, but Anakin only raised his left hand in a Force push that shoved the droids flat onto their backs.

They jinked right, somersaulting under the wide bodies of two harvester beetles, then hurdling a tangle of barbed underbrush that had managed to anchor itself in the otherwise meticulously tended orchard. They emerged from the tree line at the shore of a broad irrigation canal, fed by a lake that delimited the Neimoidians' citadel on three sides. In the west a trio of wedge-shaped *Acclamator*-class assault cruisers hung in scudding clouds. North and east the sky was in turmoil, crosshatched with ion trails, turbolaser beams, hyphens of scarlet light streaming upward from weapons emplacements outside the citadel's energy shield. Rising from high ground at the end of the peninsula, the tiered fastness was reminiscent of the command towers of the Trade Federation core ships, and indeed had been the inspiration for them.

Somewhere inside, trapped by Republic forces, were the Trade Federation elite.

With his homeworld threatened and the purse worlds of Deko and Koru Neimoidia devastated, Viceroy Gunray would have been wiser to retreat to the Outer Rim, as other members of the Separatist Council were thought to be doing. But rational thinking had never been a Neimoidian strong suit, especially when possessions remained on Cato Neimoidia the viceroy apparently couldn't live without. Backed by a battle group of Federation warships, he had slipped onto Cato Neimoidia, intent on looting the citadel before it fell. But Republic forces had been lying in wait, eager to capture him alive and bring him to justice—thirteen years late, in the judgment of many.

Cato Neimoidia was as close to Coruscant as Obi-Wan and Anakin had been in almost four standard months, and with the last remaining Separatist strongholds now cleared from the Core and Colonies, they expected to be back in the Outer Rim by week's end.

Obi-Wan heard movement on the far side of the irrigation canal.

An instant later, four clone troopers crept from the tree line on the opposite bank to take up firing positions amid the water-smoothed rocks that lined the ditch. Far behind them a crashed gunship was burning. Protruding from the canopy, the LAAT's blunt tail was stenciled with the eight-rayed battle standard of the Galactic Republic.

A gunboat glided into view from downstream, maneuvering to where the Jedi were waiting. Standing in the bow, a clone commander named Cody waved hand signals to the troopers on shore and to others in the gunboat, who immediately fanned out to create a safe perimeter.

Troopers could communicate with one another through the comlinks built into their T-visored helmets, but the Advanced Recon Commando teams had created an elaborate system of gestures meant to thwart enemy attempts at eavesdropping.

A few nimble leaps brought Cody face-to-face with Obi-Wan and Anakin.

"Sirs, I have the latest from airborne command."

"Show us," Anakin said.

Cody dropped to one knee, his right hand activating a device built into his left wrist gauntlet. A cone of blue light emanated from the device, and a hologram of task force commander Dodonna resolved.

"Generals Kenobi and Skywalker, provincial recon unit reports that Viceroy Gunray and his entourage are making their way to the north side of the redoubt. Our forces have been hammering at the shield from above and from points along the shore, but the shield generator is in a hardened site, and difficult to get at. Gunships are taking heavy fire from turbo-laser cannons in the lower ramparts. If your team is still committed to taking Gunray alive, you're going to have to skirt those defenses and find an alternative way into the palace. At this point we cannot reinforce, repeat, cannot reinforce."

Obi-Wan looked at Cody when the hologram had faded. "Suggestions, Commander?"

The ARC made an adjustment to the wrist projector, and a 3-D schematic of the redoubt formed in midair. "Assuming that Gunray's fortress is similar to what we found on Deko and Koru, the underground levels will contain fungus farms and processing and shipment areas. There will be access from the shipping areas into the midlevel grub hatcheries, and from the hatcheries we'll be able to infiltrate the upper reaches."

Cody carried a short-stocked DC-15 blaster rifle and wore the white armor and imaging system helmet that had come to symbolize the Grand Army of the Republic—grown, nurtured, and trained on the remote world of Kamino, three years earlier. Just now, though, areas of white showed only where there were no smears of mud or dried blood, no gouges, abrasions, or charred patches. Cody's position was designated by orange markings on his helmet crest and shoulder guards. His upper right arm bore stripes signifying campaigns in which he had participated: Aagonar, Praesitlyn, Paracelus Minor, Antar 4, Tibrin, Skor II, and dozens of other worlds from Core to Outer Rim.

Over the years Obi-Wan had formed battlefield partnerships with several Advanced Recon Commandos—Alpha, with whom he had been imprisoned on Rattatak, and Jangotat, on Ord Cestus. Early-generation ARCs had received training by the Mandalorian clone template, Jango Fett. While the Kaminoans had managed to breed some of Fett out of the regulars, they had been more selective in the case of the ARCs. As a consequence, ARCs displayed more individual initiative and leadership abilities. In short, they were more like the late bounty hunter himself, which was to say, more *human*.

In the initial stages of the war, clone troopers were treated no differently from the war machines they piloted or the weapons they fired. To many they had more in common with battle droids poured by the tens of thousands from Baktoid Armor Workshops on a host of Separatist-held worlds. But attitudes began to shift as more and more troopers died. The clones' unfaltering dedication to the Republic, and to the Jedi, showed them to be true comrades in arms, and deserving of all the respect and compassion they were now afforded. It was the Jedi themselves, in addition to other progressive thinking officials in the Republic, who had urged that second- and third-generation ARCs be given names rather than numbers, to foster a growing fellowship.

"I agree that we can probably reach the upper levels, Commander," Obi-Wan said at last. "But how do you propose we reach the fungus farms to begin with?"

Cody stood to his full height and pointed toward the orchards. "We go in with the harvesters."

Obi-Wan glanced uncertainly at Anakin and motioned him off to one side.

"It's just the two of us. What do you think?"

"I think you worry too much, Master."

Obi-Wan folded his arms across his chest. "And who'll worry about you if I don't?"

Anakin canted his head and grinned. "There are others."

"You can only be referring to See-Threepio. And you had to *build* him."

"Think what you will."

Obi-Wan narrowed his eyes with purpose. "Oh, I see. But I would have thought Senator Amidala of greater interest to you than Supreme Chancellor Palpatine." Before Anakin could respond, he added: "Despite that she's a politician also."

"Don't think I haven't tried to attract her interest, Master."

Obi-Wan regarded Anakin for a moment. "What's more, if Chancellor Palpatine had genuine concern for your welfare, he would have kept you closer to Coruscant."

Anakin placed his artificial hand on Obi-Wan's left shoulder. "Perhaps, Master. But then, who would look after you?"